Praise for the Novels
of Lesley Kagen

Tomorrow River

"Shenandoah leaps off the page in vivid color: sparky, resourceful, trying to cope . . . and doing it with the matter-of-fact, heartbreaking courage that kids learn when there's no other choice. This book is packed with warmth, wit, intelligence, images savory enough to taste—and deep dark places that are all the more terrible for being surrounded by so much brightness."

—Tana French, *New York Times* bestselling author of
Faithful Place and *In the Woods*

"[A] stellar third novel. . . . Kagen not only delivers a spellbinding story but also takes a deep look into the mores, values, and shams of a small Southern community in an era of change."

—*Publishers Weekly* (Starred Review)

"*Tomorrow River* is the story of a sweet, resourceful girl trying to find her mother. . . . The charming genuine voice of Shenny, whose country-Southern dialect is beautifully rendered with rhythmic cadences, is impossible to resist. It's interesting to see this world from a child's eyes and frustrating when she can't see the obvious. Overall, it's the tender bond between the twins that redeems the world from the cruelty around them and keeps you rooting for them right up until the end."

—*Milwaukee Magazine*

"The first-person narration is chirpy, determined, and upbeat. . . . Shenny steals the show with her brave, funny, and often disturbing patter as she tries to rescue herself and her sister from problems she won't acknowledge."

—*Mystery Scene*

"Be prepared for all your other obligations to be neglected when you begin *Tomorrow River*."

—Katrina Kittle, author of *The Blessings of the Animals*

continued . . .

Land of a Hundred Wonders
A Great Lakes Book Award Nominee

"I've been a Lesley Kagen fan ever since I read her beautifully rendered debut, *Whistling in the Dark*. Here she adds to what is shaping up to be her greatest strength as a novelist: She creates a most unusual narrator whose quirky innocence and frankness reveal more story than she is aware she's telling; it's deftly done and endlessly sweet. Set against the volatile backdrop of the small-town South of the 1970s, *Land of a Hundred Wonders* is by turns sensitive and rowdy, peopled with larger-than-life characters who are sure to make their own tender path into your heart."

—Joshilyn Jackson, *New York Times* bestselling author of
Backseat Saints and *The Girl Who Stopped Swimming*

"Lesley Kagen has crafted a story that is poignant, compelling, hilarious, real, and absolutely lovely. Her characters are enchanting and will have you racing to the end of this terrific novel."

—Kris Radish, author of *Hearts on a String*

"A truly enjoyable read from cover to cover. . . . Miss Kagen's moving portrayal of a unique young woman finding her way in a time of change will touch your heart. And that, dear reader, is Quite Right indeed."

—Garth Stein, *New York Times* bestselling author of
The Art of Racing in the Rain and *Raven Stole the Moon*

"Lesley Kagen's lucid, confident prose shines on every page of *Land of a Hundred Wonders*, giving a unique and unforgettable voice to her moving and heartfelt story. The humor and passion of Gibby and her compatriots will stay with you long after you reach the end."

—Tasha Alexander, author of *Tears of Pearl*

"With all the charm of *Cold Sassy Tree*'s Will Tweedy, Kagen has created an equally memorable, quirky character in Gibby McGraw. Gibby will make you laugh and touch your heart, proving that even someone who's Not Quite Right can still remedy the broken lives around her. For everyone who loved *Whistling in the Dark*, Lesley Kagen has worked her magic again in *Land of a Hundred Wonders*."

—Renée Rosen, author of *Every Crooked Pot*

Whistling in the Dark
Chosen as a Hot Summer Read by the *Chicago Tribune*
A Midwest Booksellers' Choice Award Winner

"Bittersweet and beautifully rendered, *Whistling in the Dark* is the story of two young sisters and a summer jam-packed with disillusionment and discovery. With the unrelenting optimism that only children could bring to such a situation, these girls triumph. So does Kagen. *Whistling in the Dark* shines. Don't miss it."

—Sara Gruen, *New York Times* bestselling author of
Ape House and *Water for Elephants*

"[A] sophisticated charmer of a first novel. . . . What makes the novel appealing . . . is Kagen's literary style and her ability to see the world—and the truth—unfold gradually through the eyes of a ten-year-old. Sally's voice . . . is innocently wise and ultimately captivating. Sally and Troo are both finely wrought characters, achingly alive amid a few other splendid characters, such as a girl with Down syndrome."

—*Milwaukee Journal Sentinel*

"Every now and then, you come across a book with characters so endearing that you love them like family, and a plot so riveting that you can't read slowly enough to make the story last longer, no matter how hard you try. *Whistling in the Dark* is one such book. I absolutely loved this novel from the first page to the last!"

—Sandra Kring, author of *How High the Moon*

"The loss of innocence can be as dramatic as the loss of a parent or the discovery that what's perceived to be truth can actually be a big, fat lie, as shown in Kagen's compassionate debut. . . . Kagen sharply depicts the vulnerability of children of any era. Sally, 'a girl who wouldn't break a promise even if her life depended on it,' makes an enchanting protagonist."

—*Publishers Weekly*

"We trust this gritty and smart, profane and poetic little girl to tell us the truth about her neighborhood and its mysteries. And best of all, we trust Sally to tell us what it was like to be ten years old in the summer of 1959."

—*Milwaukee Magazine*

OTHER NOVELS BY LESLEY KAGEN

Whistling in the Dark

Land of a Hundred Wonders

Lesley Kagen

Tomorrow River

NAL NEW AMERICAN LIBRARY

NEW AMERICAN LIBRARY
Published by New American Library, a division of
Penguin Group (USA) Inc., 375 Hudson Street, New York, New York 10014, USA
Penguin Group (Canada), 90 Eglinton Avenue East, Suite 700, Toronto,
Ontario M4P 2Y3, Canada (a division of Pearson Penguin Canada Inc.)
Penguin Books Ltd., 80 Strand, London WC2R 0RL, England
Penguin Ireland, 25 St. Stephen's Green, Dublin 2,
Ireland (a division of Penguin Books Ltd.)
Penguin Group (Australia), 250 Camberwell Road, Camberwell, Victoria 3124,
Australia (a division of Pearson Australia Group Pty. Ltd.)
Penguin Books India Pvt. Ltd., 11 Community Centre, Panchsheel Park,
New Delhi - 110 017, India
Penguin Group (NZ), 67 Apollo Drive, Rosedale, Auckland 0632,
New Zealand (a division of Pearson New Zealand Ltd.)
Penguin Books (South Africa) (Pty.) Ltd., 24 Sturdee Avenue,
Rosebank, Johannesburg 2196, South Africa

Penguin Books Ltd., Registered Offices:
80 Strand, London WC2R 0RL, England

Published by New American Library, a division of Penguin Group (USA) Inc.
Previously published in a Dutton edition.

First New American Library Printing, May 2011
10 9 8 7 6 5 4 3 2 1

 REGISTERED TRADEMARK—MARCA REGISTRADA

New American Library Trade Paperback ISBN: 978-0-451-23308-0
The Library of Congress has catalogued the hardcover edition of this title as follows:

Kagen, Lesley.
Tomorrow River/Lesley Kagen.
p. cm.
ISBN 978-0-525-95154-4
1. Girls—Fiction 2. Sisters—Fiction. 3. Children of disappeared persons—Fiction.
4. Parent and child—Fiction. 5. Family secrets—Fiction. 6. Shenandoah River Valley
(Va. and W. Va.)—Fiction 7. Psychological fiction. 8. Domestic fiction. I. Title.
PS3611.A344T66 2010
813'.6—dc22   2010002055

Set in Sabon
Designed by Leonard Telesca

Printed in the United States of America

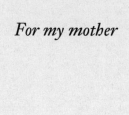

For my mother

ACKNOWLEDGMENTS

Thanks from the bottom of my heart to:

My editor, Ellen Edwards.

Publishers, Brian Tart and Kara Welsh.

The hardworking advertising, art, publicity, production, promotion, and sales teams at Dutton and NAL.

My agent, Kim Witherspoon, for her unrelenting optimism.

Stephanie Lee, Jeanine Swenson, Hope Erwin, Eileen Kaufmann, Emily Lewis, and Rochelle Staab for their valuable feedback and friendship.

Legal beagles, the Hon. Darcy McManus, Bruce Rosen, J.D., and Casey Fleming, J.D.

Brian Dally, Megan Olshanski, and Aryiana Deneffe for the brilliant photos.

Madeira James for her genius work on my Web site.

Mike Lebow, you know why.

Book clubs and readers. You make my day.

Booksellers. Especially the gang at Next Chapter Books, my home away from home.

My husband, Pete, who is a saint for putting up with my nonsense.

Acknowledgments

Casey and Riley, my incredibly bright and good-looking children.

O miraculous Charlie William. Welcome to the family, little man.

The city of Lexington, Virginia, for the literary license.

$\mathcal{P}$rologue

If you'd had the occasion to come calling on the Carmody clan of Rockbridge County that long-ago summer, being a stranger and not familiar with our twisting mountain roads and all, you might've found yourself pulling into the Triple S for directions. So there you'd be, perspiring from your every pore, waiting on the owner to come rushing out, thrilled to meet your every need. But my oh my, how disappointed you would've been. Because proprietor Sam Moody? He would've stayed sat on his station porch until he was darn well ready to come sashaying your way. And you? Awfully put off by his barely brown boldness, you'd've already formed the impression that the man was some sort of ill bred and wished you'd stopped at the Shell out on the highway instead.

But let's just say, as I'm attempting to set the scene

for you here, that you gathered your wits together long enough to inquire, "The Carmody place? Lilyfield?" And let's further say that Sam, still not thrilled, but certain you meant us no harm, replied, "Past the woods, make a left on Lee Road." So off you'd go, pressing pedal to metal, relieved as hell that you came from somewhere else that boasted cooler air and more courteous help.

But I guarantee you, the moment you braked at our wrought-iron gate, thoughts of the unbearable heat we'd been having and the station that hadn't been very serviceable would've fled your head. "Will you look at that," you'd've muttered as your eyes journeyed up our impressive tree-lined drive and came to rest on the magnificent house. "This Carmody place is fine. *Real* fine."

But just how you were thinking only moments ago about Sam Moody being nothing more than a gumptious high-yellow Negro, I'm afraid your first impression of Lilyfield would've been way off as well. Once you'd come closer, looked deeper, you'd've seen that our place wasn't at all fine and neither were we Carmodys.

The lady of our house had vanished.

During the course of all our lives, there comes a time when something or someone very dear to us will break beyond repair. Growing older teaches us we have no choice but to humbly accept that no matter how hard we try or how many tears we shed we're powerless to glue those precious pieces back together again. But during the summer I went searching for our missing mother, I was just a girl. I hadn't learned that lesson yet. No. It wasn't until the damage was done that I truly understood the meaning of "Pride goeth before a fall."

Then again, maybe my hindsight could borrow your eyes for a bit.

I'm sure you've heard it said that a person can't begin to understand another's troubles until they take a stroll in their shoes. So maybe you'd . . . would you do me the favor of slipping on my little gal sneakers and taking forty giant steps backwards in time? Go stumbling around the summer of '69 the same way I did? Once you see what I was up against, I'm hoping you'll come to believe that my heart was tender and my intentions pure, and that's got to count for something.

Assuming you're willing, allow me to offer a bit of advice before we get under way. Try to keep in mind what I mentioned to you earlier on. Because even though I'm still torn about the way I dealt with Mama's disappearance and more than likely will meet my Maker being so, I *am* dreadfully certain about one thing. Those first impressions? They can be dead wrong.

Chapter One

We got one heck of a view from up here.

Under less heartbreaking circumstances, I might even describe it as *astronomical* and that's not just me waxing poetic, which I am prone to do. I got the Monacan Indians to back me up on this. According to one of their legends, the beauty of our Shenandoah Valley so impressed the stars gazing down from above that they held a celestial powwow and agreed to cast the brightest jewels from their twinkling crowns into our abundant waters, which was real nice of them, if somewhat shortsighted. We got a whole lot more than rivers and creeks to merit their stellar attention. The Blue Ridge Mountains cradle us in a glorious blanket of green. If you breathe in deep, the smell of Christmas trees fills your nose no matter what time of year it is. Horses run faster. Flowers grow taller. Even the birds tweet sweeter.

I believe my father, Judge Walter T. Carmody, a gentleman well-known in the Commonwealth of Virginia for rarely making mistakes, pulled a real doozy when he named me after this heavenly valley on earth. Shenandoah means "beautiful daughter of the stars." That's what His Honor should've called my sister instead of Jane Woodrow, because I don't think I am. Beautiful, that is. Not like Woody. We're supposed to be identical twins, but we're not entirely so. My blond hair kinks in the heat and my green eyes look like they sprouted from a slightly different family tree than hers. From a distance, though, hardly anybody can tell us apart. Unless I smile. Got a gap between my two front teeth and who cares, I get all A's.

My sister and I are snuggled up in the strongest branches of an old oak that's eighty-two steps from the back porch of the house, depending on how much of a hurry we're in. Papa built us this fort. Carved his name in the trunk of the tree like an artist so proud of his work. Back when he still called my sister and me his "little Gemini," we'd lie with him on the fort's floor. So happy to breathe in the smell of English Leather that ran along his jaw. Overjoyed to hear his heart beating steady beneath the pocket of his starched white shirt while he pointed out Orion, the Hunter, or Ursa Major, the Great Bear. I could almost always make out those sky pictures, but Woody couldn't. Instead of saying, "Oh sure, there's the Little Dipper," the way I did to please him, my sister would begin humming along with whatever tune our mother was crooning while she washed the supper dishes, her angel voice floating out of the kitchen window below.

But everything changed after Mama disappeared.

Even Lilyfield.

That's the name of our house and the fifty rolling and wooded acres that it sits on outside of town. Not that long ago, anybody who knew the Carmody place would've told you it was pretty enough to win a pageant prize the same way Mrs. Murdoch did. She was a runner-up in the 1937 Miss Virginia contest, but has sort of slowed down to a walk these days. Don't get me wrong, Lolly Murdoch still turns heads. You just got to look harder to see the beauty that's lying beneath her weathered skin. Same with Lilyfield.

Even though the fencing out back is missing boards and all three stories of the house need more than a touch-up of white paint, as I look down upon it this morning, no matter what anybody says, I think our home is still tiara-wearing gorgeous. It's a little alarming, though. How fast something tarnishes if you don't keep it polished. Mama's been gone less than a year.

Our fort is well stocked. We got feather pillows, a ruined chiffon scarf, and sleeping blankets. My stargazing binoculars hang from a nail and there's almost always a tin of pecan fudge that I make for my sister, who mostly eats sweets these days. Always close at hand are our matching flashlights that we got on our last birthday. The Carmody twins will be twelve on the one that's coming up on August 15th. Off in a corner, there's a little altar that Woody set up. It's just a rusty coffee can with a plastic statue of Saint Jude resting on top and a couple of cut-off candles below, but she adores it. My sister still believes in all that holy baloney. Not me. I don't bother kneeling down to the patron saint of lost causes anymore. It hurts too bad in more ways than one.

We also got a saved-from-the-trash record player, but it's gathering dust. We don't have any electricity up here. I tried running extension cords from the house but came up short, so Mama's soundtrack albums don't get played. Woody likes staring at the shiny covers, though, especially *South Pacific*, which I'd say is her all-time favorite.

There's also some of our missing mother's precious books held in a neat row by a shank bone that I got for our dog, Mars, who like his planetary namesake had one hell of a chip on his shoulder. He is also missing. I picked the bone up from the butcher to fool my critter-loving sister into thinking that dog might turn back up.

And, of course, we've got art adorning the walls. My constellation map is tacked to the fort's broad boards and hanging right next to it there's a *mostly* black-and-white family portrait that was taken in more carefree days. We're in the wild lily field that our place is named after. We were having a picnic. Mama used to pack up a basket with pimento cheese sandwiches and yellow Jell-O and we'd race out to the field laughing and shouting at one another the way all families do, "Last one there's a rotten egg." After our tummies got full, the four of us would go for a dip in the creek, which I remember being a lot warmer than it is now. Papa would flirtatiously splash Mama and she'd giggle and splash him back and he'd take turns giving Woody and me piggyback rides until we all got soaked to the bone and that was the best of times.

When I wasn't paying attention the way I should've been, my sister took her crayons to the picnic picture. Drew wavy yellow lines through our mother's hair, dotted green on her eyes, and colored her cheeks real rosy. Mama looks like a flower blooming in a patch of weeds in that snapshot now. Woody can stare at it for hours, but I've got to chew Rolaids if I look at it too long, so I just don't.

Like a jarring alarm clock, the screen door of the house squeaks open below.

"I saw ya duck down, don't think I didn't, Shenny. Get down outta that tree right this minute."

That's our housekeeper, Louise "Lou" Jackson, going off like that on the back porch.

She just got done dragging herself over from the creekside cottage she shares with Mr. Cole Jackson, who is Lilyfield's caretaker and, through no fault of his own, also her uncle. Every morning about this time Woody and I can count on this kind of rude awakening.

"You two hear me?" she roosters.

I don't want to call back, but she won't let up until I do. Lou has become one of those unrelenting-in-their-personality types of people. "Not only can we hear ya, so can the rest of Rockbridge County," I shout. "Includin' those born without ears."

"Get down here 'fore I change my mind about feedin' your sassy mouth," she yells, letting go of the screen door with a slam.

I lie back down next to my sister on the fort floor. Press my tummy into the scoop of her back. When she's curled up like this, it's about the only time she seems like her old self, so half of me doesn't want to shake her by the shoulder that matches mine down to the freckles. The other half of me knows that we've got to get a move on. We've got important work to do.

"I told Lou yesterday to make bacon and flapjacks. You'll like that, won't you?" I ask her, even though I'm fairly certain she won't answer me. I mean, she *could* sass me back one of these mornings, "Stop bein' so silly, Shen. You know I adore bacon and flapjacks." That's what she would've said before Mama disappeared. But these days, no matter how much I yell or beg or promise to rub almond cream on her hands for two weeks straight, my sister will not say one word. Woody's gone mute on me.

"You know what today is?" I nuzzle my face into her hair that smells more like a penny than Prell. "It's the tomorrow I was tellin' you about last night." Nudging her onto her back, I lick my pinky finger and smooth down her pale eyebrows. "This morning we're going to jump right in. Start looking for her in earnest." My eyes wander down to Woody's bare legs. One of the Band-Aids I put on her knees after Papa let us out of the root cellar this morning is hanging by a thread.

Last night was particularly awful.

We fell asleep in our room and shouldn't have. Because I got woke up to our father weaving over my sister's side of the bed, growling, "I order you to talk to me."

I wasn't sure how long he'd been at it, but it'd been long enough that he'd ripped to shreds the chiffon scarf that Woody sleeps with. My twin was beside herself, grasping for it. It's the only thing left of Mama's that smells like her.

I reached for her and said, *"Hushacat . . . hushacat . . ."* without even thinking, and that's when Papa blew up.

"Cease and desist!" he said, lunging for me and dragging me by my ankle off the edge of the bed. "Don't you tell her to hush."

"But I wasn't telling her—" *Hushacat* is one of our twin words. It means "Everything'll be all right no matter how bad it seems at the present time." But Woody . . . she must not have heard me because she leaped on Papa's back and he flicked her off and she landed on the wood floor next to me.

"Stand!" he shouted down at us.

Trying to pull her up with me, I warned, "Woody . . . please . . . you gotta do what . . ." But then Papa slapped me on the back real hard because he was so far gone. Mumbling and cursing and smelling so bad from the vomit on his judge's robe, he chased us out of our bedroom, down the front staircase, and through the back door, straight to the side of the house.

I kept swearing to him the whole time, "I didn't mean anything. I wasn't telling her not to talk. I was just trying to comfort her."

The night grass was cool on our bare feet, the moon half full when he jerked up the latch. I could hear the Calhouns' hounds barking from across the creek. "March," he commanded, flinging open the root cellar doors.

Woody ran right over to her corner, and knelt down

on the sandy floor like she's supposed to, but I only went down the first crumbling step, still hoping I could persuade him. "Sir . . . I—"

He said through clenched teeth, "If your sister doesn't speak soon, Shenandoah, mark my words, I'll . . . I'll send her off the way your grandfather wants me to."

"Your Honor? Please?" I said, reaching out to him.

I thought he was going to give in because he took my hands in his, but then he bent my fingers back and pushed me down the rest of the steps. "This . . . it's for your own good," he said, and then the cellar doors banged shut and the padlock snapped closed and it was so dark.

He let us out soon after the morning birds began singing. He always comes before Lou and Mr. Cole report for duty, so they don't know. Sometimes Papa's still drunk and will inspect our knees to make sure we were repenting all night long. Sometimes he'll have slept it off and come begging our forgiveness at dawn. Woody and I never know which of himselves he'll be when he opens up those root cellar doors, so that's why we got to kneel, just in case. When the sun came up *this* morning, he was still drunk.

"C'mon now," I say, pressing that dangling bandage back onto Woody's knee. "Up and at 'em." When she doesn't make a move to sit up straight, I give her hand a hard tug. "We don't want Lou reporting to His Honor that we're being recalcitrant, do we?" Despite the too-hot-for-June morning slicking her skin, my sister shivers. I give her nose an Eskimo rub. "No, pea, we certainly do not."

Chapter Two

Louise of the Bayou has been acting more like Cleopatra of the Nile.

I guess it was about a month after Mama vanished that caretaking Mr. Cole must've mentioned to Papa that Woody and I needed some tending to and he was right. We weren't eating regular and since neither one of us is exactly sure how to run the washing machine, you could smell us coming long before you saw us.

Papa would take care of us if he could, but he can't. He's too busy being sad. So that's why Mr. Cole, who can read well enough but whose spelling is simply awful, had me sit down on his porch steps and write a letter to his niece in my absolute best penmanship:

Greetings and Salutations Miss Louise Marie Jackson,

How are you? We've got a lot in common because I

was named after the place I was born the same way
you are. Say, would you mind hopping a bus to come
do for my sister and me? The quicker, the better?

Though I regret it now, I signed that letter with *xxx*'s
and *ooo*'s so she couldn't hardly refuse, could she.

Hoodoo-believing Louise arrived two weeks later on
the Greyhound and ended up mostly liking it here at
Lilyfield. The weather and the wildlife suit her. It's not
as sweltering and there are fewer skeeters and no gators
like there are in Louisiana and she's having a romance.
What Lou *doesn't* like about living with us is Papa. She
warns Woody and me all the time with wide white eye-
balls, "You gals better be sleepin' with your shoes on.
There's no predictin' what your pappy will do next. He's
actin' like the worst kind of zombie there is—one of
them irritable *half*-dead ones."

Being from the deepest part of the South the way she
is, Lou tends to exaggeration so that statement is only
partially true. She knows good as Woody and me that
Papa is *entirely* lively when it comes to his rules.

Woody and I come barging into the kitchen to find our
housekeeper swaying her seventeen-year-old behind in
front of the stove, keeping the beat to "Darlin', darlin',
stand by me," which is blaring out of the blue transistor
radio that's sitting on the windowsill above the sink.

I wish I could tell you that Lou looks like three miles
of bad road, but she doesn't. She's got creamy toffee skin

and legs up to here. A round rump. And a good chest, too. Pointy as two cookie cones. But just like folks are always saying, "Pretty is as pretty does," and she doesn't do much around here lately except treat Woody and me like two of her not-so-loyal subjects.

Lou ladles the flapjack batter into the black fry pan and gives us one of her dirty looks before she says, "It's 'bout time. Why ya always gotta go up to that dumb fort anyways?"

On my way over to the sink, I *don't* say to her, "Those little wood steps that lead up the trunk of the tree are real loose. Papa can't get up 'em."

The reason I don't tell Lou or Mr. Cole or anybody else about His Honor coming after Woody and me is that I do not want his shiny reputation dulled. Nobody would ever suspect that he's behaving the way he is towards us. When he goes out and about, it's as one of the most respected men in this town, but when he's home, I think being here reminds him more that his wife *isn't*. He can't help what's happened to him, poor man. The liquor and his missing-Mama feelings are what're doing him in. They're getting mixed into some kind of heart-wrecking cocktail. Papa never used to drink all that much, but he started up after his wife vanished and it's just gotten worse and worse. He'll get better if I can find Mama. Not a doubt in my mind.

"Forts are for children," Lou says. "You're gettin' too old for that sort of thing. Y'all should be thinking about attractin' some boys. Look at the two of ya. All ratty and scuffed up. Don't you know that young women's got to take care of their skin? Men like it soft." She smooths suet on hers. "Crawlin' around on that fort floor, thas what's wreckin' your knees."

"What's that?" I turn on the sink water good and hard. Holding Woody's hands beneath the warm stream and doing the same to mine, I point to the faucet and shout back, "Can't hear you."

"I know you can, Shen," she shoots back. "Ya think I'm a fool?"

"I refuse to answer that on the grounds that it may incriminate me," I say under my breath, wishing yet again we could get back the old Lou. She wasn't always this harsh. Woody and I took to her the minute she came down those bus steps so timid in a patched gray dress, holding twin sticks of peppermint in front of her. I stepped forward to take her paper sack of belongings and said, "Welcome to the Commonwealth, Miss Louise. Thank you ever so much for comin'." With a bashful smile, she said, "Yes, ma'am," so quiet that I had to ask her to repeat herself, that's how soft-spoken she was back then.

"We got big things ahead of us today," I tell Woody once I'm done lathering, rinsing, and toweling us off. "Eat good." I get her situated in her chair at the round wooden table. Tuck a napkin under her chin. Boy, we could use a bath. Her neck's got a ring around it, so I bet mine does, too.

"I told ya yesterday and the day before that, you girls better be doin' something useful with your time. Something *besides* gallivantin'," Lou rants over her shoulder.

"FYI," I say. "What we're doing isn't called *gallivantin'*. That means roaming without purpose, and we're full to the brim with purpose, isn't that right, Woody?"

Sometimes I throw out a line real quick like that, hoping to catch her forgetting that she doesn't talk anymore, but like always, my sister doesn't take the bait. She's too busy wiggling her fingers through her hair. She's been doing that sort of thing more and more lately. Repeating a task over and over and won't stop unless I make her, which I immediately do. Lou will threaten to cut off Woody's hair again if I don't.

"FY . . . FI . . . gallivantin' . . . roamin' . . . call it whatever ya want." Lou lowers her voice to its muddy bottom. "Ya know good as me, if His Honor finds out I'm lettin' ya run loose like I is, there's gonna be the devil to pay." She reaches for one of my braids and wraps it around her hand. "You get caught runnin' wild, your pappy'll blame me. He could send me back home to the swamp, but . . . hey now, that'd suit you just fine, wouldn't it, sis?" she says, bending my head back to hers. "Ya better remember that deal we got. Or else."

What her highness is referring to is the fact that our father made Woody and me vow not to step one foot off Lilyfield. He even hired Miss Bainbridge to come school us but she had to go have a baby. I wish I could, but I can't tell you exactly why Papa's been acting more and more like a jailer and less and less like a father. My suspicion is that he's worried sick that if he allows his precious girls out of his sight we could disappear the same way his beloved wife has. That's why I recently had to make Lou a turn-in-two-circles-jump-over-a-broom hoodoo promise that if she'd let Woody and me escape while Papa's out on his ride every morning, I'd do the bathroom scrubbing for her. Papa passes out early most evenings, which has allowed my sister and me to sneak off to town, but I discovered that's not a good time to ask folks questions since most have settled in for the night and don't want to be bothered. There's a lot at stake here and it's getting more dire by the second. We have to up our ante. Woody and I need to leave Lilyfield during daytime hours if we're going to shed any light on the subject of Mama's vanishing.

Over the sound of popping bacon grease, Lou screeches, "Pick your head up off that wiped table, Shenandoah Wilson Carmody. What in tarnation is wrong with ya?"

"Why, there is not one thing wrong with me, Louise Marie Jackson, but aren't you the sweetest thing to ask." I've had it with her griping. "I'm *dead* tired is all." I big-wink at Woody so she knows I'm only being saucy, rise up out of my chair, stiffen my arms, and shuffle across the linoleum towards Lou like one of those resurrected bodies she was fond of telling us about before she got so full of herself. "One of your bloodsucking spirits drained me dry last night. That rotted thing came climbin' up the fort steps, bit the top off my big toe, stuck in a straw, and sipped *aaall niiight looong*. And ya know what else? Before it slithered off, it asked me where *you* slept."

"Dead tired, huh?" superstitious Lou says, squinting down at my bare feet. Once she's sure I'm not bleeding all over her kitchen floor, she shoves me clear back to the table. "That's what a body *gets* when it's up late peepin' on folks with those big glasses of yours from up in that stupid fort. I know ya was watchin' me Wednesday night, Shenny." She waves the spatula an inch from our noses. "And you, Jane Woodrow, if ya don't quit messin' with your hair, I'll get my shears out right quick."

If it was just her and me sitting in the kitchen, Louise wouldn't dare go uppity like she is. She knows all about my temper. And how I'll do whatever's necessary to keep my sister steady. Arguments of any sort bother Woody. She's started rocking.

"Hey, now," I say, getting her fingers laced between mine.

Stupid Lou. I'm not saying that I don't sometimes, but it wasn't on purpose that I spied her climbing out of her cottage window that particular evening. (She's been meeting up with a man after midnight for quite some time, but I'm going to keep that to myself for now.) No. The reason my sister and I finished the night up in the fort had nothing to do with our horrible housekeeper extraordinaire. Last Wednesday was Mama's thirty-fourth birthday.

We'd normally have a party for her with presents and white lanterns hanging from the trees near the garden and a yellow sheet cake with chocolate butter frosting, but Mama is in absentia, so there was none of that and no singing neither. Only the sound of Papa's weeping coming down the upstairs hall and straight into Woody's and my ears no matter how many pillows we piled atop our heads. His sad can turn to mad so fast that we won't know what hit us. That's why we slipped out from between our sheets and ran out to the fort that night. Not to spy on big-headed Lou.

"I'm warnin' ya, better watch where ya step when you're in town," she says, stabbing the bacon out of the fry pan and onto the white plates. "One of them 'zilary ladies sees ya runnin' around, ya know how they is. They'll snitch ya out."

"Oh, yeah? Well, those *Auxiliary* ladies better watch their mouths." I do not have warm feelings for those prissy women who prance through town like they own the place and neither did my mother.

"In the legal field, their back-fence talk is called slander and it's punishable," I say, even though I know for once in her miserable life she's right.

Only a few folks know that Papa's keeping us locked up at Lilyfield. I heard from Vera Ledbetter, who works at the drugstore, that he's telling everybody who dares to wonder why the Carmody twins are not attending choir practice or skimming rocks down at the reservoir or fishing at the lake with the other kids the way we do every other summer. "The girls are not feeling up to socializing just yet. They need time to recover from the loss of their mother."

That's why Woody and I have to be careful. If somebody should notice us flitting here and there, that nosy parker could blab to our father at his weekly Gentlemen's Club meeting, "Golly, it sure was nice to see the twins running around again, Your Honor."

(Believe me . . . that could happen. You live in this town, you got all the privacy of a stampede.)

Lou drops our breakfast plates down in front of us and props her spindly arms on the table. I get busy cutting the flapjacks into baby bites for Woody, which is the only way she'll eat them.

"If'n she was here," Lou says, "what do you s'pose your mama'd have to say about all this spookin' about?"

I could snap back at her, "Well, if Mama *was* here, we wouldn't have to be spooking about looking for her, would we, you big ignoramus?" but Woody is about rocking off her chair, so I breathe in deep and answer in my most tempered tone, " 'Hope is the thing with feathers that perches in the soul.' "

"Knock it off," Lou says, cuffing me on the side of my head. "I ain't in no mood for any of your mumbo jumbo this mornin'."

"That's *not* mumbo jumbo. That's poetry. Miss Emily Dickinson." I'm *this* close to getting up out of my chair, picking up the fry pan off the stove, grease and all, and using it to flatten the back of her head. She's all the time doing this. Trying to make me feel like I'm letting our dear mother down when what I'm attempting to do is the exact opposite.

I wonder if right about now you might be agreeing with her. Thinking to yourself:

What's wrong with this child? Why didn't she start searching right away? Her mama's been gone almost a year.

Well, I wouldn't be too quick to judge if I were you. I did all that I could.

I questioned those that live at Lilyfield. I didn't want to get our father more jittery than he already was, but I asked Mr. Cole Jackson one afternoon where he thought Mama might've gone off to and when she might be coming back. He set down his pruning shears and cast his eyes heavenward. "Some things in this life are not ours for the knowin'. The Almighty's got a plan for all His children," he said. "Found it's best not to question Him."

I should've known that's what he'd say. That's his answer to almost anything, so he was no help at all.

I even stooped so low as to bother Lou. "Thought ya was s'posed to be so damn smart," she sneered when I asked if she knew anything about Mama's disappearance. "There's that ten-thousand-dollar reward your granpappy put up, so if'n I knew somethin' about your mama's vanishment, don't you think I woulda told it by now? Shoot. I had that cash money, I'd be livin' in high cotton 'stead of waitin' on you spoiled girls hand and foot."

Reaching a dead end no matter which way I turned, I began to believe that Mama's goneness was just some sort of silly misunderstanding. Even after Sheriff Andy Nash showed up at our front porch on All Hallow's Eve, telling Papa in a suitably haunted-sounding voice: "I'm sorry, Your Honor. I . . . we . . . all of us have done what we can to find Miss Evelyn. The leads just seemed to dry up."

The sheriff admitting defeat like that did get my hackles up, but just a hair. I still believed Mama'd come home any moment no matter what dopey Andy Nash thought.

Especially when December 24th rolled around. Our mother loves *all* the holidays, but Christmas Eve is her absolute favorite. Woody thinks it's because she was named for it, that's why. *Eve*lyn. Mr. Cole trudged out to the woods that afternoon with his ax and drug back the prettiest spruce to set in the parlor. I placed the Mitch Miller Christmas album on the hi-fi the same way our mother would've to set the mood for tree trimming. After my sister and I hung our stockings, set out the cookies and hot cocoa, we stood by the front window and I sang over and over, "Oh, Come All Ye Faithful," but you know—Mama didn't.

And on May Day, I was so positive she'd show up with the better weather that I got up extra early and ran down to the potting shed. But when I threw open the door, all I found was Mama's gardening shoes, sitting on the workbench wrapped in spiderwebs like a haunted present.

Just like I'd been doing the whole time Mama's been gone, I told weeping Woody, "Must you always be so dramatic? Just because she hasn't showed up yet doesn't mean she's not goin' to. We'll head into the kitchen one of these mornings, and there she'll be, sipping her tea and reading. 'Good morning,' she'll say, so thrilled to see us. 'How were your dreams while I was gone, my two peas in a pod? Not half as sweet as you, I bet,' and then . . . and then everything will go back the way it was. Better even. Her and Papa have had a nice vacation from one another. Absence always makes the heart grow fonder. Just you wait and see."

Even though my sister couldn't come out and actually say so, I could tell she wasn't buying into that, which was unusual, considering that she believed in the Tooth Fairy until she was almost ten.

But right about then is when it occurred to me that maybe *I* was the one who was believing in kid stuff beyond the time that is considered normal. Maybe our mother really wasn't coming back. Not next week. Not next month. Not ever. Maybe Mama was dead.

That's when despair got ahold of me and drug me to the deepest depths. Life resembled those paintings in Mama's art books, the ones by Mr. Claude Monet, that's how bad my eyes watered. I even stopped answering the ring of the supper bell. Doing the simplest things became such a struggle with the heavy sadness I was lugging around. Woody, being my twin, understood I was going under for the third time and wouldn't let go of me. Bless her heart and perching hope is all I got to say. They're what saved me.

You already know the third reason I've put off looking for my mother in a more motivated way. It's horribly risky to leave Lilyfield. Papa likes to keep his girls within grabbing distance.

And fourthly, quite frankly? The final reason I've been putting off the search is that, even though I believe myself to be enormously brave, about the last thing on the planet I want to do is go looking for Mama. Not because we don't desperately need her back—no, no, no.

It's just that, if you set out to hunt down a critter, the woods is where you start. But how do you track down a lost mother? I could look for her from dawn 'til dusk and still come back empty-handed. That's why I keep asking myself—*Mighten it be for the best to just keep doing what we have been? Biding our time and hoping for her return?* That sounds so relieving that I almost get myself convinced. Until I jolt awake in the middle of the night to find my sister kneeling beside me, her face a testimony of tears.

But as much as I'm tempted to kitten out, and believe me, I sorely, sorely am, there are the facts to face. My darling Woody is turned completely inside out and my poor papa has unraveled so much that he's threatening to send her away. That doesn't leave anybody else but me. I need to quit my mewling and find my mother before it's too late. I can do this. I can. I'm Shenandoah Wilson Carmody, beautiful daughter of the stars, for heaven's sake.

Chapter Three

Last Chance Creek runs alongside Lilyfield like a dog. Some days it lies in the sun, barely twitching. On others, it moves loose, like it's got nowhere important to go. But on this important morning, the creek is charging out of the mountains, ready to rip an intruder to shreds. Woody and I are edging along its stony bank with our fastest sneakers tied around our necks. We're wearing our usual matching jean shorts and T-shirts. One of her sweaty tan hands is in one of mine, and in my other hand, I have my trusty tin lunch box that I got from our neighbor a few years ago. It used to have LOST IN SPACE and a couple of planets printed on it, but they've worn off. My hair is braided, but Woody's isn't. She wouldn't let me near that tangled mess this morning. "Keep hold of me. I mean it," I tell her for the umpteenth time.

We *could've* cut through Lilyfield's front woods, taken

the well-worn path that lets out onto Lee Road, but since we're working on stolen time, it's much faster to cross the creek towards town along with being cooling on bare feet and ankles. On our way over here, I stuck my head into the barn to make sure the stall of Papa's stallion was empty. His saddle was gone, too. He rides out every morning, I don't know where, but Pegasus comes back lathered.

Admittedly, I don't have much to go on when it comes to finding Mama, but I can't do any worse than Sheriff Andy Nash did. Far as I know, he batted zero when it came to drawing information out of anybody concerning her whereabouts.

"Are you aware of your mother having any enemies?" the sheriff asked me, shortly after Mama disappeared.

Since I do not hold him in high esteem, I replied rather snooty, "Enemies? Mama? That'd be like pickin' a fight with a warm-from-the-oven sugar cookie."

That made Papa grin. He was sitting right next to me in the sheriff's office because he forbade Andy Nash to question either me or Woody unless he was present. My father didn't want us upset any more than we were, that's how protective he is.

Pencil poised above his pad, the sheriff leaned across his desk. I could smell his nervous sweat. Papa can have that effect on people because he is so powerful. "What about her friends?" he asked. "Do you think any of them might know where she's gone off to?"

I crossed my fingers behind my back and told him, "Mama didn't have any friends, isn't that right, Your

Honor? She spent all her time taking care of her family."

The reason I lied to the sheriff was because the only friends our mother *did* have were the ones that my father labeled "verboten." Legally, that means "forbidden fruit," but in actuality, it means that Papa doesn't approve of his wife visiting with them. I didn't want to make my already-sad father even sadder, which he would be if he found out that sometimes his wife prefers other people's company to his own.

I went ahead and questioned all those forbidden fruits shortly after that session with the sheriff. Even though I came away no better informed, it can't hurt nothing to try again. I know from experience that when you least expect to recall something, a memory can pop up like an uninvited guest on your doorstep.

So, not having much to go on, I'm counting on just one thing—plain old gossip—to find our mother. Woody and I are looking to Blind Beezy Bell to supply us with that. That's why we're headed to her place in Mudtown this morning. I asked her a long time ago to listen especially hard to any chitchat that mentions Mama's name and I'm hoping that today's the day Beezy's finally come up with something.

It's nine o'clock, Monday morning, June 9, 1969. That means that this upcoming Friday, the beginning of the biggest bash the town has—Founders Weekend—unfortunately falls on the thirteenth. Now, I don't believe in any of that superstitious foolishness the way Lou Jackson does, but if I see a black cat or a ladder when we're in town, I *will* absolutely avoid them. I have found time and time again that it is better to be safe than sorry.

E. J. Tittle points down at the raging water from the other side of the creek and hollers, "It's foamin' at the mouth this morning. Mind yourselves."

"Fiddle-faddle," I yell back.

Woody and I have been hopping these stepping stones from our side to his since . . . I guess, forever. E. J. is well aware of that fact, but being the big brother of three sisters has given him *somewhat* of a protective nature. In other words, E. J., whose Christian name is Ed James, would laugh his butt off if *I* fell into this cold creek water, but not if Woody did. He goes gaga for her.

E. J. lives uphill from where he's standing in a house that couldn't be more unlike our grand one if it tried all day long. His place reminds me of a pile of spilt toothpicks. Not because his papa doesn't care about his family or is shiftless. Mr. Frank Tittle tries to work at an all-day job, but he almost always poops out after the noon whistle. He was a West Virginia miner and that's how come his breathing gets raggedy and he coughs like he's in a contest.

Given their circumstances, it should go without saying that the Tittle family is always strapped for cash. And food. E. J.'s so skinny. When he sticks out his tongue, he looks like a zipper. The only way he can keep any meat on his bones is by fishing the creek, spit-cooking trapped rabbits, or gathering wild berries. And if all that wasn't hideous enough, the Lord has given him another cross to bear. Not to be unkind or nothing, but the doctor probably spanked his mama instead of E. J. the day he was born—that's how homely he is. Looks like a hummingbird's nested in his hair. His nose is tiny. And his eyes? They're duller than mud. The only feature that merits praise on E. J.'s face is his mouth. It's berry stained—but normal. I wonder sometimes if Woody still finds his lips as inviting as she used to. The two of them used to go on and on about getting married someday. I couldn't stand telling them that even though they have my blessing, the very idea of them getting hitched is more than preposterous. Grampa Gus curses the day that Papa made a "bad marriage" and he'd *never* allow another Carmody to make that mistake again. The Tittles are the kind of family that Grampa calls "minin' sludge."

Yeah, that's his crab-ass opinion, not mine. I'd rather eat squirrel guts than tell E. J. how I really feel, but I think he's a hard-working citizen who makes up for what he lacks in looks and money with his brave and caring personality. And he proves me right each and every time I hint to him what kind of trouble we'll be in if the three of us get caught sneaking around. He shoves back his coonskin cap, thrusts out his chest, and growls, "A mountain man's gotta do what a mountain man's gotta do." (The boy's more molehill sized, but you have got to admire his pluck.)

I'm practically wearing Woody as we wade into the creek. I scold, "Don't you dare," because I can feel her pulling away. My sister may look light as a kite, but she's strong, and with one last tug, exactly what I was trying to keep from happening does. She gets loose. Flying across the stepping stones, not even using her arms for balance.

"Heads up," I yell across the creek to E. J. "She's escapin'!" If he doesn't grab her the second she hops onto his side of the creek, he knows good as me that we'll spend our precious time not the way we set out to, but combing the countryside looking for wayward Woody.

E. J. squats into a catching position and shouts back, "Don't worry. I got her! I got her!"

"Trap her like I showed ya. From behind!" Woody has jumped out of the creek and landed on the bank not more than a few feet from him, but she's not making a break for it. She's standing contrite. Like she's seen the error of her ways. But she's my twin. She can't fool me. "Don't fall for that, E. J. Don't take your eyes off her. She's faking." Sure enough, my sister jukes to the left, to the right, spins sideways, but our sidekick is fast, too. Once I'm sure he's got a good grip on her, I mince my way towards them, slipping into the water up to my knees twice, that's how ticked I am. "Hell, Woody. Ya ever hear of the word *cooperation*?" I wrench her out of E. J.'s arms, rip the sneakers from around her neck, and push her down to the ground. "Have you gone deaf as well as mute? I told you that we only got a little bit of time this mornin'. We've gotta find Mama." I jam her feet into her shoes and tie her laces too tight. "If I didn't know better . . . you're actin' like you don't care if she comes home."

Staring down at her on the ground, I'm remembering who my sister used to be. The days of her singing show tunes with Mama. Night frogging here at the creek, but letting them go right off because Woody couldn't stand hurting any living creature. Lying in the tall grass on our bellies, making daisy necklaces, hers always so much better than mine on account of her artistic abilities. Of course, we had our sisterly fights. Woody would always apologize first. She'd call me "Shenbone," which was supposed to be funny, like shinbone, and she'd bring me a drawing of the stars or play this little piggy with my toes even if what we were arguing about was entirely my fault. Sometimes I just can't bear up under the missing of my good old twin. Sometimes I really hate this new Woody. "Get up!" I scream at her.

"Why ya got to be like that?" E. J. says, shoving me to the side. "Ya know she don't understand." He gets down on his knees and draws a twig out of her mussy hair. Thumbs a smudge off her cheek. What I wouldn't give for her to look up at me and say in that silky voice of hers—"I'm sorry I was thinking of runnin' off. Don't know what got into me, pea. May I have a cuddle?"

Oh, this temper of mine!

You know I can't help it. I inherited the tendency to go off like that. But unlike some others in my family who shall remain nameless (my grandfather), at least I know that I need to apologize. I get busy loosening Woody's laces, saying, *"Rabadee,"* over and over again. That means "I'm sorry" in our twin talk. I'm going to have to ask for E. J.'s forgiveness, too. Not the way I did with my sister because that's unbecoming to a Carmody. I'll make amends the same way I always do with him, by way of this joke I got in a piece of Bazooka gum. I think it's close to idiotic, but he seems to get a kick out of it no matter how many times I tell it.

"Hey," I say, poking him in his narrow back.

"Yeah?" he says, still fussing over my sister. He's tucking her shirt back into her shorts.

"It's a good day for the race, wouldn'tcha say?"

He turns to me, struggles to stay straight-faced. "And what race might that be, Shenny?"

"Why, that would be the human one, E. J."

Laughing uproariously, quick-to-forgive E. J. helps Woody up off the ground, brushes the dirt off her legs, runs his hand down her hair.

I am feeling sinfully envious of him. My sense of humor seemed to disappear right around the same time Mama did. "I almost forgot," I say, popping the top of my lunch box. I hand E. J. the leftover bacon and flapjacks I swiped off my breakfast plate when Louise was too busy admiring her reflection on a pot bottom to notice.

E. J. stuffs the food into his mouth and says between chews, "Got somethin' for you, too." Of course, he does. His mama and papa may be forced to take seconds for the sake of their children, but everybody knows the Tittle boy would rather be hung by his thumbs than take a crumb of charity. I watch as he trots over to a felled tree and comes back with a pile of luscious-looking blackberries cupped in an oak leaf. "They're from that patch near the falls," he says, passing them to me. "Picked at dawn. Her favorite."

I slide the squishy sweetness into Woody's already-open mouth. "See how she's twitching around the corners." I point at her full lips that we inherited from our mother. "That means—thank you," I tell E. J.

"I know that already." With love oozing out of his muddy eyes, he wipes a bit of berry juice off her chin and says to Woody, "My pleasure, puddin'," and then he punches me good-naturedly in the arm. "A good day for the race. That's such a knee-slapper, Shen."

I know I shouldn't encourage him, but really, no matter how bad he can work up my dander, all in all, he is a good and faithful sidekick. I can't help myself. I whinny out, "And . . . they're off!"

Do I have to tell you that giggling boy ran into the woods at a full-out gallop?

The three of us are atop Honeysuckle Hill looking down at almost all there is of our town. It was named in honor of the famous Battle of Lexington–Concord. It's not big, say like Charlottesville, nor is it important like Richmond, our state capital. What Lexington does have going for it is a goodly amount of historical charm. The Confederacy left behind 144 soldiers in the memorial cemetery to remind us of their valiant effort. People come from far and wide to do rubbings on their graves and pay homage to their sacrifice. You can also tour Stonewall Jackson's house if you've got a mind to.

In the evening, gaslights shine perfect polka dots onto pebbled sidewalks. And during the day, there are shops that sell party dresses and jewelry and furniture on Main Street. But if your refrigerator quits on you, you should get a new one at the Sears Roebuck that got built off the highway east of town because it really is very modern.

As far as restaurants go, the fanciest of them is The Southern Inn, which has high-backed booths and serves the best chicken-fried steak under low-hung ceiling fans. Used to anyway. We Carmodys don't dine out anymore, so you might want to take my opinion with a grain of salt.

And right over there, on the corner of Johnson and Hayfield Streets—that's Filly's, another place Woody and I like to sneak off to whenever we get the chance. Wednesdays they have late hours and all sorts of useful things can be learned when you're crouched beneath the open window of Filomena Morgan's beauty parlor. Womanly information your mother would be giving you if she was here. That's where I found out that it's best to cut your toenails right after you get out of the tub because that's when they're the most pliable. And that Oil of Olay is good to use on your dried-out face. Also, there's not a thing you can do if your husband comes home from work and wants to "get busy right there in the kitchen." According to Mrs. Mandy Nash, the sheriff's wife, it's a sworn duty to grin and bear it. I heard her proclaim just last week, "Ladies, I don't know about you, but I just close my eyes and dream about the new pumps I'll be buyin' first thing tomorrow morning." (Mrs.

Nash has the most pairs of patent leathers in town, which leads me to believe that the sheriff must *really* like cooking.)

Over to the west sits the college of Washington & Lee, which is where Papa went to school. It's redbrick and makes you feel smarter just walking past it. Robert E. Lee is buried in its lovely chapel. Traveller, his loyal horse, is lying eternally close to his master.

The next-door neighbor of the college is the Virginia Military Institute. I've always thought it odd, considering the school's job is to train boys to fight in wars, that the grounds do not resemble a battlefield. But the VMI lawns are rolling, the flower beds chock-full, and the trees offer pools of welcoming shade.

If I wanted, I could see part of my land baron grandfather's thousand-acre spread from up here, too. It's called Heritage Farm and it starts way out on the edge of town with the longest driveway, which winds up to the house that sits atop a hill, and has pasture and springs behind it that lead straight up to the foothills of the mountains. He's got a lot of folks around here working for him. That beautiful wheat-growing property is where my father and his brother grew up in a mansion that has always reminded me of Tara from *Gone with the Wind*, only it's much older since it has been around since almost the beginning of historical time. Grampa lives there with his *much* better half—our ladylike grandmother, Ruth Love. But I won't look in that direction. I won't give him that satisfaction. Gus Carmody is a leathery bastard.

I lift my binoculars to my eyes and jigger the wheel until Blind Beezy becomes crisp and clear. Like usual, she's got on the most outlandish outfit because a mirror isn't much use to a sightless someone. Beezy's grinning this morning, she almost always is. With her teeth being scarce like they are and the orange shift and green felt hat she's got on, she could easily get mistaken for a jack-o'-lantern. One of those darling kinds that you can hold in the palm of your hand, not the fat squat ones. She's an early riser, so I knew she'd already be on the porch of her place that stands out from the rest of Mudtown like a sunflower in a junkyard. Two years ago the ladies from Old Presbyterian painted her house ridiculous yellow like that. Those Presbyterians are a sneaky bunch. They're always doing good deeds for Beezy. Trying to lure her away from Beacon Baptist, I guess.

I check Mama's watch and take off down the hill, shouting back at E. J. and Woody, "Hurry up. We only got forty-one minutes left."

Chapter Four

Her house on Monroe Street is not large nor is it small. Just perfect, is how I'd describe it. It's made of wood and it's only one story high, which is good because we wouldn't want Blind Beezy falling down a flight of stairs. She's got a nice porch and lots of trees. Handmade birdhouses, courtesy of Mr. Cole, are hanging from almost every branch. Beezy adores birds because, "They can go anywhere and do anything no matter what color they is." Of course, she can't see her feathered friends, but she knows their songs and the one she especially likes is the call of the purple martin, which sounds like a gurgling brook. I also think Beezy likes birds so much because it is their God-given right to poop on people's heads no matter what color their skin is and nobody can punish them for doing so. If I had been born a Negro instead of a white, I'd hold resentment towards some folks around here who treat the colored like they are—as my grandfather likes to say—"the shit end of the stick." I used to, but I don't believe in them being inferior to us anymore because it doesn't make sense. I know some first-class Negroes. I also know some second-rate white people. (Two of the latter being members of my family.)

Beezy gets reports on how we're doing from our caretaker, Mr. Cole. They're sweet on each other. Sometimes he brings Woody and me over here after he's put Lilyfield to bed. After we're sure Papa's fallen asleep, the three of us skulk off in the cover of darkness. Beezy makes us chicken potpie prison-style. It's got a lot of crust, which is our favorite part. After we thank her for her hospitality by doing the dishes, we stretch out on this porch and by the light of the moon listen to the soulful sounds of Billie Holiday or the toe-tapping Duke Ellington on her Victrola with her and Mr. Cole. Knowing how Papa doesn't spend much celestial time with me anymore, Mr. Cole has been kind enough to talk with me on some of those nights about how the astronauts are planning to land on the moon next month. He looks up to the sky and says, "I expect they'll do just fine, don't you, Shenny?" I always say back, "I do," but I don't mean it. Mr. Cole doesn't understand what a long shot it is to fly safely around meteors and asteroids and Lord only knows what else. Even if they manage to steer clear of all those dangers, what're their chances of landing safe? No, I do not hold out much hope for those moon men.

Woody and I also come to Beezy's because that's what

Mama told us to do a bunch of times. "If anything should happen to me, peas, you can count on Beezy or your grandmother to watch over you until things get sorted out." Woody and I told her, "Sure," but what I was thinking at the time was, how foolish can a person be? With the way Papa keeps tabs on her every minute of every day, what could possibly happen to her? (Nowadays I think my mother might have been blessed with the gift of second sight.)

Woody, E. J., and I have dashed through the backyards of the colored neighborhood to avoid prying eyes. We are playing the same game we always do. Beezy told us if ever we could sneak up on her, she'd give us all quarters. We've tried for years. The three of us are creeping alongside her tall hedge, not more than ten feet from her porch, right next to her birdbath. I'm not that nuts about this game and neither is Woody because we know what it's like to get snuck up on, but we do it for E. J. With the way he's grinning I know he's already thinking how he's going to spend that quarter. Beezy sings out, "Are those chick-a-dees settin' to shower themselves or is it those fine-looking Carmody twins and that hard-workin' Tittle boy?"

We have never once gotten past that birdbath. The old girl is sort of uncanny.

E. J.'s muttering something in frustration because he could really use twenty-five cents, but I'm yelling, "Wait up."

I can see Woody taking the porch steps two at a time and landing not so lightly in Beezy's familiar lap. My sister is so jazzed up. Beezy is special to her and me because she helped Mama take care of us when we were itty-bitty. Woody's the one that gave her the pet name—Beezy. Her real name is Elizabeth, but my sister had a hard time pronouncing that when she was a little kid, so she started calling her Beezy, and then so did everybody else.

There was also a time that Beezy got paid to clean my grandfather's house at Heritage Farm, but she got fired from that job because my grampa is Simon Legree mean. After that, she married no-account Carl Bell, but then she killed him and had to go to the Big House. Being curious of nature the way I am, I asked her once what it feels like to murder somebody. "I don't rightly know, hon. I don't feel like a murderess," she answered with a good-natured shrug. "More like a laundress ridding the world of a soul that was stained beyond repair."

It was my own father that sent her to Red Onion State Prison. Even though most all the coloreds and some of the whites in town, including my mother, believed that Beezy should be set free. She testified in court, "Carl beat me about the head 'til I went blind and then he began choking me with chicken wire." She opened her blouse collar so the jury could see the still-red welts around her neck. "I didn't mean to kill him. I was only attemptin' to defend myself." (Beezy plunged that skinning knife into Carl's neck and he bled to death right on the spot because, according to Mr. Cole who told me this story, "The skinner nicked his juggler's vein.")

After six days of deliberation, the jury didn't let Beezy off scot-free, but they did take pity. She didn't get convicted of first-degree murder, but manslaughter, which is exactly what it sounds like. This is one of the reasons I think Beezy is not so fond of Papa. I can understand her holding that against him, but I don't think she's seeing the big picture. Of course, he could've been more lenient when he sentenced her to five years with time off for good behavior, but like always—Judge Walter T. Carmody was right. Because when she wasn't busy washing and wringing the prison's sheets, Beezy got taught by one of the lady guards how to knit and purl and that's how she makes her living now. Folks travel to Lexington from all over Rockbridge County and beyond to buy her sweaters and scarves and caps. Maybe they just come to have something that they can brag to their friends was made by a murderess. I don't know.

I charge up the steps of the house in hot pursuit, shouting, "Get off her right this minute, Woody. Can't you see that you're crushin' Miss Beezy?" She pops up looking alarmed so even though she pretends she can't *some*times, my sister can hear me just fine *all* the time. "Come see what I brought." I open up my lunch box. Besides leftover breakfast for E. J., I packed her drawing supplies. If I don't keep her busy, she'll end up creating more trouble and we don't have time for that this morning. We're on a deadline. "Why don't you get comfy right over here?"

Following directions for a change, Woody spreads out her crayons and pencils, smooths out her sketching paper, and gets arty at Beezy's feet. E. J. is edging towards the screen door. His tiny nose is busy picking up the scent of something yummy just like mine is.

White peonies are lining Beezy's fence in all their glory and filling the backyard with their heady scent. And my mind with memories of Mama. They are her favorites. She had them in her wedding bouquet because they are a good omen for a happy marriage.

Shortly before she disappeared, she'd been acting mopey, so I cut her a bunch off one of these bushes and ran all the way home. I found her looking out the kitchen window. "Look what I brought you," I said, bursting in on her.

She startled, and said sort of sad, "Thank you, Shen."

When she reached up to the cupboard to get the crystal vase, her long-sleeved blouse fell back. I pointed at her arms and asked, "How'd you get those marks?"

Mama rushed to cover them up and said, "I . . . I got my arm caught in the linen chest."

"You should be more careful," I said, not surprised. My mother is a very accident-prone person. Always has got a black-and-blue mark either fading or blooming.

Once she got those flowers just the way she wanted them, she turned to me and told me thank you again, but her eyes didn't look so grateful.

I asked with hurt feelings, "Don't you like them?"

Mama hesitated for a moment, then cupped my warm face in her hands that were cool from the sink water and whispered, " 'I will be the gladdest thing under the sun! I will touch a hundred flowers and not pick one.' "

"What's that supposed to mean?" I asked.

Kissing the confusion off my face, she replied, "What Edna St. Vincent Millay means in this poem is . . . if you keep something all for yourself . . . while I love that you're thinking of me, it's important to let flowers grow. People, too. Do you understand?"

I told her, "I do," but I really didn't.

Beezy hears E. J. making his snorting noise and says, "Sure 'nuff, there's fritters in the warmer, but my ankles tell me there's also grass that needs shortenin'." That's the deal they've made. Apple fritters for mowing. "I expect you'll wanna do something about that sooner rather than later."

E. J. knows better than just about anybody that it's not smart to bite the hand that feeds him, so he says, "Yes, ma'am. I'll get over here first thing tomorra to give it a trim," and makes a beeline into the house.

After I sit down next to her, Beezy says, "Good thing you showed up today. I was preparin' to pay you a visit this evenin'."

"We tried to get away yesterday, but Louise is working us to the bone. Gramma will be here soon for Founders Weekend. You know how she can get if everything isn't white glove clean."

Beezy runs a lace hankie across her neck scar and says, "Indeed I do."

"That still doesn't give Lou the right to be such a pain in the patootie. I swear, that girl could start an argument in an empty house," I say, already knowing that Beezy won't agree with me. She feels violin-playing sorry for Louise. Whenever I complain about how our housekeeper bosses us about and what an all-around drip she is, Beezy tells me to, "Go easy on her, Shenny. She reminds me of myself at that age."

"Will Ruth Love be comin' to the festivities?" Beezy asks. "I know she wasn't feeling up to it last year."

Woody, who has been coloring like a demon, jerks her head up at the sound of our grandmother's name. "I think so," I say, hoping my sister can't hear me.

Beezy asks, "Ruth Love been stayin' on track?"

"Mostly." I wish she wouldn't go down this road. I know she and Gramma used to be on friendly terms so she always asks after her, but Woody's been having a bumpy time of it with our gramma, who if there ever was a race for the best Southern belle in this county would win by a mile. She does beautiful needlework. Can make a pot roast that just falls off the bone and mashed potatoes without one lump. And her pies? They win every prize at the county fair. She'll also play card games with Woody and me, not poker though, since she is also real holy and gambling is against the Bible. All in all, we couldn't ask for a more lovely grandmother.

Most of the time.

Occasionally, Gramma has what we're supposed to call "episodes," but I always tell Woody to stay clear if I think Gramma's winding up to "pitch a conniption fit." Some conniptions are a lot worse than others. She took a hatchet to the grand piano in her parlor a few years back because the Lord told her she was getting too much enjoyment out of playing ragtime music. Grampa Gus told folks that his wife had a heart problem, not a head problem, and that's why she had to stay in her bedroom with the curtains drawn for a month. Then he sent her off to The Virginia State Colony for Epileptics and Feebleminded over in Lynchburg to get better and thank goodness, she did—after the doctors told her to quit being so religious and gave her some electrical treatments.

"What do you mean *mostly*?" Beezy asks suspiciously. She knows things about Gramma Ruth Love that outsiders don't because Mama told her. Even though she wasn't supposed to. We're not to tell anybody what goes on in the Carmody family. "Ruth Love hasn't gone haywire, has she?"

"No, no. Why would you think that?" I *pshaw*. "She's just been puttin' on way too much Ben-Gay and it's been bothering Woody's sensitive nose, that's all."

That Ben-Gay part is true, but what I don't tell easily upset Beezy is that on her last visit, our grandmother made us play Holy Communion with her all afternoon. That also bugged Woody, but can you blame her? A person can only stand eating Wonder Bread that's been crushed into religious wafers for so long without getting bloated.

"Got any new wiggle-waggle?" I ask, trying to draw Beezy off the Gramma topic and back to the business at hand. Her eyes may not work, but her ears are like sponges soaking up the juicy gossip getting spread by the women that strut past her place on their way downtown. She's got to have heard something. Mama's disappearance is still big news.

"Lemme see, lemme see," Beezy says, letting what she's working on slip to her little lap. "Well, just about everybody's talking 'bout how Mary Jane Upton showed up at the grocery yesterday wearin' a bathing suit and calling herself Rita Hayworth."

Mrs. Upton is always going around town under-dressed asking after her tomcat of a husband who works nights at the Old Blue Hotel. You'd think everybody would be used to her by now. "Ya got anything *new*?"

Beezy considers, then says, "I heard that Abigail Hawkins been elected president of the Ladies Auxiliary."

"Big deal."

"I also heard she's been showin' up at your place on a regular basis. Any truth to that?"

A taste something like an iron handrail comes into my mouth. "She's been bringing up corn bread and rhubarb pie and . . . I swear, that woman is tryin' to give Betty Crocker a bad name."

Beezy *tsks . . . tsks*. "It's not a fondness for cookin' that's bringing Miss Abby up to Lilyfield and I expect you know that, Shen."

I protest, "Whatta ya mean?" like I have no idea what she's referring to, even though I have my suspicions. I heard Father Tommy tell Papa after church, "A year's time is considered long enough to grieve, Walter. The twins need a mother."

For God's sakes, where's his faith? His hope? I can't believe that priest is forgetting the same way that some of the single ladies in town are that Mama is not gone forever, only temporarily so. Abigail Hawkins is the worst of them, but I've kept a list of every one of those women who bat their eyes at Papa after Mass. Woe to them is all I got to say on that subject. (I'm planning on getting Miss Delia who lives at the boardinghouse to put a hex on all of them. You should see what she did to

Charity Thomas who got on my bad side. Miss D gave her a hump. A big one. Think camel.)

"Yes, indeedy," Beezy says, rocking back. "Sounds to me like Miss Hawkins is busy settin' a web for your father."

E. J. comes bursting back onto the porch with a fritter in each hand and chewing another. He's coated them in mayonnaise. I think you could get him to do just about anything for a jar of Hellmann's. He swallows and says, "Miss Abby settin' a web, yup. Sounds that way to me, too."

"It does not," I say, elbowing him in the ribs. "You're just angling for more fritters."

"*Singin' in the Rain* is showing again up at Hull's," Beezy says, picking up her yarn and hinting on how she'd like to spend this Thursday evening. She loves old-time movie night just like Mama. Especially if they're showing a musical one. Woody and me would wear our baby doll pajamas to Hull's Drive-In on sweltering summer nights. Mama would turn up the speaker and her and Beezy would sing along and we'd drink Coca-Cola right out of the bottle and eat Cracker Jack under the stars and that was all so . . . well, heavenly. We're missing those good old times up at Hull's so I try to make up for that on the Thursdays when Papa is nowhere to be found. I chauffeur us up to the drive-in in Beezy's old brown Pontiac that I can handle if we go slow.

"I had to sneak into the Belmont Theater when that picture show first come out," she says. "People of my color weren't—"

"Beezy Bell! Please don't make me drag it out of you. I'm running out of time," I say, impatient. I hold our mother's watch up to her ear. It's inscribed on the back with the word *Speranza*, which means "hope" in the Italian language. Mama got this watch from our friend Sam Moody. It's my most prized possession. Not only does it make me feel with every tick that I'm getting closer to finding her, it's also an excellent reminder that Woody and I got a fast friend in Sam, who is Beezy's illegitimate, by the way. "Have you got something helpful or not? If the answer is *not*, then we're gonna run over to the drugstore and talk to Vera."

"Sugar, it's been so long," Beezy says, disheartened. "Your mother—"

"'Defer no time, delays have dangerous ends.'" Sam used to say that to my mama all the time. "William Shakespeare wrote that. It means—time's a-wastin', so you better hurry up and do something before something else real bad happens." Beezy doesn't want my heart to get broken if I can't find Mama. That's why she's holding back. "If I hadn't waited so long to go lookin' for her in the first place, maybe she'd be home right now," I say, softer. "You understand?"

Clearly not wanting to, she sighs out, "Yesterday afternoon Dorothea Dineen was tellin' Harriet Godwin that she heard Evie applied for a library position before she disappeared."

It's true Mama was at her happiest when surrounded by books, but well-to-do married women have their gardens and the pampering of their husbands and children to fill their days. They do not have jobs. I mean, Mama *could've* gotten a position at the library if that was allowed. She went to Sweet Briar College to study singing with hopes of appearing on Broadway someday, but then she fell in love with the great poets of the past and the masters of art so she switched over to learn about them until she fell in love with Papa. They got married short of her receiving her sheepskin.

I ask Beezy, "Ya sure you heard that right? A library position?" Papa wouldn't let us go over there anymore after Mama vanished, so I started phoning on Tuesday afternoons, which was our usual checking-out-books time. I knew it was stupid, but I kept hoping that one of those times somebody would come onto the line, saying, "Miz Carmody? Why, sure she's here." Moments later, I'd hear Mama's breathy "Hello?" and when I asked her where she's been all this time, she'd say, "Oh, dear. I've lost track of the time. Your father's not home from the courthouse yet, is he?" I finally had to give up the calling. That hog of a librarian, Jeanine Anderson, squealed to Papa and that's why all that's left of the downstairs phone is its roots.

E. J. stuffs the last bit of fritter into his mouth and asks, "What's that you're workin' on, Miz Bell?"

"It's something new I'm tryin' out. It's a muffler." She holds up the piece of chartreuse and puce knitting. It's anything but muffled. Since she can't see what yarns she's combining together, her stuff is louder in color than a marching band. "Ya like it, Shenny?" she asks, waving it my way.

"Love it," I say, getting more and more riled by the second. We don't have time for a regular visit like this, but trying to get Beezy to hurry through polite talk is like pushing a mule up a hill.

"Speakin' of work," she says, back busy with hers. "Little Walter thinkin' of gettin' himself back to the courtroom any time soon?" That's what she calls Papa. *Little Walter*. So what if he's got to sit on a phone book to see over his judge's bench, she doesn't have to say so, does she?

"I'm sure after Mama returns, His Honor will be rarin' to get back to his gavel," I answer, because it seems too disloyal to tell her that I can't picture his erratic self in a courtroom any time soon. Who cares when he gets back to work anyway? It's not like we need the money. We're the richest family in town and my grandfather owns half the county.

Beezy hears me yawn and asks, "Not gettin' your eight straight?"

"Not even six. Woody spends most of the night . . ." I glance down at my sister.

Her coloring arm is back and forthing with the only crayon she's uses anymore—funeral black. It really bothers me that she won't write words. If she can't talk—fine. But she's got the paper, she's got the crayons, would it kill her to jot down one of these times, *Hey Shen, I love you?*

"Have ya been takin' her to visit the doc?" Beezy asks, sensing my upset the way she can.

"A course I have."

Papa gave me permission to take Woody to Doc Keller's office above Milligan's Hardware every Sunday evening after the sidewalks get rolled up. Mostly all he does is ask lots of questions about what we think might've happened to Mama. I stonewall him, because what business is it of his anyway? "Can't you just fix her?" I ask every time, hoping he'll change his answer.

"I could. If there was something physically wrong," he tells me when he's done examining my sister's throat. "Her vocal cords are in fine working order. She's got hysterical muteness."

Chester Keller may be Papa's fraternity brother and oldest friend, but I think he's gone over the hill and isn't ever coming back. What's so funny about my sister losing her voice?

Beezy's forehead gets as furrowed as her knitting. "This lookin' for Evelyn . . . it's . . . it's a lot to take on all by yourself, Shenny."

I almost cry out, *What am I supposed to do exactly? Papa's threatening to send Woody away because she won't talk. . . . We need to get Mama back more than ever.* Beezy may be privy to a lot of what goes on around town, but she doesn't know half of what's happening up at Lilyfield. She knows that Papa is keeping us close, but has no idea how close. If I *did* clue her in to the root cellar and the interrogation sessions and all the other stuff, there's not one thing she could do to help so there's no sense in getting her worked up. That could be dangerous for her.

"Please don't fret," I say. "I'm *not* takin' this on all by myself. There's somebody else I've got in mind to lend a helping hand."

Beezy knows *exactly* who I'm talking about and her lips are saying, "*Mmm . . . hmm,*" but she doesn't mean it. If I could spend a minute more reassuring her, I would, but my sister has gone into a prey stance, rigid as a hound. If she had a tail, it'd be pointing.

"No . . . no . . ." I reach out for Woody, but she slips right through my fingers.

"What's happenin', Shen?" Beezy asks, always alert.

"It's all right. It's fine." I pat her knee, which feels exactly like a glass doorknob.

"Woody's just run off again. I'll take care of it." From the edge of the porch, I holler, "Get back here!" She not only ignores me, my sister doesn't even bother to look both ways as she tears across the street to what she's honed in on—the cemetery. "Don't ya wanna finish your picture of . . . ah?"

I look down at what she's been coloring on, already knowing that it's going to be something morbid. Like a woman getting beat by a horned Satan or a hairy beast with foamy madness dripping off its stalactite teeth. Sure enough, today's drawing reminds me a lot of our dog, Mars. Only it's real bloody and gutsy. I should tell Woody that dog is never coming back. I really should.

"Quit catchin' flies with your mouth and do something!" I shout at E. J. He's lazing against the railing, watching with jaw-dropping adoration as my sister zigzags through the headstones to the side of Bootie Young, who is up to his belly button in a fresh grave. The reason

E. J. is not rushing after her is that he knows what Woody has got herself all worked up about and it's *not* Bootie Young.

Making my point, she doesn't even seem to notice that handsome hunk as she begins pacing. Up and down . . . down and up . . . flapping her arms the length of the grave. Flapping is the second most irritating thing she does next to eye blinking, which always makes me think she's trying to send me an SOS in Morse code and I don't know Morse code. I better get over there quick before she does something wholly unpredictable.

"She's not hurtin' anybody," E. J. says, clamping on to my arm as I rush past him. "Leave her be, Shen."

I rip out of his grasp. "Get off me!" I'm surprised by how mad I am, and by the look on his face, E. J. is, too. "Quit telling me what to do and if you ever touch me again you . . . you . . . minin' sludge . . . I'll . . . I'll—"

"Shenandoah Wilson Carmody!" Beezy admonishes. "Apologize to Ed James right this minute."

"But he . . . he—"

"Shenny," Beezy demands with a stomp of her little foot.

"Yes, ma'am." I back off and say to E. J. in my most ladylike voice, "Pardon me ever so much," so Beezy will forgive me, but she can't see me lifting my fingers up to his cheeks and pinching him hard as I want.

Stupid kid. He's acting like Woody and him have already tied the knot.

Chapter Five

Following the exact same route through the headstones and mausoleums that Woody did, I pass a slew of our dead relatives on the way towards Bootie and his hole. Grampa's also got a graveyard up at his place where some Founders are laid to rest because this cemetery wasn't around back when they succumbed to Indian raids or plow accidents or plain old scarlet fever.

"*Hurrah! Hurrah! For Southern rights, hurrah!*" Bootie is singing. He's rehearsing. He always performs the traditional Civil War song "The Bonnie Blue Flag" at the opening ceremonies of Founders Weekend because he was born with a creamy baritone that can reach out into a crowd and grab it by the throat.

The Young family works a dairy farm, but according to a couple of reports that I heard him read up front of the classroom when Woody and I were still attending school, waking at the crack of dawn to milk crabby cows holds no interest for Bootie. He wants to attend college so he can be an archaeologist, which is a bone digger, so this cemetery job is good practice. Because he's had to miss so much school during planting and harvest times, even though he's in the same grade as Woody and me (going into seventh), he's a year older at thirteen but looks even older, like all the farm boys do. I bet there's still plenty of girls that draw his name inside hearts all over their schoolbooks or pass him mushy notes that are SWAK—Sealed With A Kiss. I don't have time for that lovey-dovey stuff. I'm too busy worrying about Mama, taking caring of Woody, and keeping watch over Papa, so I am always courteous to Bootie when I run across him, but never overly so. Wouldn't want to give him the wrong idea.

Coming up to the grave, I press Woody's arms down to her sides and say, "Hey, there."

"Mornin', Shen," Bootie says, thrusting his shovel into the dirt. He's towheaded with a cleft in his chin that I've always wanted to stick my finger in to see how deep it'd go. First knuckle, I bet. "Haven't seen you in forever." Bootie looks more plumped out in the body than the last time I saw him but none of it's chub. His bare chest is smooth, but the hair under his arms matches his brown eyes and he's still got the most luscious smile. Like a gooey dessert. "Where ya gonna sit on parade day?"

"In the park with Beezy," I say. "Like always."

After Woody and I have led the Parade of Perpetual

Princesses most of the way down Main, we peel off so we can join Beezy and the rest of the Negroes. The parade doesn't go through Mudville so they got to watch it as it winds past Buffalo Park. Even though we are light-skinned, Woody and me are always nicely tanned by this time of the year. We also wear straw hats that cast shadows upon our faces so we do not stick out like two whitefish in that sea of brown bodies. (We have to be careful not to get noticed by Grampa, who does not in any way, shape, or form approve of us associating with Beezy or any of the other coloreds in a social way.)

When the parade turns the corner and heads our way, I tell Beezy every year beneath the shade of that big maple, "Here comes the high school band."

Tittering from her folding chair, Beezy will say, "I'm blind, child, not deaf."

"You're blind? Really? How come nobody told me?" I'll say in mock surprise, because she's got one of those great booming kinds of laughs that you would never suspect could come out of somebody so small. "Next up are six baton twirlers whose sparkly uniforms are a mite skimpy on top and riding up in the back, especially Dot Halloran's. (Never have been able to stand Dot, not sure why.) "Right behind them are Joe Morton and Cal Whitcomb dressed up like Uncle Sams and waving to everybody. After them, the float with Grampa in that Confederate uniform is coming. He's sitting on top in that golden horseshoe throne." I always spit into the grass once he passes by. "There's six black horses makin' a mess all over the street behind him."

Beezy will sniff the air at that point and remark, "Always thought those animals were a lot smarter than folks give 'em credit for," and that never fails to crack me up 'cause I think Grampa stinks, too.

"Whose body ya diggin' that hole for?" I ask Bootie, narrowing it down to a Caucasian since Stonewall Jackson Cemetery doesn't allow coloreds. They got to start their trip to the Promised Land over at Evergreen.

"This here is Mr. Minnow's grave," Bootie replies with a respectful bow of his head.

"*Clive* Minnow?" I may sound surprised, but I'm really not. I've been wondering why I haven't seen our neighbor around lately. Usually when I'm doing some afternoon reading, he'll appear in his adjoining woods with his metal-detecting device. Of course, Papa told me to stay away from him. They do not get along because you got to walk on eggshells around His Honor and Clive wasn't light on his feet.

"Are you absolutely positive it's Mr. Clive Minnow that you'll be buryin' here?" I ask, recalling how the last time I saw him, he didn't look fatally sick. He *had* been complaining of stomachaches off and on, but that wasn't unusual. A few years ago when Clive was convinced that he had gotten a brain tumor, I got worried because I'd seen a man on the Dr. Ben Casey television show get the same thing and he expired during the first fifteen minutes. But when I told Mama, she wasn't upset one bit.

"He's all right, Shenny. It's not a brain tumor, just a headache," she said, handing me a bottle of aspirins from the cupboard. "Mr. Clive is what is known as a hypochondriac."

"A hypo*whatee*ac?"

"A hypochondriac," she said slowly. "That's a person who thinks that they're either sick or about to become sick or much sicker than they really are, but it's only in their head."

"But a brain tumor *is* all in somebody's head!" I protested, but after I looked the word up in the dictionary that made sense. *Hypochondriac* means that Clive was the kind of person who had quite the imagination when it came to illness and that's really true. Over the years, I've lost count of the number of times he told me that he thought he was coming down with polio or chicken pox, even leprosy and malaria. I explained to him we don't have those last two diseases in the Commonwealth, but he hissed, "Ain't nobody ever taught you that there's a first time for everything, little girl?"

"How'd he die?" I ask, feeling guilty.

Bootie says, "Virgil went up to the Minnow place to deliver groceries Saturday morning like always. Nobody answered the door, so Virgil went looking. He found Clive facedown at the edge of the creek, his dog whinin' by his side."

"Oh, that's awful," I say with genuine regret. He and I had recently been bickering over a ring he'd found in the woods with his detecting device, but that's not an excuse. I should've stopped by the Minnow place more often than I had been to check up on him. "Poor Clive. Poor Ivory."

"Who?" Booty asks.

"That's the name of Clive's dog. Ivory Minnow."

Bootie pulls the shovel out of the dirt, using muscles that look like they could keep you safe. "I heard drownin's one of the worst ways to go."

"Yeah, I heard that, too."

My other grandparents drowned. For a while there, I think the sheriff thought that's what happened to our mother, too. He had half the county searching the creek's banks and bushes for her. The day Woody and I were out there watching, I pulled him aside and told him, "She's a good swimmer. She was on the water ballet team in college."

Sheriff Nash, who is not particularly smart, but *is* well-mannered, said, "Don't think your mother drowned, Miss Shen. The rowboat is missin'."

I told him, "But Mama would never take the boat by herself," but would he listen?

He pulled me behind a yew bush and said in a lowered voice, "Are you aware of your mother and father havin' any . . . ?"

That's when His Honor spotted us and hurried over. He said to the sheriff, "That'll be all, Andy," and then he dragged me farther into the bushes and reprimanded me. "Take your sister back up to the house immediately. Her crying is upsetting the hounds."

Papa.

"Nice job on the hole, Bootie. Keep up the good work. Time to go, Woody," I say, grabbing her by the arm and praying that this isn't one of those times when she makes herself as stiff as her name. She can do that when she doesn't want to leave one place and go to another. I don't have time to look for a coaster wagon to set her in. We should've been back at Lilyfield by now.

"Wait a tick, Shen," Bootie says, toeing the dirt at the bottom of the grave. "I . . . I was wondering if you'd like to . . . Y'all are goin' to the carnival, right?"

"A course we are. Right, Woody?"

No matter how much our father warns us about staying out of the public eye, the Carmodys are the descendants of those that get celebrated during Founders Weekend. Grampa Gus will insist that we not miss any of the "brouhaha," and that includes the two nights of the carnival, which is just fine and dandy with us. Woody and I have always gone crazy for those rickety rides and penny pitching games and, most of all, the Oddities of Nature sideshow, which has an Armadillo Boy and the beefiest gal in the world named Baby Doll Susan, who lives behind a wall of glass with a refrigerator and a floral sofa set on cinder blocks. The best oddities, though, have got to be the Siamese twins. There was a time when I praised Jesus for not planting Woody and me so close inside of Mama that we grew into each other the way they did, but with my sister running off the way she's been, I've begun to out and out envy joined-at-the-hip Milly and Tilly. If my sister keeps this up . . . well. I can't find Mama *and* chase after her. There's only so many hours in the day.

"Shen? Earth to Shenny." Bootie laughs.

"Yeah?"

Giving me what I'd consider to be a smile of invitation, he says, "I heard from my cousin in Winchester that the sideshow's bringin' a baby in a bottle this year."

"No kiddin'? How'd they ever—" I'm dying to RSVP. To tell him, "I would love to go for a ride with you in the Tunnel of Love. After that, we could sit on the tent benches and watch the show. I'll bury my head in your strong chest when the snake man charms the serpent out the basket because secretly, Bootie Young, you make me want to unbraid my hair and put on a frilly dress." But I put on a disinterested voice and say, "Maybe we'll run into you there," because he's not only distracting me, he's distracting Woody, and the clock in Washington Square is chiming quarter past the hour.

"Please." I yank on my sister again, but she's not budging. Her eyes are locked down, her face a mural of yearning. She's thinking about how good it would be to lay herself down on the bottom of the grave and have Bootie cover her missing-Mama heart in cooling dirt, I just know she is. "We've got to get back before . . ." I don't want to, but I got to. I lean my head to Woody's and whisper, "The root cellar," and thank goodness, she picks up her pace.

Chapter Six

We're standing at the edge of the creek on the Tittle side.

I'm arguing with E. J. He keeps fussing, insisting, "Let me walk back across the stones with you."

I got my reasons for not wanting him to get involved in the Carmody family business more than he already is. "Quit bein' more of a pain than you already are," I say, piggybacking onto the first stepping stone behind my sister, who is still real agitated on account of me bringing up the root cellar over at the cemetery. I get a better grip on her. "I mean it, E. J. Make like a bunny and hop up that hill."

"But I'm worried that—" He looks past me at Woody.

I warn him, "If you don't get out of here on the count of three . . ." One of the other reasons E. J. is being extra-overbearing is that even though he's never said anything to me, I'm pretty sure he's heard my uncle and grandfather whooping and hollering through our woods in the wee hours. That's when they like to play hide-'n'-seek. Woody and me hide—they seek. "One . . . two . . ." When E. J. doesn't make a move to turn towards home, I pull out my heaviest artillery. "I won't let you see you know who anymore if you don't git," and that settles that. Not sure that I've ever seen him move so fast. He doesn't even say, "Catch ya on the flipside," which he normally does as he scrambles off.

Woody, who appeared to be paying no mind to E. J.'s and my squabble, quick twists out of my grip and starts running across the stepping stones. Usually so sure-footed, she's in such an all-fired hurry that she slips and falls into the creek when she's almost onto our side. I want to holler out to E. J. to come back and help, but if I do, I'll never hear the end of it, so I hustle across the remaining stones, jump in after her and the two of us go panting up onto the bank. We're trying to catch our breaths. She's flushed and frenzied. I take a piece of her hair out of her mouth and set it behind her ear. "Pea . . . you . . . you have *got* . . . to stop runnin' off like—what?" Woody is sniffing the air. She can hear the wind change directions since she's gone mute, and her nose—it's keen. She's almost locked onto something and then I hear him, too.

"Have you cleaned these stalls?" Papa. His voice is coming out of the barn, not more than fifty yards from us. I thought for sure he'd be occupied in his study already, but he's come back from his ride much later than usual. "Did you throw down fresh shavings and clean the water buckets?"

Mr. Cole answers back soft-spoken so I can't hear him.

I say urgently to Woody, "If he comes out, he'll see us. Quick. Dive under the willow."

Not a beat later, His Honor comes out of the barn. The handsomest man in all of Rockbridge County, the one who's got midnight hair and eyes that are the same color as the whiskey and soda he drinks around that time looks even worse than he did last night. Taking unsteady steps our way, Papa shouts, "Girls? Is that you?"

The branches of the willow tree are wiggling and there's no wind today. That's what's gotten his attention. I will them to be still.

"Twins?" he calls, coming closer.

"Scoot . . . scoot back," I whisper frantically to Woody. We use our hands and heels to dig deeper into the branches. "And please, please, please, don't start howling."

"I see you," Papa says, but I'm sure he can't. He's tripped down to the grass. He's been worse the last few days because he gets extra soused whenever Grampa's due to visit. I can't really blame him. I have been forced to slug back a few when that old nincompoop shows up. I want to rush to his side and help him up, but I've fallen for that before, and Woody knows it. She holds me tight by the wrist until Papa struggles back up, first onto all fours, and then semi-upright. He shakes his head like he's forgotten what he was doing and turns back towards the barn.

Woody is fluttering. She wants to make a break for it, but I warn her, "Wait." I inch forward until I can see Papa through the curtain of shimmering leaves. Maybe he really did see us. Sometimes he can fool us. Sometimes he can double back. I lean back to my sister and start counting slowly, "One Virginia, two Virginia," and when I get up to "thirty Virginia," I tell her, "All right. Get set, go!" On our dash to the house, I run backwards so I can keep an eye on the barn door. "Keep movin'," I tell Woody when she looks at me bug-eyed.

Once we're on the back porch of the house, I trap my twin between my arms, press her against the peeling white wood. "Don't even swallow." I squeeze her to make a big impression. "I mean it. Hold still." I'm waving my hand and blowing on the bottoms of our shorts to dry them off the best I can. "We're gonna sneak through the kitchen."

I get Woody by the chin and raise her eyes up to mine so I'm sure she sees the seriousness daggering out of them. I'm leaving her out here until I can make sure the coast is clear. If Papa *did* double back and came in through the front door, we'll run into him. He'll do what he always does, inspect us like we're pieces of fruit, looking to find the soft spots. I am especially gifted at fibbing so I could come up with a reason how our shorts got damp, but once His Honor goes after Woody, I'd be forced to tell him the truth and nothing but the truth about where we've been this morning.

I spit on the hinges so the screen door won't squeak and stick my head into the kitchen.

There's a pot top clattering on the stove and the transistor radio is playing a rhythm-and-blues song and the
floor looks clean but tacky in places. That means Lou's
got to be close by. I'm praying that she's not hiding in
the broom closet, getting ready to pounce out at us
screaming, "Gotcha!" the way she likes to do. She thinks
that's funny. I don't think Woody could handle that right
now. She's already full-to-the-brim with scared.

"Shh." I place my fingers to my sister's lips until I
remember how dumb that is. We begin creeping across
the linoleum. "Get up on your ballerina toes," I whisper,
forgetting all about how loud that creak is in front of the
stove.

"'Bout time," Lou calls high and mighty out of the
dining room.

Damnation.

"Get in here, you two."

I lead Woody into the grandest room of our house.
Red flocked wallpaper runs from the ceiling to the floor
and a portrait of Woodrow Wilson in a gilt frame hangs
above the sideboard. The twenty-eighth president of the
United States was born in Staunton, a town up the road
a piece. Papa admires him quite a bit. Enough to name
his only children Jane *Woodrow* and Shenandoah *Wilson*.
On the dining room walls, there's also a couple of pictures of Carmodys that date back to the 1700s. Grampa's
got the most important of them up at his house, but we
have Hiram Carmody, who rode with the Knights of the
Golden Horseshoe. They were a band of explorers who
discovered the Shenandoah Valley from a crest of the

Blue Ridge Mountains. Our gorgeous valley must've seemed like a mirage to them. I'm grateful Woody and me don't take after those Founders. I think Grampa Gus inherited his sour disposition from these old codgers. Every one of them looks like he swallowed a bottle of cod liver oil and asked for seconds.

Lou's up on a stepladder cleaning the crystal chandelier that hangs above the polished mahogany dining table that sits twelve. "You're late," she says, not even bothering to look down at us.

"I know . . . we got . . ." I so resent explaining myself to her.

"Ya just missed your pappy. He came askin' for ya."

I can feel my sister bunch up again beneath my fingertips. "What'd ya tell him?" I ask, gliding my hand up Woody's neck. Stroking where her hair meets her skin keeps her calm.

"The truth, a course," Lou says haughty. "That y'all wouldn't mind me and went flittin' to town, blabbin' with anybody who'd bother talkin' to you about your mama."

"You wouldn't dare," I say, rubbing Woody's neck even harder.

"Maybe I would, maybe I wouldn't," Lou says with a rise of her right eyebrow. "Ya just can't know for sure, can ya."

Oh, yeah I can.

I can barely stand breathing the same air Lou does these days, but I love her uncle, Mr. Cole Jackson, to bits. He's the one who taught me how to play cards.

Papa doesn't give us any spending money so beating Lou and Mr. Cole at poker is how I can afford to buy Band-Aids and drawing supplies for Woody. That's how I know that Lou raises up her right eyebrow when she's got nothing but a pair of sixes but wants to trick you into believing she's got a royal flush.

"You better tell Woody you're lying right this minute, Louise, or . . . or I'll make sure Papa knows you been sneakin' out of your cabin to meet up with Blackie," I say, pulling that ace out of my sleeve. (If those two get caught, you understand who'd get into trouble, don't you? It wouldn't be my uncle, that's for sure. Lou would find herself back in the bayou so fast she wouldn't even remember taking the trip.)

"If ya think I'm scared of your fath—" Lou smacks her jaw shut. She just remembered that unlike her—I never, *ever* bluff. "Go on and tell, see if I care," she says with a toss of her head, but she's as scared of breaking Papa's rules as Woody and I are. She's not supposed to get romantically involved, especially with his brother. She's supposed to be cooking and cleaning and taking care of Woody and me and that's it, so that's why Lou's backing down. On both counts.

When she gets eye to eyes with us, I tell her with clenched fists, "Woody needs an apology."

Lou knows that when I get like this that I'm not messing around, so she steps right up to Woody and puts on one of her old-fashioned smiles. "Thought ya knew I was only kiddin' 'bout tellin' your pappy that you and your sis been runnin' into town. Ya know how I like to fun."

She didn't used to.

Woody and I spent many an evening over at the Jacksons' cottage back when Lou was still acting like an older sister. She told us all about her life before she came to Lilyfield and how it was her dream to work someday down at Filly's beauty salon. Since that will never come true because she is the wrong color, Woody and I felt sorry for her and let her do our hair into pickaninny braids while she told us stories in a drawl so thick and fluid it would suck us right in. You'd think she'd swallowed some of that Louisiana swamp the way she wove those spine-tingling tales of zombies and haunted graveyards and potions made of cat bones that can make a person invisible or bring back a lost lover. Or how red pepper powder is the best thing to use if you want to drive your worst enemy away.

Our best and favorite tale, though, has got to be the legend of the grandest of all gators named Rex. Lou would lean in close and say spooky, "Yes, indeedy. That scaly boy would come sneakin' out of the swamp, turn the knob to your shanty, and then you know what he'd do?" That'd be my cue to ask, "What? What would that gator do, Lou?" She'd say even spookier, lean even closer, "Why, he'd make hisself at home like he was payin' the rent, and then those long nails of his would go *click click click* straight into your bedroom and then he'd . . ." We'd almost be out of our minds scared by now, waiting for her to say, "And then . . . and then . . . he'd eat you whole while ya was asleep, thas what he'd do!" Woody would throw her arms around me and I'd let loose with a scream, the both of us picturing that willful beast climbing *not* out of the bayou, but out of Last Chance Creek. That's when Mr. Cole would come rushing to our rescue with a plate of hush puppies and cold ginger ale. He'd laugh and tell Lou to quit. I would always tell Woody after one of those hair-raising evenings, "I know for a fact that we don't got gators around here, but I think we should sleep in the fort tonight no matter what, don't you? Our luck hasn't been so hot lately."

Lou only started playing pranks on Woody and me the past few months. That's the same way my uncle treats us and she is trying to impress Papa's older brother, who fancies himself quite the wit. He was baptized Dwight Alfred Carmody, but nobody calls him that. They call him Blackie, because of his job. My uncle is a lady-killer, but also a blacksmith, and he's very good at fooling you into thinking he's somebody he's not by laying on the charm, which I regrettably admit can be considerable when he wants something from you. Lou, like many of the other young women around town, has fallen head over heels for him even though I've tried to tell her time and time again, "Are you crazy? You better get ahold of yourself and be quick about it. He's gonna break your heart so bad. I know you think he cares for you, but you are sadly mistaken. You're just another in a long line of what Blackie calls his 'Kleenex gals.' When he's done usin' you, he'll toss you into the trash like all the rest of them," but she won't listen. I feel sorry for her. Until she pulls something like this.

"The apology?" I say, wondering where Papa is right this moment. "We don't have all day." Is he coming up the front walk?

To my surprise, Lou has enough remaining good sense to turn to my sister and say, "I's so, so sorry for playing a trick on ya, Jane Woodrow. Here. Let me make it up to ya." She widens out her skinny arms, like she's intending to give my twin a honey bear hug.

"Don't be such a sucker." I yank Woody back by her shirt collar. "Can't you see it's a trap?"

"No, it ain't." Lou is acting wounded with a pouty, dimpled look. In a hurt-little-girl voice, she says, "Why ya always gotta be so mean to me, Shenny?"

I laugh in her face and hope my breath smells bad. "That's a real good impression, Lou. You should enter yourself into the Founders Weekend talent show. You'd win first prize, that's how good that is." I say to Woody, "Let's get outta here before she breaks into 'The Good Ship Lollipop.'" I take a couple of steps in the right direction, expecting my sister to follow, but she doesn't. "What are you doin'?" My head whips back and forth between her and Lou. "Oh, for the love of Pete," I say, figuring out why my music-loving sister is acting like she's nailed to the floor, "I didn't mean that she's *actually* gonna perform that song, Woody, I meant that she's—"

"Oh my, you're in for it now," Lou butts in. "Ya hear that?"

Papa?

I hold my breath and listen for the sound of his high-heeled boots. The way his silver cleats click against the foyer's cool marble floors. I check my sister's face. She's got on her usual you-can-knock-all-you-want-but-nobody's-home look. That's good. If Papa was close by, sensitive Woody would be squinching her eyes closed and throwing back her head, readying herself to make this sound that's very theatrical. The only other time I've heard it was in that movie we took Beezy to see up at Hull's Drive-In called *The Hound of the Baskervilles*.

"You better quit bothering us, Louise," I say, setting my hands on my hips. "We don't hear a thing, do we, Woody."

"Maybe ya should try harder." Lou cups a hand to her ear. "I believe . . . why yes, I'm sure that's the toilets callin' out your name. Sheeen . . . Shenandoah Carmooody. Ya better get right up here and scrub us 'fore the lovely Miss Louise runs and tells yer pappy what ya been up to."

Technically, I've got aces over Louise's kings. Woody and me leaving Lilyfield to search for our mother is bad, but maybe not as bad as Lou taking off her clothes for that joker, Uncle Blackie. But a fat lot of good that does me. I *can't* tattle the dirt I got on her. Not right now. Lou knows how much I love my father and that the last thing I want to do is cause him more trouble than he's already got, what with Mama's recent birthday and the anniversary of her disappearance and a long visit with Grampa hanging on the horizon. I *could* rat her out to Mr. Cole, but being so kind and forgiving like he is, probably the worst he'd inflict upon her would be the recitation of a Mary Magdalene passage out of the Bible.

No. A good card player knows when to fold.

"Just so you know, Lou, Woody and I wish you were dead," I spout as I huff out of the dining room, pulling my twin behind me.

"Cleanin' bucket's under His Honor's sink." Lou devilishly laughs. "Use the bleach and lift the seat."

"That's fine. Don't worry," I say, attempting to console my sister as we head up the front staircase. "This is just one hand in the game. The second I get a chance, you know what I think I'll do?" Woody pauses and listens intently. She looks so cute that I cannot resist hugging her. When I do, a little *sssss* escapes out of her. I'm sure that's her way of showing me that even though she can't talk, we're still on the same wavelength. "That's exactly right, pea. I'm going to ask E. J. to do a little copperhead hunting for us. We'll add it to the pot."

Chapter Seven

O ur white canopy bed has always reminded me of a sailboat anchored in the middle of a deep sea.

When she was painting the walls this pretty blue, Mama told Woody and me she hoped they'd make us feel less like we were "weathering a tempest," and more like we were "drifting through a sea of tranquility," and sometimes they do. But mostly we're sleeping in our fort lately. It's safer up there.

I'm gazing out our bedroom window at the Minnow place, recollecting what Bootie Young told me over at the cemetery this morning. It's hard to believe Clive has shipped off to the Great Beyond. Just over the treetops, I can see the porch we used to visit on. His dog, Ivory, is lying next to his master's bentwood rocker, his back legs stretched out like a frog's, his head between his paws. Mr. Clive asked me one morning, "Know why I named this mutt the opposite of what he looks like, little girl?" He nodded down at the chocolate pup. "The dog's the only one tolerates me besides you Carmody gals, so I guess that makes him only ninety-nine point forty-four percent smart. Get it? Ivory? Like the soap?"

I think that remark shows some humility, so I guess that'll be my eulogy for my hypochondriac friend. I don't imagine there will be much of a turnout at the cemetery service. Clive wasn't all that appealing. His hair cascaded in greasy rivulets that pooled at his shoulders. A stench rose off his body in almost visible waves. And his teeth . . . I think that might've been moss growing off them. Thank goodness he was a hermit. Even if he *had* wanted company, who'd want to spend an afternoon with somebody who looked and smelled the way he did? To the best of my knowledge, nobody besides me and Mama and Gramma. Woody never was too interested. Every time I asked her to join me for a neighborly visit, she'd say, "You go on without me. Clive reminds me of standing water."

Gramma Ruth Love, she liked Clive. She brought him pies. That's one of the things that Auxiliary ladies do, go around and deliver tasty things to shut-ins. That wasn't totally unselfish of her, though. I know by the smile it put on her face that it made her feel good to watch Clive, who really did appreciate home-cooking, gobble that pie down in one sitting. And Mama, she was a friend to Clive as well. She would run errands for him when Papa wasn't home and sometimes straighten up his house. Since he hardly never threw anything away, it could get pretty crowded in there. His Honor didn't care for Clive. Sometimes, from the fort, I could hear them going after each other, but just the sound of their furious voices, not what they were saying specifically.

I let the lace fall back over the bedroom window and wonder what's to become of that little Lab that's got gray running through his muzzle and stiffness in the hips now that his owner's dead? Maybe Papa could find it in his heart to let us keep him. Woody could sure use another dog.

Mars is never coming back.

My sister is sitting at the vanity table poofing powder on her cheeks, her chin, arms, and hands. "Hey, knock that off. You're starting to look . . . why don't you work on a picture instead? Something pretty for a change," I say, back flopping onto our bed.

Drawing is Woody's real gift from God. Our mother explained that even though her twins shared the same room when we were growing inside of her, there were two chutes that fed into us. I got Mama's love of words delivered to me and Woody got her fondness for music. But it was our mother's love of art that got specially delivered to my sister's soul. When she was still here, Mama would admire Woody's work, saying somewhat tearful (that's how moved she'd be), "That's perfect. Just the right amount of shading. And the colors . . . gorgeous. You'll be a respected artist someday, honey. Maybe in New York City. You'll live in a walk-up with your sister, who'll be a wonderful writer . . . *sniff* . . . *sniff*. The Carmody twins will be the toast of the town."

Now, why would she say things like that when she knew Woody and me would be doing nothing of the sort? Our father has made it clear time and time again, "Carmody women *have* never and *will* never hire themselves out."

I scooch across the chenille bedspread to make room for Woody. "If you don't want to draw, then come be with me, would ya?" Watching as she floats over, anticipating the feel of her matching head resting beside mine, I cannot help but wonder for the millionth time, how can two girls look so much alike on the outside and have such different filling? I am firmly planted in this world despite my interest in the stars, but my twin? It's hard to believe she slid out of Mama only two minutes and ten seconds before me. She's more so now, but Woody has *always* seemed unearthly. Like only moments ago, she arrived from a far-off place where harp music fills the air, and for breakfast, lunch, and dinner they serve angel food cake and drink nectar out of ruby-encrusted chalices.

She lies down so gently beside me, I have to check to make sure that she actually has. "Don't do that. You're givin' me the creeps," I say, trying to pry her arms apart. She's firmly X'd them across her chest and lowered her lids. With Mama's dusting powder covering her from top to toe, she looks exactly like one of the corpses over at Last Tidings funeral parlor that's waiting for somebody to tip the casket closed so they can be on their way. "Look, Woody," I say, getting strict with her. "I know you're hurtin' so bad that you *wish* you were, but you're in fact—not dead. Remember how I felt the same way when I got so melancholy? You got to shake this off. Pull yourself up by your bootstraps." I'm trying to hold my breath so I don't smell Mama's Chantilly powder. "I didn't make much progress today, but I'll find her, just you wait and see. It'd help a lot if you'd quit runnin' off."

I know it seems like I don't miss my mother as much as she does, but I do. It's just that Woody is counting on me to rescue our damsel in distress, so I cannot wear my feelings on my sleeve the way she does. I got to stay strong, armored up, but I want you to know, there is no way to describe how much I pine for our mother. The way she presses her cool full lips down to soak the fever off my forehead. Her cheeks as smooth as the underbelly of leaves and how her honey hair . . . aw, shoot.

I guess this is as good a time as any to come clean with you.

It was Easter Sunday.

The last we had together.

Shortly after we got home from Mass, the entire Carmody family sat down at the dining room table to a lunch of burnt ham, soggy green bean casserole, and partially cooked biscuits.

Grampa dug right in, but after chewing for a bit, he spit it all back out onto his plate.

"This the kind of swill Yankees eat? No wonder you're skinny as a pot handle, Wally."

Uncle Blackie set the plastic vomit he keeps in his pocket up on the table and made some retching sounds.

Gramma mumbled a prayer in Latin, but it was too

late even for the Almighty to intercede. Grampa Gus had already ripped the napkin off from around his neck, threw it down on his plate, and said, "I'm headin' to The Southern Inn to see if they got anything left. Hell, even their garbage would be better than this slop. Y'all comin'?"

Grampa and Uncle Blackie stormed out the front door, but on her way out, Gramma Ruth Love took the time to say politely to her daughter-in-law, who she really loves despite her failings, "The cranberries were nicely done, Evelyn."

Papa went fuchsia in the face about his wife not being a good cook after they slammed the door behind them. I completely understood that. I mean, it's a woman's job to keep house and cook meals, and Mama would be the first to admit that she really wasn't A-1 at neither.

Papa broke the ponderous silence when he said, "You may clear the table now, Mother." That's what he called her: Mother. No matter how many times she corrected him by saying, "Please don't call me that. My name is Eve."

Woody carried the dishes into the kitchen and Mama and her got busy washing up. Papa and I stayed at the table and talked planetary business, but I could hear my sister in the kitchen saying over the running water and scraping, "I thought it was a real good dinner. The ham, especially. I like it crunchy like that," and other nice compliments about the gummy biscuits.

When the last dish was dry, my mother came back out red-eyed and told Papa, "I'm sorry, Walt. I tried."

He tried, too. To keep the disappointment off his face. But it's so important to him what his father and brother think and his wife just made that so bad for him. Grampa Gus and Uncle Blackie will be making dumb jokes for the rest of the year about that Easter dinner, that's what I thought to myself, which is probably the same thing my father was thinking. Then Mama asked, "May I go out to the garden and do some planting now?" The garden is her haven the way the fort is Woody's and mine.

Papa graciously replied, "Yes, you may." Then he pushed his chair back from the dining table and I remember so clearly that grating sound it made. Could feel it in my chest. "I'm leaving now to join the rest of my family at the restaurant. Jane Woodrow, you come with me. Shenandoah, stay here with your mother." Papa nodded at me across the table. He was telling me to follow Mama out to the garden because he adores her so much that he couldn't stand not knowing what his true love was doing every minute, every second of the day.

I swung on the gate and Mama dropped down onto her knees and began tending to all the new life rising up once we got out there. It was a lovely afternoon. The lilies were perfuming the air something fierce. Roses were budding in all their pink glory. I could hardly breathe for the scent.

Her head down close to the earth, Mama asked, "Would . . . would you and your sister like to go away with me?"

"What?" I about split a gut. "Papa's right. You really

are getting more addled by the minute! What are you thinking? You know he can't leave on a trip right now. He's in the middle of the Merriweather trial."

That's when my mother's whole body went droopy, like she desperately needed to be watered.

So maybe that's what she did. No longer able to ignore her yearning for travel, she snuck off. Maybe to Italy. She *had* been learning to speak the language with that Berlitz record.

But if that *is* the case, if she *is* in Italy, why hasn't she sent us a "Wish You Were Here" postcard?

Because she doesn't. Not me anyway.

Even though she went back to her planting that Easter afternoon, like the whole traveling idea had never come up, I saw her tears showering down on those seedlings.

That's why her goneness is probably all my fault. If only I'd knelt down next to her in the garden that day and said, "Go away with you? Well, gosh, we can't right now, but I'm sure we could real soon. Right after Papa's trial is over. Let's plan on that."

If only.

You got to admit, standing alone those words are pretty awful, but married together like that, they must be two of the saddest in the English language.

Chapter Eight

Then again, there *is* what happened to Mildred Fugate to take into consideration.

Madame Fugate tells everybody that she was born in Paris, but we all know it's not the one in France, but the one up near Leesburg. Guess she thinks it gives her a little more *oo . . . la . . . la.* She gives comportment and dancing lessons to the girls in town in a room she's got off Main Street. (When she comes back home, I am going to surprise Mama and enroll her in one of Madame's manner classes so she can learn her proper place in the order of things because Gramma Ruth Love is right, this is something my mother really needs to improve on.)

The reason Madame comes to mind in regards to finding Mama is that teacher took a nasty spill on a patch of ice during that bad winter we had a few years ago and ended up with her left leg broke in three places and her head bounced off the sidewalk and landed right into unconsciousness. Dancing in a tutu is a little too frou-frou for a girl of my temperament, but I was there, waiting to walk Woody home after her ballerina class. I ran to Doc Keller's office, stuck my head in, and shouted, "Come quick. Madame has either fainted or died." When he got to where she was sprawled out, Doc wiggled his smelling salts under her nose. I burst out laughing, because just like in the movies, the second after she opened her eyes, the first words out of her mouth were, "Where am I? Who am I?"

That compound fracture healed up just fine, but Madame's memory didn't.

She never could recall a lot of things from before that icy fall. Like her husband. (I think she might've been faking that part, though. If I were her, I wouldn't want to remember "Bait" Fugate neither.)

So maybe something like *that* is what happened to our mother. She might be wandering along the side of some backwater road, not knowing where she rightfully belongs or why she pines for a pair of matching girls. I know it's hideous of me to wish that, but you know, that would be such a relief. So much better than believing that wherever she is, it's all my fault that she's gone.

Wallowing. That's what I'm doing, when I'm supposed to be cleaning his bathroom.

Papa's sink is spotless today, but every so often I find it dotted with leftover whiskers. I have a collection that I've picked up with pieces of Scotch tape. I'm planning to take that stubble to Miss Delia Hormel at the boardinghouse. She was born on the right side of Sulphur Mountain and besides throwing hexes, those folks are known for their skill in remedying people. If you bring along two dollars and something that belongs to an ailing loved one, Miss Delia will make you a get-well dolly out of burlap with corn kernels for eyes. She might be the only one who can help Papa feel better because nothing I've tried seems to work.

I gave his horse a bath and cleaned his guns and he never seemed to notice. I've offered many times to spend the night constellation searching. I remind him how the astronauts are going to the moon next month and how we were going to celebrate that historic event with a party. I slip notes under his study door. In them, I tell him how much I love him and ask if there's anything else I can do to comfort his heart. Sometimes I remind him about how much fun a certain day we spent together was. Like that October I was nine and we walked the Appalachian Trail and collected fiery leaves for a school project. I sign the notes, *Your beautiful daughter of the stars*. I'm sure I'll hear back from him any day now.

I'm looking at myself in the mirror above the sink. My hair lacks luster and the shadows under my eyes are pronounced, made even more so by the powder that slipped off my sister's cheek and smeared onto mine. I swipe it off, wishing I could do the same to my worries. Woody's getting worse and I know why. She's having bad memories. Founders Weekend will be here before we know it and it was during the carnival last year that Mama disappeared.

A few folks suggested that it wouldn't be a waste of the sheriff's time to go looking for Mama up in Loudoun County, where Colonel Button's Thrills and Chills settles in after it leaves us. "Perhaps Evelyn ran off with one of those roustabouts. Bless her heart, she never did seem to fit in, did she?" I heard one of those Auxiliary ladies snigger behind her tea party hand. That's not only ignorant, it doesn't make sense. Why would my mother leave my yummy-smelling Papa for some drifter that reeks of sawdust and sweat? His Honor says Mama's not that smart, but she would've had to be born without a brain to go off with a toothless man who lives in an aluminum trailer when she had lovely Lilyfield to come home to. Maybe she . . . oh, I don't know what to believe anymore. Mama *does* adore the Ferris wheel. She loves that above-it-all feeling. And the merry-go-round, she likes that, too.

Loathe as I am to admit it, there's a possibility those club women could be right. On the night she never returned home, I *did* find Mama standing in front of the freak tent. She had on my most favorite outfit—white slacks and a white blouse with the pockets edged in red yarn. She looked so pretty with the wind ruffling her hair. So breezy. When the barker's voice came over the loud speaker, "Come one, come all. Moments from now Tiny Jimbo—the smallest man on earth—will be taking our stage," I came running to her side and asked, "Where have you been? I've been lookin' all over for you. We need two quarters. Quick! The show is about to start."

But Mama did not rush to open her pocketbook. She

shook her head at the garish flags whipping in the wind and said in the loneliest voice I have ever heard, "People can be so cruel to the different." Then she locked her eyes on to mine and said, "Where's your sister? I've got something important to tell—"

I didn't even let her finish her sentence. I ran off. Woody and I looked forward to watching that Oddities show all year long. I saw Mama searching for us later in the night, probably to apologize, but I stayed far away as possible, that's how mad I was that she wouldn't give us that admission money.

Opening up the medicine chest, I remove a bottle of pills. There's a few left.

Papa shook this exact bottle and told me one morning in the kitchen, "These will help Mother feel calmer."

"Really?" I asked because I thought that would be miraculously wonderful. Maybe then she'd stop screaming at Papa and he'd stop screaming at her and they could go back to the way they used to be. Enthralled. Not giving each other the cold shoulder one minute and being boiling mad the next. So it was with excitement that I watched Papa crush the relaxing pill with the back of a spoon and stir it into Mama's favorite teacup along with her cream and two sugars. That went according to plan, for a while anyway. Our mother definitely had less fight in her. She took to her bed most afternoons. Until the day she found out what he'd done. I will never know how for sure, but I suspect Woody might've told her. There was a horrendous to-do.

Mama threw the teacup on the kitchen floor and it

broke into pieces. She whimpered, "You're doing this because I quit the Ladies Auxiliary."

"My grandmother founded the club. And my mama was president for how many years? What is so wrong with a wife obtaining worth in serving the needs of her husband and home? What's gotten into you?" Papa hollered.

"Oh, Walt. What's gotten into *you*? You're trying to snuff out my spirit the same way your father has yours," she said, looking at him the same way Jesus is looking at Judas Escariot in our picture Bible.

Papa scoffed, "Nonsense. I'm giving you the pills for your own good. Isn't that right, Shenandoah?"

I didn't pause, didn't even consider not agreeing with him. I said, "That's right, sir."

Remembering that argument, I pocket the pill bottle and rush out of his bathroom. "I'm doing this for your own good" is the exact same thing Papa shouts over Woody's and my root cellar crying.

I come to a stop in front of our bedroom door, set my face against the shiny wood, and call to my sister, "This cleaning shouldn't take me much longer. Soon as I'm done, I'll come back and sing you something from *South Pacific*, all right?"

I want so badly to picture my once-lively twin jumping up and down on the bed the way she used to, clapping her hands and squealing, "*South Pacific?* That's Mama's and my favorite album!" But try as I might, all I can see in my mind is Woody the way I left her. Lying still on the quilt, barely moving. The goodness knocked right out of her.

Chapter Nine

You know how I'm beginning to feel?

Like a piece of saltwater taffy getting pulled this way and that. Stretched to my absolute limit.

If my mother was here, I could whine to her—"Tell me what to do next. I'm so mixed up."

But she's not here. Even if she was, my asking for help wouldn't do me a bit of good. I can hear in my head her certain reply. "Shenny, I can't tell you how to solve problems. You need to find your own answers. It's important that you grow up to be a strong woman," she'd say like she was imparting some kind of sacred knowledge. "An independent thinker doesn't rely on others."

I'd shout back at her, "And to thine own self be true, right? You sound like one of your record albums. A broken one." I'd be spitting mad. "Ya know what I think? 'The lady doth protest too much!'" because really, she was being such a hypocrite. Papa always tells *her* and the rest of us what to do. After one of our spats, I'd storm off, spend the rest of the day fuming up in the fort about what a bad mother she was and how pathetic people from the North are. And Shakespeare—he was an idiot, too. I'd thumb my nose at the pecan fudge she'd bring out, sneer at the heart she'd scratched on top. I'd wait for my father's car to wind up the drive after a day at the courthouse, scramble down the fort steps and leap into his arms, so relieved to get whatever problem I was having out of my head into his much wiser one.

But counting on Papa to provide me with a solution to my confusion is no longer possible. His socks don't even match.

What to do? What to do? A quote Mama made me learn by heart, one that she thought might help me when I was troubled about this thing or that comes swooping into my mind:

> *To be, or not to be: that is the question:*
> *Whether 'tis nobler in the mind to suffer*
> *The slings and arrows of outrageous fortune,*
> *Or to take arms against a sea of troubles,*
> *And by opposing end them?*

That's right. I can't just sit around and get shot in the heart by outrageous fortune. I need to dive in headfirst.

I'll start off by getting another scarf of Mama's to soothe Woody.

I also have to fulfill my promise to our good friend Sam Moody. He's been asking me if I found a note since the night Mama vanished. I thought he was wondering if Papa had received a *ransom* note. Sam has a lot of big city police experience. If he had been in charge of finding her instead of imbecilic Sheriff Nash, I bet former Detective Moody would've been asking everybody the day after Mama disappeared: *Did you notice anybody at the carnival lurking around with a blindfold and a gunny sack? Did you see anybody suspicious drag Miz Carmody off into the bushes?*

Her being absconded with seemed so right that I gathered up my courage and went straight to Papa, asked him, "Sir? Did you by any chance happen to receive a ransom note?"

I took his swooning as a no.

Sam got a little teary when I reported that back to him. He told me, "I wasn't talking about a ransom note, Shenny. Keep looking."

There's only one place where I might find all three things. The scarf for Woody, Sam's note, and something that would mean the world to all of us. A hint to Mama's present location. There might be something in her diary.

Only here's what Mr. Shakespeare called "the rub." I have been forbidden to enter their bedroom under any circumstances.

So which of my thine selves am I supposed to be true to exactly? Shen, the good sister? Shen, the loyal friend? Or Shen, the obedient daughter?

If my mother was here, what would she tell me to do? She wouldn't. She would probably quote Shakespeare again. Yes.

To sleep, perchance to dream.

Well, that seems clear enough.

I don't know where His Honor is right this minute, but I'm fairly certain he's not in here. I'd hear him snoring or yelling out in his sleep if he was. I rap my knuckles against the sturdy oak door. Once. Twice. "Sir?" Cracking it open an inch, I barely say, "Your Honor?"

I haven't been in here in the longest time.

Except for a shard of sunshine cutting through the wine velvet curtains, I can't see real good, but well enough to tell that their four-poster bed is empty. Socks and shirts are spread across the wood floor and there's a smell of crusty food and, just for a second, Chanel No. 5.

Oh, Mama.

You know how you come across something? Like a ticket stub from a movie you really liked or a four-leaf clover that you pressed between wax paper so you would be able to feel lucky any old time you wanted to? But to your surprise, when you dig them up, instead of making you have a happy memory, those parcels from the past get you filled to the brim with so much wanting for something that you might never have again. That's how I'm feeling, just like that.

Our mother placed the family pictures on the wall across from their bed so she could look at them before she fell asleep and have sweet dreams. This past New Year's Day, I caught my father stuffing them all into a cardboard box like he'd made a resolution to do away with them, like his family was a bad habit. Right here next to the window is where Woody and my favorite portrait used to be. The one we've got in the fort now. I asked him, "Do you mind? Could we just keep that one?" Papa handed it to me and said, "Salt in the wound," and went right back to his packing. I thought it would work like a splint on Woody's and my broken heart, but Papa was right. Whenever I look at the picture of us in the lily field, it burns so bad right below my wishbone.

I run my finger over the frames' smudged outlines. Shots of Woody and me looking like baby bookends in Mama's arms once hung here. There was another of us attending the first day of school in matching white blouses and navy skirts. I especially loved the shot of my sister and me wading in the creek with Boppa Joe and Gran Jean. Mama's mother and father passed away in a boating accident a few years back on the chilly waters of Lake Michigan up in Wisconsin. That's why she steers clear of boats unless it's too risky to get where she is going any other way.

Woody and I weren't allowed and Papa was involved in a trial, so our mother had to travel to her old home and to make the funeral arrangements all by herself. When she returned, my sister and I noticed that she was different. Of course, she was thinner from grief, but what she'd lost in weight, she appeared to have gained in spirit. Mama became so recklessly outspoken after her parents' deaths. Grampa Gus always says, "Money talks," and my mother had inherited a bundle in her parents' will, so maybe that had something to do with her newfound mouthiness, I don't know.

There never were any pictures hanging on the bedroom wall of Grampa, his arm thrown around the youngest of his sons, the both of them beaming with pride. It's the job of a camera to capture truth for one second in time, and the truth is—Grampa is *not* proud of Papa. He got rheumatic fever when he was a child and that's why he's stunted and not rough and tough like his father and his brother. Grampa calls him "the runt." He makes fun of his job at every opportunity. Gus Carmody thinks being a judge comes in handy in certain situations, but that it's not a very manly way to make a living. "What kind of man wears a robe to work?" he razzes.

There *were* pictures from Mama and Papa's wedding day on the wall. Our mother in Gramma's high-necked gossamer dress holding a white ribboned bouquet. Our father looking natty in a long-tailed tuxedo and top hat. They looked like Ginger Rogers and Fred Astaire. In the old days, when something with a beat came on the radio, Mama and Papa would jut their hips and move smoothly into one another. Or sometimes watching a movie together late at night, they nuzzled close on the sofa, the light of the television bouncing off their sweetheart faces. And on Saturdays, they'd go into town for a date to have dinner and when they'd come home, I'd hear their bubbly laughter out on the porch.

I've given this a lot of thought. Tried to pinpoint when their happy-ever-after story came to The End. I don't think it was just one thing that made everything start to go bad. It was a thing here and a thing there, and over time, the same explosiveness that's inside Grampa Gus sprang free from some place deep within Papa to spew all over Mama. Once it was loose, he couldn't seem to cap it off. I held Mama responsible for him changing. *She* was the one causing the problems. I begged her to stop being so defiant, shook a finger in her face, and told her, "All you got to do to make things right again is remember your wedding vows. You got to love His Honor and, most importantly, obey him."

This is her dresser.

Down here in the bottom drawer is where she keeps her scarves. I've got to replace the one Papa ripped up last night. My sister *needs* that chiffon. She balls it up in her fist and holds it up to her nose and sucks her thumb. It makes her night go faster, having that little bit of Mama in hand.

Long as I'm here, I also want to look again for my mother's white blouse with the red yarn trim and . . . Lord, what's wrong with me? I'm not going to find anything of hers in here. Papa donated all her clothes to the secondhand shop because he couldn't bear having them around to remind him of what he's lost. I saw Mama's short-cut emerald jacket at Mass last week and was halfway out of the pew before I realized that it was Beebee

Mathison wearing it like it belonged to her. That's all right. After I bring Mama home, we'll go buy her some new things in the fancy stores of Richmond or Washington, D.C. Oh, Papa would love that! He insists on picking out *all* her clothes. Wouldn't think of letting his wife shop for herself.

Right under this Oriental carpet of blue and gold swirls is where Woody and I helped Mama hollow out a secret spot she called "my stronghold." We worked all afternoon prying up the boards when Papa was at the courthouse. It seemed so important to her to have a private place. She told me when we were all through, "We must keep this a secret. Your father would be disappointed, you understand, Shen?"

I sort of did. I always pretended that I could make out Centaurus when I couldn't so I wouldn't let Papa down.

I've had a hundred excuses for not looking for Mama's diary before now. It's just that . . . fine, I've been too chicken-hearted to read the pouring-out of her innermost feelings. Too scared to see her lacy handwriting spell out something that I would be better off not knowing. Something that would take away all my hope.

I get down on my knees and fold back the carpet. Lift up that notched board with shaking fingers. I'm trying hard to scold my scared into behaving, but it won't stop back-talking me.

Do not go looking for trouble, Shen, it's saying. *You already have more than your fair share.*

I desperately want to answer, *Of course, you're right.*

What was I thinking? Then I could run downstairs and make Woody and me some pimento cheese sandwiches and head out to the fort. I could practice my card tricks.

There you go, the voice inside my head is saying. *Now you've got on your thinking cap.*

"Hush!" I say out loud because I can't listen to it the way I have in the past. I know from vast experience that fear talks a lot louder than courage. I need to listen to that other voice inside me, that faint one that's struggling to be heard. *You were born under the constellation Leo. You need to be brave hearted. A lion.*

When I think about how my mama was the last one to touch this place, I go so weak that I almost stop, but I don't. The light may be dim, but I can see right off that the stronghold is empty. Sam's note is not here. And neither is Mama's diary, which really hurts. I feel like I opened a gift that I've been waiting a year to receive and there's nothing inside the box. Where is it? Could Papa have found it? The thought of him . . . no, I'm being silly. He'd have no reason to go looking for something that he didn't even know existed. If he *had* found the diary by accident he would know that his wife had been visiting with Sam and how Woody and I helped them and . . . no, Papa doesn't have it. There would have been punishments. My mother must've moved it. Hid it somewhere else and didn't tell me. I bet she told Woody, who is such a Mama's girl.

I get up off my knees, toe the rug straight. I'm feeling miserable. I bet Sam will, too, when I tell him that I looked in the last best place for his note and found nothing, not even dust. And poor Woody. How will she ever fall asleep without Mama's scarf?

"What do you think you're doing?" another voice accuses.

I almost shout out, "I'm just tryin' to find my mother before my family falls apart worse than it already has. Can't you just leave me be?"

But I'm not imagining the voice this time. I can smell horse sweat and Maker's Mark.

I look up to see Papa scowling at me in the mirror above Mama's dresser. He couldn't get much realer.

Chapter Ten

"Is that you, Jane Woodrow?" Papa asks, striding through the doorway in his boots and breeches. For such a small man he takes such large steps.

I spin and most especially grin so he can see Woody's and my only identifiable difference—my gaped teeth. He's always had a hard time telling us apart. "Golly! You startled me, Your Honor," I say, tempering it with a chuckle lest he accuse me again of impertinence. "How was your ride this mornin' . . . I mean morn*ing*?" He is very particular about how we speak. No calling ourselves Woody and Shenny in front of him neither. Pet names are not allowed. "Was Pegasus—"

"What are you doing, Shenandoah?"

"I . . . I . . ." Can't help myself. I don't care how messy he looks or how mad he is. I would love for him to take me into his arms, press his stubbly cheek against mine, rub his high-bridged nose with my snubbed one. I want to take a comb to his hair, no matter how many teeth got broke. I venture closer and try to untie my tongue. "Did . . . did you notice those shooting stars last night and that Jupiter has been real close and . . . and don't forget the men are going up to the moon next month and you promised last summer that we'd—"

"You've been warned about coming in here," he says, striking his riding crop against his leg.

"I know, sir, and under any other circumstances I wouldn't." I wish I could tell him what I was really up to. How I was looking for the diary in the stronghold, hoping to find a clue to where his lovely wife has gone, but he'll get sadder if he knows that Mama kept something hidden from him. You have never seen someone so enraptured like my papa was with my mama. When she left a room, his breath would go with her. He'll thank me once she's back in his arms. "I'm really, really sorry, but . . . Wood . . . Jane Woodrow, she's having the hardest time sleeping. I thought that if I could find . . . she needs to—" I bet he doesn't even remember shredding Mama's scarf last night before he took us down to the root cellar.

"Was that you and your sister I saw at the creek?" he asks, coming closer and closer.

"No, Your Honor, no, it wasn't."

"How odd," Papa says, acting comically confused. "I could've sworn I saw the two of you lying beneath the weeping willow tree when I came out of the barn." His hands are clasping me right below the *Speranza* watch that Sam Moody gave Mama. How could I have been so careless? I got so worried about being late that I forgot to put it back under my pillow when Woody and I got home.

"Are you referring to the big willow tree?" I ask. "The one with the cracked stump? Is that the one you mean?" I pretend to consider that. "No, uh-uh, sir. That wasn't us. But speaking of the creek, you remember Mr. Clive Minnow, don't you? Our neighbor? Virgil from the grocery found him lying dead in the water and so now his old dog, Ivory, is all alone and . . . do you think I could go get him? You know how Woody loves dogs and—" I've gone and trapped myself. I can tell by how crafty Papa is smiling that he's figured that out, too. Before he was a judge, he was a prosecuting attorney known for persecuting witnesses. I've seen lawyers for the defense go whiter when they found out the one they'd be going up against was the great Walter T. Carmody.

He says smoothly, "Perhaps you'd care to explain to me how you heard about Mr. Minnow's unfortunate passing?"

"I—"

"Your shorts are damp. Did you and your sister take the stepping stones into town when I expressly forbade it? Is that how you heard about Mr. Minnow's death?"

"No, sir. Woody and I did not go—"

He lets me loose and drags his dirt-packed fingernail along the bottom of my cut-offs. I swing my hands behind me, slip off Mama's watch, and push it deep into the back pocket of my shorts. "If you weren't down by the creek then why are—" There's a ruckus in the hallway. Papa cocks his head and calls, "Jane Woodrow?"

My stomach shrinks up the way it usually does when he calls out her name. *Please, Lord, do not let it be Woody come looking for me.*

There's more clattering. A few clanks. "Yoodihoo. It's me, Your Honor," Lou calls from the hall. My knees buckle in relief, knowing it's not my twin. "Lunchtime. I got all your favorite—"

"Leave the tray," Papa says. If I wasn't looking straight at him, I'd swear I was hearing Grampa. Or Blackie, he's got that sneering tone as well.

"Did Miss Shen tell ya about your neighbor?" Lou prattles on. "Yessir. Your brother came by earlier to . . . ah . . . let ya know that your horse needs new shoes soon. He told me and the girls *all* about Mr. Clive bein' found dead. Ain't that a cryin' shame?"

As much as I wish it were, barging in like this is not an attempt on Lou's part to rescue me. It's just her roundabout way of reminding me to keep my mouth shut about her loving up my uncle and she'll do the same about Woody and me escaping from Lilyfield this morning.

Papa's voice bounces off the bedroom walls. "You're dismissed."

I'm hoping so bad that he means me that I try leaving. "Your sister?" he says, clamping down with his hands. His law school graduation ring is digging into the bone at the top of my right shoulder. "Where is she?

And why are your shorts wet if you weren't down at the creek?"

"She's . . . I . . . we've been waterin' the gardens so they look nice when Grampa comes," I lie. "It must've been somebody else you saw under the willow or—"

"I was down to the creek this mornin' pickin' flowers for your mama's room," Lou hollers from the hall. She has not come into view, it's just her voice. "Got a nice bunch of those lilies she likes so much right downstairs on the—"

"Louise." Papa uses his quiet voice that is much more frightening than his loud one.

"Sir?"

"Get . . . back . . . into . . . the . . . kitchen. *Now*. There's work to be done before my father arrives."

I hear Lou scurry away, mumbling *yessir*s and *hoodoo* words to keep herself safe from the wrath of Papa, and I so badly want to run after her. He's pressuring me much harder than I'm sure he's meaning to. "You and your sister were up in the fort the night your mother disappeared. The moon was full. What did you see?"

I knew he'd ask me. It *always* comes down to this even though I've told him countless times what I saw that night.

Most of it anyway.

Colonel Button's Thrills and Chills Show sets up their rides and games in Buffalo Park, which is on the other side of Honeysuckle Hill, a stone's throw away from our place.

Woody and me were sleeping up in the fort that night

because I just love the sound of folks having fun. All that hooting and hollering—it makes me feel like part of the greater good.

We'd had such a swell time at the carnival. We each got a teddy bear and rode the Tilt-a-Whirl and laughed to tears at how wavy we looked in the Maze of a Million Mirrors. Dreaming of all that fun is what must've been giving me such a nice slumber, but it wasn't doing the same for my sister. She woke me up after midnight, babbling, "Mama . . . Mama . . . gone."

I tried ignoring her, and when she wouldn't let me, I groused, "Did ya eat too many Red Hots? You're having a bad dream. Lie back down and go to sleep."

Woody plastered herself against me, which I usually love, but her hands were sticky with cotton candy. I rolled away, but she came after me. "Papa . . . Papa," she moaned, and that's when I heard him, too.

He was thrashing about in the woods, bellowing, "No . . . no. Mother . . . how could you?" And then all went still, except for Woody's whimpering and Mars, the dog, barking and the strong man bell ringing faintly from over at the carnival. For a split second, I thought Papa had passed out, but when I pressed my eye to the fort peephole I could see him swatting at branches and coming fast our way. Somebody else was back there, too, but I couldn't see who. "Your mother . . . she's . . . gone," Papa hollered up at us from the trunk of the tree. "Get down here, girls."

Knowing better than to tangle with him when he got like that, Woody and me stayed right where we were, which proved to be for the best, because a little while later Mars quit barking and gave off a blood-curdling yelp and Papa left us to return to the clearing, nearly crawling.

At the time I thought to myself, Papa needs to stop trying to match his father and brother drink for drink. I got so ugly with my sister for interrupting my sleep. "Quit bein' such a titty baby," I snapped at her. "You know he acts and talks foolish when he's soused. You know that. All we got to do is wait him out. Mama's around here somewhere. She's not gone. She's got nowhere to go." I looked up at the house to make certain. I'd often catch our mother peeking out the curtains, like she was expecting somebody or maybe she was just watching over Woody and me, I don't know. But that night, their bedroom window was dark and empty. So with a leave-me-alone grunt, I curled back up and was almost to sleep when Woody whispered into my ear the last words she's spoken since that night, "Mama . . . gone."

That's when I recalled how little our mother enjoyed the carnival no matter how hard Papa and Grampa tried to force her to. And how later on in the evening, I got mad because she didn't give Woody and me the money to see the Oddities show but she was taking a ride on the merry-go-round with our friend Sam Moody. He was straddling a white horse and Mama was a few rows back in a swan. They should've been smiling, but they looked like they'd just lost their best friend. Good, I thought, I'm glad they're sad, because I was still feeling so het up about Woody and me having to crawl under the tent to see the freak show like some poor children.

When that merry-go-round memory came back to me up in the fort that night, I didn't even bother pulling on my sneakers, just a balled-up shirt and shorts. I reached for my flashlight and hissed at Woody as I undid the get-down hatch, "You're actin' like Sarah Heartburn, but since it looks like you're gonna go on and on and not let me get a minute's sleep until I do so, I'll go look for Mama. She's gotta be around here somewhere."

My sister tried to stop me, but I shook her off. I didn't let on to her, but all of a sudden it seemed possible that Papa wasn't talking from out of the bottom of a bottle. Maybe our mother really *wasn't* where she was supposed to be. What if she and Sam, neither one of them being gregarious of personality, had gotten off the ride and made their way back to his cabin to finish discussing their book of the week in peace and quiet? What if when they got done conversing, Mama dozed off? Realizing how world-coming-to-an-end horrible that would be, I told Woody, "If Papa comes back, do *not* leave this fort no matter how much he begs, ya hear me?"

I slid down the fort steps and charged barefoot through the front woods all the way over to the Triple S. Hopping up Sam's cabin steps, I waved my flashlight the full length of the porch, but did not see my mother sprawled out in the swing. *She might be inside*, I thought. Sam had that table fan and it was so sticky that night. I pounded my fists on the front door.

Sam called out, "Who's there?"

"It's me."

He opened the door sweaty and with a shotgun. "Shenny? Where's Woody?" Sam looked out over my head into the darkness.

"Is Mama here?" I dived straight into explaining what'd happened back in the clearing. By the time I got done telling him about Papa yelling about his wife being gone and Mars yelping and Woody weeping, I was crying some, too.

"Your mother," Sam said. "Did she say anything to you earlier in the evening? Did she leave you a note?" His scared was making my scared even worse.

"I . . . I don't know nothin' about that." I backed away. "If Mama should show up, would you make her come home as fast as she can? Tell her that His Honor . . . that . . . he's very disappointed," I said, and took off.

I was in the middle of the station lot when Sam called out, "Be careful."

Those warning words made goose bumps rise up on my arms, because I immediately understood that Sam didn't mean to be *careful* like I should watch out for reckless drivers when I crossed over the road or shouldn't let any branches scratch my face on my way back home through the woods. He was warning me to *be careful* like—be *full of care*. I will never forget it. The way the neon of his station sign washed my arms red, the dog barking up the road, my heart that had galloped up to my throat. That steamy night is when I realized that Sam *knew*. That Mama must've told him private family business. I still don't know how much she divulged, but what would possess her to go skating on thin ice like that?

"Shenandoah," Papa says now, getting me by the upper arms. "Are you sure you've told me *everything* about that night?"

I put on my best poker face. "Yes, sir. Like always. Everything I can remember. I swear."

He never believes me. And he shouldn't. Because I always leave out a few details, including the part about me running off to Sam's cabin in hopes of finding our mother there. No matter what Papa does to me, I can't tell him about Sam and Mama's friendship. My sister and I swore on each other's lives that we would never say anything to anybody.

"Your sister?" Papa says, terser. "Has she told you anything?"

My poor grieving father, he's so out of touch. "You do remember that she doesn't talk anymore, don't you?"

He draws his arm back. "Are you mocking me?"

"No . . . no . . . I was just trying to . . ." I close my eyes, ready to feel the sting on my cheek.

The last time he cross-examined me like this he ended up loosening one of my molars. He didn't mean to.

"Open your eyes." He has come so close that he's about pressing his lips against mine.

I turn away from his overpowering bourbon breath just in time to see my twin through a crack in the red velvet bedroom curtains. It's like watching a scene out of a matinee movie. Woody's sprinting across the yard like a heroine getting chased by an invisible villain.

Thinking fast, I jiggle from foot to foot and point across the hall. "Your Honor . . . I apologize, but . . . I can't answer any more of your questions right this minute. There's an urgent matter I need to attend to. May I be excused to use the little girls' room?"

He draws back, looks at me like I have suddenly appeared out of nowhere. "I . . . I'm . . . of course you can, I didn't—" Papa collapses back onto the bed. "I'm sorry."

"That's right, that's all right," I tell him.

This has been going on for some time now. One minute he's stormy, the next minute my calm papa. Mercurial is what he's become. "Why don't you take a lie down?" I rake my fingers through his tangled hair. "I'll come back later and if you want, I'll shampoo you with that Castile soap you like so much and get out your razor. We really must tidy up," I say, baby-stepping backwards and hoping with my whole heart that he does not take his head out of his hands. If he should look up, he'll see Woody through the window.

She cannot take another night of kneeling. She just can't.

Chapter Eleven

My sister has been running off for months.

I wasn't all that concerned at first. I thought she was just needing a change of scenery, you know? That she was feeling as cooped up as I was in the jail that Lily-field's become. Only recently have I begun to realize that her escaping is more in line with what Miss Emily Dickinson described when she wrote, "A wounded deer leaps highest."

When my mother quoted that to me the first time, I asked her what it was supposed to mean because it didn't make sense. If an animal is hurt, they're more apt to curl up in a ball and lick their wounds, not go jumping all over the place. Mama told me that what Miss Dickinson meant was, "The worse something hurts inside us, Shen, the harder we try to get away from it."

I have *got* to break into the secondhand shop to get

her another of Mama's scarves. Woody can use it like a bandage. She's going to need it after I get done tearing her limb from limb.

"Would you quit chasin' that chicken and get over here," I shout to the other side of the creek, which hasn't settled down at all since we crossed it this morning. If anything, it's gotten itself more worked up. It's practically rabid. Looks like there's a storm coming.

"What's wrong?" E. J. drops his ax and hollers back.

"She bolted!"

He comes barreling down the slope and across the stepping stones, skipping every other one. "How'd she get by you?" he says, arriving breathless at my side.

Neither one of us will forget that horrible day she got away and we looked and looked and it grew dark and we never found her. E. J. and I had to run over to the Jacksons' cottage to ask for help, but wouldn't you know it, right after I'd told Mr. Cole in tears, "Woody's missing. You better go get the sheriff," my twin came into the yard, looking bedraggled with her shoulder messed up. Mr. Cole took one look at her and said, "Her arm's hangin' odd." Real fast, he took her wrist in his hands and he relocated those bones back into place. I screamed my head off at the sound, but my sister barely flinched and that got to me most of all.

"Did she shimmy down the trellis again?" E. J. asks.

"She musta."

Worry is making E. J.'s face impossibly homelier. "Didn't you tell me last week that ya was gonna do something about that window?"

"Yeah, so what?" I take out my frustration by kicking up a spray of creek water. I hate it when he's right. I should've nailed our bedroom window shut or boarded it up or something! "I saw her streakin' across the yard towards the front woods. Ya know what that means."

Woody will take off higgle-niggle some days, but she's mostly got two destinations when she runs away.

One of them is to the outskirts of town. To the railroad tracks, so she can visit with the hoboes.

I like it up at the camp now, too, but the first time I chased Woody over there, I felt like most folks around here do towards those vagabonds with their stringy clothes and sole-slapping shoes. I felt disgusted to find Woody looking so content amongst the patchwork of tattered sleeping bags and cardboard houses that they set up behind the water tower. After I spent more time up there, though, I kind of understood why my sister found it a good getaway. There's something so . . . I don't know . . . familiar about it.

I got curious as to why the hoboes chose our particular town to squat in instead of, say, Roanoke or Goshen Pass, so I got up my nerve and asked a man named Limping Larry, who is the King of the Camp even though he only has two teeth and one ear. He showed me the special secret signs the hoboes write on trees and the sides of barns to tell others of their kind that Lexington is a good place to hop off a train because it slows there to fill up with water. He told me, "Travelers don't have to jump out of a fast mover and risk a bad injury the way I did," which is why he is called Limping Larry.

The hoboes don't make the town government so happy. Because when they aren't sleeping or telling stories around the campfire the hoboes drink, a lot, which makes them surly. Every so often, Sheriff Nash and his deputy round them up. If they aren't fast about scattering, which they rarely are because they're sort of rundown, some of the hoboes get sent to the Colony to dry out and the rest get tossed in the clinker until they stop seeing pink elephants.

Woody's most absolute favorite friend at the camp is Dagmar Epps. She is Limping Larry's girlfriend and, therefore, Queen of the Camp. Dagmar is not a regular hobo. She didn't travel here from some far-off place. Dagmar was born in town, but she went up to the camp to live because she's sort of retarded, I think. She got pregnant three times and wasn't married. To help her get control of her loose morals, His Honor put Dagmar's children in an orphanage and then committed her to the hospital to have her insides taken out. Dagmar is rather cool to me, but she loves my sister, who she sometimes refers to as "Genevieve," which I think was one of her babies' names.

A hobo named Curry Weaver is Woody's newest friend up at the camp. He's only been up there for a little while, but my sister has *really* taken to him. That hobo is like the pied piper with that harmonica of his. He takes it out of his pocket and places it on his lips and asks in his Northern accent, "What would you like to hear this evening, Woody?" but he always performs the same tune. An excellent version of "Mr. Bojangles," because somehow he knows that's a very relaxing song or else that's the only one he knows. I believe that Curry is being so friendly to us because if you're on the run from the law, which Limping Larry told me most of the hoboes are, it helps to have friends in high places. Curry has been asking me lots of questions. About the town. My grandfather. My mother. The two of us like to sit up on the trestle that runs over the Maury River when we talk. That is as calming to me as Curry's harmonica music is to Woody. Seeing all that water flowing below. It reminds me of Mama.

"His Honor . . . what is he like?" Curry asked last time I was up there.

"Well, he's a real busy and important man. A great father. The best. Cares so much about the town, too."

"Your mother? I heard she's disappeared. That must be painful for you and your sister." He looked over his broad shoulder at the camp. Woody was back there with Dagmar, who was combing my sister's hair with a Popsicle stick. "When did she stop talking?"

"The night Mama vanished. But when I find her, she'll start up again. I've got a plan."

"What kind of plan?" he asked, like he was truly interested.

"Oh, a snatch of this, a snatch of that." I didn't know him well enough to fill him in, so we were quiet together, watching the birds swoop down for their dinners like the river was a big old buffet.

Curry asked me then, "What can you tell me about Doc Keller?"

"Doc Keller?" That kinda threw me. "Well, he and

Papa have been best friends since they were kids. They're fraternity brothers, too. Why do you ask?" I looked the hobo in his dark-circled eyes. "Are you not feeling well? I could arrange an appointment for you."

Curry shrugged off my offer. I figured he must be suffering from something embarrassing that he didn't want to talk about. I scooched away from him then. A lot of the hoboes have lice.

Obviously, I haven't told him any Carmody family secrets, but he isn't exactly forthcoming with me neither. I've asked, but he won't tell me, who or what he was before he jumped a train and landed up here. I believe he might've been a teacher before he hit the skids. He's well-spoken and wordy like that. Or maybe he's a writer and he's doing research for a book and just pretending to be a hobo. Like that white man who colored himself dark and wrote that story called *Black Like Me*, which Mama and I read and liked. That was a real eye-opener. Maybe Curry's writing *Hobo Like Me*. His research must get dangerous at times. He's got a revolver hidden in the waistband of his dungarees.

I told Vera from the drugstore about him when I stopped by for Band-Aids last week because I thought if Curry could clean himself up a little they might be a nice couple and I think she's lonely being so far away from home the same way he must be. Vera handed me my sack and told me, "Oh, yeah. I know the hobo you mean. Looks kinda like a burnt stump? Short and dark? I've seen him talking to a few people and makin' phone calls in the booth next to the courthouse."

Well, whoever he is or was, I like Curry and so does Woody, who is extremely hard to please when it comes to people.

The other times my twin has flown off, she's headed over to the Triple S to sit with Sam. That's where she's going right this minute. I could just choke her, that's how exasperated I'm feeling. And E. J.'s pokiness isn't helping my mood any.

"Could you possibly move any slower?" I shout back at E. J. We're not even halfway down the path that goes through the front woods. I'm worried about the time. There's no telling with Papa. He might be laid out in his bed for fifteen minutes or a couple of hours. "You're a turtle, Tittle."

My sister runs over to the gas station for a lot of reasons. She is comforted by Sam's voice. Languid, I think best describes it. Or maybe sultry. He's also smart. Not like my summa cum laude father, but along with his extensive knowledge of baseball and crime, Sam possesses a certain way of looking at problems and solving them. Here's an example: When I complained to him about my lack of shut-eye because I had to stay alert against Woody's sleepwalking, Sam suggested I tie a cowbell to my sister's finger to warn me when she was fixing to take off. I exclaimed, "That's genius!" because I really thought it was. But with Woody's restlessness, her tossing to and fro . . . what an infernal clanking that cowbell made. Sounded like our fort was under attack by a herd of heifers.

I told Sam the next morning how bad his idea worked and he shrugged and said, "I guess we'll have to come up with something else then, won't we. No sense crying over spilt milk."

Please don't go thinking that sort of merrymaking is typical. Sam Moody is no socialite. He refers to most folks as "lying assholes" *without* saying, "Excuse my French." He's fond of me and Woody, though. And E. J., who he's teaching to be a grease monkey so he's got some way to make a living when he's grown up that's better than mowing lawns and chopping wood.

I guess you could say it was an act of God that sent Sam back down to us two years ago. And the murder of his police partner in Decatur, Illinois. Sam misses his beloved Cubs and his pizza-loving partner—Johnny Sardino.

And Mama.

Of course, she'd known Sam in a polite way from his visits home to check on his mother, but their friendship really got launched the day after the Welcome Home Sam party Beezy threw for her son at her house. Man alive! That bash was really something. The yard was decorated with sparkling lights and men-in-blue balloons. No other whites had been invited to the festivities except for us. Sam was the guest of honor, but he doesn't count as white. His skin is more the color of a perfectly toasted marshmallow. It made me feel uncomfortable at first to be with these folks in this type of party atmosphere. Usually the only Negroes I associated with were Beezy and Mr. Cole, but I got in the groove quick enough when I saw how much they wanted us to have a ball, too. And, boy, did we. I already knew that they sing better than we do, because every spring I make Beezy bring me to Beacon Baptist to listen to their *Hallelujah* choir. But can the coloreds ever dance! They can do all sorts of low-down movements the likes of which I have never seen before. (There are exceptions, though. Woody and I tried to do the Monster Mash with Mr. Cole, but he had quite a bit of trouble staying with the beat. And Sam didn't do much dancing because he was having a hard enough time standing up.)

My mother and I were over at the library a few days later when we ran into Sam again.

He was standing in line—actually, *weaving* in line—behind us at the checkout counter. When the pile of books Mama was holding slid out from between her arms, he bent down, checked the covers, and handed them back with a "Good afternoon, Miss Evelyn. Nice to see you again. I'm . . . an admirator . . . an admir . . . I like poetry, too. Do you read . . ." He burped. ". . . the Great Bard?" Sam's smelling like a still didn't seem to bother my mother. I think she was so eager to talk to somebody besides me about this Elizabeth Barrett Browning sonnet or that Shakespearean play that she was willing to overlook the ripeness that was coming off him. Before I knew it, we'd left the library and walked all the way to the Triple S.

That was the first of many visits.

Every Tuesday afternoon, Papa's longest day at the courthouse, Woody and Mama and I began sneaking over to Sam's. We took the rowboat. The one that's missing. Our mother thought the creek was the safest way to go, but she asked that I do the rowing because she didn't trust her trembling hands. The first time we rounded the bend and Sam's place came in sight, Mama said, "You've got to promise not to tell your father that we are spending time here. He . . . wouldn't understand." Of course, Woody crossed her heart and hoped to die right off, but I wasn't feeling great about their get-togethers until I saw how happy Sam made Mama. And us. So I promised, too. (The Carmody girls are good at keeping our mouths buttoned up. Practice makes perfect.)

The two of them didn't sit out on the station porch, Mama in a crisp, pressed dress and Sam in his greasy overalls, sipping pink lemonade and eating tea cakes. That would be foolhardy. Dr. Martin Luther King Junior could dream until he was blue in the face, but folks around here still aren't even trying to be more tolerant of the coloreds. Mama and Woody and I would wait for Sam to flip his NOT OPEN sign over, and then we'd hike back to where he's got a cabin behind the station so they could have some privacy. If it was raining, they'd sit on the porch. During more pleasant weather, they'd exchange ideas at a picnic table below a glorious maple. Sam described it as "the kind of tree that Joyce Kilmer would feel grateful to bump into."

Woody and I'd leave Sam and Mama alone and skip rocks at the creek because my sister would get antsy listening to so many he *doth* this and he *doth* thats. Not like me, who could listen to the two of them word-waltzing into the night. I was fascinated not only by their conversation, but also by the way he talked *with* her. Of course, Mama would pay such close attention when Sam would talk to her about baseball or *Macbeth* because that's what ladies are supposed to do. Act real interested in what men have to say.

"I'm gonna come back there and light a fire under you if ya don't hurry up," I yell back to E. J. I've already reached the road. "You aren't moving very fast for a mountain man that is attemptin' to rescue his future bride. Maybe I should tell Woody you changed your mind and wanna marry Dot Halloran."

"For God's sakes, Shenny. Don't do that. I can't stand that cow Dot Halloran," he calls from somewhere behind me up in the bushes.

I cannot lay my eyes on the Triple S without memories of my mother washing over me. She always had a smile on her face when she was spending time with Sam, and seeing her ruby lips . . . that was like witnessing the parting of the Red Sea, that's how miraculous her happiness seemed to me.

Woody is crate-sitting on the station porch next to Sam, just the way I knew she'd be. His aviator glasses are covering her eyes. They take up half her face, but Woody just adores those glasses. Sam's got his baseball hat pulled down over his eyes, but don't let that fool you. He knows we're coming.

E. J. finally emerges from the brush, scratched and sweating. His hair has got some twigs sticking out of it.

"Well? What're ya waitin' for?" I say, shoving him halfway across the road. "Go get her, Casanova."

Chapter Twelve

The Triple S is not new and shiny like the Shell out on the highway.

This station looks kind of like, well, not to be ungenerous or anything, but Sam's place reminds me of a three-legged dog. There's only two pumps and no car wash. It's got a restroom, but considering it looks like the entryway to hell, I'd rather relieve myself in the creek, thank you very much. Sam's office has a beat-up wood desk and a swivel chair, a baseball calendar, and an adding machine. Fan belts hang on hooks above a refrigerated case where you can get yourself a cool drink and all of it reeks of Valvoline.

Sam inherited the station in his second cousin's last will and testament. "Good thing it was Sander that passed away and not my cousin Hembly or I'd be shrimping off the Gulf Coast instead of whiling away the afternoon with you, Shen." I told him, "That *was* a lucky break. You didn't even have to get a new sign made up."

After sprinting across the two-lane and scrambling onto the station porch, E. J. quick drags over another crate and gets comfortable at my sister's side. I get right up into her. "You're using up all our lookin'-for-Mama time and Papa almost saw—" She's looking so natty in the aviator glasses. Like she could skip over to Jessop's Field and fire up one of those planes, rip into the wild blue yonder without so much as a "take care now, ya hear," and that only makes me worse mad, because honestly. "Ya hear me?"

E. J. chops my arms down from her shoulders. "Quit shakin' her so hard. You're gonna dislodge her brain."

"But she's gonna get us . . . you don't know . . ."

Sam's listening in on our bickering, but not umping. He's working neat's-foot oil into the pocket of his already broke-to-death Rawlings. There's a foamy bottle of half-drunk cream soda at his feet. He stays away from sloe gin these days. Mama helped him dry out. (He fell off the wagon for a while after she disappeared, but he got himself up, brushed himself off, and hopped right back on board.)

It would be six kinds of rude to ask, so I haven't, but I think Sam's around forty years old. Those ravines that run from his nose to his lips, I've noticed that's about the age they begin appearing on somebody's face even if they aren't prone to smiling all that much. His nose is beaked. His eyes are the color of hazelnuts and like the

Zulus in the *National Geographic* magazine, he wears his hair bushy, not oiled. He dresses a whole lot better, but the rest of him takes after his mother in looks, except for skin color. Nobody knows who Sam's father is except for Blind Beezy and she's not telling. I know that it *wasn't* Carl Bell. (Thank the Lord. I've seen pictures of him. The man looked like he got dropped off a bridge at dawn and nobody bothered picking him up 'til dusk.)

"How are you, Shen?" Sam asks, still working on the glove. From spending sixteen years up North, most of Sam's Southern drawl has faded away, but you can hear it coming out on some words. And it's not only how he sounds. It's what he says. He always treats us like we're on the same playing field. His kind voice made me uncomfortable at first. Like maybe Sam wasn't very manly. A little too up on his toes, if you know what I mean. I'm used to him now.

"I been better, Sam," I say, getting comfortable next to his calico named Wrigley, who's named not after the gum, but a baseball field in Chicago, Illinois. Even if I didn't tell you that somebody tossed him out of a fast moving car, that's immediately what you'd think upon seeing this cat.

"Did you happen to see those shooting stars last night?" Sam asks, looking up like they might've left a scorch mark on this afternoon's cottony sky.

"I certainly did."

"Did you make a wish or two?"

"I certainly did not."

"Why's that?"

"You know why." *Wishes. Bah.* "So I been thinkin'."

"A portent of doom if ever there was one." Sam shakes a couple of lemon drops out of the box that he keeps in his shirt pocket, places one in Woody's cupped hand and wiggles the box at E. J., who, of course, accepts. "Care for one?" he asks me.

"No, thank you, and kindly quit trying to distract me."

He tosses one of the lemon drops up in the air the way you do peanuts. "What's giving your bounteous brain such a workout that you don't have time to enjoy the finer things in life?"

"Well, amongst other things," I say, looking past him at my sister, "Papa is threatening to send Woody away because she won't talk."

Sam jerks his head up and gives me a long, lingering look, like he wants to tell me something, but he doesn't. That's another of the qualities I really appreciate about him. He isn't getting ready to say, "The Lord giveth and the Lord taketh away." He knows that spouting that kind of hooey doesn't make you feel better at all.

"And Beezy told me this morning that she believes that I might be takin' too big a bite out of this rescuing-Mama idea," I say. "She thinks I could use somebody to help me out. You know anybody like that? I can pay. Been beatin' the snot out of Mr. Jackson and Louise in five card."

"Son, would you mind bringing me that bar of candy that's sitting on my desk?" Sam says to E. J.

See that? Just like Beezy, Sam is excellent at changing

directions whenever the subject of my mama comes up. I have hinted and hinted, but he hasn't yet offered to apply his detecting skills to find her. He's a generous soul, so I don't think he's being withholding. No, it's a combination of perfectly good reasons that he's not stepping into the batter's box.

I believe Sam lost some confidence after his partner got shot dead right before his eyes. A bad guy, whose name I'm sure was Stumpy or The Maggot or something simply awful like that, ambushed Johnny Sardino, who was Sam's police partner and best friend. How that killing creep managed to get out on bail I can't imagine, but the police found him dead two days later in a Decatur alley. It took some time to identify The Maggot because his face had been beaten to a pulp, but when the cops finally figured out who it was, the shadow of suspicion immediately fell upon Detective Sam Moody. Charges were pressed against him, but on account of what is known in legal circles as insufficient evidence, Sam got off. But not entirely so. His chief called him into his office and explained to him that even though he would be sorely missed by one and all, he thought it would be for the best if Sam took an early retirement. (He doesn't know that I know this. I pried this out of Beezy.) Grampa lectures that "revenge is a dish best served cold," but just like almost everything else he says, I disagree. When the wrong is still piping hot, when your blood is still on the boil, *that's* the best time to serve revenge up. I believe that's what Sam thinks, too. That's not even taking into consideration his breeding. His mother knocked off her husband, didn't she? So I completely understand if Sam committed that justifiable homicide, but I get scared that the police up in Decatur might not feel the same way. They might discover new evidence in the death of Stumpy or The Maggot and come looking for Sam. I know how unrelenting officers of the law can be.

"Here ya go," E. J. says, coming out of the station office with the Baby Ruth in hand. He winds up and tosses it to Sam, who catches it one-handed.

"You know, now that I see this chocolate up close, I just recalled I need to lose a few pounds," Sam says, throwing the bar back to E. J. "Go ahead and eat that temptation for me, will you?" (What he's really doing here is being considerate of E. J.'s always-complaining stomach. Sam does not at all run on the chunky side. He's built like a Popsicle stick. Arms and legs just dripping.) "That reminds me. Did you know that in the 1918 World Series the Babe—"

I interrupt him with, "Pardon me?" Sam pitched for a few seasons in the Appalachian League and once Number Eight gets onto the subject of baseball, he can go on and on about who hit this and who caught that. Babe Ruth's not his favorite player, though. I try to make sure never ever to say the word *Jackie* or *Robinson* or *Brooklyn* or *Dodgers* in any conversation or I'll never get another word in edgewise. "The help?"

Sam gives me the kind of look a pitcher gives a batter when he's deciding if he's going to throw a fastball or a screwball. He says, "I ran into the sheriff this morning."

He settled on the screwball.

"No kiddin'," I say, not excited. I have suspected for some time that the sheriff is not on the up-and-up. I think Papa wrote Sheriff Nash a nice fat check for his Be-Handy-Vote-Andy campaign. Sam doesn't agree with me. He thinks Sheriff Nash is "doing the best he can given the circumstances." I have seen the two of them now and again chatting away. It's because they're both cops that Sam likes Nash. Not me. The sheriff never did find Mama. The man couldn't locate ants at a picnic. "Did you get anything out of him about Mama's missing?"

"He's not at liberty to discuss it," Sam says.

Figured as much. I know the Eleventh Commandment—*What goes on with the Carmodys is nobody's business*—just as well as I know the other ten. By heart.

Noticing, Sam points at my wrist and says, "You're wearing Evie's watch."

I hold up my hand so the sun can catch it. "I know you told me to be careful, but . . . you don't really mind, do you?"

I let him know right off when I found it last month by the old well. I went straightaway to his place. Sam was down by the creek fishing. "Look what I found!" I said, running up. "It's the watch you gave Mama and it's still running!" Since I was feeling like a month of Sundays, I was expecting a much livelier response out of Sam, but the air just went out of him like he'd sprung a leak. I hadn't considered how seeing the watch might upset him, until I realized that if I gave someone a present nice as this one, I'd expect them to hold it dear. I'd feel that same way if I let myself wonder if Mama ran off and left me and Woody behind.

"Did you come across anything else?" Sam asked, setting his pole down that afternoon.

I said, "No, there wasn't . . . oh, yeah, there was." I went into detail about what else I'd found not *by* the well, but *in* the well. If I'd known Sam was going to go even further deflated, I wouldn't have just blurted it out.

He also asked, "Was there . . . did you find—" I closed my eyes and shook my head. He was asking about the note. Again.

"Sam?"

"I see him, E. J."

A boy in a shiny white convertible has come flying into the Triple S. Skidding to a halt in front of pump two, he lays on his horn, and yells our way, "I ain't got all day. Hop to."

I've never actually seen Sam hop to. Mostly he stays on the porch and stares at whoever pulls into the station until he's sure they've reached the worst part of uncomfortable before he decides to sashay their way.

"I'll go," E. J. says, starting to get up. "It's—"

"I know who it is," Sam says, unfolding his six-foot-and-more self.

It's Remmy Hawkins. He's what you'd call the bad boy of our town. A regular James Dean minus the good looks. Remmy's built like a doorway, but his face is squashed in like he ran into a wall. And he doesn't hardly ever wear a shirt and won't care if you just about toss your biscuits looking at his spotty back. Worst of all? The boy's got red hair. Not that Howdy Doody kind that's not so bad. Remmy's is more like Clarabelle's and he's just as honking dumb. The kid could throw himself on the ground and miss. His grandfather is the mayor. Remmy works for him doing this and that. Errands and such. And his aunt, Abigail, is the one that keeps bringing food to our place.

E. J. and I watch all atwitter from the porch. Even Woody seems on the edge of her crate when Sam sashays over to the side of the car. He reaches in and turns down the radio that's blaring "Stand by Your Man," which I really love and now I can't anymore because this moron seems to like it, too. Sam says, "What can I do you for today, son?"

Remmy spits out, "I'm not your son, nig—"

Good thing he cut himself off. Woody and I used to settle disputes by playing Eeny Meeny Miney Moe Catch a Nigger by the Toe until Sam taught us, "You can catch a colored by the toe. You can catch a Negro by the toe. Even getting hold of a spade is not all that bad, but calling somebody a nigger? That's not only behind the times, it's hurtful."

Remmy doesn't look up, but says, "Ya sell gas in this dump, don'tcha?"

"Ya know, Mister Remmy," Sam says, changing his usual educated voice to sound very much indeed like he just fell off the back of a turnip truck, "I don' believe there's nuthin' I druther do more in the whole wide world than fill up this fancy go car with a tank of gas, no siree, Bob. That'd be a real privilege."

"I ain't got all day," Remmy says, still not looking up.

"Why, I'm sure ya don't, an important fella like you," Sam says. He turns to us and gives a wink. "But . . . well . . . much as I'd like to oblige ya, Mr. Remmy, my pumps is actin' up. Coulda swore they was topped to the brim this mornin' but they up and run dry not more'n two minutes ago. Don' that beat all?"

I can see Remmy biting his tongue from twenty yards away. Acting a whole lot smarter than he is, he revs up his engine and throws his car into gear. But before he takes off, he smiles real ghastly up at Sam with teeth that are buck enough to eat corn on the cob through a picket fence, then he calls over to the porch, "Heard from your mama lately, twins?"

I hop off my crate and shake my fist at him, shouting, "Get your dumb ass outta here, Remington Hawkins." I don't want Sam to get into trouble and he will if the mayor's grandson shows up at supper with a black eye. Mama was Sam's best friend and he won't put up with that sass. "I mean it."

With a beep of his *ah oooga* horn, Remmy dusts out of the Triple S, his wicked laugh not reaching our ears until it's too late for me to do a darn thing about it.

I say, "Ohhhh. . . . I'd like to . . . I'd like to . . ." I wasn't counting on something like this. The station being off the beaten path the way it is, mostly only the lost and the colored stop by and none of them would tell Papa they saw us. What if Remmy goes yakking to somebody, "You know who I saw this afternoon? The judge's girls, shootin' the breeze with Moody over at the Triple S." And what if *that* somebody is a meddler of the highest order and answers, "You don't say," and rushes right over to Lilyfield to tell Papa? Like I told you before, nobody in town but a few know that Papa is keeping Woody and me prisoners, but *everybody* knows that we're not supposed to be hanging out with the coloreds unless they work for us. Being the most prominent family in town, we are expected to set a good example. Grampa is one of those people who believes that Negroes should be hardly seen and never heard. That's something that Mama and Papa never have come to terms with. When she would tell him that this sort of prejudiced thinking is nothing but Southern ignorance born out of fear, he would respond with, "Feel free to take your enlightened Northern attitude back where it belongs, Mother."

Sam steps back onto the station porch after his tangle with Remmy and he's smiling. Smiling!

I'm still fuming! "For two cents, I'd . . . I'd take a garden claw to Remmy and once he was down on the ground writhing I'd—"

"Shen," Sam admonishes. "Watch yourself." He gets after me all the time to remember that a temper like I got can only lead to me doing something I might regret. I think of Stumpy or The Maggot lying beat to death in that Decatur back alley when he says that, and I can't help but wonder if he is speaking from experience. "Now, what were we discussing?"

I say with a fed-up snort, "You can be super-infuriatin' in a real calm way, you know that?"

Sam picks his glove back up and gets back to softening it, but what he's really doing is ignoring me until I can get a grip on myself.

"Fine. If that's the way you're gonna be." I take in air to the bottom of my lungs the way he taught me and count to ten. "I believe we were at the part where you're about to agree to help me look for Mama and if you could do that sooner rather than later I would appreciate it," I say on an exhale. "It's gettin' on in the day, and well, we got to get back before Papa—"

"*Bawwwk . . . bawwwk . . . bawwwk.*" My head swivels to my sister. She has started making a fox-in-the-henhouse racket. "*Bawwwk . . . bawwwk.*"

How absolutely brilliant!

Maybe she's not quite as bad off as she seems. Woody's got to know that Sam'll feel sorry for her. Believe me, no matter how hard-boiled he seems, he's over-easy.

E. J. pops up off his crate to soothe my sister and I flip my palms up to Sam like—*see?* This is all your fault. She's never going to stop squawking unless you agree to help us find Mama. You better speak up before we all go deaf as a post.

"I'll . . . ," Sam says.

"But . . ." I'm sure he's about to give me another one of his excuses.

"Hear me out, Shen."

"I would if I could." I shout, "That's enough now, Woody." Instead of feeling proud of her the way I was a few minutes ago, I feel like wringing her neck. "Will you pipe down!" E. J. is doing all the right stuff, like patting her and crooning, but he's not having much luck.

Sam scoops up Wrigley and sets him down in Woody's lap. He picks up her hands, places them gently on top of the cat's back, and like somebody turned her on switch off, she smiles and shuts right up. Bringing his attention back to me, he says, smooth as can be, "We've been over this before. You know why my asking around about your mother would not be a wise idea."

The colored and the whites are like the birds and the bees. The birds are supposed to stick with their kind and same goes for the bees. If Sam goes around questioning folks, "Do you know anything about the disappearance of Evelyn Carmody?" somebody could start the rumor that Sam and Mama could've been, well, pollinating. (There's always someone willing to fan the flames no matter how dumb the gossip.)

"How about if you discover something that seems important to your mama's disappearance you bring it to me? I'll assist," Sam suggests.

"Do you mean like a double play?" I got him now. He cannot resist baseball lingo.

Sam grins from ear to ear, just like Blind Beezy does, and says, "You've got a lot of your mother running through you, you know that?"

"Funny, I was just thinkin' the same about you." Him and Beezy both make me prett'near drag everything out of them. "How do you mean I've got a lot of my mother runnin' through me?"

"You fishin'?"

He means for a compliment.

"Guess I am."

"Well, there's lots of ways you two resemble one another, but mainly, I was thinking about her tenacity." He looks down at her watch on my wrist and says real seriously, "Wish you'd leave it here with me for safekeeping."

That's the same thing he'd said to me the day after I found it and came rushing over here.

I tell him the same thing now that I told him then. "I can't do that. I'll take good care of it. Mama'll be wanting to wear it as soon as she gets back home so I have to keep it at the ready." I get a little choked up. "It . . . it makes me feel closer to her and . . . you understand?" I don't feel bad about not granting his wish. I brought another memento for him to remember Mama by. "Hold on." Withdrawing the dog-eared copy out of my back pocket, I tell him with my most cheerful smile, "I know she'd want you to have it until we can bring her back home." It's the story they were studying together right before she vanished. Mama could barely read the part to me where Juliet takes a potion that makes her appear to be dead but she really isn't, but Romeo thinks she is, so he drinks poison and then Juliet wakes up and daggers herself so they can at least be together in heaven. What a mess.

Sam doesn't say, "Thank you. How kind of you," when I hand the book over to him and that's all right. I'm not giving it to him because I'm trying to win an award for being the most generous person on earth. I just can't have it near me anymore. Picturing Mama holding it between her hands with the bit-to-the-moon nails makes me pine too much for her, and my lunar-loving papa, too. I've been thinking that the book might be a hint in her disappearance. Everybody knows that it's a story of unquiet love that takes place in Verona, which only adds credence to one of my original ideas of where Mama might've taken off to. "Do you . . . do you think she could've run off to Italy?" I ask.

"No," Sam says, looking affectionately down at the little red book and then off to House Mountain. Those twin peaks are Mama's favorites. "I . . . I'm hoping that your mother is much closer to home."

"I hope you're right. Because I've tried and tried, but all I've managed to learn from that Berlitz record so far is *Buon giorno. Dov'è la biblioteca?* That means—"

"Good day. Where is the library?"

His dead partner taught him some of the language when they were on stakeouts up in Decatur. I feel remorseful about bringing up Johnny's memory. It always makes his Adam's apple work extra hard. "Shoot, Sam. I didn't mean to mention—"

"Y'all better start towards home."

"Okay." I understand that he's not trying to get rid of us. Or chastise me. He's being thoughtful. He doesn't know exactly what will happen if we get back to Lilyfield too late, but he does know how strict Papa is. "Time to hit the trail, Woody." I reach over E. J. to remove the aviator glasses off her eyes, but she twists at the waist so

I can't get at them and starts squawking again and it's about all I can take. I'm sticky and tired and getting real worried now about how late we stayed at the station. I holler at her, "Why ya always gotta be so obstinate? I should start callin' you Mule Girl. How'd ya like that, huh? Mule Girl . . . Mule Girl . . . Mule Girl. Maybe I should sell you to the Oddities of Nature show when it gets here. Yeah, that's what I'll do. You . . . you could stand up on that stage next to Armadillo Boy and the two of ya could—"

"Shut your mouth, Shenny!" Without warning, E. J. stiff-arms me straight off the porch. I land hard in the dirt on my behind. Shocked, I yell, "You little . . ." I clamber up and come charging back at him.

"That's enough, Shenandoah," Sam says, grabbing me by the arm before I can sock E. J. a good one.

"But—" I am struggling to break free. "That's not fair! I'm the youngest, *she* should be babying *me*." I get so sick of pulling on my kid gloves. Brushing Woody's teeth. Braiding her hair. Braying those stupid show tunes. I even got to butter her toast. I deserve those aviators with shiny frames that hook behind the ears. "She's always gettin' what she wants!"

"Is that right?" Sam asks, pointing over my shoulder at my sister who has gotten up off the crate. She lifts her arms out to her sides and begins slow, but is soon twirling herself round and round, like a whirlygig falling out of the branches of an oak tree. "Perhaps you'd like to reconsider that statement."

"I know she's bad off, but . . . but what about me? I'm the one that's always got to—"

Sam says so low in his high humidity voice, "Your sister needs them more than you do."

I hate it when he does this. He's trying to make me feel like I'm acting spoiled rotten.

Sam glances over at Woody again with sorrowful eyes. "Seeing the world through rose-colored glasses. That expression mean anything to you, Shenny?"

Even though I know exactly what it means, I yank my arm out of his hand and say, "No, it certainly does not." I want to hurt his feelings as much as he just hurt mine. So with my nose up in the air, I say as snippy as a girl can get, "That must be something that only Negroes who are too big for their britches go around sayin'." And then I step off the porch and glide across the gas station lot like I'm white and you're not so put that in your pipe and smoke it, *former* Detective Samuel Quincy Moody.

Chapter Thirteen

I'm leading the way back home.

Woody is sandwiched between me and E. J. so he can grab her if she tries to get away. We're at the spot on the path where the house will soon come into sight when E. J. whisper-shouts to me, "Shen . . . Shenny . . . ya gotta slow down."

"I'll do no such thing." We stayed much later at the Triple S than we should've. Papa will probably still be napping, but if he isn't, if we should run into him, he'll smell the motor oil that's sticking to our clothes the same way I am. Woody and I are taking a hot bath tonight, no ifs, ands, or buts.

E. J. shouts even more frantic, "Stop!" and then there's this flurry of activity.

Scared that Woody has sprinted off, I spin around and am relieved to see that my sister has done the exact opposite. She's planted herself on the path and in doing so has tripped E. J., who is lying spread-eagled in a patch of ivy next to the trail.

"Kindly give a little warnin' before you dig in, all right?" I say, backtracking to her side. I'm sweet-talking her because I'm already feeling contrite about being mean to her up at the Triple S. Sam was right. I *was* acting spoiled. Put upon by my twin, who I love with every ounce of my heart. What gets into me? I know darn well that she'd stop all this twirling, flapping, and running if she could. Woody has never liked perspiring all that much. Thinks it's unladylike. "Pea?" I brush up her clumpy bangs and blow on her forehead. "Are you overheatin'?" I tap the rose-colored glasses low on her nose and wave my hand in front of her lime eyes, but she doesn't blink. She's locked onto something that she's seeing over my right shoulder. I don't see anything except for a couple of hot-headed cardinals, but I trust that my sensitive sister has picked up the scent of something that's beyond me. Her nostrils are flaring.

I've got to get closer.

"E. J., quit piddlin' around," I call to him in the ivy patch. "Come get her. She's sensing something."

"That's what I was tryin' to tell ya, Shen," he says, getting up and dusting off. "Be nice if you listened to me every third time or so."

"Yeah, well next time, speak up. I couldn't hear your puny voice." Once I'm sure he's got a good hold of Woody, I take a few steps into the woods. She whimpers, but I pull back on a hickory branch anyway.

Bringing up my binoculars, I scan the surroundings for whatever it is that's made my sister start twitching like a cornered rabbit. There's Mr. Cole hoeing the vegetable garden with his straw hat on. Louise is having a hissy fit at his side. The two of them are bickering about something until Lou stomps off into the house. Maybe Mr. Cole found out about Lou's chasing around the meadow with Uncle Blackie. I might've gone ahead and left an anonymous note in the shed for Mr. Cole that clued him in on their midnight meetings. I'm not saying that I for sure did, but there's times that I get so worked up. It's like . . . like I drank down a bottle of hundred-proof pissiness. I can blab out this thing and do that thing while I'm in that state. Look how I just treated Sam. Next time we go over to the Triple S the first words out of my mouth will be *Jackie Robinson*.

My eyes are searching the front of the house now.

I really must remember to speak to Mr. Cole about painting the second story shutters, and the doorbell, it's hanging by a wire. But none of these odds and ends are what's got Woody worked up. This is just business as usual. I still don't see . . . wait. That shadowy figure in the corner of the porch. I'd know his outline anywhere. Papa was who Woody's nostrils were picking up. I'm surprised she didn't start howling. His Honor is lounging in one of the tall-back woven chairs. His mouth is moving, so he must be talking to somebody. I swivel my binoculars to the swing that hangs off the porch ceiling. There's Sheriff Andy Nash gliding back and forth with icicle-shaped perspiration stains under his arms. He looks like he's melting. Not like Papa, who's looking cool as an igloo. Dressed in a snowy white shirt, his hair slicked back. I can almost smell his English Leather cologne from here. He took my tidying-up advice to heart and changed himself from the sloppy, grieving man I left up in his room into his sparkling, magisterial self.

He's doing what I call his *regal routine*.

I've seen him do this too many times not to recognize it. After Sunday Mass, he'll stand on Saint Pat's steps and slap the men jovially on their backs and spread the compliments so thick. "Why, don't your wives look younger than springtime and aren't your children cute as June bugs," he says, like a medieval ruler passing out morsels of food to starving villagers on the way back to his castle. It's perplexing and hurtful. How can he be so giving to them and so miserly to his own flesh and blood? I know he doesn't mean to, but sometimes Papa makes Woody and me feel like we're a couple of peasants who've got the plague.

Andy Nash has to be here for a reason. Papa must've come looking and rung him up when he couldn't find us or maybe Lou opened her fat trap and ratted us out or . . . maybe the sheriff has come with news of Mama and I can call off my search, which quite frankly hasn't been going too well so far.

If the sheriff *is* here to deliver a surprising report about our mother, then Woody and I will blow up balloons and I'll bake a yellow cake and get out the butter brickle! But if he's gabbing out on the porch with Papa to pass the time until his deputy arrives, I've got to come up with an escape route. Because after they find us, Papa'll laugh and say, "Kids will be kids," but once the sheriff leaves, he'll march us to the root cellar. I can take that kind of discipline because my hide is tough, but Woody? She's made more out of feathers than leather. I don't think she can endure one more night on her knees, no matter how many stories I tell her.

After the first two times Papa dragged us down there, I got the idea of putting some important things inside a sack and took it to our home-away-from-home.

I pawed against the cool walls last night until I got to the bushel basket that the sack's hid under. Opening it, I felt around for what I was looking for. Woody gets so scared of the dark that she can't even cry so I right away lit one of the matches and set the flickering candle down close to her and said in my most loving voice, "Do you think you could draw a little?" I placed a spiral pad and a couple of pencils in the sack, too. "Something that would make you feel like you're somewheres else." The candlelight bounced off the cracked root cellar walls. Off my sister's face. Even in all that decaying ugliness she looked beautiful.

She didn't reach for her drawing stuff right away, so I nudged her and said, "Ohhh, I get it. You want to eat a little something first. Why don't we crack open a jar?" That's a joke. Woody and I cannot stand to even look at those jars of strawberry preserves that sit on that rickety shelf along the back wall, that's how much we've eaten them. We got so hungry we ate the pickled beets, too. "Come on, pea. Drawing will make the time pass faster, you know that," and then I started singing "Some Enchanted Evening." Woody goes crazy for that song. When my voice wore out, I whispered her the story about two girls who go to a faraway beach with their mother, she likes that one most of all. "Once upon a time, it's a perfect day. Not a single cloud in a baby blue sky. The girls' mama is relaxing under a striped umbrella reading and watching her twins build sand castles." My story was so believable Woody started drifting off. "Wake up," I told her when she began listing. I found a mouse nibbling on her hair one night and after that, we don't fall asleep no matter how whipped we are.

I mean, *I* understand why Papa puts us down there. All the liquor he's been drinking has made him stricter, but he has never spared the rod. How else are sinful children to learn? The Good Book is clear on this subject. And Woody and I deserve to be punished. We're *not* telling him the whole truth about the night Mama disappeared and somehow, some way, his under-the-influence brains knows that. Whenever he interrogates us, I leave out the part about Sam and our mother's friendship and how I ran through the woods that night to his place looking for her. And then there's Woody, who will not speak to him at all, which makes him worse mad to be disregarded like that. His Honor expects you to follow the rules. If you don't, then you got to take the punishment. It's his job.

Of course, E. J.'s noticed. He pointed at our scabbed knees and asked, "Why ya always got those?" I told him, "From kneelin' on the root cellar floor, a course." He grinned and asked, "And which root cellar floor would that be?" like he was waiting for me to deliver the punch line of another Bazooka joke. I didn't want to embarrass him over his poor upbringing, so I told him, "It's something rich people do, you wouldn't understand."

I reach into my pocket for a piece of pecan fudge that I keep in all my shorts for moments like these, but there's nothing in there, not even lint. "Wait here and whatever you do, don't let go of her," I say, passing E. J. my binoculars. "I'm going in for a better look."

Our sidekick doesn't understand why we've got to be so secretive like we always are, but unlike Mama did to Sam—I am *not* spilling the beans. I expect E. J. to trust me and for the most part, he does. I drop to the ground and unlace my sneaker. Slide off my sock and ball it up. We had to give up using just our hands to clamp my sister's mouth shut because she bit us too many times. "We got to keep her from howling. Stuff this in her mouth."

"Aw, Shen," E. J. says, holding the sock by the toe. "That's so . . . it's—"

"Ya think I don't know it's disgustin'? You got another idea then have at it. It's the only way she'll keep quiet without the fudge and I forgot to bring it, okay? Can't remember everything, can I?" I say, feeling guilty that I haven't.

E. J. looks at his love girl, and says, "Sorry, dear," as he slips the sock into her mouth and gets her hands in his so she can't dislodge it. I want to suggest that he take the rope off his pants and tie her wrists, but I know he won't.

I warn Woody, "You can forget gettin' an almond cream rub tonight if you spit that sock out. Mind E. J.," and then I take off to make my way up closer to the house to find out what's going on between the sheriff and Papa.

Over in the east yard, Mr. Cole has abruptly stopped pulling milkweed and started cutting down an apple tree that got diseased. He sees me, I know he does. Our caretaker mostly stays in the background of our lives, but Mr. Cole is *real* attentive to what plays out at Lilyfield. Especially if it involves Woody and me. He's promised Beezy that he'll keep her up-to-date on our well-being and takes that responsibility very, very seriously.

Mr. Cole gives me a wave and picks a baby green apple up off the ground and shines it on his pants. He knows they're my favorites. He's getting ready to shout out, "Hey, Miss Shen. Look what I got for ya," so I shake my head as wild as I can. Mr. Cole stares back, confused, until I point to the porch. He nods, lifts the ax up to his shoulder, and begins chopping . . . *chu* . . . *chu* . . . *chu* . . . harder and faster. For good measure, he breaks into a round of "I've Been Workin' on the Railroad." He can't write his letters all that well, but that doesn't mean he's not a smart man. He knows that sometimes I got to slink about to get an understanding of what's going on around here. The disturbance he's making will cover up any noise I make.

I weasel through the bushes to squat down below the kitchen window, being ever so careful not to step on anything that might make Papa *snap* to attention. Him and the sheriff are only a few yards away. Above me, I can hear Lou in the kitchen beating a spoon against a bowl near to death. She's making such a racket that I've got to work hard to hear the sheriff say, ". . . don't really know for sure. Thought at first he'd drowned in the creek, but I got Perry Walker, the medical examiner from Charlottesville, to come take a look. He said there was no water in Clive's lungs. Perry hasn't run all the tests, but it looks suspicious. Murder maybe. Did you happen to hear anything out of the ordinary comin' outta the Minnow place Friday evenin'?"

Murder? Minnow?

"Friday?" Papa replies. "Wish I could help you out, Andy, but as I recall, the girls and I had a light supper, played a game of cribbage, and turned in early that night."

That's not true. We don't eat or play cribbage or do anything else nice together.

Papa then says to the sheriff in his most persuasive voice, "I'd certainly like to keep this incident quiet. With Founders Weekend coming up, we wouldn't want to put a damper on the festivities with talk of something as nasty as a possible murder, would we? I don't think my father would appreciate that."

The sheriff says, "I take your point."

Of course, he does. I admit, I've got some resentment towards him on account of the way he never found Mama, but I'm not letting that affect my assessment of his personality. Sheriff Andy Nash with his brown hair and brown eyes and brown uniform—if he was standing next to a pile of bull crap you'd never be able to make him out. It's not like he's evil or anything, he's actually sort of nice. Just always seems like he's more interested in glad handing than crime solving. Sam is usually so picky about who he spends his time with. What he sees in the sheriff is beyond me.

I can't tell from where I'm crouched down, but I bet the sheriff is dabbing his chin with his red bandana. He does that a lot because he sweats a lot. "This heat is really something. Have you noticed the trees? They've been soaking in so much of this wet warmth that they can barely stay upright. Remind me of hoboes on a bender," he says. "Can't remember a summer this bad. Maybe in '61, yeah, that was a scorcher. You could fry—"

"Was there anything else you needed to discuss, Andy?" Papa interrupts. "I'm afraid I'm rather pressed for time."

"Well, now that you mention it, sir, I'd like to have a few words with the twins. Ya know how children can sometimes hear and see things us grown-ups don't. I know they got that tree fort that overlooks the Minnow place. Would you mind?"

"I'm afraid that would be inconvenient," Papa says politely, but he minds very much. I can tell by the sound of his voice that his feathers are ruffled. "I'll ask the girls this evening if they saw anything and get back to you. By the way, have you heard anything more about the parade rerouting?"

The sheriff says, "I haven't . . . golly, could I trouble you for another glass of tea? This heat . . . it's . . . I'm parched."

Papa calls impatiently, "Louise?"

Instead of going out to the porch the way she's been taught to ask if they're needing anything, Lou slams the mixing bowl down on the counter and thrusts her head out the kitchen window that I'm hiding under. Hearing my *gasp*, she startles, too, and bangs her head on the bottom of the raised window. She narrows her eyes at me and says, "Yes, Your Honor?"

"We need another pitcher of sweet tea. Quickly, please."

I clasp my hands together in a praying way and beg Louise with my eyes, please, please don't tell him, "Your spoilt daughters've been runnin' off to town against your expressed wishes. Been talkin' to folks about your wife's disappearance, and oh sakes alive, look! Here's one of 'em balled up beneath my kitchen window listenin' in on y'all." Remarkably, she doesn't utter a word. I'm already thinking a few good thoughts about her until she points at Mama's watch. She covets it. I give her an over-my-dead-body look. She answers with a suit-yourself shrug.

"Sir?" Lou shouts. Now she's eyeing me with Rex the alligator eyes, half-lidded like that. " 'Fore I fetch you that tea, thought you'd like to know that I found what you was lookin' for earlier."

She means me. I can't do anything else but slip the watch off and drop it into her outstretched claw.

Gloating, the same way she does when she's beat me out of a big pot in cards, Lou says, "Yessir, those molasses biscuits you was askin' after, they was in the pantry after all. You and the sheriff care for a few?"

Damnation.

I'll get Mama's watch back, I'm not worried about that. I've been gone longer than I planned on and am worse concerned about Woody, so I stick my tongue out at Lou and back out of those bushes the same way I got in them.

When I get back to where I left them, I find my sister in E. J.'s arms, but not in a romantic way. She's wiggling, trying to get free. If I hadn't cut her nails real close, she'd be scratching his face to smithereens.

"It's all right. I'm all right. Let her go, E. J." Woody throws herself at me like she didn't expect me to come back alive. I hug her tight and sing, "Don't be *bellow-bellow*," over and over. I'm telling her not to be scared in our twin talk, but it's not working. Woody's teeth are chattering worse than a set of Grampa's practical joke ones.

"What'd you do to her?" I ask E. J., like it's all his fault that Woody's gotten worked up.

"She was doin' just fine 'til she heard your father and Louise yellin'," he says, rubbing his cheek. There's a pale handprint where Woody must've slapped him. "What were they goin' on about anyways?"

"Nuthin' you'd understand." If I tell him how I was spying on Papa and the sheriff up on the porch, or that Louise caught me beneath the window and got Mama's watch off me, Woody will hear and get even wilder than she already is, which is almost more than I can handle. I get her by the shoulders, square her, and say, "We're gonna go round through the side yard and slip into the house. Get busy polishing silver like we've never been gone. Papa'll be none the wiser. I promise. You hear me? I said I *promise*."

She doesn't completely stop, but her gyrating slows. I remove Sam's aviator glasses from her eyes. "I'll keep these for you. Wouldn't want them to get lost." What I'm really thinking is if by some awful turn of circumstances we don't out-dodge Papa, if we get caught, his first interrogating question will be, "And from whom did you receive these interesting glasses, Jane Woodrow?"

E. J. says, "I think ya should—"

"Do we care what you think?" I set my fist an inch from his nose. "Even if we did, which we don't, we don't have time to listen to one of your dumb ideas right now." I do *not* want him drawn into this mess any worse than he already is. His mama's got a brand-new baby and his father's got black lungs. They need their boy to bring in cash money. If Woody and E. J. and I get caught returning from the Triple S, the Tittle boy is going to find himself in a hell of a fix. Anybody who gets in trouble alongside a Carmody does. Whatever bad thing happens, it's not our fault. It's yours. This is what Uncle Blackie calls the family motto: Not me*um* but you*em* has got your ass*um* in a sling.

When E. J. stands his ground, I shove his shoulder and hiss, "Am I not makin' myself clear, Ed James? We don't need your help. Scram."

He bends at the waist and lifts Woody's creamy hand to his berry-stained mouth. Upon straightening, E. J.'s less Musketeer and more mountain man again. "Tomorra," he says to me like I'm the last person he wants to see then or any other time in his life.

All I can think about as I watch that scrawny boy disappear into the dwindling day is our mother. And how every night after tucking Woody and me into bed, she'd kiss our eyelids closed and whisper, "Today's worn itself down to a trickle, my sweet peas in a pod. But tomorrow is a river waiting to carry us to our fondest dreams."

I'm beginning to get the awfulest feeling that my mama might've been wrong about that.

Real wrong.

Chapter Fourteen

Grampa will be arriving soon with his bag of tricks.

Back when I was a kid and too stupid to know better, he'd bribe me to play practical jokes on Mama. Had me conceal a thin wire in the dining room doorway so when she was carrying the dirty plates back to the kitchen, she'd trip and go flying. Or told me to set a paint can on top of a closed door and call for Mama like I was hurt. It took two weeks to get that orange color out of her hair. Grampa got me to do stuff like that by promising me a palomino. I held up my end of the bargain and thought he would, too. Until he showed up one afternoon with a broom horse saying, "Look what I brought ya, Shenny. Your very own Trigger." The harder I bawled, the more his jowls shook with laughter. I bet that's the only part of Mama my grandfather misses. Making fun of her.

Gramma Ruth Love will come, too. I know *she* misses all of Mama. She has taken the loss of her quite hard. They would have wonderful conversations. Both of them love to garden so mostly they'd chat while weeding or watering. I'd listen to Mama telling our grandmother, "This is a new age, Ruth Love. You need to be your own person. You spend too much of your time worrying about how to get the ring around the collar out of Gus's shirts or what to serve him for dinner. He's bullying you into submission."

Gramma would always answer back with a demure smile beneath her broad-brimmed hat, "I know you mean well, dear, but we do things differently down here."

Mama would weed faster, saying something like, "Personal freedom is not dictated by the Mason-Dixon Line."

They'd discuss stimulating ideas like that for a while until Gramma would eventually start her holy quoting. "What about wives submit yourselves unto your husbands? Saint Paul said that." And then Mama would have to give up until their next visit, because that's true. The Bible is a real hard thing to argue against and my grandmother knows it word for word.

The reason our grandparents stay with us during Founders Weekend is so Grampa doesn't smash his precious truck up again. Three years ago that rummy ran his Chevy into a ditch on the way back to his place. Gramma got a jaggedy cut when her forehead hit the door handle and it has left an ugly scar, but did Gus

Carmody care? No, he did not. That's why I ran a rusty nail alongside the shiny black paint from taillight to headlight when I found his truck parked in front of Willie's Public House last month. He's still raging on about how when he catches whoever defaced his truck is going to be sorry they was ever born. But what about our grandmother's face? (That's another something that I inherited from my father. I like to keep the scales of justice in balance and do so whenever I can.)

Gramma Ruth Love is very particular. She'll get agitated when she shows up for her stay if our home is not glistening clean and we wouldn't want to wreck her visit. That's how come I'm saying to Woody in a no-nonsense, but entirely pleasant way, "That's real good, keep comin'." We're cat-footing through the empty kitchen on our way to the dining room and all that silver that needs polishing when the rattle of the broom closet door gets my attention. By the time I remember her witchy trick, by the time I yell, "Watch out, Woody! She's comin'," Lou is already bounding out of the closet, bent over and cackling, "Gotcha! Gotcha! Gotcha!"

But this time, the joke's on her.

Woody is not dashing away, nor is she screaming her head off like she usually would while Lou doubles over in laughter. My sister's standing stone cold still in the middle of the kitchen floor. She's gone marble white. I've never seen anything like it. It's awful. Even Lou must think so, because she's quit hopping like a hag and is eyeing Woody with an astonished face. She comes closer and reaches out to stroke my twin the way you do a statue in a museum that looks so lifelike. "Woody?" she says tentatively. "Are ya—"

"You and Blackie think that's so damn funny, you—" I leap, land on Lou's chest, and knock her backwards against the broom closet door. "Look what ya did!" I slide my palms down her cheeks and jerk her head towards Woody. "Ya petrified her!" Lou is kicking at me, trying to duck under my arms, but I get her by the hair. Some strands come off in my hand and I wave them in her face. "I'm takin' this to Miss Delia. She'll hex ya. She will. She made Charity Thomas grow that hump on her back and she'll do the same to you. Ya think Blackie'd come sniffing around something protrudin' like that? Well, do ya?"

"You don't scare me! Charity tol' me she was born with that hump," Lou yells back.

"She's lying. Her back was flat until—" From the corner of my eye, I can see that my argument-hating sister has thrown back her head and opened her mouth wide. Papa is right outside. "No . . . no . . . don't . . ." I gasp, letting go of Lou and lunging for Woody, but her howl has already broken free. I slap my hand over her mouth to make her stop, but under the *tick tick* of the cuckoo clock that hangs over the pantry and the bouncy tune that's coming out of the transistor radio, I can hear the front door open and close with a slam. He heard. He's coming.

"What is going on in here?" Papa asks, materializing in the kitchen doorway. "What's all the shouting about, Shenandoah?"

He's not sure which twin I am, so I bare my gaped teeth and say, "Good afternoon, Your Honor. So sorry to disturb you. There's nothing going on here of any importance. Woody . . . ah . . ." My sister is only staying upright because I'm holding her so. "Jane Woodrow . . . she . . . stubbed her toe is all." I chuckle. "You know how she can be." I said that not directly to him, but to Lou. I avert my eyes to her hair that I got hidden in my hand.

"Is that right, Louise?" Papa asks for confirmation. He's got to look up to her because she's taller than him by a few inches.

"Oh, thas right, sir, thas right. Nothin' goin' on here but a stubbed toe," she says with a rise of her lying right eyebrow and an arch of her back. I am digging my fingernails between her shoulder blades to remind her of my hump-hexing promise.

"You look so nice," I say to Papa. Despite the sternness in his voice, I can feel my need for him bubbling up. "Have you got something to attend to this evening? If not, maybe you and me and Woody could go up to the fort and star—"

"Everything all right, Walt?" someone calls out of the hall that leads off the foyer into his study.

"We're in the kitchen, Abby," Papa says, his penetrating gaze still not letting up on us.

Abby?

Abigail Hawkins. I didn't see her Cadillac parked out front. She probably parked down by the barn. Yes. She'd feel right at home down there.

The Hawkins and the Carmody families have at least

a hundred years of hunting and drinking under their belts. Our grandmother loves to tell the tale about how everyone in Rockbridge County took it for granted that her precious baby boy and the Hawkins girl would eventually tie the knot. It came as no surprise when they set a date to wed after they finished high school. Abigail worked on the family horse farm and Papa went to college and everything was going according to plan. Until Abigail came down with something the night Papa had planned to attend a sock hop at Washington & Lee. That's why he was all by his lonesome when he spotted Evelyn Anne MacIntyre across the crowded dance floor. Just one look, that's all it took. He fell head over heels for Mama. Swept her off her size sevens. Abigail Hawkins's clodhoppers didn't have a chance.

Gramma always concludes the story with a long sigh. "As you can imagine, losing Walter like that to another woman, poor Abby took the breakup hard. She never did wed." Hardly a surprise, I always think to myself. Who'd want to wake up every morning for the rest of their lives next to a woman who bears a resemblance to one of the Clydesdales her family breeds?

"Walter?" Miss Hawkins comes into the kitchen with a *bick . . . bick . . . bick* of huge white heels with shiny buckles on their toes and a belted blue gingham dress in a size too small. She must've come to do more of her Betty Crockering or what Beezy called "web spinning." I didn't notice until just now two of her picture-perfect pies sitting on the kitchen counter.

Bait.

Miss Abigail throws her hands to her chubby cheeks, says so concerned, "Everything all right in here?" When she speaks, her ponytail bobs back and forth. It's the same rambunctious red as her lowbrow nephew Remmy's.

Oh.

No.

After he left the Triple S, did that boy drive right over to her farm to tell his auntie that he'd run into us? Is that why she's here? Has she come bearing bad news along with those pies? My heart starts thrumping in anticipation of her saying, "Well, here are those naughty girls Remmy saw this afternoon at the gas station with that half-breed Sam Moody."

I bring my eyes up to my father. Concentrate. When he gets like this, our mother taught Woody and me, "It's important to not only listen to what he's saying, but to study him the same way you would a map, girls. Pay attention to the way his shoulders draw up into little mountains. Check to see if his brow is rutted or if his cheeks are deep like pot holes. Those are signs that he's angry."

And he *is* mad, but not in the worst kind of way. Not how he'd be if Miss Hawkins just informed him that his girls had disobeyed and taken off from Lilyfield. If that was the case, his face would look like a froze-over pond. But beneath that icy crust would lie a man ready to blow.

Papa puts on a gleaming smile before turning towards Abigail. "Nothing to concern yourself about, Abby," he tells her. "Just a stubbed toe."

"Oh, goodness. Those always hurt worse than you think they should. Perhaps I should get some ice," she says, heading towards the freezer like this is her own house.

"There's no need for that." Papa shoots us a be-on-your-best-behavior-or-else look. He hates for us to make a fuss in front of other people. "Girls, where are your manners?"

I am still shaking from my tussle with Lou and worried about Woody, but I do what he expects. I step up and curtsy the best I can in blue jean shorts. "Good afternoon, Miss Hawkins. What a pleasure it is to see you again. Thank you for bringing us those lovely pies." I point over at the counter. While Gramma Ruth Love wins all firsts at the fair, Miss Abigail always comes in second. "Are they peach? *Mmm . . . mmm . . . mmm.* Can't wait to get me a slice."

I'd rather eat tree bark. I'd rather be dead.

Miss Hawkins says, "Why, aren't you the sweetest thing. It's very nice to see you again . . . ah . . ."

"I'm Shenandoah Wilson, ma'am. This is Jane Woodrow," I say, nodding towards Woody, who's still looking mighty rocky. "She's the strong, silent one."

Still plastered against the broom closet door where I pinned her, Louise pipes in with, "How do, ma'am. Would ya like me to fetch ya a glass of something cool?"

"We don't have time for that," Papa says. "Miss Abigail has a meeting of the Ladies Auxiliary to conduct."

"Excuse me, Your Honor?" I need to ask him for a

favor, even though my twisting tummy is telling me the timing's not right. Mama always said that was important, too, that you had to pick the right moment. Maybe Abigail Hawkins being here will help. Seems like he's trying to impress her. "That dog I asked you about earlier? Ivory? I don't think he's eaten for days. He's lying out on the Minnow porch looking very skinny."

Papa turns to Abigail and says apologetically, "I'm afraid my daughter has a hard time following directions." To me, he says, "Did you go over to the Minnow place?"

"No, sir."

The corners of his lips are tucking into the triumphant smile he gets when he thinks he's caught a witness lying on the stand. "Then please explain how you know that the dog is out on the porch."

"I can see him from our bedroom window, Your Honor. Do you think I could go get him?" I ask, before he comes up with another question that I might not be able to answer. "We'll take good care of him." Grassy breath and all that fur. My sister *needs* that.

He says to Woody, "Is that true? Do you want that dog?"

She does not bring her eyes up to his, she looks down to the floor and reaches for my hand, squeezes so hard.

I say, "She really does. She is missing Mars so bad."

Papa thrusts out his chin. Narrows his eyes. I know that look. If he had a gavel, it'd be pounding. His Honor is about to announce a verdict. He says to Woody, "If *you* ask me for that dog in your own words, Jane

Woodrow, I might give my consent." He wants her to start talking again so she can answer his questions about the night Mama vanished. Threatening to send her away is the worst thing he could do, but this is bad, too. Papa knows that Woody is madly in love with all creatures great and small. She even gave up fishing because she couldn't stand hooking the worms.

My sister has begun swaying, ever so slightly.

Papa doesn't like it when she rocks. His temple vein is beginning to bulge blue. He is opening and closing his fists. That's not good. If Mama was here, she would say, "May I give you a neck rub?" to detour his anger.

I start to say, "May I give you . . . ?" but he doesn't hear me. He's too intent on Woody.

Crouching down in front of her fast enough to make her flinch, Papa says sternly, "You know what befalls animals that outlive their usefulness, don't you?"

"I know, Papa, I know," I say, waving my hand in the air like an overeager student. I'm trying to distract him from my sister. "When our animals get aged or injured beyond fixing, you tell Mr. Cole to put a bullet in their head and bury them out back of the barn." Woody has marked every one of their graves with crosses she made out of twigs and twine. "They're no good to us anymore if they can't do their jobs."

"That's correct, Shenandoah, and your sister would do well to remember that." Papa gives Woody a too-firm pat on the head.

"She most certainly will, Your Honor," I say, peppy. "Thank you for that wonderful advice."

"Come, Abigail," he says, turning to leave. "You'll be late for your meeting."

"Oh, goodness, you're right," she says, checking her watch, which is not half as nice as Mama's. She bends down low enough that I can see the top half of her freckled bosom escaping from her scooped-neck dress. "So nice visiting with you, girls. I look forward to spending a lot more time together real soon." When she rushes off to my father's side, she leaves behind a cloud of that sickening gardenia perfume she wears.

Lou calls, "Sir? Will you be home for supper?"

"No," he says, not bothering to look back.

Usually I'd be thinking after an encounter with Papa, *Yes, he's right to get strict like that with Woody. She's got to start talking one of these days.* Or maybe I'd come up with another explanation for the way he's acting. Something like, *Papa doesn't mean to be so cruel. His suffering over his wife's disappearance is what's making him think crooked.*

But that's not at all what's going on in my mind.

You see that, Shen? That right there? Shocking thoughts are screaming at me. *See how His Honor is trying to break already-fragile Woody, who is so sad about losing her mama that she cannot sleep or speak or eat anything not sweet? See how he's telling her that harm will come to a helpless animal if she doesn't do what he wants her to? Well, do you?*

Oh, more than anything, I don't want to. But Papa's meanness is feeling as familiar to me as the Bible story about Solomon who was willing to slice a baby in two to settle a score.

I shouldn't be thinking like this. Even my lungs know that. They're in and outing faster.

"Shenny?" Lou asks, shrinking away from me. "What's got into ya?" She's probably thinking that I've been taken over by a devil spirit and I'm scared, too. How I'm feeling is a sin against the commandment that obliges us to love our father, respect and support him in his time of need. I'm sorry, Lord. Forgive me, I can't help it. I know you want us to turn our other cheek, but every time we do, it just gives Papa another place to slap. Or make us kneel in the root cellar. Interrogate us for hour upon hour about what we saw the night Mama disappeared. I know how much pain he's in, but shouldn't a loving father care about his daughters no matter how bad he himself is grieving? Couldn't he be more under-standing about Woody instead of threatening to send her away? He should've fetched Ivory off the Minnow porch. Tied a pink bow around his neck. Given that dog to my sister like a get-well-soon present. That's what he would've done back in the days we laid together on the fort floor, searching the skies every night after supper, Mama's singing drifting out of the kitchen window below. Back when he held his little Gemini so close, telling them, "I love you as much as the stars."

It's no use. I can't go on pretending anymore. Can't deny any longer that there's been a crack in our universe. First our sun . . . and now our moon has come tumbling from the heavens.

Woody has wet herself.

Chapter Fifteen

Optical illusions.

I came across my first at Doc Keller's office just last week when I was waiting for Woody to be examined. I picked up a *Jack and Jill* magazine off the pile in the waiting room and started paging through it to pass the time. In the puzzle section, I came across a picture of a fancy goblet sitting under a headline that said—*AMAZING. What's so amazing about that?* I thought. But as I was turning the page, that picture caught my eye again and something truly *AMAZING had* happened. The goblet picture had somehow transformed into something completely different. Just like that, I was staring down at two identical girls—twins—going nose to nose. Feeling tricked, I tried desperately to get that goblet to reappear again. I opened my eyes as wide as I could. Blurred them. Squinted. Did it all over again ten times. Finally gave up.

That's the closest I can get to describing to you how I'm feeling about our father. No matter how hard I try, I won't be able to bring him back.

Woody, Lou, and I are still huddled together in the kitchen, like soldiers trying to regroup after a surprise attack. The sound of Miss Abigail's laughter and the crunch of my father's car tires drifts through the kitchen window. I'm pretending not to notice the puddle of pee at my sister's feet.

"Shenny?" Lou says, tiptoeing her fingers up my arm. "Listen. 'Bout jumpin' out at y'all like that . . . I . . . I was only funnin' around. Blackie told me . . . I didn't mean—"

"Shut your stupid bayou mouth, Lou. And if you don't wipe that pityin' look off your face, I'll wipe it off for ya," I'm barely able to say. "Woody?" With what feels like the last ounce of strength I got in me, I reach out to my twin. We use each other like crutches as we limp through the foyer and up the front staircase.

Leftover love is what I've been using as an anchor to keep me from drifting off, I see that now. I'm pressing my burning cheek against the cool blue wall that Mama tried to paint so tranquil. I'm getting swept away by sorrow and there's not a thing I can do about it. I have been lying to myself this whole time. Not only when it comes to my papa. It's so true that you don't know what you've got until you don't have it anymore. If I could only take Mama into my arms and apologize to her for almost always taking Papa's side in their arguments. For defending him. I'm feeling now how she must have felt. Helpless.

Nobody could be that accident-prone.

My sister is poised on the edge of our bed. The white washrag I got out of the bathroom so she could clean herself up is hanging off her fingertips like she's surrendering.

I kneel down in front of her and say, "Just so you know, wettin' yourself, that's no big deal. Happens to me all the time. I did it twice on Sunday." Her sneakers are soaked with pee, so I slip them off. "Oh, Woody . . . I'm so sorry. It won't always be like this. I'll find Mama, just you wait and see," I say the same way I have been, even though I don't believe it anymore. I'm not even sure that I ever did, but I can't let my fragile sister know that. "C'mon now, we got to cheer up. I could sing that song from the *Camelot* album you and Mama like so much." I wipe the crying snot off with my arm and lower my voice as far as it will go. "'If ever I would leave you, it . . . it wouldn't be in summer. Seein' you in summer I never would go. Your hair streaked with sunshine, your . . .'"

I want so badly for her to yank on one of my braids and say the way she once would've, "You know what would make me feel a whole lot better? If you'd stop singin'. You can't carry a tune in a bucket, Shenbone."

I lift the washrag off of her fingers and run it down her legs, being careful around her still-raw knees. She's lost the Band-Aid I stuck back on this morning. "Please, please talk to me. You can if you want. Doc Keller says there's nothing wrong with your voice. If you could just try to say a few words."

Slowly, she opens her mouth. For one blessed moment I think—this is it. She really is going to speak! She parts her lips, but instead of words, out comes her tongue. She runs it fast across my cheek.

"Geeze, Woody, geeze. That's so . . ." I'm shocked, but I don't wipe that spit off. I go ahead and lick her right back, thinking to myself, *Maybe she's got the right idea.*

Whoever it was that said, "Sticks and stones can break my bones, but words can never hurt me," must've been hard of hearing. Papa shouldn't have threatened Woody. And he shouldn't have talked to Mama in the hurtful ways he did neither. Calling her despicable names because she wanted to do things her own independent way instead of his. He uses his silver tongue like a sword. Nicking away at your heart, cutting word by cutting word. Maybe silence really *is* golden.

Not at all feeling ready, but knowing that I need to rally for my sister's sake, I say, "Let's get you dressed." Passing by the window, I pause. Ivory's out there. Feeling Woody's warm lick on my cheek, I know what I have to do.

Grabbing the cleanest clothes I can find out of the pile that's growing on the closet floor, I strip off the wet ones and shimmy dry drawers and shorts up my sister's legs. "There. That's much better," I say, standing back to survey her the way you're supposed to do to a work of art. "You look exceptionally gorgeous. Except for your hair. Looks like a cat's been suckin' on it. Let me braid you." I take Mama's gold hairbrush off the vanity table and try to work it through my sister's tangles, but she pushes my hand away, reaches behind me, and picks my tin lunch box up off the end of the bed where I'd tossed it. She hugs it to her stomach.

"What? Are you *meetone*?" I ask. "Do you need something to eat?"

Communicating with Woody since she's gone mute is very much like playing a game of charades. You got to try and piece together what she's acting out bit by bit and make some sense of it all. She's begun marching up and down. "Do you want to go for a walk?" Now she's beating on her chest. "Heartburn? I'm out of Rolaids. I'll get some more when we go to Slidell's tomorrow." My sister throws the lunch box down to the rug and gets down on her belly in front of it. She's scratching at the latches, so I think I might have been right in the first place. She's hungry. Starving, by the looks of how hard she's clawing.

"There's nothing left in there. I gave it all to E. J. this morning, remember? Here. Let me." When I pop the lunch box lid, she doesn't search for a few crumbles of leftover bacon or a bit of cold flapjack. She snatches out the picture she drew at Beezy's this morning. Waves it frantically in front of my face. It's the drawing of Mars bleeding all over the place.

I found the dog the same afternoon I found Mama's watch.

On the kind of spring afternoon that makes you want to crawl into Mother Nature's lap and give her a kiss of gratitude, I was snuggled out on Mama's and my reading bench. It's where she and I would hide out most afternoons, below the shaking aspens. Sometimes, if she and

Papa had gotten along that morning, she'd be feeling lighthearted enough to perform a song for me. She was Laurie from *Oklahoma!* belting out "People Will Say We're in Love" or Maria from *West Side Story* chirping "I Feel Pretty" with a twirl of her skirt, but most of the time we kept our noses in our books. If we came across something that we thought the other would get a kick out of—we'd read aloud. Mama would usually quote the poets. I'd stick to reading her parts of an adventure story, which are my favorites. I go nuts for tales of intrigue set in far-off lands like China or the Dark Continent or California. When I'd come across a particularly exciting passage, I'd say, "Listen to this." That was the cue for my travel-yearning mother to close her eyes and let the sound of my voice transport her far, far away.

But I wasn't reading something thrilling like that the afternoon I found the watch. I was flipping through the pages of *The Miracle Worker* trying to get some pointers on how to help my sister start talking, when the sun caught something shiny over near the well. I set my book down, shooed away the leaves that were huddled around the well base, and picked up what had caught my eye. I lost my balance for a second, so I had to grab onto the stony edge. That's when I got a glimpse of the carcass. Mama was always begging Papa to have Mr. Cole seal the dried-up well for good, but it never seemed to get done.

Oh, well, I thought, gazing down at the pile of bones that'd got caught up amongst the well's collapsing walls. Dust to dust and all that. I figured they belonged to a coon or possum, they were about the right size. I was about to head back to the reading bench when I remembered what had caught my eye in the first place. I opened my hand and lo and behold! It was Mama's watch. The one Sam gave her. Giddy, I wound it tight, slipped its stretchy band onto my wrist, and listened to its still strong *tick . . . tick . . . tick* when I pressed it up to my ear. I ran my fingers over the word *Speranza* engraved on the back. *The Lord has led me to this watch*, I thought. *It's a sign. But what is He telling me exactly? That time is on my side? To have hope? Yes!*

Feeling ever so grateful for this unexpected gift, I dropped to my knees and prayed, "Our Father who art in heaven, hallowed . . ." That's when something began niggling at me. I'd only had a quick look into the well, but . . . what was that down there next to the bones? It glittered. Thinking it could be something more of Mama's, I said, "Hold on a minute, Lord." I got my tummy up on the well to get a closer look. But it wasn't one of my mother's brooches or necklaces shining amongst the crumbling stones. It was a silver bell. The one Woody had taken off a Christmas ornament and attached to Mars's collar to warn the squirrels that he was on the hunt. The bell was lying at the base of his skull.

That night in bed, I slipped Mama's watch from the cool side of my pillow, wiggled it in front of my sister's eyes, and whispered, "Look what I found." Instead of being excited the way I was, Woody started to cry. I said, "*Shhh . . .* he'll hear you. Don't be jealous. You can wear it sometimes, too."

The reason I still haven't told my sister about finding Mars the way I should have was because I convinced myself that making her aware of something so tragic might shove her off the edge that she appears to be teetering on. But now I'm realizing that it wasn't *her* that I've been protecting, it was selfish *me*. I didn't want to watch Woody's face collapsing into itself one more time. The way she wept in her sleep broke my heart most of all. Watching those tears slip out of her lids when she was supposed to be sweet dreaming—that just about killed me.

I think it was Ralph Waldo Emerson that wrote, "Truth is beautiful; but so are lies," but I don't feel so beautiful about lying to my sister anymore. Yet how am I supposed to tell her that her beloved Mars is never coming back? And that as much as I want it to be true, I am not at all sure our mama is either. I see now that hope is just another illusion. Not of your eyes, but of your heart. Hope is for the weak. I must be as strong as the fifth largest constellation—Hercules.

I must tell my sister the truth.

I lift the dog drawing out of her hand, run my finger along the waxy red crayon that's streaming off Mars's back, and drag it over to the plaid suitcase that he's holding in his mouth. She's drawn pictures of Mars before but the suitcase is something new. She must've added it on when I was busy cleaning Papa's bathroom.

"Yes." I squeeze my eyes shut so I will not have to look at my sister's face. "That's right. Mars is . . . uh . . . he's gone on a trip . . . but one that he's never coming back from. He's dead, Woody. I found his bones in the well and please, please don't start crying, I'm gonna get you another dog, a lot furrier one I promise."

Every muscle in my body goes rigid to shield me against her onslaught of sad. I can hear her breathing getting mixed up with my breathing, but that's all that's coming out of her. Opening my eyes one at a time, I see her eyes gleaming back at mine, but it's not sorrow that's making them shine. It's . . . it's pure relief. She's practically drenched in it.

"Woody? What . . . ?" Was she not as attached to Mars as much I thought? No, she loved that mean dog, I'm sure of it. Maybe she's just feeling so tired of *hoping* the same way I've been that she's given up or she might . . . oh, sweet Mother of Jesus. There's only one other reason that I can think of that she's not fallen to the ground writhing in grief. It's because she's *not* surprised at all to learn of the dog's demise. That's how she's acting. But how can that be?

I look back down at the picture. I can almost feel his wiry hair, hear his annoying bark. The night our mother disappeared there was that blood-curdling yelp and then nothing. When the dog didn't show up the next morning, I figured he'd just run off. And that's what I thought Woody believed, too. But now I'm thinking that this picture of bloody Mars may not be a creation of her artistic mind, but a true-life depiction. Like a photograph.

I don't want to know the truth. I have to know the truth.

I ask Woody, "Are you . . . are ya tryin' to show me in this drawing that . . . ?"

The plaid suitcase Mars is holding in his mouth. It's Mama's.

Chapter Sixteen

Woody must've actually *seen* Mama in the woods on carnival night.

That's what the drawing about Mars and the suitcase is all about. That's why it looks so real. My sister was an eyewitness to my mother's departure.

I'm filled with sadness, but not completely shocked. I thought for a while that she might've witnessed something, but I never followed up on that. Now, I got no choice. Woody's picture confirms what I've been too scared to admit to myself. Mama's run off.

I can't be sure, of course, but admitting this truth about her leaving of her own free will instead of fooling myself into believing that she'll be back any minute or she's just taken a trip to Italy or she's got amnesia or even that she's been nabbed—I really do feel a little freer. The lies have loosened their hold some. The worst one was thinking that Mama was being held forcibly against her will somewhere dark. Woody and I know all about that.

Our mother couldn't possibly have known how sad, no—*mad*—Papa would get when she took off. They were barely speaking to each other around the time she disappeared.

When they were in a room together it was like watching two icebergs scrape against each other in a polar night. Mama must've believed that her husband would be so pleased to have a break from his sassy wife that he'd go back to being warm and cuddly, which would be the best possible thing to happen for her beloved girls.

Her leaving was one thing, but an entirely different beast if she'd taken us with her. Mama is only married to him, but Woody and I have Carmody blood running through our veins. We *belong* to Papa. She knew that His Honor would've come after us with the full force of the law. When he found us, he would've been disappointed within an inch of our lives.

Woody is still on the edge of the bed, staring down at her drawing of suitcase-toting Mars. I pat her hand and say, "I understand now. You're trying to tell me in this picture that you saw Mama leavin' that night from up in the fort, right?" She doesn't nod yes, but that has to be what happened. "We've got to find her. I already searched for her diary. It's not in the stronghold where it's supposed to be. There's got to be something in it that would help us find out where she's gone off *to*. I bet she's been writin' us every single day with directions on where to find her. Papa must be keeping the letters from us. Or

maybe Daryle Lawson didn't bother delivering them."
Our mailman could author a book entitled *I Am Lazy*.
"Do you know where her diary is, pea? You do, don't
you?"

Woody rushes over to our dresser and I can't believe
she's had it this whole time. I feel crushed as I watch her
rummaging through the drawers. She never kept secrets
from me in the past.

When she finds what she's looking for, she comes
back and sets it on my lap. But it's *not* Mama's little blue
diary. It's another one of Woody's drawing pads. She
wants to show me more of her pictures. The pad feels
like dead weight. It's my guilty conscience that's weighing it down, I know it is.

Since she was born the more delicate of us, I knew
that Woody would need the kind of tending that only a
mother can provide, so I stepped into Mama's shoes
after she vanished.

Thinking it might help, the way putting on church
clothes makes you feel more holy, I put on her cardigan
sweaters that still smelled of her Chanel No. 5 and stuck
her tortoiseshell combs into the top of my head, strands
of her honey hair blending into mine. But to look down
and see my legs in her rolled-up pants and to smell her,
you know. That was bad.

So I stopped trying to look like her and started *doing*
all the rest of things Mama would have done were she
here. I sang show tunes to my sister. Tickled her behind
the ears. I even tried to look at her drawings and write
something complimentary at the bottom of the page like

Mama would have. But the pictures weren't like the ones Woody used to do of butterflies frolicking over a minty meadow or a rainbow with a pot of glittering gold. After Mama disappeared, my sister's pictures became so gruesome. I told myself that she was just having a "Blue Period," like Mr. Pablo Picasso had. I even scribbled things like, *Wow! Look at those snarling teeth. And that ghost dripping blood? Only a genius would think of that*" on the bottom of her drawings. I kept thinking this morbidness was only temporary like everything else that was happening to us. Soon, I told myself, Woody's pictures will get perky again, but they never did. I finally admitted to myself that my once-sunny sister had been sucked into a world of darkness that I couldn't afford to follow her into. I couldn't let myself get so despairing again, which these hellish pictures could do to a person if they stared at them. No. Not if I was going to be the one that took care of us. So when Woody tried to show me her drawings, I began closing my eyes or looking away. Said stuff like, "How about a game of tiddlywinks?" or "Let's go see what E. J. is up to."

I see now that was not only cowardly, it was another one of my big mistakes.

She wasn't being morbid. Well, maybe she was just a little, but just like this picture of Mars, I think Woody has also been trying to tell me something important in her art. Something about the night Mama vanished. Like a drawn-out charade. Yes, I'm sure of it.

"I let you down before," I tell her, biting back the disgust I'm feeling towards myself. What a coward I've been. "I'm ready now. Show me."

When she notices how bad my hands are shaking, she flips open the cover of the drawing pad for me.

The first picture takes the rest of my breath away. It's our gorgeous mother with her short hair. It makes me recall the morning she lopped it off.

We were sitting on the back porch steps, the three of us. The hose was running across our feet and Mama was humming "Gonna Wash that Man Right Out of My Hair" while she trimmed Woody's and my bangs. When she was done snipping, she let out a sigh, and said, like she'd been thinking about it for a long, long time, "I've had just about enough of this." She gathered the thick coil off her neck and took the shears to it. I had no time to beg her not to, her crowning glory was already lying at my feet. She ran her fingers through what was left. Picked up the hose, doused her head, and shook it. "That's much better. Lighter. Freer."

Woody squealed, "You look like the movie actress Mia Farrow," but I thought she was acting crazy. Had Mama forgotten what Papa had told her about never cutting her hair?

Later that afternoon she came out to the fort with a couple of sandwiches and two soda pops. His Honor was due home from the courthouse at any minute. She called up to us, "Stay put for a while, peas. I fear there are rough seas ahead," and she wasn't acting so full of herself anymore.

Woody got dewy-eyed and shouted back all stuttery, "No matter what he says, I love your pixie cut."

I pretended I didn't hear Mama as she headed back

up to the house heavy-legged. She stopped at the rose garden to give us a weak wave. That's when I lost my temper and told Woody, "I don't see what you're so upset about. She's bringin' this on herself. She knows how much he loves her long hair."

Oh, how I wish I had that afternoon back. I would've complimented her, too. Thrown her kisses, shouted, "Good luck" or *"Buona fortuna."*

There's somebody standing above Mama in Woody's drawing. It's hard to tell if it's a man or a woman.

"Who's that supposed to be?" I ask, pointing to the barely there figure. "Papa?" If I got to face this, she might at least lend a helping hand. She could pick up a crayon and write, *Shenny, quit being dumb as a bag of hammers. Can't you see that's a picture of _____? Is that too much to ask?*

Woody jumps off the bed and rushes to the window, starts wildly gesturing. I head to her side and cinch my hands around her waist. I look in the direction of the reading bench and then the clearing that Mama vanished from that sits right behind it. There's nothing there. My twin is going absolutely bat shit. Flapping her arms and making this weird noise that sounds like a going-dead car battery. Whatever she was trying to tell me about the drawing is long gone. She's just acting up now.

"C'mon. That's enough." I'm tugging with all I've got. She can get like this sometimes. Especially after an encounter with Papa. Hard to work with as a piece of Saran Wrap. "Let go of the sill. Let go!" When she does, we fall backwards into a heap onto the carpet. We roll around for a while until she straddles my stomach and pins my hands. "Maybe I *should* sell you to the carnival, not as Mule Girl but . . . Wrassling Woody." I laugh, but when she gets her hands around my neck and starts squeezing it's not so funny anymore. "What are ya doin'? You're . . . I can't . . . breathe!" I say, chopping at her arms to break her hold.

She lets go and looks down at me, hurt and confused.

That's when I get what she was gesturing to from the window. It had to be the Minnow place. "Woody, don't cry." She's still sitting on my tummy, her chest heaving and her hair going every which way. Suddenly, I realize I don't care anymore what Papa will say or do if he catches me. I'm doing what he should've done for his little girl. Getting her what she wants, what she *needs*. "If you would let me up, it might be easier for me to go over and fetch Ivory. That's what you're tryin' to tell me, isn't it?" I ask, positive that it is.

Her tongue darts out from between her lips again.

"Don't even think about it," I say, bucking her off. "One lick of appreciation is fine, but I do not want this to become another one of your peculiarities. I mean it."

My sister starts happy wagging, not just her tail, but her arms and legs, even her head.

"All right then." I slip on my sneakers and head out our bedroom door. "Get out the soap and start running the tub. That pup takes after Clive. He's gonna look like hell and stink to high heaven."

Chapter Seventeen

Ivory Minnow is small for a Lab.

Looks like he's got some Corgi in him. Or maybe like what happens to people, he's just shrunken with age. He's lying between the bentwood rocker and Mr. Clive's metal-detecting device that's propped up against his house, which is about the same size and shape as a boxcar.

That's how our neighbor spent most of his day when he was still alive. Rocking in his chair or wandering around in the woods that're between his place and ours, using his metal-detecting device to unearth what he called, "Buried treasure. Free for the taking." He found scads of Civil War coins and other left-behind-in-the-heat-of-battle momentos. Muskets and snuff boxes, lots of uniform buttons from both sides, belt buckles and swords. If Clive found something he thought was extra valuable, he would snap a picture of it and then ask me to bring Mama over. She'd take what he found into town for him the next time we went. Artesia Johnson, who owns What Goes Around Comes Around, would place Clive's find in her store and some enthusiastic tourist would buy it.

The money he got from those doodads would help supplement the check Clive got each month from the government for his service to our country. When he was a younger man, he was in the U.S. Coast Guard and got tossed overboard during a hurricane. He didn't get rescued for two whole days. Clive told me at least once a week, "You think we're alone in the universe, but we're not. I saw four flying saucers *whish* over my head while I was bobbing in that ocean waitin' to get saved. Not one, not two. Four."

I'd sit out here with him some nights on this very porch, because just like me, Clive loved the sky. Not for the same reasons, though. He didn't mind me pointing out the constellations to him, but would tell me to *hush* if he saw something that looked like an unidentified flying object. That was his passion. UFOs he called them. "They're up there. They're watchin' us," he'd say, real creepy. Thinking that there might be aliens peeking down on us would about scare the undies off me, but for him, it was a comfort. Since he had few friends on *this* planet, I think he believed there might be beings from far, far away who would be willing to visit him. (I've seen aliens in movies. None of them are that good-looking either, so Clive and those UFO beings would have a natural jumping-off point.)

He's going to be so disappointed that he died and didn't get to see the men land on the moon. He was really looking forward to that.

The wind has kicked up a notch and is pushing his rocker to and fro. The sky is on its way to going deep gray and I can hear thunder trumpeting from the other side of Elephant Mountain. A storm is moving in.

"Hey, boy," I say to Ivory as I come up the porch steps, holding out my hand so he can get a whiff of me. Even though I told Papa that the dog was starving to death to try and elicit some sympathy from him, I'd told E. J. that it would make his wife-to-be happy if he'd go over to the Minnow place once a day and feed the poor thing. That's why there's clean water in a dish and a bowl half full with the food Clive kept in a garbage can out back. Just like I thought, the dog smells worse than wet wool and brambles have worked themselves into his chocolatey fur. Below his eyes, there's fudgey trails. "Remember me? I was the one that used to play checkers every Wednesday afternoon with your master."

I peer through one of the front windows of the house. Clive wasn't the best housekeeper, but this is the worst I've ever seen his place. The parlor looks like General Sherman marched through. Sofa cushions are split open and lying catawampus on the floor. The oak mantel above his river rock fireplace has been swept clean. Maybe some burglars got in here, knocked him on his head, drug him to the creek, and rifled through his stuff. If that's what happened, they weren't real professional. The pipe rack is still on the end table next to his favorite chair. Clive told me a bunch of times, "Keep your germy hands off my white pipes. They're from Germany. They're worth something."

Or maybe it wasn't burglars at all.

Sheriff Nash told Papa out on the porch this afternoon that he thought our neighbor might've been murdered. It was probably the sheriff and his deputy, Homer Willis, who messed up the place looking for clues. But who'd want to kill Mr. Minnow? He was practically an antique. Doesn't seem like anybody'd go to the trouble to do away with someone who the Grim Reaper already had on his folks-to-visit-next list. Clive didn't have any family that I know of (except for Ivory) or a lady friend (no one but Jesus of Nazareth could be that charitable), so his death could not have been the result of what is known in legal circles as a "crime of passion," which means that you've got to love somebody a whole lot in order to murder them.

Ivory hasn't moved from his post. He's watching me in that same distrustful way Clive did.

"Quit lookin' at me like that," I say. "He told me I could have the ring. You heard him."

The front door has a handwritten KEEP OUT BY ORDER OF THE ROCKBRIDGE COUNTY SHERIFF sign posted, but it's unlocked, and my curiosity is getting the better of me.

Stepping over the threshold and into his parlor, I think, *This is a dead man's house*. It feels different from just empty. It's like all his belongings know that Clive is never coming back and they're in mourning, too. The plants he had near the front window are limp. Everything that should be standing upright isn't. The floor lamp is living up to its name. Lightbulb bits are scattered around its crushed shade. Clive liked to read science fiction books and they've been pulled out of the bookcase. The screen of his fancy colored television set has been smashed in with a fireplace poker that's still stuck inside.

Last summer, Clive must've found something real rare because he got flamboyant. Ordered this nineteen-inch colored television set out of the Sears Roebuck catalog and a fancier camera with a long lens to take better sky pictures with. I was over here the day his new and improved detector and camera got delivered.

"All the bells and whistles," he said, thrilled.

Of course, I was happy for him, but also concerned. I knew before Mama vanished that she'd been slipping him some of her household money because he was having a hard time paying his bills. So I pointed down to the empty delivery boxes and told Clive, "Don't you think ya might've gone a bit overboard?" which, in hindsight, might've been a poor choice of words, considering his Coast Guard experience.

He got very wound up and told me back, "Don't worry about me, little girl. I got what you'd call a long-term investment," and then he ran off into the woods hither-nither and I didn't see him for a few days after that.

I hop over the mess of pictures carpeting his living room floor. Whoever was in here has also upended the old sea chest where Clive kept his photo collection.

There must be a thousand or more pictures. Mostly of the sky, but there are ones of Ivory and some of his metal-detecting finds and trees and dirt.

What I've come for, besides Ivory, is in the starfish box that's lying untouched next to his special chair where he smoked his pipes. Clive got the box from the Far East on his travels. "The Chinese are very tricky and inscrutable. They love puzzles and hidden drawers," he told me. He'd always turn his back to keep me from seeing how the box secretly opened, but there's a mirror above his fireplace and I could see him just fine.

I fell deeply in love with the ring the morning Clive discovered it under a birch tree with his metal-detecting device. I begged him for it and kept asking every time we played checkers, "Please?" but each and every time he told me, "The day you get the ring will be over my dead body."

So there you go.

The drawer on the side of the box that you can't see unless you know it's there pops open to reveal the mother-of-pearl sitting prettily on red velvet like it's been waiting for me. Just for a second I have the most fanciful thought. What if the reason Clive was so adamant about me not having this ring was because he was intending to give it to Gramma Ruth Love? Wouldn't that be something? I think he had a fat crush on her. He gave himself a spit and polish on the days he knew she was coming for a pie visit.

When Clive was alive, being suspicious like he was, he wasn't that big on letting me see too much of the house. I want to look around now that I got the chance. I leave the parlor and go around the corner to the bath-room door, which is shut. The doorknob sticks, but when I finally jiggle it loose, I'm knocked backwards by the odor.

From the look of things, the sheriff is wrong (big surprise) about Clive getting murdered. He'd been com-plaining about stomachaches off and on, but I didn't take that hypochondriacting seriously. I guess I should've because it looks like a real sickness is what did him in. Probably influenza. There's a bad one going around. Old upchuck covers the toilet, the sink, and the green tiled walls. This room also doubled as Clive's darkroom and his expensive developing equipment is right where he left it, untouched by his retching. The last photo-graphs he took are hanging from the crooked shower rod, held in place by red plastic clothespins. There's one of me and that's the most upsetting part of all. Clive re-ally did like me. Sometimes he called me "Peaches." And he gave me the *Lost in Space* lunch box after he found it in a ditch by the road.

"Mercy," I say, moving into the kitchen. The cup-board doors are flung open and what was inside is now on the outside. Dented cans of Campbell's pork and beans, Clive's absolute favorite, and a couple of jars of Kraft pimento cheese because sometimes he'd make me a sandwich when we'd play checkers, are lying on the tile next to a bunch of other food items and a whole family of dead mice. Their rotting bodies are part of the real bad stink. The rest of the putrid smell is coming from the overflowing trash can.

The house shutters have begun rattling. The windows, too. It usually takes time for a storm to climb over the mountains and settle into the valley, but every once in a while, one can surprise you like this. I get jumpy around lightning, so I hurry back out to the porch, shut the door of the house, and get Ivory by the collar. "C'mon, ol' boy. We gotta get home. Something nasty is comin' our way."

Chapter Eighteen

Branches are beating against the four-paned window. Our house has gone deep black, which always happens when the wind comes up this fierce. We lose our power. Lou tells Woody and me that it's a ghost playing a trick on us. I half believe her, because Mr. Cole has tried to fix whatever is wrong in the fuse box time and time again with no luck. I've lit a couple of stubby candles, let the wax drip onto the porcelain sink and stuck them.

My shadow is dancing across the white bathroom wall like a chorus girl in a movie musical when I sing for the fifth and, I swear, last time, "When you walk through a storm keep your head up high and don't be afraid of the dark. At the end of the storm is a golden sky and the sweet silver song of a . . . *bark*." This song from the *Carousel* album is another one of Woody's all-time favorites. I have sung it to her enough times down in the root cellar that I know perfectly well that last part's supposed to go—the sweet silver song of a . . . *lark*, but I knew changing it up like that would make her smile.

I already took my bath. Now my sister's in the claw tub beneath a scattering of bubbles, her freshly shampooed hair floating like seaweed in the ocean. I've already inspected her for the dime-sized marks.

The first time I found the purple splotches, I scrubbed and scrubbed and when they wouldn't come off I asked her, "Did you do a swan dive into a blueberry patch or something?" It was mysterious. And got more so when I noticed that the marks kept showing up even when there weren't any berries blooming. I figured it out the afternoon I saw Woody running down to the animal cemetery behind the barn. She was going to bury a baby bird that had fallen out of its nest. When I got down to the barn, Pegasus was pawing in the cross ties. Out the door, I could see that Blackie who was here to shoe Papa's horse had caught Woody. He pried the dead bird out of her hand, threw it as far as he could, and when it landed up against a tree, he laughed and said, "Guess it needs some more practice." He mimicked Woody's flapping. "Ya can fool your idiot father, but ya can't fool me. You're just puttin' this shit on." That's when he started pinching her all over the place. He only stopped because I yelled out to him, "There's a woman on the telephone for you, Uncle Blackie. Got a voice like Marilyn Monroe's. You better come quick." I wanted to tell Papa on him, but I knew if I did, Blackie would get back at me.

The next time he got ahold of my sister, he'd pinch her quarter size.

I sit on the edge of the tub and bury my toes in Ivory's chocolate back. He looks up at me and gives me a very jolly look. "I were you, I'd wipe that smile off my face. You're next," I tell him. "Get out now, Woody. We got to get up to the fort before the rain comes."

When she stands, I notice how we're not flat anymore. Our chests are budding. And between our legs wispy hair has come in and we've got gentle curves at the waist. Tears spring to my eyes when I do Mama's job of wrapping my sister up tight in a towel. Woody and I are changing into little women without her.

Due to his unusually small size, Ivory was easy to stuff into the Bucket Express.

Mama was the one who came up with the idea of jerry-rigging a rope to a branch on the tree fort, placing a pully on top and an old wash pail down on the bottom so we could haul stuff up without having to leave the fort. "Mother is the necessity of invention," she said when she stood back to admire her work, and I just loved that.

Woody, me, and Ivory are snug like spoons in the sleeping corner of our fort, so maybe that's why the rhyme that Papa liked to recite to us when we'd come up here together to view the spring constellations is popping into my mind no matter how hard I'm trying to push it away.

Hey diddle diddle,
The cat and the fiddle,
The cow jumped over the moon,
The little dog laughed to see such sport,
And the dish ran away with the spoon.

"Right there, girls. See?" Papa would speak softly, like he was hunting and might scare the stars away. "The cat is your birth sign—Leo the lion. And the fiddle is Lyra—the lyre. The cow the rhyme is referring to is Taurus the bull. The little dog is Canis Minor, you see him? And the dish is Crater running away with the spoon, who is the Big Dipper."

Memories are so two-faced.

One minute they're hugging you like a long-lost friend, the next minute they're ripping you apart like your worst enemy.

I whisper into my sister's hair, "I'm gettin' so *grimmery*. 'Bout everything."

Woody and I are having our pillow talk time the way we always have. I wish she'd start holding up her end again. My thoughts come so fast and furious this time of day. I desperately miss my twin telling me when I would get like this, "Ya know what your problem is, Shenny? You think way too much. *Hushacat.*"

We came into this world knowing a foreign language. Mama thought it was cute and would try to chitter-chatter with us, but Papa made us quit because he said we sounded like little monkeys. So, just like anything else you don't keep up, we mostly forgot how. We still remember *some* of the twin talk and use it when we are alone. Before Woody went mute on me, that is. You already know that *hushacat* means everything is going to be all right no matter how bad it seems at the present time, but what I just told Woody? That I'm feeling *grimmery*? That's hard to define in regular English. The closest I can get is—"catastrophically worried to death." *Meetone*—means "I'm hungry." *Rabadee*—"I'm sorry." The best twin word of all, though, has got to be *boomba*—"love." Not the dependable kind, like when your mother and father who still care for each other are sitting on the back steps discussing their day and their voices come drifting through your bedroom window where you're sleepy between hung-in-the-sun sheets after a warm bubble bath. And not the kind of romantic love that E. J. feels for Woody and I feel for Bootie Young. No, a *boomba* is more like how you feel when you get an unexpected gift. Me getting Ivory Minnow into my sister's arms, for instance. That gave her a *boomba*.

Speaking of which, poor Clive. I wish I hadn't run out of Rolaids. Just thinking about him is making my stomach leap about the same way his must've before he died. Deceasing all alone like that must've been terrible.

Or maybe my tummy's jumpy because I'm having one of those gut instincts that Sam is always going on about. "If you two girls begin to feel like something bad is about to happen that means it probably is. Trust your gut," he tells us all the time. "You start feeling that way, come to the station as fast as you can."

"Does your stomach feel like you swallowed a pogo stick?" I ask Woody.

Beneath this starless sky, Sam's words are especially worrisome. I'm not so sure Papa would be able to stop himself from doing something I can't even imagine if he found out what Woody is holding back. Other than Mama leaving with a packed suitcase, I don't know what else she knows, but she knows something—believe me. I can tell. She's my twin.

"Pea? Why do you think Papa keeps askin' us what we saw that night?"

Seems like he doesn't even want his loving wife to come back anymore, so going over the details of her disappearance is as pointless as a pocket on the back of your shirt. He put his arm around Abigail Hawkins this afternoon in the kitchen. He might've fallen into her web, which should make my grandfather pleased as punch. He's glad that Mama's gone. The only reason he's offering that hefty reward for information on her whereabouts is so those good old boys will comment to each other what a thoughtful man Guster Carmody is over their biscuits and gravy at Ginny's Diner.

His cronies have no way of knowing that whenever Grampa would come over to Lilyfield for Sunday lunch, he'd bark at Mama fetch me this, fetch me that. He threw insults and ordered her around. But it wasn't only her. He talked to Gramma like she was one of his prize retrievers, too. If they tried to enter into a conversation the men were having around the table, Grampa'd cut them off with, "*Yap . . . yap . . . yap . . .* you girls don't have one useful brain between ya."

After they'd cleaned up the kitchen, they'd go for a walk near the garden. Mama would tell Gramma, "Gus doesn't own you, Ruth Love. You're not one of his parcels of land. Possession may be nine-tenths of the law, but it isn't the same as love. Don't . . . don't you see that?" Mama would beg her to get a backbone and Gramma would smile and nod her head, but I think it must be true that you can't teach an old dog new tricks because I have *never* heard her tell our grandfather to sit down and shut up. Not once.

I say to Woody, "I've been thinkin'. No matter how put off you've been by Gramma lately, Mama'd want you to go out of your way for her when she comes this weekend. Play with her dolls, let her show you the pictures in the album, all right? I'll put Vick's VapoRub under your nose so you won't smell her Ben-Gay." I nudge my sister pretty hard. "Are you or are you not asleep?" Her slow breathing is leading me to believe she is, but she could be playing possum again. I lift up her arm and it drops heavily onto Ivory's back, which is balled into her tummy. Carefully pulling myself away from the two of them, I remove Sam's aviator sunglasses off of the dog and place them over Woody's eyes. They'll prevent the lightning that's coming from waking her up. E. J. nailed a bit of galvanized tin over part of the fort last month when I told him we were spending more time up here than in our room, so the two of them will stay dry when the rain finally comes. E. J. sure does come in handy with a hammer. I was such a piglet to him today. I'll bring him some extra breakfast tomorrow.

I tickle my sister's cheek one last time, wanting to make sure she's out. I slipped one of the pills I took out of Papa's medicine cabinet this morning into our last piece of pecan fudge and fed it to her. They're the same calming pills he put into Mama's tea. But unlike what he did to her, me doing this really is for my sister's own good. I got something important to do and I can't get worried while I'm gone about Woody wandering off to the Triple S or the hobo camp or Lord knows where.

I tug her thumb out of her mouth and open her fingers. A jagged square of Mama's shredded chiffon scarf is bunched in her hot palm the way I knew it would be. I kiss every single one of her bit-to-the-quick nails, pat Ivory on the snout, and say, "Watch over her." The both of them smell like rose soap.

Sticking my flashlight into my shorts, I get the rope between my fingers and lift the fort hatch, reminding myself to watch my step. Papa came back a little while ago from wherever he went. I heard his Lincoln Continental drive up. And I think Uncle Blackie must be around here somewhere, he usually is. His house is down creek from us but since he's been messing with Lou in the meadow, much to my and Woody's dismay, he's over at Lilyfield a lot more than he used to be, which is another good reason to stay on my toes.

A dog is good but not as good as a mother at giving comfort and Woody really needs extra sweet loving. ASAP. I'm sure that the anniversary of Mama's leaving is going to hit her like a tidal wave. I can already see it coming. She's going to need something to hold on to, something all in one piece. I'm going into town to break into What Goes Around Comes Around to get my sister a backup *boomba*.

It's not stealing to take back something that is rightfully yours.

Is it?

Chapter Nineteen

The C&O runs close enough to Lilyfield that I can hear the train's *clickety clack* and the good-bye whistle as it chugs out of Lexington on its way over the mountains to Lynchburg.

The tracks smell as black as they look with tar and oil, but I've always thought the train makes a lulling sound. Unfortunately, that *chug . . . chug . . . chug* is not enough to dispel my fears this evening. Besides all the other worries that I got on my mind, these woods that I love to stroll through during the day turn into something straight out of a horror movie once the sun sets. Animals eat each other down to the bone and bats come flying at you. I saw a wolf once, at least I think it was a wolf, E. J. told me it wasn't. Another night, I heard footsteps behind me and when I turned a man stepped out of the shadows. I could see by his appearance that he was a hobo. His barn door was unzipped and he was lost and in tears. After I gave him directions on how to follow the railroad tracks to the water tower so he could be with his own kind, he hugged me, and I let him, because I hadn't been hugged in so long. When I told Curry Weaver about that encounter, even though he is a "man of the rails" himself, he warned me to be careful. "I know that seeing someone down on their luck is heart-breaking," he said, fanning his arm around the hobo camp, "but you've got to remember that having nothing to lose is a dangerous way to feel."

I sure wish I knew Curry's circumstances and how long he's intending to stay. Woody is really fond of him and his harmonica. And I like sitting on the trestle with him. Answering his questions makes me feel important. That's the hardest part about becoming friendly with those travelers. You get to know and like them and off they go.

How nice it must be to hop a train and leave your troubles behind. I've been thinking for some time that Woody and me should get away from Lilyfield. Like Mama did. Maybe our leaving for a bit would jar Papa into remembering how much he loves Woody and me. I didn't know what I had in Mama until *she* was gone. But the second somebody saw us hustling towards the depot with our suitcases they'd call up to Lilyfield and tell Papa. (Most everybody in town thinks the sun comes up just to hear him crow.)

We *could* go to Beezy's, but he knows how much we love her, so that's the first place Papa would come looking for us. And Mr. Cole has nowhere to put us but in his cottage and Lou lives there. We get enough of her as it is. Sam? He's who I'd really like to go to, but he'd get in the worst trouble of his life if we got found over there. Besides, his cabin smells like used spark plugs.

That leaves Vera Ledbetter. Even if Papa put pressure on her, she wouldn't tell where we were. She doesn't care for him. Vera is one of Mama's forbidden fruit friends, who's got a bungalow on Montgomery Street. She lives alone with her parrot so I'm sure she'd be happy to have the company. Vera's also a professional cook at Slidell's Drugstore and since all of Woody's and my clothes are getting as loose as E. J.'s are on him, she could fatten us back up. That could work out just great. I'm going to talk to Woody about that hiding-out idea as soon as I get back from town. (Since Vera has that talking bird, I'm sure my critter-loving sister will be thrilled.)

When I come out of the woods that end at the meadow that butts up to the creek, I can see the Jacksons' cottage lights shining through the rustling leaves. I'd never tell Lou, but I dearly miss those evenings that Woody and me spent over at their place. Her telling us those bayou stories when she was still nice. Those yummy hush puppies Mr. Cole would do up for us. I can't remember the last time I ate. I'm so tempted to wander over there, but I can't. I got a sisterly duty to perform. Maybe when I get back from town. If Lou's in one of her less wicked moods, I can persuade her to tell us a Rex the alligator tale and Mr. Cole will feed us. I could get Mama's watch back from her, too. Mr. Cole would make her give it.

Thrilled with that plan, I'm hustling even faster towards the creek stepping stones when I hear, "Where're ya goin'?" coming from somewhere out in front of me.

I think that Lou Jackson is talking to me and I'm getting ready to answer her back until I hear my uncle say, "It's over."

I douse my flashlight.

The Carmody brothers have got the same booming voice, but Uncle Blackie laughs like I imagine Satan does, that's how I know it's him and not Papa. He's informing Lou that the romance has drawn to an end. He's fixing to toss her into the trash just like I warned her he would. Just like he has so many other gals who fell under his spell, including Dagmar Epps, the bad-moraled lady who lives up at the hobo camp. They were an item for almost a year and look at her now.

"But, I . . . I . . . ," Lou whines. "Ya can't mean it. Don't ya want . . . I got something real nice for ya. Lookee here."

I peek around the tree that I've hidden behind. They're only about fifty feet away, but I can't see them clearly until the lightning strikes again. Lou is being pressed up against the side of the gardening shed by Blackie, who is handsome just like Papa, but his dark hair is wilder looking. He's got a tattoo on his muscular arm of a lady whose bosom is barely covered by two horseshoes, and his chest bulges, too.

Lou's blouse is all the way unbuttoned and her brassiere up around her neck. Blackie is smiling down at her pointed cookie cone chest. "I told you this right off. When I say the party's over, it's over, but I guess there's nothin' wrong with one for the road."

Lou's moans come out of the darkness, low and long. When the lightning comes again, I see that Blackie has slid his hand up under her skirt. He's moving it back and forth like a saw. Lou is moving back and forth, too, until my uncle does something down there that makes her give out a choked scream.

As furious as she makes me, my heart is going out to her. Until the flame from Blackie's Zippo lighter illuminates Mama's watch on her wrist when he lights up a Lucky Strike. The flash of silver catches my uncle's eye, too. "Where'd you get this?" Ripping it off, he holds the watch out of her reach. When Lou jumps for it, he smacks her away. "I've never seen this before. Did you steal it, girl? Answer me." When she doesn't, he pinches her real hard on the arm.

"It's . . . Shen's," Lou wails.

"What'd ya say?" I know that Blackie heard her because even though the treetops are swishing and thunder is rolling closer, I'm having no trouble at all picking up on his belittling tone.

Lou cries, "Give it back. It's Shenny's."

"Where'd that brat get something this fine?"

"I . . . I don't know," Louise says, but if I could see her I know she'd be raising her lying right eyebrow. I told her I found Mama's watch near the old well when we were still getting along.

Blackie says, "Looks fancy. Not for a kid. You sure this watch doesn't belong to daaarlin' Evelyn?" I can hear the leer in his voice. He likes Mama, and not in a relative way. He was always putting his hand on her caboose and giving it a goose and didn't care that Papa saw.

Letting go of Lou, my uncle tucks his shirt back into his pants and says, "I'll just take the watch and return it to Walter."

That would be disastrous if my uncle was a man of his word. I know him too good. He'll keep it and give it to his next Kleenex gal.

"His Honor didn't gift it to the girls' mother so there's no need to return it to him." Lou is sobbing so hard that she's begun hiccupping. "Please . . . *hick* . . . give it back . . . *hick* . . . to me."

How does she know that somebody else besides Papa gave Mama the watch? I wasn't the one who told her. Woody can't. Could Sam have? Beezy?

"What do you mean Walt *didn't* give it to Evie?" Blackie asks, suddenly interested again. "Where'd she get it from? A beau? Was she gettin' herself a little gravy on the side?"

"Blackie, please," Lou says, not mad but like that girl in the patched dress who got off the Greyhound bus.

"Did Evie have a back-door lover?" My uncle sounds frantic. "Did she?"

I want to stop all this before something even worse happens, but if I dare to interfere, my uncle will drag me up to the house and shout at Papa, "Look who I found stickin' her nose where it don't belong again."

Thankfully, Mr. Cole Jackson opens up the door to their cottage and thrusts out his head.

"Louise, honey? The storm's startin' up. Better finish up what you're doin'." A crack of lightning finishes his sentence off like an exclamation point. "Lou? Ya out there?"

I want to shout, "Come quick, Mr. Cole," but I know that would only make things worse. I think of them as family, but the Jacksons are the help. If they try to go up against the Carmodys, my grandfather will make sure nobody else in town hires them once they get kicked off of Lilyfield.

After Mr. Cole steps back into the cottage, Uncle Blackie says to Lou so sickening, "Thanks for the hospitality. Take care now, ya hear?" and struts off into the woods.

I hate that.

Despise it when somebody strong takes advantage of the weak, but what can I do? Nobody, not even the meanest man I know—Grampa—would want to tangle with my uncle when he gets to acting like the cock of the walk.

I'm going to drag Lou out of this storm and back into the cottage. Mr. Cole will set out dry clothes and heat a cup of milk with a splash of brandy. When she falls asleep, I'll snip a bit off her hair and take it up to Miss Hormel at the boardinghouse tomorrow. I'll pay her to give Lou that hump. That may sound mean, but it really is for the best. Lou'll get tempted to take up with him again if Blackie comes scratching at her window one of these nights because she is conveniently located. She'll get her heart broken all over again. Of course, I'm mad at her for letting my uncle take Mama's watch, but it'll be easy to get back. Blackie will pass out tonight, probably on the front porch swing. I'll sneak it out of his pocket then. He won't even remember when he wakes up tomorrow morning that he took it off Lou, that's how hanged over he'll be.

I switch my flashlight back on and start heading towards the shed, but before I get even a few steps, from behind me, a hand clamps over my mouth and drags me back behind the tree. I have visions of that hugging hobo, or maybe it's Blackie. He must've seen me watching him being so mean to Louise. I hunch up, listening for his snide *Gotcha! Gotcha! Gotcha!* I am too terrified to put up a struggle and get even more so when I feel his smooth small hand. Smell his English Leather.

It's not a wandering hobo or my disgusting uncle that's got his arms around me.

It's Papa.

He doesn't shout something vile or twist me around in disgust. He doesn't push me to the ground and tower over me yelling. He's not even slurring when he says in his kindest of all voices, the one I still hear in my dreams, "Shenandoah? Is that you?" When I don't turn to show him my gaping teeth the way I usually do to let him know it's me, he assumes I'm my sister. "Jane Woodrow. I was just at the fort looking for you."

Thank Jesus I gave Woody that sleeping pill.

I feel ashamed of myself for needing him so much that I don't tell him that it's me and not my twin. I can't help myself. I want him to keep holding me. Maybe he's come to apologize, to beg forgiveness for the way he's been treating his precious girls. I can feel myself melting into him.

Papa says, "All this time . . . I . . . I haven't been sure if it was you or Shenandoah I saw that night watching from up in the fort, but Doc Keller told me earlier this evening that he's almost certain it was you, and my father . . . your grandfather . . . he agrees. He wants me to send you away." His Honor sounds like a scared little kid. "I've been hoping this would all sort itself out, but it's only gotten worse. It *was* you, wasn't it? You saw what happened that night, didn't you?" Hearing his desperate fear, I don't know what else to do but nod. "It's the Lord's work. He took your voice away to keep us safe. If you *could* talk . . . tell what you saw . . . it would be the ruination of everything that we have worked for, do you understand, sweetheart?" Gripping me harder, he says, "You . . . you haven't told Shenandoah, have you?" When I shake my head, I feel his muscles go stringy again. "I . . . I want you to know that I'm sorry it ended the way it did. Your mother . . . she . . . Mother misunderstood." He spins me around and snugs my head to his chest, and I can hear the beat of his heart.

"Your mama's life may be over, but ours isn't. Things are going to be different around here from now on. You'll see. It's all going to go back to the way it was before . . . before . . . We'll stargaze together and I'll read you the Sunday comics and whenever you and your sister want to, we'll go to the beach. You particularly liked that when Mother . . ." He breathes in, shuddery. "All you have to do is promise me that you'll keep doing what you've been doing. Not saying a word about what you saw. Can you do that for your papa? For your twin?"

I want to scream, run off and hide where I will never be found when I realize what he's telling me, but I nod again the way he wants me to. And when I do, it's not the cooling rain that has finally come, but his warm tears that I feel falling into my hair when he presses his lips to the top of my head and rewards me with the words I've been longing to hear, "I love you, my little Gemini."

Chapter Twenty

The earth has tilted off its axis.

Struggling back to the fort through the downpour, I'm shaking so bad that I can barely get a grip on the splintering steps that lead up the tree. I throw open the hatch with a bang and crawl towards where I left her. Sweeping my hands across the floor, feeling for my sister, I get a handful of Ivory instead. "Woody!" It's not until the lightning flashes again that I see she's not sleeping. She's kneeling in front of the Saint Jude coffee can altar, her head bowed to her chest, her lips silently moving.

The rain pelting the tin overhang is not loud enough to drown out Papa's words. All those interrogation sessions. The root cellar. The way I protected her from him. Woody's been listening to me going on and on about finding our mother. I feel so betrayed when I think of all the times I told her, "We'll do this . . . we'll question this person . . . . don't you worry, I'll find her. I won't let you down."

I strip off my soaking shirt and throw it as hard as I can. It lands on her praying back with a *plop*. "You're gonna make your knees bleed and I don't know where the bandages are and even if I did I . . . Get up. Get up!" When Ivory barks, I kick at him. "Papa caught me in the woods. He thought I was you. He told me that you saw something happen to Mama the night . . . he told me . . . he was sorry it had to end the way it did. That Mama's life was . . . over." I yank her up by the hair and shove her across the fort. "Is that true? Talk to me! What did you see?" When Woody looks blank faced and close mouthed at me, I rip those sunglasses off her eyes and pry her mouth open with my fingers and shout down her throat, "I hate you, you stupid mute. Do you hear me? I hate you! I hate Mama! You . . . her . . . you're nothing but deceiving, disgustin'—"

My sister draws back and slaps me across the face.

The sound of the storm and my weeping and Ivory's whimpering are all I can hear until she takes me into her arms. We drop to the floor, curl into each other as if we are still safe inside our mother. I cry out the unspeakable, give voice to the fear that's been crouching in the corners of my mind. "She's . . . she's not run off. She's not ever comin' back. No matter how hard I look. No matter how hard you pray. Mama's . . . dead."

"*Hushacat*," my twin whispers under the thunder. "*Hushacat*."

Or that could be nothing more than the wind whistling in the dark.

Even after I had thumbed my nose at hope, I admit, I kept it in my heart. I felt it not perching, but fluttering inside me like a bird trying to get air beneath a broken wing. Hope made me think that Mama'd come home to us, even though I suspected she wouldn't. But then I believed she would, but after . . . I don't know. I've always thought of my heart beating steady, but I see now that it doesn't. It dashes up and down and all around, searching desperately for what it craves, it never gives up. Until it flies headlong into a brick wall.

Seemed like Woody and I stayed nested together like that for two days, maybe more. We wailed on each other's chests until there was nothing left inside us to shed. All this time I was believing . . . trying . . . I imagined our reunion, every detail. How I'd kiss Mama's satiny cheeks until my lips got swollen. Rub her earlobes between my fingers, envisioning a velvet party dress. Beg her to sing "Oh, What a Beautiful Mornin'."

It's so hard to accept that she's gone and never coming back. Like how her garden would feel if the sun never rose again.

His Honor came to the bottom of the fort tree one of those sorrow-ridden nights. He didn't call up, "I love you as much as the stars and the sky." All he said was, "Remember your promise, Jane Woodrow. You may leave Lilyfield now, girls."

That's when I realized why he'd been keeping Woody and me in solitary confinement. He wasn't worried that his twins would disappear the same way his wife did. He didn't want us to go running around town telling folks what we saw the night our mother disappeared. What *Woody* saw anyway.

I begged my sister to "please, please, tell me. I can't stand not knowin'. Your suitcase drawing shows that Mama was going to leave, but . . . then what happened? Did she fall down the well the same way Mars did? Or get a heart attack? She *was* looking very pale under those carnival lights. I saw another person back there that night besides Papa, did you?" But no matter how much I begged or how hard I tried to convince her to share her secret with me, she stayed resolutely mute.

E. J. must've gotten worried out of his mind when Woody and I didn't show up in the morning to start our search for Mama the way we'd planned, because he came to the fort as well.

He didn't call up, "Ollie . . . ollie . . . got room for one more?" like he always does. He stood beneath the branches and sang, "Love me tender, love me true" in a reedy voice and then he climbed up the fort steps, poked the hatch open just wide enough to slide in a basket of fresh-picked blackberries.

Lou came, too. Instead of squawking from the porch like she usually does, she called up meekly from below, "I got flapjacks and bacon for ya in the cottage. Extra syrup. You gotta eat."

I didn't understand why she was being so out-of-character nice until I remembered that after Papa told me about Mama's being dead and he disappeared into the rain, I saw Lou still plastered up against the shed, spying on me the same way I'd been spying on her with Uncle Blackie. She must've followed me back to the fort, listened to my ranting at Woody, then run back and told Mr. Cole because he came, too.

Our caretaker asked, "You two all right?"

I don't know why, but I yelled back at him, "Right as rain," which made me sound a lot braver than I was feeling.

Mr. Cole must've went and fetched Beezy because some time later I heard her froggy voice scolding Lou from below, "Don't you dare go up there. They don't need you throwin' no bones or chantin' conjurations. Leave those girls be. They's in mourning." She gentled her voice when she called up to Woody and me, "Ya got to keep your strength up. Here come some fritters in the Bucket Express. When you're ready to talk, Shen, I'll be waitin' to listen."

I know she will. She is an expert on death. Not only did she kill her husband, she lives across the street from Stonewall Jackson Cemetery. That's where Mama must be. No, Bootie Young would've told me he dug her grave and expressed his utmost sympathy.

When I find where she's buried, and I will, I won't set white peonies at her headstone because of what she told me the day I brought them to her from Beezy's. "It's important to let flowers grow, Shen. People, too. Do you understand?" It's so obvious to me now that she was talking about Papa. And how he made her feel trampled beneath his feet. I'll also tell my mother's dearly departed soul, "I'm so sorry for the way I treated you. Woody has stopped talking, but I know she wishes you well, too. Don't worry. I'll take good care of her. When we move to New York City, we'll be the talk of the town." Then we'll weep and I'll quote Emily Dickinson since she was Mama's favorite. The poem where death stopped and took someone away in a carriage.

But the carriage didn't hold just Mama and immortality. Papa was in the clearing the night Mama died. And there was a shadow of another person weaving around in the trees—I didn't imagine that, I know I didn't.

From the way they're all acting, seems to me like everybody either knew or suspected that Mama had passed away the whole time I've been looking for her. Feels like they hung me out to dry. But maybe, I guess, they *were* trying to tell me and I was just too wrapped up in my plan to find her that I didn't take notice. Beezy was always discouraging me from looking for Mama. Telling me it was too hard a task to take on all by myself or trying to distract me with some gossip. And sometimes I would catch Mr. Cole staring at Woody and me with such pity in his eyes. And Sam. He never was enthusiastic about doing detective work for me. He must've known that searching for his good friend would be useless. Even E. J. Thinking back on it now, he seemed to lose his merry smile whenever I brought up the subject of finding Mama.

I am the last to know.

No. That's not true. Somewhere inside me, I've known all along that our mother's life had ended.

Woody told me.

She played possum with Mama's Chantilly powder, covering herself white from head to toe. Those utterly black drawings. I convinced myself it was my sister's despair over Mama's disappearance that had gotten hold of her and drug her to the depths the same way it had me early on, but it wasn't. Her acting like that, it was the only way she could let me know that Mama was dead. Woody's running off makes sense to me now, too. She wasn't climbing down the trellis and cantering off to the Triple S or the hobo camp to torment me. My twin was doing the same thing that I've been doing, trying to run away from the truth.

When I find enough strength to pull out of my sister's grip, the sun is melting behind the mountains and streaking the sky the color of orange and raspberry sherbet. We ate the berries that E. J. brought and the fritters from Beezy, but I'm hungry again, so my twin must be, too. The pill-laced fudge that she spit out is sitting next to a candle on the Saint Jude coffee can altar. This whole time it wasn't our mother's return that my sister's been praying for night after night the way I thought she was. She knew Mama wasn't ever coming back. My twin was begging Saint Jude to intercede on my behalf. *I* was the lost cause.

"Stay put, would you? I'm gonna get us something to eat." Woody is still lying huddled on the fort floor.

Using Ivory like a pillow. I run my finger down her cheek, following the tear trail. "*Ciao*," I say, thinking that speaking some Italian might remind her of Mama and make her smile and that's the best I can muster.

That's what people do at a funeral. Bring food. Recall fond memories. Pretend the whole time like they will be able to take the next step down the road of life without holding on to the hand of the one they loved and lost, when they know in their hearts that's nothing more than the most hopeless of dreams.

Chapter Twenty-one

I'm on my way to E. J.'s by way of the stepping stones.
The creek is running fast. How tempting it is to wade
in. Watch the emerging stars as I float downstream to
finally get swept over the falls. Is that what Mama did?
Did she feel so sad about her unhappy marriage that she
threw herself in? That might be the reason why Papa
has kept her passing so hush-hush. He wouldn't want
folks to know that his wife did away with herself rather
than face one more day being married to him. That
would embarrass him, and His Honor hates being embarrassed as much as he does being pitied.

It was the talk of the town when Mama's fellow choir
singer Mrs. Clayton put on her wedding dress, threw a
rope around a barn rafter, climbed onto a milk can, and
stepped off into eternity after her husband told her that
he didn't love her anymore. But Mrs. Clayton was child-

less and Mama had Woody and me to think about. No. She'd never do that. But if she did, in a moment of weakness, I'd understand. Nobody can get at your heart once it's lying six feet under.

That makes me say out loud Mr. William Wordsworth's poem that Mama cried over so often. " 'What though the radiance which was once so bright be now for ever taken from my sight, though nothing can bring back the hour of splendor in the grass, of glory in the flower, we will grieve not, rather find strength in what remains behind.' "

I know I will not be able to "grieve not," as he suggests, but I am determined to reach deep within myself to find "strength in what remains behind." During those forlorn nights in the fort, I vowed to myself to discover the truth about Mama's passing. Finding out what happened to her is the only way I've got left to respect her memory, to honor her.

The first and best place to start looking for answers, as always, begins and ends with my family.

Papa knows what happened to Mama, so that means Grampa and Blackie must know, too. His Honor is putty in their hands. But our grandmother? Since the Carmody men keep everything that's important to themselves, Gramma Ruth Love might *not* know about Mama's passing, unless she overhead them talking, which she probably has. Even though Grampa has her kowtowed, she doesn't let that stop her from placing a drinking glass on walls to listen in on conversations or picking up the telephone extension in a very stealthy way. But if our grandmother knows about Mama's passing, why hasn't she told Woody and me?

Grampa probably caught her eavesdropping and forbid her to tell us. When she comes for Founders Weekend, I'll get her out of his clutches the same way our mother used to. I'll have her join us in Woody's and my bedroom and ask her questions about our dearly departed. I'm sure she'll confess to me that she's known all along and just couldn't stand to be the bearer of such bad news. And after we all get done crying together, she'll say a Bible passage for her good friend and daughter-in-law. Probably that lying-down-in-green-pastures part.

Oh, Mama.

I want to be with you.

It would be so easy to let the creek water wash away this pain forever.

I better take the road way to E. J.'s.

Crickets are singing soprano and alto frogs are harmonizing. They're romancing. I've made up my mind never to join that choir. You get swept away by love and before you know it, you're married. And marriage rusts. No matter how hard you work to scrap it off and polish it up, it will never come back to its original shine. It's not just Mama and Papa's or Grampa and Gramma's wedded unbliss that I'm thinking about. Look at Mary Jane Upton wandering around town half clothed, looking for her tomcat of a husband. And the ladies down at Filly's beauty shop are all the time complaining about how their men chew with their mouths open and how lazy they are until it comes time for them to go hunting or fishing.

There's only one exception to that marriage disaster that I know of. Dorry and Frank Tittle. This dirt-poor couple have got the Midas touch when it comes to love.

I was trying to be quiet as I came up their dirt drive, but the Tittles' next-door neighbors, the Calhouns, raise hound dogs. They must've picked up my scent. They're baying loud enough to make Mrs. Tittle come out onto the sagging porch of her ramshackle house with the new baby pressed to her breast. She is a plain woman with straight brunette hair that ends at her chin. She's barefoot, but wearing a fancy white dress that was my mother's, and I have to bite my cheek to keep from crying out. Mama couldn't tell our father that she didn't care for all the frilly outfits that he bought her. When Papa asked her, "Why aren't you wearing the new frock? The one with the big bows?" Mama would say, "I'm sorry, dear. I can't zip it. I must've gained a few pounds." Then she'd bundle up those flouncy gowns and bring them over here.

"Shenny? That you?" Mrs. Tittle calls into the dark.

Stepping out of the shadows, I say, "Yes, ma'am. Sorry for disturbing you. How has Mr. Tittle been feelin'?" The sound of his hacking cough is coming out of the screened windows. E. J. told me when his daddy tries to rest, all the black sludge in his lungs wakes up.

E. J.'s mama says, "Mr. Tittle is doin' just . . ."

She's about to tell me that her husband is good and fine. I save her from committing a venial sin by saying, "Lovely evening, isn't it?"

Mrs. Tittle doesn't lift her eyes and she doesn't ask me what I'm doing here. She knows I've come for her boy. When Baby Fay starts whimpering, she jiggles her gently. Coos that song that only mothers seem to know.

"Well, night then," I have a hard time saying.

After she goes back into the house, all I want to do is chase after her, crawl into her arms, and have her rock me like I'm her baby, too. The empty space where Mama used to be is weighing so heavy on my heart . . . it takes all I got to put one foot in front of another.

I find E. J. setting rabbit traps out back. He always does about this time of night.

"Hey," I call to him.

He knocks over his red lantern when he jumps to his feet. "Hey."

This is not the first nor do I imagine it will be the last time I come over here for his help.

I right the lantern and say, "Get your shoes on."

"What's goin' on? Is it Woody?" he asks, alarmed as he reaches for his sneakers that are next to him on the log. "Has she run off again?"

"No, no, she's all right." I cross myself in the name of the Father and the Son and the Holy Ghost to guarantee that she is.

E. J. points and says, "That's a nice ring. Where'd ya get it?" I bet he's thinking something like it would make a nice engagement present for Woody when the time comes.

I sit next to him and hold the mother-of-pearl in front of my face. "Clive told me I could have it after he died." The ring really is gorgeous. It even smells good. Like the ocean. "I took it from his place when I went and got Ivory."

E. J. gives me a smile and a nod. He knows that my bark is worse than my bite. Having that dog by Woody's side will calm her down better than almost anything.

I watch as he laces up the high tops he got at the church rummage sale. They're royal blue and two sizes too big. "Thanks for bringin' the berries up to the fort. I coulda done without the song, though. Can't for the life of me understand why Woody liked it so much."

He grins.

"Our mother's dead," I say.

"Yeah," he says, not looking up. "I suspected she might be."

"Really? Why's that?" I ask somewhat eagerly. The Tittle place is so close to ours and E. J.'s always running around in the woods and going back and forth across the creek searching for something good to eat. Could he have seen what happened to Mama and just been too nervous to tell me?

He says, "When she didn't come back for such a long time . . . she wasn't the kind of person who would just up and leave her babies. She just wasn't." Mama was always kind to E. J. Paid him too much money to do odd jobs around Lilyfield and gave him plates of her pecan fudge to take home to his other two sisters, who thought it was delicious because they're not very picky eaters. "My mama thinks so, too. She told me that if she could, Miss Evie would've come home by now. That had to mean that she couldn't. That she was . . . ya know."

I pick up a rock and toss it hard as I can towards the creek. "Ya coulda told me that you were thinkin' that way."

E. J. picks up a rock, too, but doesn't throw it. Just runs it through his fingers. "I thought . . . ya seemed so sure that she was still alive and . . . you're so much smarter than me." He's embarrassed that he had to drop out of school last year to work hard for his family. "How did you find out about her . . . um . . ."

I look over to Lilyfield. Even though Papa told me that things were going to be different from now on, out of habit my skin crawls when I think about Woody all by her lonesome up in the fort. "His Honor told me."

"Has she been passed for a long time or did they just . . . did your father tell ya how your mama—?"

"She . . ." The pain of going over this is gumming up my mouth, but I got to tell him. E. J.'s stood by us through thick and thin. "She's been gone for almost a year. She died on carnival night last year."

"How?" he asks, stunned.

I'm not sure if I should tell him this part, but I do. "His Honor didn't tell me how, but Woody saw what happened. She's known the whole time that Mama's dead."

He hops off the log. "Did she say something to you?"

"Don't be stupid. I'd tell you if she did," I say, before he goes completely bonkers. He misses her talking as bad as I do. Their long chats about their future together.

They want to get married at Lee Chapel and have enough kids to make up a baseball team.

From the house, we can hear Mrs. Tittle humming a lullaby to the baby. I speak up about why I've come. "You know how Woody's all the time makin' those scary drawings?"

"I don't think they're scary."

"They're scary as hell and you know it."

"I don't—" He stops when I give him a you've-got-to-be-kiddin'-me look. "Fine," he says. "What about 'em?"

"There's this one . . . have you seen it? It's of Mama and there's somebody else, too. She got real agitated today when she showed it to me. I think it has something to do with what she saw that night, but I can't figure out what."

E. J. looks off into the woods. "Sometimes when ya hunt, no matter how hard ya chase after something you can't get a bead on it. That's when you got to be patient and wait 'til it circles back to ya."

"You know better than that," I say.

Of course, he doesn't disagree. Patience is not my long suit. "Will you help me find out what happened to our mother? You know, how she died and where she's buried?"

E. J. screws up his face. He must be thinking along the same lines that I am. It's one thing to go looking for a long-lost mother but an entirely different ball of wax trying to figure out how she died. That's a much, much sadder chore.

Seeing how he's waffling, I tell him, "Woody can't tell us what she saw, so we got to find out on our own so we can share the burden with her." I can see that E. J.'s mostly going along with that. I have inherited His Honor's persuading personality. "Once she has somebody to share that secret with, she'll feel so much better." I smile before I present my closing argument. "I bet she'll even start talkin' love and marriage again."

E. J. squares his cap, which I have always believed is the font of his bravery, and says, "What's the new plan?" He throws caution to the wind and doesn't care where it lands when that coon sits on his head.

"New plan?" I haven't thought this through. I don't have any idea what to do next, other than talk to Gramma or persuade Woody to tell me what she saw that night back in the clearing. "Well, I could . . . maybe we should . . . oh, E. J. . . . . Mama . . . she's . . . never comin' home."

He saves me from collapsing onto the ground by taking me into his arms. Lets me cry on his shoulder beneath the twilight sky.

"Shen?" E. J. says, once I get my sniveling under control. "I know you've been wantin' to talk to Vera. We could head over to the drugstore."

I scrub the sad off my face with the bottom of my T-shirt and say, "Ya only want to go to Slidell's 'cause you know Vera's gonna give you a free brown cow. Do you have no shame?" This is my way of thanking him for coming up with a good idea. Vera Ledbetter *was* a good friend to Mama. I have already thoroughly questioned her about our mother's vanishing. She didn't have much to offer then, so she probably won't have nothing more to add to my understanding of how Mama died. But she does make a mean brown cow and gives me free Rolaids whenever we stop by. And I promised Woody chow. One of Vera's scrumptious egg salad sandwiches would do my sister a world of good. When we were hugging during our mourning days, I could've played her ribs the way Beezy's favorite musician, Mr. Lionel Hampton, plays his vibraphone.

"We've got to be quick about it. I don't want to leave Woody alone too long," I say, looking down at my wrist to check the time out of habit. It's two freckles past a hair. That's something else I need to take care of. Getting Mama's watch back from my uncle tonight. "We also need to make a stop at What Goes Around Comes Around."

E. J. asks, "What for?"

"I'm gonna get Woody one of Mama's scarves. Papa rip— I mean, I accidentally lost the one she had." Getting her that scarf is not a completely unselfish act. I figure she might tell me what she saw the night Mama died if she's got some of that chiffon wrapped around her neck. Later tonight, when she's got a full stomach and is surrounded by all that soft, she'll be prime for the picking. If that doesn't work, I'm going to have to get strict with her. Absolutely no almond cream rubs until she coughs up that information.

I stand up and dust off my bottom. "Ready?"

E. J. looks around for my lunch box. "Did ya bring the disguises?" We always wear them if we have to sneak into the busy part of town. I have a black-haired wig from the year Mama got this idea that she and Woody and I would go trick-or-treating on Halloween as the three witches from *Macbeth*. E. J. wore the leftover beard I have from when I played one of the wise men in the church Christmas pageant.

"We don't need the disguises anymore. Papa says it's all right for Woody and me to go into town again."

E. J. gives me a squinty look. I'm sure he must be curious why all of a sudden we're being allowed to roam free, but just like everybody else around here, he knows better than to go prying into Carmody family business.

I extend my hand, he grasps it, and we turn towards the fastest way to get to town.

We're about a quarter up this side of Honeysuckle Hill when he says, "It's a good night for the race, wouldn't ya say?"

Bless his homely heart. He's trying to cheer me up by telling me the Bazooka joke the same way I always do when he's down in the dumps. "And which race might that be, E. J.?" I say, playing dumb the same way he always does.

He can barely contain himself. "Why, that would be the human one, Shenny."

I am so surprised by what escapes out of my mouth. I don't know if it's relief from not having to search for my mama anymore or the comfort of having a steadfast mountain man by my side who's going to help me find out how she died. It's the first time I've laughed in a coon's age.

Chapter Twenty-two

Once we're atop Honeysuckle Hill, E. J. and I can hear boogie-woogie music coming over the loud speakers. Lights that look like full moons are illuminating most of Buffalo Park. Flatbed trucks that're loaded with rides and game booths and men are struggling with a tent, shouting, "Get 'er up."

Colonel Button's Thrills and Chills has come to town.

The half-raised red tent is for the Oddities of Nature show and a couple of them are already here. The fattest lady in the whole world—Baby Doll Susan? Her trailer has a picture of her painted on the side. Her dimples are the size of truck tires. The towel-headed man is relaxing on a folding chair under a shade tree reading a magazine, which strikes me so funny. I never imagined he did anything else with his life but lie down on a bed of nails in a diaper twice a day. The other oddities like Milly and Tilly the Siamese twins and Tiny Jimbo, and that baby in the bottle that Bootie told me was coming this year, can't be far behind.

I ask E. J., "What day is it anyway?"

He stopped to watch a couple of the hoboes struggling to set up a game booth. "Damn it to hell and back!" E. J. says, throwing his cap onto the grass.

"Ed James!" I'm shocked. He rarely curses.

"Sorry. It's just that . . . I shoulda got over here earlier." He runs his hands through his bird's nest hair. "My papa's been feelin' . . . we could use some extra cash."

Watching the hoboes shuffling to and fro from the trucks, I say, "Don't worry. Most of them won't come back in the morning. You know how they are." They can get work when the carnival comes to town because mostly everybody else in the show is as dirty and scruffy as they are. But they're not hardy nor reliable. They'll buy Thunderbird wine with the cash they make working tonight and sleep it off tomorrow.

I recognize a few of the local boys working up a sweat, too. John-John Ellis is here and so is Bootie Young. When Bootie notices me, he stops unloading admission boxes and waves, and I wave back and think once again how dreamy that boy is. I mean, really. He is super something. And he likes me, too. A girl can tell.

Unfortunately, they open the show to everyone no matter how repulsive they are, so Remmy Hawkins is here, too. He's sprawled on the hood of his fancy car, wearing the same pair of greasy bibs that he's always got on without a shirt. Judging by the stack of empty beer cans piled alongside the whitewalls, he's been here most of the day.

Another group of burly men are unloading the merry-go-round piece by piece.

Mama.

That's the last time I saw her alive. Riding on the merry-go-round that night with Sam Moody in her white blouse with red yarn trim on the pockets. Seeing that smiling swan . . . it makes my stomach hip-hop so I move my binoculars to the trees that run alongside that part of the park.

"Is that . . . Curry Weaver?" I ask E. J., not at all sure that it is. He's standing by himself at the edge of the trees that line the north side of the park.

"Curry?" E. J. is spinning around. "Is he back from the Colony already?"

"He got sent to the Colony?" I ask. Usually the hoboes that get put up there are the habitual offenders. Curry's only been in town for a few weeks. How much trouble could he get in? "How'd you know that?"

E. J. says sheepishly, "While Woody and you were up in the fort for those days . . . I got sorta lonely. I went up to the camp to see what Curry was doing. Maybe get some lessons." E. J. is learning some hand-to-hand combat from the hobo who might not be a teacher or a writer like I first thought, but a soldier who has gone AWOL from the army. Since that war started over in Vietnam, deserters have been showing up at the camp, trying to blend in. I used to think that they were cowards, but when Ricky Oppermann came home from the war without half his skull, that changed my mind. I really liked Ricky even if he was planning on being a dentist like his father. Now he spends every day on his front porch drooling into a bib, so if that's what Curry is—a deserter—I don't like him any less for it. "But he wasn't there. I got worried that he'd hopped a train so I asked around. Dagmar Epps told me that he got hauled off to the Colony by the sheriff."

"Well, if *Dagmar* told you . . . ," I say, like could you be any dumber to take the word of the town idiot.

"She's not retarded like you think she is," E. J. says, real defensive. "Dagmar's just had a bad string of luck. And she makes a great rabbit stew. Where do you see Curry?"

"There." I point out to where the carnival lights barely reach, wishing that my sister was by my side. She'll be sad that she missed seeing Curry. She'd be juiced by how good he cleans up. Instead of his usual hobo outfit, he's got on a pressed blue shirt and khaki pants. He looks sharp. Probably thought getting fancy would help him get a job with the carnival. (He's not been living at the camp long enough to know that all Colonel Button requires of his hires is that they got arms and at least one leg.)

"Well, look at that. It's Sam." He's come out from behind one of the trucks and is standing a few yards away from Curry. "Let's go over there," I say to E. J. "I want to tell Curry how dapper he looks and I need to talk to Sam in the worst way." First, to give him hell for not being forthright about Mama's death, and second, to throw my arms around him. He has to know about Mama's passing. He's a detective. How he must have been suffering all this time.

I'm still watching when Sam turns and spots Curry. Extends his hand. They shake and start gabbing like they're long-lost friends. I didn't even know they knew each other. And is that Sheriff Andy coming to join in the conversation? Well, I'll be. I know that Sam and the sheriff are on friendly terms . . . but Curry? I didn't know that he knew either one of them. I guess, if what E. J. told me is true about that hobo getting taken up to the Colony, that's when he made the sheriff's acquaintance. So why is Curry being so buddy-buddy with him? I went up to the hospital to visit my gramma after she had her nerves break down. It's not a place that you'd thank somebody for sending you. What could they be talking about? Sam is wagging his head in disbelief at whatever Curry is telling him, and the sheriff is, too. Sam is also shaking his sinewy arms. Is he warming-up for the baseball toss game the roustabouts are setting up next to the Guess Your Weight scale? No, he seems too agitated. Has Sam fallen off the wagon?

"C'mon." I let my binoculars drop to my chest and we start heading towards Sam, the sheriff, and Curry when Remmy Hawkins stumbles in front of us and blocks our path.

"Oooeee, look what the cat drug out from under the porch," he says. He means E. J. Remmy likes me. In a very disgusting way. "If it ain't E. J. *Shittle* and my little honey bun. That *is* you, ain't it, Shen?"

It makes me sick that he can tell me and Woody apart. "Don't call me your honey bun, you . . ." I want to tell Remmy that he's an imbecile, but you know, this boy is drunk enough to be a keg with legs. And he loves to fight. He wouldn't hurt me, but E. J.? Remmy loves picking on him. It's practically his hobby to make fun of how poor and small he is.

Hawkins leers down at E. J.'s too-big shoes and says, "You come to get another pair offa Jinx the Clown?" He spits and that gob lands on the tip of E. J.'s royal blue sneakers, which are his only ones no matter how flappy they are on him. Elbowing him out of the way, Remmy sidles up next to me. "Ya might want to think about gettin' off that high horse you're on. You're gonna have to start bein' a lot more hospitable to me real soon."

"Why would I do that? You givin' away free tickets to the freak show or something?" The storm that swept through earlier might've cooled things down for a day or so, but I'm still feeling hot about Remmy showing up at the Triple S, taunting Sam and laughing diabolically when he called out from his fancy car, "Heard from your mama lately, twins?" As much as I know that I shouldn't go after him, I simply cannot rein myself in. "Just in case I have not made myself clear durin' our previous encounters, you make me sicker than a case of ptomaine poisoning, Remington Aloysius Hawkins, and . . . you . . . you got hair just like Clarabelle's." I've been dying to say that to him for years.

Remmy grabs one of my braids and reels me in. "You'll be whistlin' another tune once His Honor proposes to my auntie Abigail," he whispers wetly into my ear.

I twist out of his grip, kick him in the shin, and jump out of his reach. "And what exactly is my father going to *propose* to your horsey aunt?" I wink at E. J. Being humorous like he is, he'll appreciate this. "That she enters herself into the Four-H show?"

Remmy's rubbing his leg not anywhere near where I kicked him, that's how drunk he is. He mutters, "Marriage."

"What did you say?" The smile I gave E. J. is still on my lips.

"You heard me," Remmy says. "Your daddy's gonna propose marriage to my auntie this Saturday night."

I throw my head back and laugh like the lady that dares you to enter the carnival's Ye Olde Haunted House does. "Did you hear that, E. J.? Remmy here is telling us that Papa's thinkin' of marrying Abigail Hawkins," I say haughty, until I recall how I thought Papa might be falling into her web that afternoon she brought those pies over to the house. Then there's what good friends my grandfather and Mayor Jeb Hawkins are. His Honor told me the other night in the woods, "Things are going to change around here. You'll see." Is this what he meant? Was he telling me that he was intending to marry Abigail?

That thought must be plastered across my face because Remmy rocks back on his heels and says, "That's right. Now ya got it. You're always playin' hard to get, but you can't fool me, Shenny Carmody. You're excited as me that we're gonna be kissin' cousins."

The thought of this boy being related to me—it is too much. I ball my fists and take a step closer. I don't care how big he is. I'll pound him into a bloody pulp.

Seeing how crazy fired up I am, E. J. jumps in front of me and says, the same way Sam would if he was standing here next to me instead of furiously conversing with Curry Weaver and the sheriff over near the woods, "Count to ten."

"But he . . . did you hear what he just said?" I say, outraged.

"Allow me," E. J. says in a very distinguished way.

I guess just like anything else in life, you can't predict what's going to happen next, but I'll tell you one thing for sure. I didn't think it would be little E. J. smashing that buffoon Remmy Hawkins in his nose so hard that he knocked him out cold. That fight training he's been getting from Curry has really paid off.

"Why, thank you, kind sir," I say, smiling down at Remmy. Grampa Gus couldn't be more wrong about the Tittle boy. He's not minin' sludge. He's Sir Galahad.

"My pleasure." E. J. whips his coonskin off his head with a great flourish and a growling stomach. "Better get over to the drugstore now before Vera closes up."

I say, "Give me a minute to talk to Sam," but when I look over to where him and the sheriff and Curry were gathered, there's nobody there. "Where'd they go?"

"You can catch up with him tomorrow," E. J. says, looking down at Remmy and tugging at me. Remmy's already coming to. "We got to skedaddle if you want to get Woody something to eat. And that scarf."

Stepping over Hawkins, I accidentally on purpose genuflect on his gut and he lets out a groan. I ask E. J., "That's nothin' more than his usual hot air, don't you think? Papa has been keeping company with Abigail, but he can't really be planning on marryin' her."

He says, "A course he's not," but I know by the way he's avoiding my eyes as we make our way off the carnival grounds that he's not being truthful with me. No. E. J.'s lying through his knight-in-shining-armor teeth.

Chapter Twenty-three

Welcome banners are hanging from the old-fashioned streetlamps.

Downtown is decked out for the party. Tomorrow these cobblestone streets will be swarming with folks who've come to buy souvenirs. Just about anybody who wants to can peddle pictures of Robert E. painted on velvet and whittled figures of Traveller and stone replicas of Natural Bridge. Every knickknack under the summer sun can be got at the temporary booths that are lining Main Street. The permanent shops are spruced up, too, with MAKE YOURSELF AT HOME signs perched in their windows. Sidewalks are scrubbed clean. Streets swept. Founders Weekend is a big deal, but honestly? I'm dreading the whole darn thing. Feels to me like another storm is bearing down on us instead of a good time. I should be home right now battening down our fort. And it's not only my sister who is on my mind. You know, we had that blowup with Remmy Hawkins. When he comes all the way to, he'll start looking for E. J. and me, wanting to even the score. Was Remmy telling the truth or was it just more of his usual foolishness? The thought of Papa marrying Abigail Hawkins . . . her vile red hair lying on Mama's percale pillow. Her thin lips drinking out of our mother's teacup in the morning. Stroking our mama's things with her stinking gardenia hands. Papa would probably make Woody and me call her *Mama*. People like to say that you can get used to anything, but that's not true.

E. J. and I are short-cutting to the drugstore through Mudtown. Negroes young and old are out on their porches sipping out of beer bottles and listening to their bluesy music. A lot of the men are bare-chested and the women have fans in their hands and their skirts hiked up. There's kids playing Red Rover, Red Rover, Let Billy Come Over. Most everybody shouts out, "Evenin'" or "How do." They're used to seeing us come down this street to visit with Blind Beezy, who isn't out, but the lights are on in her front parlor. She must be knitting and purling like a madwoman. Tomorrow folks will be lined up and clamoring for her loud shawls and sweaters and scarves.

As we turn onto Monroe Street, E. J. gets a twinkle in his eyes and says, "Ya wanna do a sneak up on Beezy? I sure could use a quarter."

All the years we've been trying to take her by surprise, we have never once been successful. I'd love seeing her, but we really shouldn't. I promised Woody I'd be back soon. Then again, E. J. went out on a limb for me tonight when he popped Remmy in the nose. I owe him.

We come in low-to-the-ground through Beezy's backyard like we always do. Once past her garage, we make a sharp turn at the peony bushes and tiptoe around her gardening patch. She grows okra, which is flowering nicely. E. J. is in the lead and he's crouched over so far that his belly is all but dragging on the grass. Once we're even with the birdbath, E. J. gives me the zipped-lips sign and points up to her parlor window, which is open, of course. The heat of the day has spread into the evening.

Beezy's talking to somebody. A visitor's come calling. Could it be Mr. Cole? Forgetting that we're trying to be stealthy, I almost jump up and say, "Hey!" because I am really missing those nights on the porch with him and Beezy. I could point out some constellations to him real quick, chat about the men going to the moon. That would be nice. Maybe Beezy's got some chicken potpie prison-style in the oven. I could take some back to Woody.

"Ya got to do it this way?" Beezy's croaky voice drifts through the window that we're hunkered below. She sounds . . . scared? That's very unusual. She's the bravest woman I know.

"Believe me, if there was another way to go about this . . . Sam asked me to stop by. He doesn't want you to worry."

I look at E. J. and he's as perplexed as me. We recognize that Northern voice. It belongs to Curry Weaver.

"It's a God-forsaken, horrible thing," Beezy says. "I never imagined he was capable of planting—" She stops. All I can hear is her radio selling toothpaste and the kids down the block playing Red Rover, until she calls out in her usual trilly way, "Is that chickadees settin' to . . ."

Uncanny, I tell you.

Curious as all get out about what the two of them are talking about, but not wanting to be drawn into a long visitation with Beezy, I don't answer her and neither does E. J.

We just back out of there the same way we came. Sneaky as two rampaging elephants.

It didn't sound like Curry was asking for a handout like a lot of the hoboes do when they go door-to-door. Beezy said something about "planting." Were they talking about gardening? But that's a pleasant subject that she can really warm up to and she sounded kind of horrified. I ask E. J. when we make the turn onto Montgomery Street, "What do ya think Curry was doin' over at Beezy's? What were they were discussin'?"

"Do I look like a newspaper?" he says, using one of my own smart mouth remarks on me. He shoves his hands into his jeans pocket and his pants are so big they almost fall down. He's being unusually peevish because he didn't win his quarter. "Could we go back and try again?"

"Absolutely not. I promised Woody . . . wow!" I say as we turn into the town's main square.

The Beautification Committee has trimmed the band shell in flags and the gardens have been weeded and planted with red geraniums. The life-size statue of the Father of Our Country is rubbed to a nice sheen. Tree trunks are wrapped in gray crepe paper—the color of the Confederacy. This square is where the Parade of Princesses will start on Saturday morning.

"Race ya for a sundae," E. J. says, perking up and pointing towards Slidell's, which is across the square directly next to the courthouse.

"Naw, I don't feel like racin'," I tell E. J. like I always do, but then I peel off fast, like I always do. Being quicker on my feet than the winged messenger Mercury, I win most of our footraces by a mile. But I've decided to let him be victorious this time. Our sidekick is looking very starved this evening.

We run across Jefferson Street, shoving and bumping each other. We use the front door of the drugstore to stop ourselves. "Beat ya by a step," E. J. says, bent over laughing.

"Hold up there," somebody shouts from behind us. Still not used to being able to come and go from Lilyfield whenever I want, I freeze in place.

From the reflection in Slidell's window, I can see the sheriff's car idling at the curb. And he's got a passenger.

Sam Moody is in the backseat. He leans forward and says, "Evenin', Shen. E. J."

I go up to the car and squat down so I can see more of him below his baseball cap.

"What's goin' on, Sam? You and the sheriff doing some Founders Weekend joyriding?"

He shrugs, smiles. He has got the nicest teeth. Lined up like veteran's headstones. He must've inherited them from his father because Beezy's are tan and detachable. I'm just about to ask him if he knows why Curry Weaver was over at his mama's house when Sam says, "When I saw you and E. J. dashing across the square, I asked the sheriff to stop so I could let you know before you heard from somebody else."

"Hear what?" E. J. asks.

"The sheriff is taking me in," Sam tells us.

"Dang it all!" I am feeling more upset for me than him. After I got back to the fort, I planned to feed Woody and then the two of us would head over to the Triple S and sit on the steps of Sam's cabin and talk about Mama's passing. He has to know that she died and just didn't say anything to us because he didn't want to take away our hope. Our *Speranza*. Now he's gone and ruined it all.

"What did you do?" I say. "Did you fall off the wagon?" I picture him and Curry over at the carnival grounds. Did that hobo say something to get him mad? Then Sam planted his fist on his chin and the sheriff was called in? Yes. That must be what happened. That's why Curry was over at Beezy's. He was apologizing to her for getting Sam arrested. But they all looked so friendly when I was watching them through my binoculars. I'm confused. "Did you get in a fight with Curry Weaver?"

Sam gives me an incredulous look. "Why would you think . . . it's . . . it's not like that."

"Well, then how is it?" I ask, practically feeling the steam coming out of my ears.

"Shen . . . somebody reported to the sheriff that I had something to do with the disappearance of your mother," he says.

"What? Why that's . . ." I grab on to the half-raised car window to keep myself from tipping over backwards. "That's—"

"Real wrong," E. J. says, running over to the driver's side of the car. "Beg your pardon, but that's not right, Sheriff Nash. Sam and Miss Evelyn were the *best* of friends. They spent every Tuesday after—"

"E. J.!" I shriek, giving him the cut-throat sign over the roof of the car.

He looks back at me, stricken. "I mean . . . they knew each other a little but not so much that—"

"Calm down, son," Sam says with a hint of a smile. "You're going to blow a gasket."

No matter how hard we were trying to keep Sam and Mama's friendship on the q.t., seems like somebody found out. And unwitting E. J. has just confirmed it.

"Sheriff," I say, putting on my most powerful Carmody smile, "I don't know who it was that told you Sam had something to do with my mother's disappearance, but whoever it was, they're mistaken."

Andy Nash doesn't acknowledge me. He stares straight through the windshield and says, "I think you better go home now, Miss Shen."

Vera, who must've been watching what was unfolding from behind Slidell's plate-glass window, juts her head out the drugstore door and says, "Everything all right out here?"

Gazing into his light-colored eyes, I ask, "Is it, Sam?"

"If you could run over to the station to feed Wrigley, that would be much appreciated. And don't worry." And then to the sheriff he says, "All right, Andy."

When the car pulls away from the curb, I'm shivering in my sneakers, but not because I think that Sam had something to do with my mother's passing. I know he didn't. There was somebody back in the clearing with Papa that night, but it wasn't Sam. There is no way he could've made it all the way back to his cabin by the time I told Woody that I'd go looking when she was wailing, "Mama . . . gone." I don't care if Sam did answer his cabin door sweaty and with a shotgun.

E. J. is watching the county car disappear behind the courthouse. That's where the jail is, down in the basement. He's looking like he hopes a truck comes by and runs him down.

"I see that accusin' look on your face." He comes fast to my side, waving his hands like he's got something awful stuck to them.

"You two, keep your voices down and get your butts in here." I forgot about Vera. She's still standing in Slidell's open door in her peach waitress outfit and white shoes. "Got two brown cows already made up," she says, and goes back into the shop looking vexed.

E. J., who normally wouldn't have to be told twice when it comes to anything as delicious as one of Vera's root beer floats, doesn't budge.

I say, "You heard Sam. Somebody already reported to the sheriff about Mama and his friendship. What you said makes no difference at all. At least you didn't mention that she's dead." I have *never* seen E. J. cry. Not even when he got bit by that sick dog and had to have those shots in his stomach. He's got to be thinking the same way I am about how bad this could be. I guarantee you it's halfway through town already that half-breed Sam Moody has been taken in for questioning in the disappearance of the white wife of Walter T. Carmody. Of course, I'm mad that he blabbed, but I can also feel his upset. E. J. panicked when he saw Sam in the back of the car, that's all. Under normal circumstances, he is very tight-lipped. I knock his coonskin cap off his head so he can bend down and wipe off his watering eyes without me noticing. Opening the drugstore door, I say, "Ya hear that?"

E. J. shakes his head about off.

"Are you tellin' me that ya can't hear two brown cows mooing their heads off?"

"Shen—"

"Shut up and get in there, you fool," I say, giving him a kick in the keester.

Chapter Twenty-four

It's ten past closing at Slidell's.

The tan counter with the red vinyl stools runs along the right wall of the shop. The lights are off, except for the one above the grill, but I can still see the aisles chock-full of soaps and hot-water bottles and coloring pads and crayons and anything else you might need. In the way back of the shop is where Mr. Slidell sits on a stool and doles out his pills. He's a grouch. Vera told me that he's all the time crabby because he's been married to his wife too long. *That* I can understand. Sara Jane Slidell is the treasurer of the Ladies Auxiliary. She always went out of her way to be snooty to Mama, who she referred to as "the gal from up North." It didn't seem to bother our mother all that much when Mrs. Slidell was rude to her, but it did me. (I might've dropped a box of weed killer in her award-winning rose garden one night. I'm not saying that I did. But I might've. Twice.)

E. J. and I are dawdling near the front door, not exactly sure what to do. We've never been in here when it's empty. The drugstore, especially the lunch counter, is usually bustling. When Papa was still sitting behind the bench, he almost always came home to check up on Mama's whereabouts when Saint Pat's bells struck twelve. Then he'd come back here to join the other members of the Gentlemen's Club who traditionally eat breakfast at Ginny's Diner and meet again at Slidell's counter at noon. That's how Vera knows His Honor personally. She serves him his tuna fish on toast, no pickle, no chips.

Vera looks up from the counter she's wiping with a checkered red towel and calls, "What are you waitin' for? An engraved invitation?"

Vera is twenty-eight years old, but looks younger with that pinkish skin that strawberry blondes have, a smattering of fairy kisses across her nose, and eyes the color of a July sky. These days she's a wonderful cook, but Beezy told me that she used to work entertaining the sailor boys over in Norfolk, where there's the world's largest naval base. Vera's tough in her personality on the outside. Rough trade, you know. But on the inside, she is as mushy as one of her marshmallow cloud sundaes. She's an animal lover, just like Woody and Mama. Over at her place, there's a parrot named Sunny Boy living in a wrought-iron cage. He can say, "Ahoy, sailor, hop aboard," and a few other things that I'm not allowed to repeat. Vera told Woody and me that she moved from Norfolk to Lexington "to get a new lease on life," and now she works at Slidell's and sings in the church choir. That's how her and Mama became friends. They met over "Amazing Grace." The Auxiliary Ladies don't like Vera neither, but their husbands sure do. They'll drop their keys on the other side of the counter and look up her skirt when she bends over to pick them up. As Grampa likes to put it, Vera is "built like a brick shithouse."

Sausage curls are escaping from her hairnet and her red fingernail polish is chipped at the tips. "What was that all about? With the sheriff and Sam?" she asks, setting down the two brown cows.

I can't look at E. J. when I explain, "Somebody told the sheriff about Sam and Mama's friendship." (I'm not sure if Vera knows that her good friend is dead. She probably does since she's tight with Beezy, but unless she says something, I'm not going to tell her that Mama's passed. That would be mean.) "He's takin' Sam in for questioning in her disappearance."

"Admiral Jesus H. Christ," Vera says, very rattled. The lines between her eyes look like her first initial—*V.* "That changes things."

I take a slurpy sip of the float and say, "Not really. I'm sure it's just routine." But then suddenly, something pretty bad occurs to me. What if the sheriff knows that Mama is dead, too? If he does, then I know from spending many hours in my father's courtroom that the first thought that will come to his mind is foul play. Lawmen can't help it. They're born suspicious. That's why they become policeman and not poets. Yes, murder is what will dart across the sheriff's mind. Before Papa threw our television set out the window, my favorite show was *Mannix*. When people went missing in that show, every stinking time they *never* made it back home alive. Joe Mannix would look and look, but those missing loved ones *always* turned up shot in an alley or stabbed on a park bench or smothered in their sleep the way Yolanda Merriweather was by her husband, Jimmy.

Seems like when a wife gets murdered, it's almost always by her husband, but Papa didn't do that to Mama. The most superior court judge in Rockbridge County placed his hand on the Bible and swore to uphold the law, not break it, no matter how furious he got at his willful wife. His Honor could lash out at her, even kick her when she was down, but he could never take her life.

But if *I* thought that Mama could've been murdered, that would mean the sheriff might think the same. Not about Papa, but *Sam*. It would never in a million years occur to Andy Nash or anybody else in this town that my father would be capable of doing away with my mother.

Vera searches in her apron pocket and comes out with a pack of Pall Malls. She shakes one out, tamps it down on her thumb, and struggles two times to get a match lit. Picking a piece of tobacco off her tongue, she says, "Y'all better finish up and get back home. It's gettin' late. Where's Jane Woodrow anyway? Don't think I've ever seen you two apart, Shenny."

"She's back at the fort. She was too weak from hunger to come with me." The red glowing Coca-Cola clock is letting me know that it's fifteen past nine o'clock. I've left my sister alone for an hour and a half and Vera's right, I hardly go anywhere without her. Feels weird, but not completely bad. I love her with all my heart, I do, but being with Woody, it's like spending every minute of every day inside a Mixmaster. "Would you mind makin' me two of your famous egg salad sandwiches?" E. J. nudges me hard in the ribs. "Make that three. One with extra, extra mayonnaise. To go?"

Vera sets her cigarette into a slot on the gold metal ashtray and says, "Three sammies, one with x mayo comin' up." She bends to slide the sandwich fixings out of the Frigidaire, but her shoulders are shaking with the effort. Woody gets like that sometimes. I've always thought that means she's struggling to keep something inside her and it's struggling to come out. Like having a tug of war, with yourself.

"Vera?" She looks at me in the mirror behind the counter that she uses to keep an eye on her customers. She's having a hard time holding my gaze. I want to reach across the counter and pat her on the back. It's unnerving to see a woman with an Anchors Away tattoo inked into her bicep burst into tears. "Are you wantin' to tell us something?"

She snivels, packs the sandwiches into a wax bag, and places them on the counter in front of me. "About your mama, Shen," she says in a drawl thicker than one of her malts. "I've been meanin' to . . ." She doesn't know what to do with her hands. They're at her neck, then her hair, and finally, she's rubbing them together.

"Did your mother ever mention to you . . . did she tell you that she was plannin' to . . . damn it all."

Maybe Vera was the one who told the sheriff about Sam and Mama, and she wants to get it off her abundant chest.

"There's something you need to know," she says. "Evie . . . your mother . . . she was gonna leave your father."

E. J. shovels a spoonful of vanilla ice cream into his mouth and asks, "Where?"

I already know that, but since his mother and father are so happily married, he doesn't get what Vera means.

"When Mama . . . do you know if she was planning on asking Woody and me to join her when she left?" I ask Vera in the smallest voice. Even though she's dead, it matters to me more than anything ever has that my mother wasn't going to leave without asking her peas in a pod to come along, the same way she had that Easter in the garden.

"Your mother had been plannin' her getaway for months," Vera says, like she didn't even hear me. "She had every little detail down pat. She was gonna take the steppin' stones across the creek, and your mama, E. J., she was gonna borrow the Calhouns' car and give Evie a ride to the bus station." She's trying to remove a napkin from the container to use as a hankie and it's giving her a hard time. She finally gives up and uses her capped sleeve to wipe off her drippy nose. "I've gone over this in my mind a dozen times. I don't know what the hell went wrong."

I know how she feels.

"We all kept hopin' that we'd hear from her," Vera says.

The same way I was. Before I found out from my father that night in the woods that he was "sorry for the way things worked out."

Even though I would have told my mother that I couldn't leave Papa back then because I was a daddy's girl, her asking again would've made all the difference. I ask Vera, louder this time, "Was Mama gonna ask Woody and me to come along with her?"

"A course she was, cookie," Vera says, snubbing out her cigarette and patting my hand. "Didn't you get her note?"

"What note?"

"Your mama was supposed to leave a note behind for you. A beautiful note. She knew how much you twins loved your father, especially you, Shenny, but once you read her explanation, Evie was sure that you'd . . ." She stops to faraway smile, the way you do when you're having a nice memory. "I offered to take you girls to her when the time came, but your mother, she wanted Sam to do it. She thought it best that a family member bring you."

E. J.'s mouth drops practically down to the counter alongside mine. *Sam? A family member?* Why would she say something like that? What is wrong with . . . oh, poor thing. Working these long hours at the lunch counter. Those deep fryers can get awful hot. Vera probably has a severe case of heat exhaustion. Bootie Young told me there was this one time that his dairy-farming daddy was working too long under the sun and his mama found him trying to milk one of the bulls.

"Now, Vera," I tell her in the voice you use when dealing with the sick or maimed, "a little rest and relaxation is what you need." I've gotten up off my stool, taking care not to make any sudden moves. I'm going to walk over to the pay phone and call Doc Keller to come over here quick as he can. "You know Sam is our friend and not a relative, right? You just got mixed-up."

"Well," she says, throwing her hands into the air, "like they say in the Navy, the torpedo is outta the tube now. No sense pretending it ain't." Vera comes from around the counter and steers me back to my stool. "You're gonna want to be seated when I break this to you. Me, too. Move over, E. J." She gets situated between us. "A long time ago, when Beezy was just a girl, she worked for your grandfather cleaning his house, Shenny."

What could Beezy have to do with Sam being a family member? Vera is getting more confused by the second. She really does need help. Is Doc's number Hopkins 4563 or 4653?

"She hadn't married Carl yet so she wasn't called Beezy Bell back then," Vera continues. "She was poor and pretty Miss Elizabeth Hortense Moody, and Gus Carmody was a rich and a very handsome young man."

I'm not sure what this has to do with the price of a cup of coffee either, but she's saying the truth. That old coot wasn't always uglier than a pig snout. Gramma

Ruth Love has lots of pictures of him pressed into a photo album that has THE GOOD OLD DAYS stamped on its cover. As much as it pains me to admit it, Vera's right—Grampa *was* a looker.

"I've heard customers remark many times that Gus was quite the charmer," she says.

"You heard that wrong," I say back, gruff. "My grandfather's about as charming as a funeral."

"That may be true now, hon, but back then? They say that your grampa could talk the sweet off a sugar cube."

I'm trying to alert E. J. to Vera's rapidly deteriorating condition by leaning behind her back and vigorously tapping my temple, but he's too busy hanging on her every word to notice. Being a mountain man, he's fond of tall tales.

"Then what happened?" E. J. asks on the edge of his stool.

"That depends." Vera looks back and forth between us, her curls bobbing. "I don't know much about kids. Are the two of ya old enough to know how babies are born?"

"Yeah," E. J. and I say. He's got a goat that he delivered babies to and I watched.

Vera pauses, like she's about to change her mind, but then says, "When Beezy was young, she was desperately in love with Gus Carmody."

"What?" I say, aghast. That's proof positive that the woman has lost her mind. I have never in all my days heard something more harebrained.

Vera ignores me. "And when two people get hot and bothered like that, they . . . uh . . . they do it."

"Do what?" E. J. asks.

"Shuck the oyster," Vera says like she's reciting the soup of the day.

E. J. looks as confounded as me.

"They zalleywhack. Play the game of twenty toes?" Clearly, Vera's not getting the reaction from us that she expected. Exasperated, she says in a voice that echoes up the drugstore's empty aisles, "Beezy and Gus fornicated."

Root beer comes squirting out of E. J.'s nose and I jump up off my stool, "Oh, that's so disgustin' and . . . and . . . unappetizing and . . . Vera! What is wrong with you? Beezy wouldn't shuck with Grampa. You're her friend, you know how much she hates him. You're the one that's hot and bothered. I'm calling Doc Keller right this minute."

Vera puts me back in my place. "You mean Beezy hates your grandfather *now*. Back then was different. Hear me out."

She seems so convincingly upset, I grit my teeth and say, "Go on," but the second she's done, I'm rushing to the phone.

"Well," she says, "after he got what he wanted from her, Gus turned his back on Beezy. Threw her right outta his house despite her condition."

The condition Vera means is that Beezy was feeling sad and stupid about something he did to her. Grampa puts me in that condition, too. But this still doesn't explain her earlier loopy remark about Sam.

Vera spins her stool my way, leans in close, and says, "You've got a lot on the ball, Shenny. You musta noticed the resemblance between your father and Sam. Their hooked noses, those same caramel eyes. How they both got an interest in law enforcement?"

I'm afraid she is giving my powers of observation too much credit. I've never noticed anything of the sort.

"What I'm tryin' to tell you . . . what I mean to say is—" She breaks off like she's having second thoughts.

"What, Vera?" I ask, curious now what her over-fried brain is trying to get at. "For God's sakes, spit it out."

"Just a second." Vera digs into her apron pocket and slaps three rolls of Rolaids onto the counter before gushing out, "Sam Moody is the bastard child of Beezy and your grampa's old-time love affair. Sam . . . he's your uncle, Shenny."

Chapter Twenty-five

Vera told us if we'd wait while she closed up the store, she'd give us a lift back home. I told her thank you for the offer, but we had to make a stop, and then E. J. and I ran out of Slidell's before she started getting into the blow-by-blow account of how Sam came to be my uncle.

Half-uncle, really.

Now I know why Beezy hates Grampa as much as I do. She's the gal they're talking about in one of those "Hell has no fury like a woman scorned" situations.

How come I haven't put this together before? I should've figured this out. One time when we were driving home from church the Mudtown way, we slowed down in front of Beezy's place. Woody and I stuck our arms out the window and yelled, "Mornin'." My grandfather turned to Uncle Blackie, who hardly ever goes to church because he doesn't have a conscience that needs cleansing, that's why I remember this trip. "Ya see that, son," he said. "There ain't much left of her now, but that nappy used to be fine. Legs like a nutcracker. *Hardy har har*." Grampa saying something that nice about a colored person was so out of the ordinary that Woody and I talked about it later. She decided he must've been paying Beezy a good-at-lifting-furniture compliment since he'd just come from Mass, and that sounded about right. But that wasn't what he meant at all.

Then there's how Woody and I feel naturally close to Sam—that was another hint. And the way Beezy treats us like we're her family. I thought her special kindness towards us was just a holdover from when she worked up at Lilyfield taking care of us when we were teeny-tiny, but it's so much more than that. Woody and I are sort of her grandbabies.

I'm not angry at Beezy for not letting my sister and me in on all the spit swapping she did with Grampa Gus. I know why she never told us on one of those sultry nights on her porch when all sorts of secrets come out. She was afraid that Woody and I would think poorly of her. I confess, I do a little. Shucking oysters with our grampa shows a real lack of taste on her part. He probably tricked her. Did the same exact thing to Beezy that Blackie did to Louise Jackson. Those men seem to know just what to say to a girl to get them to do what they want, especially Grampa, who has years more experience being a horse's ass. Gramma refers to our town as Sodom and Gomorrah, and I'm beginning to see her point. Does she know about this long-ago dalliance between Grampa and Beezy? Or like all the other skullduggery that involves the Carmody men, has my grandfather managed to keep it buried?

Men laughing and jukebox music, the sound of pool balls hitting against one another and the tantalizing smell of burgers are coming out of the open door of Elmo's Bar as E. J. and I scurry by.

I'm so hungry my stomach thinks my throat's been cut, which means Woody's must, too.

I wouldn't feel right eating without her, so I pass E. J. his egg salad sandwich and keep the other two in the sack. "We gotta make this quick," I tell him as we turn the corner onto Main Street.

E. J. says, "Are you all right? Ya know, about what Vera told us about your grampa and Beezy and Sam?"

"I guess I am." I'm miffed that Sam didn't let us in on the secret and I'm shocked, but it's a good kind. I'll get a huge grin out of Woody when I tell her. Maybe she'll even start talking again, that's how thrilled she'll be. I bet E. J. is feeling swell about our newfound relative as well. When he marries Woody, Sam will be his uncle, too. He doesn't look so happy right now, though. I say to him, "A penny for your thoughts."

"Don't got a penny."

I'd explain, but I'm worn down right to my tread. "What's on your mind?"

"Your mother."

"Me, too." I wish I could've read that note she left for me and Woody. Vera said it was beautiful. I'll look harder for it as soon as things settle a little. *That* note must be the one Sam keeps asking me to keep an eye out for.

"What if the sheriff begins thinking that Sam had something to do with your mama's . . . ummm," E. J. asks as we make the turn into the alley that runs behind the shops on Main Street.

He means her death. It surprises me more than snow in August that he figured that out. I might underestimate our sidekick sometimes. "He'd need proof of wrongdoing."

E. J. follows me as I turn into the narrow alley. "Like what?"

I think back on some of the cases that I observed in my father's courtroom and on *Mannix*. "Like maybe something that belonged to Mama being found over at the Triple S. Something that would point to foul play." That gives me the quivers. "But that's not gonna happen. Mama was Sam's best friend."

I come to a halt and tell E. J., "Here we go."

The bottom half of the moon is aglow with the nicest smile, but it's not shooting off enough light to help us make our way through the junk that's scattered in the backyard of What Goes Around Comes Around. I got to switch on my flashlight. A mangy cat is giving himself a bath on a cushionless divan. A bunch of chairs are stacked on top of one another and leaning against the pile are rusted signs that folks find on the highway and bring to the owner of the shop, Artesia Johnson, who is a soft touch. By the wink she gives me at Mass, I know she leaves the back window of the shop unlocked so I can come look for Mama's stuff from time to time. A real generous heart beats beneath Miss Artesia's blubber.

(She's heavyset. She'll tell you it's her glands, but all you got to do is share a blanket with her at the church picnic and you'll know right off it's her mouth.)

"Cup 'em," I tell E. J. I shake off my sneakers and place my foot in his hands.

With one good boost, I'm halfway through the back window and I wriggle the rest of the way through.

The shop is much spookier at night than during the day, when it already gives me the willies. It's the mannequins. They don't have faces. One of them's wearing a nice red, white, and blue jacket. Besides a scarf of Mama's, I think I'll get that jacket for Woody. She's going to be so excited when I inform her that we got a big new relative. She'll probably make me sing some stupid show tune to celebrate. Or a patriotic ditty, now that we got our very own uncle Sam!

There are tables upon card tables of discards set willy-nilly around the shop. Egg beaters are mixed in with mohair sweaters. Beaded purses are lying on top of typewriters with missing keys. Miss Artesia's got the antique jewelry and more valuable items set out in a display case. There's one of Clive Minnow's Confederate buttons that he found with his metal-detecting device. I missed his funeral when Woody and I spent all that time up in the fort grieving Mama. I'm going to borrow this button, too. Miss Artesia won't miss something this small. Once everything calms down around here, I'll take it to the cemetery and push it into Clive's mound. He'd like that.

A selection of scarves is hanging on a coat hanger right above the jewelry case. The third one from the left, that's one of Mama's. I never took them home all at one time because having them sitting in a pile in the fort felt too final. By leaving them here, I could pretend, the same way I was doing about everything else, that someday Mama and Woody and me would come by to pick up the rest. I slide the scarf off the hanger and hold it up to my nose, but the scent of her is long gone. The pink chiffon smells like spaghetti and meatballs now. Miss Artesia's favorite. Woody won't care. She'll just be glad to have something of Mama's. And it *is* Italian.

"Shen!" E. J. calls through the back window. His mouth sounds full and like he's saying, "Then!" He must've already started eating his sandwich. "Get out of there. Thomebody's comin'."

It's probably Miss Johnson remembering she forgot to put out the goose lamp above the cash register when she closed up. That's all right. I don't care if she finds me rifling through her wares. It will give me the opportunity to thank her for her patience and understanding. There's a jingling, then a rattle at the back door. Like she is having a hard time fitting the key into the lock, but then the door opens and closes hard.

"Hey, Miss Artesia," I call in that direction, so I don't startle her. "Don't be scared. It's me, Shenny Carmody. I'm just picking up something for my sister. I'll pay you back."

But it's not Artesia Johnson coming out of the dark back hallway looking all forgiving. Somebody else is standing in the glow of my flashlight.

It's Curry Weaver.

Chapter Twenty-six

Curry's still got on the starched blue shirt and tan slacks that he had on over at the carnival grounds when I saw him discussing something so heated with Sam and the sheriff. He looks polished for a man who just got out of the Colony. Usually those hoboes come back from the hospital looking like "The Wreck of the Hesperus." Curry's dark hair is parted on the left and combed with shiny grease. Whiskers have sprouted up on his jaw and small upper lip.

I say, "Hey!" like I've just run across him while the two of us were doing our daily errands. "Don't you look nice."

"Hello, Shenny," Curry says. E. J. steps out from behind him. He's got egg salad stuck to the corners of his mouth.

My brain, which went into reverse upon seeing him, is just starting to rev back up. First he's at Buffalo Park,

[261]

then over at Beezy's, and now here. What the heck? Oh, I get it. He must've saw E. J. and I leaving Beezy's. I bet he followed us over here to chastise us for spying on him and her. "Look," I say, "we're really sorry we tried to do a sneak up. We didn't mean to intrude on your visit with Beezy. Tomorrow I'll tell her how—"

"That's not why I'm here," he says.

"Okay." I look over at E. J. and he seems as flummoxed as me. "Then why *are* you here?"

"I thought you two might like to know that the sheriff has finished questioning Sam concerning your mother's disappearance," he says. I take a step closer to him. E. J. looks smaller than he usually does next to Curry, who must've found his new outfit in the Extra Large section of wherever he shops, which is odd. I don't think that hoboes usually do. Shop, that is. Looks to me like they get most of their stuff from garbage pails.

"Well, I appreciate you coming by to tell us about Sam, but I don't understand," I say. "What do you care about him or my mama or . . . not to be rude or nothin', but what does anything that's goin' on in our town have to do with you? You're just passing through. You're . . . well . . . a hobo." But the second those words are out of my mouth, I remember how Curry never slurs his words and his teeth aren't rotting like the other men at the camp. "Aren't you?"

"Not exactly." Curry reaches into his back pants pocket and takes out a black leather wallet. He flips it open and flashes a badge. It has DECATUR stamped in raised-up silver.

Oh, Lord. He's not a writer. He's not a soldier that has gone AWOL. He's not a man of the rails. His name isn't even Curry Weaver. It's Anthony Joseph Sardino. And he's a cop. A detective. Just like his brother— Johnny, Sam's dead partner.

Curry says, "I'm sorry I couldn't tell you two sooner, but I'm working undercover."

"Under what?" E. J. asks.

I'm sure he thinks that being "undercover" has something to do with pulling a quilt up over his head. "That means Curry has only been *pretendin'* to be a hobo, while he gathers important police facts of some kind." I saw that happen on *Mannix* and that other show with Peggy Lipton called *The Mod Squad*. Those kids were undercover all the time.

I ask Detective Sardino, "*Why* are you undercover?"

"Sam's been placed under arrest."

Swallowing back the brown cow that's come halfway up my throat, I ask, "For . . . for what?"

"First-degree murder."

E. J. and I reach for one another.

The seed of what I used to worry about has blossomed. The Decatur police must have finally found some proof that Sam beat to death Stumpy or The Maggot, that man who killed his police partner. Curry has come to arrest our Sam for that lowlife's murder.

I'm sure this cop doesn't care about Sam beating to death that criminal who killed his brother. No. He must feel just fine about that. Lieutenant Sardino here must blame Sam for not keeping his brother Johnny safe the way a partner is supposed to. He's come to settle the score. Curry is going to slap a pair of handcuffs on Sam and drag him back to Decatur to be put on trial. Sam could be found guilty and go to prison the same way his mother did after she killed her bad husband. I think that when I see the WHAT GOES AROUND COMES AROUND sign painted in frosted letters on the front window.

I rush to tell Curry, "Just in case you don't know, Sam is still so sad about not bein' able to protect your brother from that bad man who shot him. I can't even say *Johnny* or *arrividerci* . . . his Adam's apple goes nuts." I am horrified that I was stupid enough to talk to Curry or Anthony or whatever his name is over at the camp. I know better than to trust people like that. He asked me so many questions, and like an idiot, I answered them. I thought he was lonely or trying to garner some protection from a girl whose father is the most superior court judge in Rockbridge County. I even thought for a time that he would put me in his *Hobo Like Me* book that he was writing. But all he was doing was plying me for information in his investigation of Sam the same way he was doing to others. Vera told me he made phone calls in the booth outside the courthouse. And I bet Dagmar Epps told him a thing or two. They got very chummy around that campfire.

What about Woody? I'm going to have to go back to the fort and tell her that this man she likes so much is not a harmonica-playing hobo, but a badge-wielding cop. And that he's about to take her new uncle Sam Moody away from her. I can't let that happen. She just couldn't take losing another person that she loves.

"Please," I implore Curry, "please don't take Sam away. As you already know, we've lost our mother." I haven't told him that she's dead. That's what I'll do next if this doesn't work. "Can't you let bygones be bygones?" I know he must be a Catholic. He's Italian like the pope. "Remember what Jesus said about forgivin' your enemies?"

When I break into sniffles, Lieutenant Sardino reaches for a dishrag off the table he's standing next to and sets it gently into my pleading hands. He's got hair on his knuckles. "You've got this all wrong, Shenny," he says. It's not just Curry's clothes, his personality seems different from when he was just a hobo. He's still nice, but it's a more take-the-bull-by-the-horns kind of nice. "I'm not here to arrest Sam for Buddy DeGrassi's murder."

"You're not?" I say, blowing my nose. *Buddy?* That doesn't sound like a mean-enough name for a man that killed Sam's partner so cold-bloodedly. "Are you sure?"

Curry gets a gleam in his eye. "Yes. I'm sure."

Is this another one of his undercover lies? "Then—"

"Just a hanged minute," E. J. says, showing off his mountain man moxie. "If you're not here to arrest Sam, then why's he been arrested, Curry? I mean, who's he supposed to have committed first-degree murder on?"

I know. I have figured it out. And I can tell by the way he's looking at me so pitiful that Curry knows that I know. He says softly, "Shenny's mother."

E. J. wheels towards me and shouts, "But you told me . . . you said the sheriff would need proof of wrong-doin'."

Shakily, I ask Curry, "Doesn't he?"

"Something incriminating was found at Sam's place," Curry says. "Something of your mother's."

"I don't care what the sheriff found. That . . . that just means that Sam and Mama were friendly, not that he murdered her. E. J., we got to go get Sam out of that jail right this minute," I say, stepping towards the back door with a full head of steam.

"Come back, Shenny. Sheriff Nash didn't find the evidence," Curry says. "A boy found it buried under a rock in Sam's yard. He was searching for fishing worms and found something else instead."

"What something?" E. J. and I say together.

"A woman's blouse."

Without even thinking, I ask the same way a defense attorney in my father's courtroom would, "Which boy was this exactly that found this blouse?"

"The one I noticed you talking to over at the carnival grounds earlier," Curry says, holding steady under my cross-examination. "Remington Hawkins."

"That's not real evidence!" I tell him with a stomp of my foot. "That's . . . Remmy . . . He hates Sam, isn't that right, E. J.?"

"A hundred percent!"

Curry replies even more delicately, "There's blood on the blouse, Shenny. And the boy is the mayor's grandson. That gives him some credibility."

Needing to sit down, I boost myself up onto one of the card tables and pick up a mouth-eaten sweater to hold on to for comfort. "But what does that have to do with Mama? Kids like to hang out at that part of the creek. Probably some girl drank too much beer and . . . and fell down and got a scrape. So she took off her bloody blouse and left it, that's all that is," I say. The blouse is what my father would call circumstantial evidence.

Curry looks down at his feet and then back at us. I can tell he's dreading what he has to tell us and is putting it off as long as he can. "Shen, I . . . your grandfather and father have identified the blouse as one belonging to your mother."

I glance over to where Miss Artesia has tops hanging. I have searched and searched this shop for the one she was wearing at the carnival that night. "Is . . . is it white with red yarn trim?"

Curry doesn't have to say, "It sure is." The answer is in his I'm-sorry eyes. "And your mother's diary states some pretty strong feelings."

"Her diary?!" I remember how my hand rattled around in the empty stronghold. I thought Mama had moved it or given it to Woody. Could Remmy have broken into our home when we were asleep? Pried up the floorboards in the master bedroom and stolen it? "Remmy found Mama's diary, too?"

Curry reluctantly says, "It wasn't the Hawkins boy."

"Then who?"

He's stalling. Gazing around the shop like he's come to pick up a few things.

"Curry?" I say. "Who found Mama's diary?"

He looks at me with concern and says barely above a whisper, "Your father."

"Papa found Mama's diary and took it to the sheriff?" I ask, incredulous. "Are you sure?"

Was this recently or has my father had the diary the whole time that Mama's been gone? Has he been lying in his bed at night reading it? Is that why he wails in the wee hours? I have no idea what Mama might've written about Sam in her most private way, but I know the words would have been glowing with gratitude for finding a friend who was so kind to her. A man who shared the same interests in foreign languages and poetry. Someone who had spent some time up North.

Curry answers me, "Some pages have been ripped out of the diary, but there are enough left for anybody to conclude that Sam and your mother had a relationship that would be considered improper to some people."

The diplomas hanging on Papa's study wall let you know that he graduated from law school at the top of his class. He is the smartest of the smart. He wouldn't have given the sheriff Mama's diary unless something in it put him in a good light and Sam in a bad one.

This couldn't get much worse.

"Your father also brought in a watch as evidence," Curry says. "The one that Sam gave your mother."

"But how did he get . . . ?" Blackie. After he took it off Lou in the storm that night, he must've gone up to the house and shown the watch to Papa, who told his big brother that he wasn't the one who give it to Mama. They must've gone over to Elmer Haskall's jewelry store to find out exactly who did. Mr. Haskall would've put on his half-glasses, and said, "You know, this timepiece looks a lot like the one that Sam Moody bought a while ago. Let me turn it over to be sure." He would've seen the word *Speranza* that he'd inscribed on the back. "Yup, that's the one I sold Sam," is what Mr. Haskall would've said. "Told me he was buyin' it as a gift for a dear friend."

I feel horrible. I should've given Sam the watch back when he asked for it. How could I be so selfish? Even *I* have to admit that the overwhelming evidence makes him look guilty. But if you could have seen him look at Mama with such tenderness the way I did. It was not the way a man looks at a woman he's wanting to kill. I'm familiar with that look. I've seen it on Papa's face. "What does the sheriff say is Sam's motive for killin' my mother? I mean . . . why would he think that he'd want to do her harm?"

Curry says, "Your father told Sheriff Nash that he believes your mother's murder was a crime of passion. He knew that Evie . . . your mother . . . was spending time at Sam's place trying to help an alcoholic Negro get back on his feet. He insists that Sam misinterpreted your mother's kindness. When she didn't reciprocate his feelings, he murdered her in a drunken rage."

"That's not true," E. J. shouts. "Sam hasn't had a drink of hard liquor in over two years!"

I say, really worked up, too, "And Papa did *not* know that they were spending time together. He's . . . he's makin' it sound like he was proud that Mama was doing Christian deeds of mercy. He *never* would have allowed her to go over to the Triple S. My father . . . I know I told you up at the hobo camp that he was so wonderful and the best father, but . . . he's not what you think . . . he's not what anybody . . . you don't understand."

"I understand more than you realize," Curry says with a curious little smile. Is he ridiculing me?

"I'm sure I don't know what you understand and what you don't. But I can tell you this much—Sam *did* love Mama, but it wasn't in that crime of passion way," I say, even though doubt has popped into my mind again. They could have started out as friends and then on one of those Tuesday afternoons realized that they were feeling something stronger. I look over at homely E. J. Could I wake up one morning and feel about him the same way I do Bootie Young? Could Cupid be that careless? Aimlessly shooting arrows at people, not think-ing who could get hurt? Maybe that *is* what happened between Mama and Sam. Their love of words turned into a love of each other. I have never seen a white woman and a high yellow Negro or any shade of Negro be in love. It was unusual enough that the two of them were friends. No, that's not right. Mama had to know all along what I just found out. That Sam is my father's half-brother. Family. She wouldn't have allowed herself to fall in love with him no matter how many arrows she had sticking out of her heart.

"Sam and Mama are related. Did you know that, Curry?" I ask, trying to gain back some of his respect. For once in this conversation maybe *I* can tell *him* something.

"I know that Sam is your half-uncle, Shen."

"You do not." I wish I'd never come into this dumb shop. I should've gone straight back home to Woody with her egg salad sandwich.

"What about the sheriff?" E. J. asks. I thought all this was going over his head, but he's keeping right up. "Does he *believe* what His Honor is tellin' him?"

"Of course, he does. I know Sam likes him and all. You seem pretty chummy with him as well," I tell Curry's surprised face. "But you two don't know . . . the sheriff is so crooked you can't tell from his tracks if he's comin' or goin'. My father gave him a big check for his Be-Handy-Vote-Andy campaign."

All of that said, the three of us just stand there looking at one another. Finally Curry breaks the ice. "We know that Sam didn't hurt your mother, Shen, but you've got to admit it sure looks like he did."

Suddenly, a wonderful feeling comes over me. The kind I get when I find my sister after chasing around all afternoon for her. It doesn't matter what my father or the sheriff has to say. Woody *knows* what happened to our mother. Papa told me she does. I don't know if she knows if somebody ended Mama's life or if she just had a bad accident, but Woody definitely knows that it wasn't Sam Moody who caused it. I might not be the best judge of people, but my sister is. If Sam had done something wrong to our mother, Woody would've let me know to keep away from him. She would've made a drawing with a skull and crossbones or a big red STOP sign over a picture of the Triple S if Sam wasn't safe. I may not have been paying close enough attention to her drawings the way I should have, but I'm sure I would've noticed that one.

Feeling revived, I tell Curry, "Woody saw something the night Mama disappeared. I think she might've seen what happened to her. She's an eyewitness."

Curry nods. "I suspected as much."

"You did?" I have begun to doubt him again. He could be making every single bit of this up. I don't know why he would, but he could. Grown-ups are always perpetrating tricks on innocent children. "Why didn't you just come out and tell us you were a cop?" I ask.

"That's not how it works, Shen. If I'd told you that I was down here investigating your . . . what if you or E. J. had accidentally let that slip?"

I feel E. J. go stiff. He's remembering what he shouted out to the sheriff in front of Slidell's. I can see Curry's point. Really. If I knew something secret I probably wouldn't tell us neither.

I got a lot more questions for Curry, but when one of the mantel clocks at What Goes Around Comes Around starts striking, he tells us, "Tomorrow is going to be a big day for all concerned. I'll give you a ride back to Lilyfield."

Chapter Twenty-seven

The car doesn't have air-conditioning so the windows are rolled down.

Curry is behind the wheel of Beezy's old brown Pontiac. The one I drive to Hull's Drive-In. I'm remembering the last time I was in this car, the seat pulled all the way up so I could reach the pedals. Besides musicals, Beezy goes ape for creature features. The last one we went to see was *Invasion of the Body Snatchers*, but I barely watched it. I spent most of the night looking over at Woody, thinking maybe *that's* what happened to her. She's one of those pod people now. I couldn't stand it. I leaned up close to Beezy and whispered, "Maybe that's what's wrong with Woody. Some aliens came up to the fort one night and changed her brain around." Blind Beezy reached out for my hand in the dark. "Don't be silly. Woody is still Woody. She's just not workin' real good right now. Spaceships . . . alien bein's . . . that sort of thing only happens in these movies."

Not according to Clive Minnow. When we drive past Stonewall Jackson Cemetery, I regret missing his burial ceremony. Not as much as I do about missing Mama's, but there's a twinge when I recall Clive's foolish fears about catching leprosy and malaria, and how he would get so excited when he found something with his metal-detecting device that he'd do a Rumplestiltskin dance through the woods, and his furious picture taking while he was searching for UFOs, and how he'd upset the checkerboard if he was on the losing end—yes, even that I'm going to miss. That man might've been odd, but he was someone I could count on to be where he was supposed to be, doing exactly what he always did. That's a rare quality these days.

E. J. and I are in the front seat of the car. E. J. doesn't get to ride in cars very often and he keeps sticking his head out the window like a dog. I have draped Mama's spaghetti-and-meatball-smelling scarf around my neck. I wish we could just drive and drive. I don't want to have to think anymore about Sam or Mama or my father or any of this horridness. I want to be small again. A little girl heading home after a long day at the beach. Smelling of sunburn, not putting up a fuss when my mother picks me up in her arms and carries me out of the car, sets me down on our sailboat bed, crooning, "Tomorrow."

"How'd ya come up with the name Curry?" E. J. asks. "It's kinda different."

Lieutenant Sardino smiles, flicks his signal up, and makes the turn on Kilmer Street. "Curry is my wife's favorite food. She's Indian."

E. J. perks up. "No kiddin'!" He really likes Indian stuff. Whenever Clive Minnow found arrowheads in his woods he gave them to me because he was only interested in metal objects. In turn, I gave them to E. J., who has quite the collection. Curry must be a food like pemmican.

Cruising past Washington and Lee College where Papa went to law school, I ask, "How're you plannin' to get Sam out of the fix he's in all by yourself?" I don't care if Curry Weaver is a lawman. He's not from this neck of the woods. If the Carmody family is involved with charging Sam for Mama's death, even though he thinks he does, Curry has no idea what he's going up against.

"I got a plan," Curry says. He's teasing me. That's the same thing I told him up at the hobo camp about finding my mama. "At some point I may need assistance from you and your sister to stand up in Sam's behalf. Do you think you could do that even if it was contrary to what your father had to say about him?"

I give him the most truthful answer I can. "I don't know." Mama would expect us to help Sam. To tell the truth. She'd pull out that old saying, "Honesty is the best policy." But I shudder three inches deep to think how mad Papa would be if I went against him. Woody and I would have to find someplace else to go or face living in the root cellar. Maybe we could move over to the Triple S. We could take care of the station until Sam gets paroled for good behavior. We can clean wind-shields and pump gas, and E. J. knows how to change fan belts and operate the cash register. If Papa can calm himself down, we could go over to Lilyfield and have supper with him sometimes. But not on Sunday. Not the day Grampa Gus usually comes.

The more I think about this, even if I wanted to, helping Sam is sort of a moot point. No matter how hard I stick up for him, my testimony won't do much good. If His Honor believes Sam murdered Mama, and the sheriff supports him, our new uncle is going to go away for a long, long time, no matter what I or anybody else has to say. Still, doing the right thing even if you think the outcome will be bad is important. Mama taught me that.

Making up my mind, I tell Curry, "I will speak up for Sam under one condition."

"What's that?" he asks.

"That it's just me who testifies for him. I don't want Woody gettin' mixed up in all this. She's very delicate and I'm worried that she might never start talking again if something else bad happens."

It has been 363 days of not hearing her say, "Good mornin', pea. Are those flapjacks and bacon I smell?" Three hundred sixty-three nights of not hearing her say with a yawn and a scratch, "Don't let the bedbugs bite."

Curry says, "I'm not sure that will be possible, Shen. I think Woody knows something important that might help Sam."

I know she's an eyewitness to what happened to

Mama, but I can't figure out how he knows. "Why do you suspect that? Is there something you aren't tellin' us?" Curry just keeps on driving with his elbow out the window like I haven't said a word. I can see why him and Sam are friends. Question dodgers—that's what they are.

As we pass by the Triple S, my eyes get hot when I think of the fix Sam is in. The light above the office is flickering off and on. The bulbs need replacing. Only Sam is tall enough. Wrigley is sitting out on the station porch like he's waiting for his owner to show up. First thing in the morning, I'll get over here and feed him the way Sam asked me to. It's the least I can do for my own family member who is about to be sent to prison, maybe the electric chair.

Curry turns off the two-lane and onto Lee Road. When we're at the beginning of Lilyfield, he switches off the car lights and drifts to the shoulder. The yellow glow of the turned-down radio is reflecting off his face. I've never met anybody so dark skinned who wasn't a Negro. Come to think of it, I've never met anybody who is Italian. His complexion is deeper than Sam's. Despite the impatience I'm feeling towards him, I want to place my hand on Curry's whiskers the same way I used to with Papa. Rub my palm across his chin and call him Capricornis, after the goat constellation.

"Do you think my father and grandfather truly believe that Sam murdered Mama, or is something else goin' on here?" I ask. Curry gives me an admiring glance before he turns his face back into a blank canvas. I have finally figured out what it is about all this that's getting under my skin. My mother always told me—timing is everything and there are no coincidences. That everything happens for a reason. "You know what I think?"

Curry swings his arm up to rest on the seat behind my head and when he does I can smell his manly aftershave. It's not English Leather. It's something spicy. "I have a feeling you're about to tell me."

"Well, I think it's possible that Sam is gettin' framed by my family." I saw this on another TV show once. This man killed his wife so he could get all her money. He cut the brakes on her car and made it look like an accident and tried to blame her death on this poor auto mechanic, just like our Sam. But Papa and Grandpa don't need money. The Carmody family is loaded, so that part doesn't really fit.

"Whatta ya mean *framed*?" E. J. asks.

Curry says, "What Shenny means is, she thinks that her father and grandfather might be trying to take suspicion off themselves and put it on Sam instead. Right, Shenny?"

"I . . . I don't . . ." I hadn't really thought it through all the way, but now that Curry has fleshed it out, it's beginning to make diabolical sense. "Do *you* think Papa and Grampa are framin' Sam?"

"Why do you think they'd do that?" Curry asks in an I-know-something-you-don't-know way. He's got this very mysterious quality about him. The same one Sam has. They must teach it at the police academy up in Decatur.

"I don't know why they'd try to frame him. All I know is it's a bit coincidental that Mama is about to be declared dead at the same time my father is thinkin' about asking Abigail Hawkins to marry him. Did you know that he was?"

"Accordin' to Remmy Hawkins," E. J. says, "His Honor's gonna propose to her on Saturday night."

"That's right," I say, trying to think it through. "So . . . maybe Papa is blaming Sam so he can marry that horse-faced woman without everybody wondering at the wedding what would happen if his real wife shows up one day. I mean, His Honor could just go ahead and declare Mama dead, it's been almost a year, but havin' Sam to blame for her murder really closes the book on the subject."

That sounds too sinister, even for my grandfather. His name hasn't come up, but I know that old devil would think up something dastardly like this and make my father go along with it. I rub my itchy eyes, and say, "I really don't know what to believe anymore. It's all so awful and such a jumble and . . . can't you please tell me what you know?"

"I wish I could but . . ." Curry moves his hand from the cloth car seat to the back of my head. He strokes my hair. He seems more like a daddy now than a cop. I wonder if Curry has any papooses. "Tomorrow morning," he says. "Be right at this spot at nine o'clock and all your questions will be answered."

"But—"

"Listen to me carefully." Curry lets his hand slip

from my head down to my shoulder. "I want you to promise me to get Woody and go somewhere safe right away. Stay the night at Beezy's or—"

"You can come to our place," E. J. offers eagerly. He likes to cuddle with Woody. "It's closer."

"But . . . why can't we just sleep up in the fort?" I ask. My twin feels best up there and I do, too.

"You need to do what I ask, Shenny," Curry says, serious as can be. "It's important. Do you trust me?"

He seems concerned about Woody and me and that feels nice, so I say, "Yeah, all right."

"Promise?" Curry asks.

I make an *X* over my heart and nudge E. J. with my hip. He gets out of the car, but I don't follow. For better or for worse, I have decided to put all my eggs into Curry's basket. I lean into him and say, "I'm not sure I'm doing the right thing here, but I can tell you mean well."

Curry gives me a pat on the head. "Give my regards to Woody. Stay safe." Then he adds on under his breath, "For all our sakes."

When he takes off down Lee Road, Beezy's rattling old Pontiac gives off a backfire.

E. J. and I are standing by the side of the road, watching the one taillight disappear into the thick darkness. He says, "Pididdle," and then, "You think he's tellin' the truth?"

"How am I supposed to know?" I'm extra crabby 'cause I'm hungry. I pull our dinner out of the drugstore sack. I must've sat on it in the car. The egg salad sandwiches Vera made us look like how I feel. Smooshed.

"I got my doubts about him," E. J. says. "I'm sure you thought of this already, being smart like ya are, but how did Curry know to come down here two weeks ago to help Sam out of trouble when he just got arrested a few hours ago?"

Boy, I really *have* been underestimating our sidekick. I don't want him to know this idea never occurred to me, so I just say the first thing I can think of. "Maybe he's got ESP like the swami at the carnival." Now I don't trust Curry again. Something's rotten in Denmark.

"Well," E. J. says, hiking up his too-big jeans. "Gotta go. You know how mothers get when you're not home when ya say you're gonna be."

One of the Calhouns' hounds starts baying on the other side of the creek like he heard E. J. and knows just how I'm feeling.

"Geeze, Shen . . . ," E. J. says, trying to take the foot out of his mouth. Again.

"Forget it." I'm looking towards the big oak that's easy to spot even from the road, so he does, too. Rays of candlelight are coming out from between the fort's broad boards. That means Woody's praying in front of her Saint Jude coffee can altar. I'm so much later than I told her I'd be. She's probably saying Hail Marys for my immediate return.

Trying to get me to laugh, E. J. points and says, "Hark! What light through yonder window breaks?" He makes it sound not Elizabethan at all. *Yonder* does not have that many *o*'s. "You know I love her with my whole heart and soul, right?" he adds on real soulfully.

Even though I'm planning to tell the truth about Sam on the witness stand, he will still be incarcerated because what the Carmodys want the Carmodys get. After the trial, my family will disown me. And Beezy will probably get so mad at Papa and Grampa for being so mean to her boy that she won't want to have anything to do with her new almost grandbabies. Woody will be all the flesh and blood that I'll have left. I'm not so eager to share her with E. J. I tell him, "If you start goin' on about how she's the sun and the moon is envious, I'll hit you over the head with this flashlight, drag you into the woods, and let the wolves have at ya."

Backing towards the trail that will take him home, he says, "Hurry, go get her the way Curry told you to. I'll be waitin' for y'all on the porch. I'll have a bowl of berries ready." And then, out of the trees that he disappeared into comes, "How many times do I got to tell you, there's no wolves around here?"

"I wouldn't be too sure about that," I say into the night. I know of at least one big bad one.

Through the trees, I can see the front porch light shining on Grampa's black truck.

Chapter Twenty-eight

I'm not exaggerating, Woody is drooling happy to see me.

Ivory, too. I give my sister both of the egg salad sandwiches as an apology for being late and she feeds the crusts to the dog.

Getting next to her on the fort floor, I rip open one of the bags of crackers that I've been stealing out of the pantry and say, "You're not goin' to believe what I found out." I've given some thought to what I'll tell her. Not everything all at once. I'm going to start off with the good stuff. My sister is not decrepit, but sometimes that's how I think of her. Like an old-fashioned gown that's been sitting in Gramma's attic trunk too long. If I'm not careful in the way I handle her, she could fray in my hands.

I lace her fingers in mine. "Now, take it easy, all

right? I'm warnin' you, this is big happy news." I wish I could go slow and tell her every detail about what happened since I left her, but I got to be short and sweet. I'll fill her in on the specifics later. We're running out of time right now. "Don't start hoopin' or hollerin'." I tilt my head towards the house. "We don't want them to hear us." Woody cocks her head the other way and so does Ivory. "All right then," I say, swallowing in the biggest breath I can. "Vera told me at the drugstore tonight that Sam . . . our Sam . . . he's not just our excellent friend . . . he's . . . are you ready?"

She nods with a lot of enthusiasm.

"Sam is . . . our uncle!"

It takes her a second to get what I'm saying, but when she does, it's like she hit Bingo! I knew she wouldn't doubt me for a second. I'm her twin. Woody jumps up and spins in glee. Happy flaps around the fort!

"Isn't that great?" More flapping. "Okay, okay, now settle down," I say. "I got some bad news, too. You ready?" She doesn't nod. "Curry Weaver told me that Papa went down to the sheriff's office and brought along Mama's diary and the watch Sam gave her. He's tellin' Sheriff Nash to charge Sam with murdering her."

Just like the good news I delivered, it takes a second for this to sink in, and when it does Woody slaps the fort floor over and over. Attacks her hair. Gnashes her teeth. I try to get ahold of her around the waist, but it's like trying to capture lightning. "I know . . . I know, it's the worst news ever," I tell her, "but don't worry . . . we're going to help Sam, all right?" I thought she'd get upset but not this much. There's no reasoning with her when she gets like this. She shoves me down to the fort floor, reaches for her drawing pad out of the corner. Her face looks like it's on fire.

Papa, Grampa, and Uncle Blackie are in the house. I got to calm her down before she starts howling. Remembering what I brought from What Goes Around Comes Around, I grab the scarf out of my pocket and place it around her neck. She stops wildly flipping through the pages of her pad long enough to take a sniff of the chiffon. She's searching for Mama's smell. "Sorry about that," I say. "You know how Miss Artesia loves her spaghetti and meatballs."

Woody drops the drawing pad in my lap. She's found what she's been searching for, but we really don't have time for art appreciation right now. I made that promise to Curry to come back to the fort for my sister, then go over the creek stones to the Tittles', but she'll never do what I ask of her until I look through her drawings. Once she gets her mind set on something, there is no changing it. She can be a butterfly and a bulldozer, both at the same time.

I flick on my flashlight so I can see clearer what she's all fired up about. Staring back at me is the drawing that's been bothering me. The one she did of Mama with the ghosty figure. Woody must've been working on it when E. J. and I were in town. The crayon colors look bright and it's got that waxy smell. There's wavering lines coming off the previously unknown figure like fumes. I can tell now that it's a lady. She's got gray hair resting on her neck like an SOS pad. Her hands clasped in prayer.

I whistle in appreciation. And surprise. She never draws pictures of her. "That's really something. I bet Mama is *oooh*in' and *aaah*in' up in Heaven at what an excellent version of Gramma you've come up with." I brush the cracker crumbs off my legs, stand, and offer her my hand. "We can look at more pictures later, okay? We got to get goin' now. I promised Curry—"

She starts crazy slapping the floor again.

"What, Woody, what?" She points angrily down at the drawing and then puts her hands around her neck like she's choking herself. That's when it comes to me that maybe Gramma's smelling bad or making us play Holy Communion with her are not only the reasons Woody's been avoiding her.

Oh, how could I be so dumb? So careless?

Gramma must've had one of her conniptions when I wasn't around. She really can get out-of-control sometimes, especially if she's provoked by Grampa. When he was sleeping one night, she tried to crucify him to the headboard of their bed. She had the nails and the hammer and everything. I know that might seem mental to some people, but I don't really think it is. She's got a lot of sane reasons to be mad at him. No. It's not until our grandmother smears red lipstick on the palms of her hands and pretends that she's bleeding like Jesus on the cross that I think she's gone nuttier than one of her praline pies.

"Did Gramma have one of her fits and hurt you? Is that what you're tryin' to tell me?"

My sister shakes her head hard enough to make her braids whip.

"Shenny? Woody?" It's Louise calling to us from down below. I didn't hear her coming down the path from her cottage to the fort. "I know you're up there. I see the light."

"Only ignorant girls that live in bayou shanties sneak up on people and shout at 'em. What do ya want?" I say, keeping my eye on my twin. She is back to the drawing again. Circling faster and faster from the Gramma figure to the Mama figure.

"Uncle Cole wants you and Woody to come to the cottage," Lou says. "Beezy's over there. The sheriff . . . he's arrested Sam."

"We know that." I'm sure the whole town does by now. Poor Beezy.

Woody puts her hand on the back of my head and tilts it forward until I'm a few inches away from the drawing. "I'm sorry. I still don't see what you're tryin' to tell me," I say in my most soothing voice.

Exasperated, my sister throws the pad off to the side and places her hands around *my* neck this time. Squeezes with all she's got. This is the same thing she did to me that afternoon in our bedroom when we were looking at the drawing the same way we are now. "Cut it out!" I say, prying her fingers off. "I'm tryin' hard as I can to understand."

Lou shouts, but not mean-sounding, "We got food over at the cottage. I made some of that pecan fudge from your mama's recipe."

I know I should do what I promised Curry I'd do, but my stomach is begging me to fill it. The Tittles won't have anything to eat and even if they did, I wouldn't feel right taking it off them. Woody and I could just run over to the Jacksons, eat, tell Beezy that Sam is going to be okay in the long run, eat some more, and then take the stepping stones over to E. J.'s the way I told him I would. We'll stay over there until tomorrow morning when Curry promised to answer all my questions.

I beg Woody, "Please, please, let's leave the drawing be and go over to the Jacksons'. Did you notice how pleasant Lou sounds? I think she's changed back to her old Louisiana self now that Blackie's broken off with her. Bet we could get her to tell us a tale about Rex the kid-eating alligator while we chow down—doesn't that sound wonderful?"

When she frowns at me, I start singing a couple of bars of "I'll Never Say No to You" from the musical *The Unsinkable Molly Brown*. Making her feel guilty can work sometimes if I'm really trying to convince her of something.

"Uncle Cole says your grampappy is soused as a saxophone player on a Saturday night. And your uncle . . . ," Lou says, choked up. "His Honor and his brother have begun celebratin' the Founders, too."

It's good they got busy so early. Maybe they'll forget all about Woody and me.

"I made ya girls a ju-jus," Lou says, a little shy. That's the nicest present a hoodoo woman can give. It's a little sack full of fingernail clippings and ashes and feathers and toad parts. Those bags are supposed to drive off evil spirits. "I gotta get back to the cottage now. I know Beezy would love to see ya. Me, too."

I want nothing more in the world right now than to call back to Lou, "We're comin' in two shakes," but Woody has collapsed in a heap on the fort floor. Her face is glowing, radiating. There's that flu going around. The one that got Clive Minnow. "Are you feelin' sick?" I kneel down next to her and kiss her forehead, but it's not warmer than it should be.

"You out there, girls?"

Woody jerks to attention, the way she always does at the sound of her voice. I scramble over to the fort's peephole. Gramma Ruth Love is standing on the back porch of the house under the bug light. She's wearing a cream-colored nightie and her hair that she has never cut is cascading down to her waist.

"I baked a lemon meringue for you," she calls. Next to chiffon pie, that's our mouth-watering favorite and she knows it. She loves my sister and me and wants to feed us and spend time together.

Or Grampa sent her out to entice us.

He'll do that. He knows how fond we are of our grandmother most of the time. Thinking about a slice of her prize-winning pie is making my mouth water. Woody is furiously licking her lips, so maybe she's feeling the same way. Or maybe not. Because now she's doing something odd with her mouth. Twisting it, and then opening and closing it. Maybe she really *is* sick to her stomach.

"Are you going to upchuck?" I ask. "Let's get you over to the side." But it's not a retching sound that comes out of her mouth. It's a word that I swear sounds like "*Cantaboo.*"

I'm not sure that she's spoken or if it's just wishful thinking on my part.

"Twins?" Gramma calls again from the porch. "I brought all my best dolls."

Woody opens her mouth and tries again. Yes. I'm sure she's saying, "*Cantaboo.*"

If this was any other moment in time, I would be crying for joy, thanking her for coming back to me, for speaking. But this isn't any other moment in time. It's now or never. I heard the screen door open and slam shut again.

"*Cantaboo!*" My sister is telling me to *Run!* But there's only one way down from the fort and Grampa is already coming.

Gramma is calling to him from the porch, "I'm sorry, Gus. I tried to get them to come down the way you told me."

"Show yourselves!" Grampa shouts. When we don't jump right up, he changes his tone to sound something more like one of those carnival men trying to con you into playing one of their games of chance. "There's a nice surprise waitin' for you two in the parlor."

No, there isn't. Not one thing that's about to happen will be nice. Or a surprise.

This is all my fault. I should've done what Curry told me. Climbed up the fort steps and right away taken Woody over to E. J.'s.

I gotta make this right. I'm not going to let my sister suffer for my stupidity.

I hand her the flashlight, whispering, "I'm going down. Wait five minutes and then you and Ivory *cantaboo* over to the Tittles. Take the steppin' stones and not the road so Grampa can't follow you." Nobody can scoot over those rocks faster than she does. I wish I could tell her to head over to the Jacksons, but they aren't strong enough to fend off Grampa if he goes over to the cottage looking for her. And I can't do that to them. They're at the mercy of the great and invincible Guster Carmody. The Tittles are poor, but they *are* white. Grampa might think twice about charging over there in the dead of night. But even if he does, E. J. will hear him coming with a hunter's ears. He'll keep his true love safe. "Do you understand, pea?"

Woody shakes her head, but she does.

I take her hands in mine and say, "I had a visit with Curry Weaver tonight and you know what he said? He told me that you're the only one in the whole world that can help Sam because you're an eyewitness to what happened to Mama. That means you're a very important person. We've got to keep you out of harm's way. You don't want to let Sam down, do you? You don't want your new uncle to have to work on a chain gang, do you?"

"Get your twin butts down here!" Grampa can't be more than ten paces away.

Woody lays her head on my chest. Ivory sets a paw high on my thigh.

"One more thing," I say, petting them both. "You need to meet Curry out on the road in front of the house tomorrow morning at nine o'clock. He's got some news for us." My sister's warm breath is coming fast onto my neck. She knows what's bound to happen to me once I leave the fort. "Oh, c'mon now. It's not the end of the world. Shoot. I can handle the root cellar with one hand tied behind my back. There's those delicious strawberry preserves down there. I could eat all those up and wouldn't you be jealous."

I manage to get a teensy smile out of her.

"Sum bitch," Grampa says, from right below us. "You girls make me send Ruth Love up after ya, I ain't gonna be happy."

"I'll see you soon," I tell Woody. "Go straight to E. J.'s. And keep your eyes peeled." Then I call in my most congenial voice, "I'm comin' right down, Grampa. Golly, I'm so, so sorry. I must've dozed off. Didn't hear you."

When I lift the fort hatch, Woody whimpers, whispers, *"Hushacat."*

"Amen," I say, even though I don't believe for one second that everything'll be all right no matter how bad it looks at the present time. And neither does Saint Jude. Over my sister's shoulder, I can see the plastic statue of the granter of hope for the hopeless. He's lying face-down on the rusty coffee can altar.

Chapter Twenty-nine

My arm may be broken.

Grampa practically ripped it out of its socket when I came down out of the fort. "Smile!" he shouted, so he would know which twin I was.

The lights are down low in the kitchen. Just the one above the stove top and the brass lamp on the counter are lit. A half-empty bottle of Maker's is standing in the middle of the round kitchen table. The Carmody men have been interrogating me. Gramma has wandered off somewhere.

Brave Beezy came pounding plaintively at the door a little while ago. "I know what you're tryin' to do to my boy, Gus, and ya ain't gonna get away with it. Bring me those girls. Show me my babies." Her cries were no more important to them than the owl hooting in the backyard tree.

Grampa's wearing brown trousers and a tan sport shirt stretched across his belly. Below the pocket is a speck of barbeque sauce, or it could be my blood. His crew cut is buzzed down to his sunburned skull, his hands are tantrum red and within reach of his double-barrel shotgun. The usual Lucky Strike cigarette is stuck in the corner of his mouth, so wisps of smoke are hanging over us.

Papa leans forward in his chair and says, "I'm only going to ask you one more time, Shenandoah. Where is Jane Woodrow?"

I can't hardly talk because my lip is so swollen. "I already told you, sir, I . . . I don't know. I wish I did."

Bare-chested Blackie raises his hand again, but Grampa says, "Don't mark up her face anymore. We got the festivities to think of." He pours himself a couple of fingers out of the bottle. "What difference does it make where Janie is, anyhoo? Now that she's admitted it's her we saw that night in the fort even if she could talk, who'd believe her? All that flappin' and eye blinkin'. Anybody can see the girl's got bats in the belfry." He downs the whiskey and wipes his lips with the back of his hand. "We can look for her later. When we find her, Shenny will help us impress upon her twin the importance of keepin' her mouth shut, won't ya, honey?"

"I sure will, Grampa," I say. If they knew it was me that promised my father to keep quiet and not Woody . . . I can't think what they'd do to me.

Uncle Blackie says, "Gus is right." His sons have always called their father Gus because he doesn't like to be called Daddy or Papa. He thinks it's sissy. "We'll go lookin' for Janie later. I've been hankering for a game of hide-'n'-seek," he says, giving me a playful smile.

"Speakin' of mental cases, where's that woman gone off to? Ruth Love, get in here," Grampa leans back and bellows. "Bring me a piece of that pie."

The lemon meringue is setting on the kitchen counter not a foot away from him, right below the radio, which is playing something low and bluesy. The three of them are so drunk, they're swaying to the drumbeat and don't even know it.

Grampa burps and says, "Time to get to the business at hand. Go ahead, Wally." He doesn't respect him, but he knows that my first-in-his-law-school-class father is far more skilled than a horse farrier or a land baron at posing probing questions.

Papa rolls up the sleeves of his wrinkled white shirt and says to me, "Remmy Hawkins told me that he saw you and your sister over at the Triple S the other day visiting with Sam Moody. Is that true?"

"I . . . I've been meaning to tell you about that, sir. Woody . . . I mean Jane Woodrow . . . ran over there and I went to fetch her. I know how much you don't like Sam Moody, Your Honor. Me neither. I despise that man."

"You're lying," Papa says. "I know Mother had been visiting with Moody on Tuesdays and that you girls went along with her in the rowboat. Maybe that's why your sister ran off to the Triple S. Do you think that could be why, Shenandoah?" He asks that like he really does wonder why his wife sought comfort with another man and why his children liked spending time with him, too.

"That's not true," I say. "I think you got wrong information, Your Honor."

"No, I didn't." Grampa and Uncle Blackie are smirking at me from across the table. Papa says, "I dropped a cuff link . . . I found your mother's diary hidden beneath the bedroom floor. Did you know that she kept one?"

I lower my eyes, not able to stand the pain that I'm seeing in his.

"Of course, you knew," Papa says, so disappointed. "That's what you were doing the other day up in my room, wasn't it? Looking for her diary?"

"No . . . I . . ." His Honor holds up his hand in a stop, just stop, I-can't-take-anymore-of-your-lies way. Sadness is tugging at the skin around his eyes, his mouth. He truly doesn't understand. He bought all Mama's clothes. Never let her out of his sight. Held her so tight.

Seeing him so dejected makes me want to brush the lock of hair that's fallen onto his forehead back where it belongs. To kiss his tears away. How devastated Papa's going to be when I testify at his trial. "Sam Moody did not murder my mother," I'll tell the court. "He couldn't have. I was over at his place that night and he was there and not in the clearing behind our house where my mother was last seen alive. I don't know why, but my father is lying, trying to make Sam seem guilty when he isn't." The family attorney, Bobby Rudd, will jump up and protest, but it'll be too late. I will have done irreparable damage to my father. No matter what I told Curry earlier, I can feel my feet growing cold. I don't think I can go through with it. As wrong as it would be to let Sam take the blame for something he didn't do—I can't betray my father. This little man, no matter what awful things he's done, this runt of the litter is my papa.

"Pay attention." Grampa taps the back of my head, hard. "Sam Moody's been arrested for murderin' your mother in the first degree."

He was trying to catch me off guard, but I'm too practiced to let him. I feign shock and make myself say what he expects to hear. "He . . . he . . . that nigger killed Mama?"

Grampa smiles, showing teeth that are as beautiful and bright as Sam's, and just for a moment in all that radiance, I can imagine how Beezy let herself fall in love with the richest boy in the county all those years ago.

"Shenandoah." Papa isn't sad-sounding anymore. He talks to me in the same judgmental voice that he would a prisoner that's just been found guilty in his courtroom. "You've done a bad thing. Do you understand that?"

"Yes, Your Honor, I do. And . . . I'm begging for mercy. I should've told you that Mama was going over to visit with Sam Moody at the Triple S. I realize that now."

"You need to make things right."

"Yes, sir. I will do anything I can."

"When . . . when the sheriff questions you in this matter I want you to tell him how your mother was so kind." Papa looks at Grampa for his approval. "And how she was going over to the gas station to help Moody out of the goodness of her heart. And . . . how you heard him threaten to kill her when she shunned his advances and—"

"Cuckold," Grampa barks out.

Blackie sneers and says, "Your woman was steppin' out with your own father's bastard. Ya pussy."

They will call each other names into the night. Grampa and Blackie ganging up on Papa.

When my father drops his head into his hands and starts bawling, Grampa Gus says, so repulsed, "For Chrissakes. No wonder your wife went lookin' for some *real* male companionship."

"Go ahead and tell Shenny the good news, why don't you," Blackie says slyly to his little brother. "Go on, Wally."

"I have to get remarried," Papa says. "To . . . Abigail Hawkins."

Even though I'm not supposed to ask questions in these interrogation sessions, I can't help myself. "You *have* to get married to her?"

Grampa snorts out, "He damn well does. 'Bout time he made up to all of us for the years of trouble he caused marryin' that Northern bitch."

When he mentions Mama, I start to cry along with my father and it makes my lip bleed harder.

"Awww . . . let me help you with that," my uncle says. He steps over to the freezer and removes a bag of peas. All I can think of is Woody. I hope she made it to the other side of the creek into the loving arms of E. J. and isn't wandering around in the woods, not sure what she should do next. "Here you go." Blackie sits back down and places the cold bag against my mouth, presses down too hard.

"We'll be heading over to the carnival tomorrow evenin'," Grampa says, taking a long draw and blowing the most perfect smoke ring. "I bet you're excited, Shenny. Ya always have loved that freak show."

I reply exactly how he expects me to. "I'm more excited than a banty rooster in a henhouse, Grampa."

"Thatta girl," he says, phlegmy. "Now get me a fresh bottle of bourbon from the dinin' room cabinet and don't forget a glass for yourself."

Grampa and Blackie like to get Woody and me inebriated. They think that's *hardy har har* funny.

"You heard your grandfather," Blackie says, tipping my chair backwards until I have no choice but to do what he asks.

The lights that hang above the pictures of past Carmodys are the only illumination in the dining room. Hiram Carmody. Elsie Carmody. All of them. These black-and-white people dotting our walls are the ones to blame for creating a line of men so mean that they think nothing of framing an innocent man for murder or getting a kid drunk on whiskey or treating women like . . . I'm going to run out the front door. Make a break for it. Join up with E. J. and Woody over at the Tittles'. I take a step towards the foyer.

"Gotcha! Gotcha! Gotcha!" my uncle says, sneaking up behind me.

When I jump and turn to fend him off, something in the corner of the room catches my eye. Behind the potted plant, I can see my grandmother peeking out from the bushy leaves in her creamy nightie. She's been eavesdropping on their manly conversation. I step in front of the highboy so Blackie can't see his mother hiding. The open chest door is now perfectly covering her up. If Gramma gets found, she'll be in as much trouble as me.

"Don't forget your glass," Blackie says. He smells of some musky scent I don't recognize. "Looked to me like you were headin' towards the front door. You weren't thinking of goin' for a stroll, were you? Why, the fun's just begun." He pinches the flesh under my arm and leads me back to the rest of them.

Papa and Grampa have taken their shirts off. They're comparing muscles. My father doesn't have any.

"Sit back down, Shenandoah," Grampa says. When I do, it's to the sound of a long pass of gas. He's put his whoopee cushion beneath the kitchen chair pad. He and Blackie burst into cackles.

"Sounds like you need some of them Rolaids ya like so much," my uncle laughs out. "Say 'excuse me,' Shen."

"Excuse me."

He slides the empty shot glass down in front of me and fills it over the brim. "Let's toast Founders Weekend. And the weddin'."

I only want to pretend to take a sip, but Blackie fingers the bottom of the glass, tips it until I can feel the bourbon burning in my mouth and down my throat. I look over at Papa and plead with my eyes: *Please. I need you to come to my rescue. To scoop me up in your arms and take me someplace safe.*

Blackie refills my shot glass. "C'mon, drink up. You're way behind," he says, poking me in the ribs.

A back porch step creaks. Grampa Gus reaches for his shotgun and shouts, "Who's out there?"

It might be Woody not able to leave me behind. I open my mouth, ready to shout, *"Cantaboo! Cantaboo! Run! Run!"* I don't care how bad they beat me.

"It's just me," Lou Jackson says, slipping through the squeaky screen door. "I heard y'all from the cottage. Stopped in to see if you needed me to cook ya up something."

Light-on-her-feet Gramma enters the kitchen from behind me and says, "That won't be necessary, Louise. I've brought pie."

Grampa and Blackie look at each other and break into raucous laughter. Barely able to speak, my grandfather says, "It ain't one of your special pies, is it, Ruth Love? Old Clive never saw that comin'," and then he smacks his hand down on the table so hard that the salt shaker tips over. That's bad luck. Superstitious Lou reaches for it and Blackie gets ahold of her. Kisses the inside of her wrist, runs his tongue up the inside of her arm with the most sickening look on his face.

Grampa grunts and says, "Likin' the dark meat must run in this family. *Hardy har har.*"

My gramma smiles, and says, "If you're through visiting with Shenandoah, I'd like to take her upstairs now, if that's all right with you, Gus."

Grampa doesn't answer. His eyes are glued to Lou, who looks pretty in a pink shift. Her toffee skin glistening.

Lou looks around and asks, "Where's Woody?"

I can't let things get stirred up again. I can't let myself get thrown into the root cellar. My twin needs me. I answer as casual as I can, "Oh, she'll be home any minute, I'm sure. She's gonna need her beauty rest. We got the Parade of Princesses early tomorrow morning. I know *Woody* is really looking forward to that. *E. J. Tittle* is real happy about that parade, too. He probably can't even *sleep over at his place* for all the excitement he's feelin'." By putting special emphasis on the words, I'm trying the only way I can think of to tell Lou where Woody is and that I want her to go check on her right away. I'm sending her a hoodoo mind message.

Grampa Gus mumbles, "Tittles? Minin' sludge." He's still eyeing Lou in a very hungry way. Uncle Blackie is looking at her like a starved dog, too.

Lou nods and says, "Well, long as there ain't nothin' ya need from me, best be gettin' back to the cottage." Ripping her arm from Blackie's grasp, she heads towards the screen door. She stops as she opens it and says boldly to me, and only me, "Just wanted to make sure you was all right."

My grandmother replies in her best belle voice, "Thank you for your concern, Louise. But as you can see, we're just as fine as fine can be," and puts her arm around me. She smells like Ben-Gay and the strong incense from church. "Aren't we, Shenny?"

"We sure are, Gramma," I lie. "Fine as a fly in July."

Lou shrugs and gives me the most helpless look. She backs out onto the porch so she can keep her eye on Blackie and Grampa.

"Damn, that's one fine-lookin' gal," Grampa says to Blackie. "Ya sure you wanna move on from that?"

Blackie says something disgusting about Lou's chest and Grampa's eyes get more desirous looking. "Nipples the size of silver dollars?" He pushes back his chair and says, "I'll arm wrestle ya for her."

"C'mon, sweetheart," Gramma says. "Let's go up to your room and leave these men to their celebrating."

She is trying to save me from Grampa's and Blackie's grunts and laughter. Their bragging strongman talk.

I wish I could do the same for my father. He looks defeated and helpless. I say what I used to when I was little and he'd tuck me into bed, "See you in my dreams," but Papa can't hear me. His head has fallen back onto the oak table. A string of spit is hanging from his lips.

Chapter Thirty

We're kneeling at the side of Woody's and my bed. My grandmother has turned off all the lights and set the Jesus Christ she keeps in her pocketbook in the center of the other statues around a white purity candle on our dressing table. She was the one who gave the Saint Jude statue to our mother, who then gave it to Woody. Gramma has plenty enough to share. Saint Christopher and Saint Teresa the Little Flower, etc. These statues are what she calls her dolls. She can spend a whole afternoon telling Woody and me the stories behind each saint's suffering and performing reenactments. The Saint Francis of Assisi play has little animal figures and Gramma uses grapes to pretend that Saint Lucy's eyes have gotten plucked out of her head the way they were. The Saint Joan of Arc story involves a burning at the stake.

Gramma has her favorite wooden rosary entwined

between her fingers. She brought a matching one for me along with The Good Old Days photo album, which is lying on top of my pillow. When we're done praying, she'll want to spend some time with the performing saints and then she'll make me look at the pictures with her. She'll go on and on. "Your grandfather. There he is. This shot was taken at one of our high school home-coming games," she'll tell me. "See all those girls swimmin' around him? How lucky I am to have landed him." I've always thought it was the complete opposite. How butt-scratching Grampa ended up with a woman of such refined tastes beats me. When she's done caressing the pictures of her husband of forty years, she'll show me some shots of Papa and Blackie being such darling boys and get teary. Gramma cut Mama out of all the snap-shots after she disappeared, saying as she snipped, "Such a nasty business. Out of sight, out of mind," so our mother's not in the album.

"Isn't it nice to have some lady time together?" she asks. She's about the same size as I am now. She used to be a taller brunette. Usually very pulled together in a fancy dress with petticoats and pearls, her gray hair snug in a bun, she looks fairy-tale witchy tonight with it going every which way. Her skin so frighteningly white. When we got up here, she dusted herself with Mama's Chant-illy powder and took from her purse the red lipstick and smeared it across her palms. This is bad. Very bad. This is the telltale sign that she is about to have a big fit. Grampa upset her downstairs.

I tell her, "I'm not feeling so good." The whiskey's

got me woozy and warm. My hurt arm is throbbing. And the overpowering stench of Ben-Gay is making my stomach shrink into a hard ball. But I can't give in to any of that. I need to get over to the Tittles' to make sure Woody made it over there. On the other hand, what kind of girl would abandon her grandmother in her time of need? No telling what she'll do if I leave her alone in this state. Once I'm safely downstairs, I could yell at Grampa as I leave through the front door, "Your wife is pitchin' a conniption," and then run away as fast as I can. That's a good plan. "I'll be right back, Gramma." I struggle to get up. "I need a breath of fresh air."

"Not just yet," she says, grabbing my shirt and pulling me back down to my knees. She is so much stronger than you'd think she'd be. She'll tell you it's the power of the Holy Spirit working inside her.

"Please . . . I—"

"You can have all the air you want when we're done here, honey. You just go ahead and suffer a bit," she says. "Jesus likes that. Remember? 'Suffer ye children'?"

"Yes, ma'am," I say. I've calmed my grandmother down before when she got like this, I can do it again. I just have to go along with her for a while until I can find an opening.

"Would you lead us in the rosary?" she says, handing me mine and gathering hers to her chest.

I bow my head. "Bless me, Father, for I have sinned—"

"That's the wrong prayer. That's the confession prayer," she says. "What's the matter with you tonight, Shenny?"

I know the prayer is not the right one. "I'm sorry. It's just that . . ." I was trying to relax her. Lull her. Confessing is one of her most favorite things to do in life. She'll stand in line at Saint Pat's Cat all afternoon, waiting to get into her favorite confessional. "Do you mind if we do this later?"

"Later?" She titters. "Where are your manners, child? We can't keep Jesus waitin'."

I lower my chin again, but I'm eyeing my window of opportunity. The gauzy white curtains are blowing inward with the faintest of breezes, the scent of pink roses lingering from the heat of the day. The trellis. That's an even better idea. Once I get her calm, I will make my way over there and climb down the way Woody always does, instead of creeping through the front foyer where they could get their hands on me.

"I can't hear you," Gramma says. "Speak up."

"I . . . I believe in God—"

"Louder," she demands. "Kiss the crucifix."

When I bring the rosary's silver cross to my mouth, His suffering body feels cool against my still-bloody lip. "I believe in God the Father almighty, Creator of heaven and earth. And in Jesus Christ, His only Son . . ."

She jerks her head up. "Why'd you stop?"

"I . . . I . . . my gosh, something really wonderful is happening. It's a miracle . . . I think the Lord is answerin' my prayers," I tell her, putting on my most awestruck voice. "He's . . . yes, I can hear Him loud and clear."

"What's He saying?" she asks, suddenly thrilled, but

then suspicious. "This could be a trick, Shenny. Are you sure it's the Lord communicating with you? It could be Lucifer. Is it a real high-pitched voice or is it deep like your grampa's?"

I pretend to listen again. "Oh, it's the Lord all right. He sounds exactly like Grampa. He's tellin' me that He loves you. He adores you. He wants you to know that you are loved for all eternity."

An enraptured blush comes to her crepe cheeks. I usually tell her at this point that Jesus wants her to take her special medicine and go lie down, but I need to take my time. I can't rush. If I do, she'll only get more wound up. Maybe if I mention her pies. That always gives her a warm glow. I remember what Grampa said downstairs about the "special" ones she made Clive and how he never saw that coming. Gramma must've come up with a new recipe to surprise our neighbor on Thursday afternoons. She's always experimenting with different fruit combinations. Yes, that should do the trick. "About your pies—"

"Is Jesus telling you that he's hungry?" she asks like a concerned hostess.

"No, he's full right now, but . . . He wants me to tell you that he is so proud of you for taking those pies over to Mr. Minnow the way you always did."

"Oh, for goodness' sakes! Jesus is playing a joke on you, Shenny. He's the one who told me to take them over there in the first place." She giggles too loud, too long. "Bless his heart, Mr. Clive is dead now, you know," she says, turning morose on a dime.

She'll miss those afternoons with him. They had developed a pleasant friendship over the years. Gramma was patient with Clive. Delivered a pie and stood over him until he ate the whole thing. They played whist sometimes, too.

"What was so special about the pies you took to Mr. Minnow?" I ask.

She grins impishly. "They had a secret ingredient."

"And what was that?"

"You promise not to tell?" She looks around like somebody might be listening in. She lowers her voice. "It's a family secret."

"I promise." It's probably nutmeg. She likes to throw in a pinch now and again.

"Well," she says, clapping her lipsticked hands together, "I tried mixin' in a few things from under the sink, but that didn't seem to work, so like always, I prayed on it. Sure enough, the Lord answered. He told me to put rat poison in the dough and knead it up good. That worked like a charm."

Poor thing. She's worse than I thought. She's suffering again from her made-up-in-her-mind stories. What the Colony doctors called delusions.

I can hear the men downstairs. They're bickering and somebody's knocked over a chair.

Trying another tactic, I say, "Well, we better finish up praying now and get back to the kitchen. You hear that? Isn't that Grampa callin' your name?"

She would usually blanch white when I mention his name, but she doesn't even hear me. She has slipped into a world of her own. Her eyes glossy, her lips wet.

I pat the bed and say, "Or maybe you'd like to lie down and rest a bit. Wouldn't that feel nice?"

"Your neighbor shouldn't oughta stuck his nose and his camera into a family matter. Then he had the nerve to tell my Gus that if he didn't pay him lots of money for the pictures he took of us that night, he'd call up the sheriff. Even after Gus paid him, Clive demanded more," she says. "Greed's a sin, you know."

"Pictures?" What is she going on about? "What pictures?"

"Jesus doesn't care for that sort of thing, Shenny," she says, prissy. "It is written in Deuteronomy: 'You must purge the evil among you.'"

"What . . . what do you mean?" I'm completely confused. Her normal delusions aren't usually this complicated. They're mostly about the Lord demanding something or one of the saints instructing her to do this and that. Perform the Stations of the Cross over and over. Chop up the grand piano with an ax.

"You have no idea what hard work that was. I had to search and search, but I found the pictures in a sea chest way down on the bottom. Gus didn't think I could, but he was proud of me when I did. I could tell." Perspiration is beading on her top lip. She smiles, but it's not a nice one. "I ripped Clive's place up good."

The day I was over at the Minnow place fetching Ivory, I had to step over a slew of photos that'd been scattered over Clive's parlor floor. The cushions ripped apart. The mantel swept clean. And the bathroom—that awful smell. Could she have . . .

"Would you like to see the pictures?" She reaches behind her and lifts The Good Old Days photo album off my pillow.

I remember the afternoon when I expressed my concern to Clive that he was spending too much money. How he told me, "Don't you worry about me, little girl. I got what you'd call a long-term investment." And he bought that new metal-detecting device and that nineteen-inch color television and that fancy camera with the long lens and new trays for his developing room. He'd been bellyaching to me about stomach pains. I thought it was just more of his usual Clive hypochondriac talk. Or the flu. But there were dead mice on his kitchen floor and I don't think they get the flu. Could Clive have been getting money from my grandfather the way Gramma just told me? Lots of money to keep quiet about some pictures he took? Did he start recently asking for more?

"Oh . . . Jesus," I utter.

"That's right, honey. Praise be to Him."

"What . . . what did Clive see you doing? What did he take a picture of that he wasn't supposed to?"

"Your mother and me." She's paging nonchalantly through the album. "I don't know what went wrong with that gal," she says, like she's talking about a recipe that didn't turn out quite the way she expected it to. "No matter how much I lectured her about her wifely duties, Evie wouldn't listen to me. You know how she could be, Shenny. You complained enough about her. So independent. So Northern. Not bending to Walter's will the way she was supposed to. Here we go." She taps her fingernail on a picture of Mama lying on the ground. Her head is resting on the grass in the clearing. The full moonlight is shining down on her white blouse with the red trim. A puddle of blood is turning her honey hair black. Gramma is standing over her. Triumphant.

The candle on the dressing table is spurting and the room is spinning and the look on my grandmother's face— I . . . I feel like I have risen and am looking down at her from above. "What did . . . what did you do?"

Bursting with pride and piousness, she says, "What was demanded of me in the Good Book. In Timothy it is written: 'I suffer not a woman to teach, nor to usurp authority over the man. For Adam was first formed, then Eve.' *Eve*, ya see? That was your mother's name. And if . . . if you add the *l* on the end . . . it's Evel. You can see what Jesus wanted me to do, can't you?" When I don't respond, she raises her voice. "Answer me!"

"I . . ."

"Did you know that your mother was planning on runnin' away from my Walter? She gave me a note. I was supposed to give it to you and Janie, but I'd never pass that garbage on."

Mama loved Gramma. Trusted her. Would have wanted to say good-bye to her.

That night.

Woody woke me, babbling, "Mama . . . Mama . . . gone." I tried ignoring her, and when she wouldn't let me, I groused, "Did ya eat too many Red Hots? You're having a bad dream. Lie back down and go to sleep." I rolled away from her, but she came after me. "Papa . . . Papa," she moaned, and that's when I heard him, too. Thrashing about in the woods, bellowing, "No . . . no. Mother . . . how could you?" At the time, I thought he meant *our* mother. That in his drunken state he was referring to her in an outraged way. Somebody else was back there with him, but I couldn't make out who and by the time I found my binoculars, I heard our father's grunting, cursing effort to get his feet situated on the fort steps and Woody could, too, and she grabbed on to my neck when he hollered up the trunk, "You mother . . . she's . . . gone. Get down here, girls."

That somebody else I saw darting around in the trees was Gramma Ruth Love. She killed my mother and Clive took a picture of her doing it, so she killed him, too.

"Evie was a wicked woman, yes, she was," Gramma says. "She was carryin' on with Sam Moody, too. Did ya know that he's Gus's illegitimate? Back when we were young, Elizabeth Moody tempted my Gus with her young flesh. Running around the house half-clothed. How could the man resist?"

Blind Beezy is out in the Jackson's cottage, grieving for the loss of her son, who is about to be prosecuted for a crime he didn't commit. Grampa knows what his wife has done. Blackie and Papa, too. They're trying to frame Sam. Blame him for Gramma's badness.

"Elizabeth Bell, she's the next one the Lord wants me to take care of. Isn't that right?" she politely asks the Jesus statue on the dressing table.

"Mama," I whisper over and over. "Mama."

"I got the note from her somewhere right back here, if you want to see it." She is ripping through some papers and cards that're in an envelope that's taped to the back cover of the album. "I'm sure finding this out comes as somewhat of a shock to you, dear, but once you read it, you'll know you're better off without her." Gramma slips a piece of folded yellow paper out of the envelope. Brings her glasses that she keeps on a gold chain around her neck up to her eyes. "Yes, this is it. Read it, please," she says, passing it to me. "Out loud."

Mama's writing, her delicate hand. I choke out:

Sweet peas,

By the time you receive this letter from your grandmother, I'll be gone. I know how much you love your father, so I can only hope that you will understand why I must leave. I can bear the slap, a shove, but you, my darlings, I'm afraid the anger he feels towards me may soon spread to you. Leaving is the only thing I can think of to stop him. We will start anew. Please, please try to understand. I'm not abandoning you. I'll be close by. Sam will bring you to me when you're ready. I'll be waiting. I love you.

Forever, Mama

I bring the note up to my nose, breathe in her hope.

"That's real sad," Gramma says, dabbing at her eyes with the edge of her creamy nightie. "You know, despite all her failings, I miss Evie sometimes. She could be real—"

"How dare you!" I haul back my hand and slap her across the mouth before she can take my mother's name in vain one more time. She tips sideways, catches her head on the sharp edge of the bedside table, and collapses onto the floor. She's bleeding from the head, the same way Mama is in the picture that Clive took of her in the clearing that night. She's not moving, her chest barely rising.

I bend down to her and cry, "Jesus also said, 'Life for life, eye for eye.'" I cannot help myself. My temper. I reach for my pillow off the bed and place it over her face, press and press until my knuckles whiten. Being the fine Southern lady that she is, my grandmother does not struggle.

Chapter Thirty-one

I thought my grandfather was holding me in his arms until my cheek brushed up against the cool badge on his chest and Andy Nash commanded, "You're comin' with me, Miss Shen."

The sheriff isn't carting me off because I killed Gramma Ruth Love. I wanted to, almost did, but my twin was all I could think of as I was pressing down on that pillow with all my might. Woody could not get by if I got sent away for committing murder. I had to stop, for her sake, not because I didn't want Gramma dead. I wanted to take her life the same way she took our mother's.

After I let up on the pillow, I crawled over to the window. I've got to get to Woody. That's all I was thinking. Gramma came awake when I was sliding over the sill. "You're just like your mother. Go . . . go on . . . run away the same way she tried to," she raved, waving at me with her lipsticked palms. "You won't get any further than she did."

The blood from where she cut herself on the bedside table was scalloping her forehead like a crown of thorns. The overwhelming horror of it all came over me and I lost my grip on the trellis and went tumbling down to the ground and landed hard on the grass below. I'm not sure how long I lay there before I felt the sheriff pick me up. I didn't even bother putting up a fight.

What was the use? While I was blacked out, Gramma must've hollered downstairs and told Grampa that I escaped. He must've called the sheriff, who came rushing right over. That's why I'm sitting in his county car now.

My father's oldest friend and Kappa Alpha fraternity brother, Doc Keller, is along for the ride. Him and his black bag are slouched next to Sheriff Nash in the front seat. It's after midnight. The doctor has been roused out of his bed. That's why his breath smelled like an old shoe when he patched up my arm that Grampa hurt. "It's not broken, just sprained," he told me as he wrapped the bandage from my wrist up to my elbow and back down again. "You'll be fine in a few days."

I'm in the backseat. The windows down. The doors locked. The mountain air blowing my bangs. I didn't tell the sheriff what my grandmother confessed to me about killing Mama and Clive. I'm sure he already knows. He's on my father's payroll.

"Where are ya takin' me?" I ask the back of the sheriff's head again.

He says, "We'll be there before you know it." His

eyes are studying me in his rearview mirror. "Why don't you just sit back and relax? This will all be over soon. Isn't that right, Chester?"

Doc Keller doesn't acknowledge the question. He's staring out the window. We're near the peak of the mountain. Behind us, the lights of the Founders Weekend carnival are illuminating the sky, and in front of me, the lights of Lynchburg stretch out. I know where the sheriff is taking me now. That's why Doc is coming along. He needs to add his signature to the commitment papers, which have probably already been signed by my father. He must've told them to take me to the Colony because I'm not his beautiful daughter of the stars anymore. I'm the daughter who knows that his mother killed my mother. And that my family is framing Sam Moody for that crime. What will Papa tell people? That I ran away? Yes. He will spread the word that I have always been a handful. Everyone in town will believe him. He's Walter T. Carmody, the most superior court judge in all of Rockbridge County.

That's all right. I'm getting exactly what I deserve. The search I undertook for my mother is what's caused all this. It was pride that convinced me that when I found our mama and brought her home, our lives would be restored to their previous shiny glory. If only I'd humbly accepted Mama's missing right off the bat, none of this awfulness would've happened. Sam wouldn't be in jail waiting for his trial that I will not be allowed to testify at. Beezy wouldn't be over at Mr. Cole's place crying her blind eyes out for her son. Woody would be snuggled safe up in our fort instead of hopefully hiding under the covers over at the Tittle place. And I would not be on the way to The Virginia State Colony for Epileptics and Feebleminded.

I understand why he's got to do it. Knowing what I know, my papa has no choice but to hide me away. He cannot let his mother go to jail for murdering Mama and Clive Minnow. Grampa Gus would *never* allow the Carmody name to be besmirched and Papa cannot go against him. No matter how His Honor has struggled over the years to be his own man, in the end, he has become the spitting image of his father.

It's not like he didn't warn me. Papa told me that night in the woods when he held me close and thought I was Woody, "If you *could* talk . . . tell what you saw, it would be the ruination of everything. Do you understand, sweetheart?"

I do now.

The hospital is looming at the end of the long hedge-lined driveway. A wrought-iron fence with pointy tops surrounds the property.

When we pass through the gate, the sheriff orders Doc Keller to "get out the papers."

The loud *crack* his opening bag makes is painful.

When the car comes to a halt in the circular drive, I look out the window at my new home. The three stories of ivy climbing the redbrick walls. The two turrets. From the outside, the hospital looks like a fairy-tale castle, but on the inside, I know it's more like a dungeon that smells of people who have got no way out.

The sheriff opens his door and the yellow light goes on inside the car. I can see the back of Doc Keller's bristling neck coming out of his rumpled shirt collar. "Please keep lookin' after my sister, won't you?" I lean forward and ask him. What will become of my dear, confused twin? I will not be able to braid her hair and rub almond cream on her hands when she can't sleep. Who will sing musical tunes to her?

Sheriff Andy Nash offers to help me out of the car like a real gentleman. I do not take his hand. How can he sleep at night? Bought and paid for by my father and grandfather to do their bidding. When he tries to put his arm around my shoulders, I shake him off and say, "You should be ashamed of yourself."

He smiles slightly and points to the ornate front entrance. "This way."

I look up to the starry sky one more time. It's fitting that I can see Cassiopeia so clearly tonight. She is chained to her throne for her haughtiness.

The hospital reception area is beige and well furnished. Magazines are stacked neatly on the tables. A strong, flowery spray to hide the hospital smell is lingering in the air. Nothing has changed since Papa made us come here to visit Gramma Ruth Love when she was confined for her treatments.

At the front desk, we're greeted warmly by a lady named Cindy, who has her hair in a French twist and bright pink lipstick feathering around her mouth. She's the same woman who signed us in every Saturday afternoon before we went up to Gramma's room. I recognize the watch she's got pinned to her blouse. Cindy winks at me and says, "Nice to see you again, sugar," when the doctor passes her the papers.

"Come with me, Shenny." The sheriff points to the elevator. He's got a job-well-done look on his face. He must be as relieved as my family is to get rid of me. I can't really blame him. I never have been nice to him. When the elevator arrives, Andy Nash says to me, "You go on up. There'll be a nurse. She'll take you where you need to be. The doc and I have some unfinished business to attend to." I step into the back of the car and he reaches his brown uniform arm in and presses number three, the top floor on the panel. Has the gall to say, "Good luck," as the door slides closed.

Somebody has drawn a heart on the dull elevator wall. There's a phone number, too. And a Roses-are-red-Violets-are-blue poem written in ballpoint, the last two lines smeared like somebody changed what little of their mind they had left. When the doors slide open, a girl who doesn't look all that much older than me is standing erect and waiting. She's got on a crisp white uniform, her haircut is in a pageboy and she's on the bony side. Her name tag says—Alice.

"Hello, Shenandoah," she says, taking me firmly by the arm down the long corridor. "We've been waiting for you."

The hospital floor is speckled browns. The bare walls are green, nearly the same color as Woody's eyes. Above the sound of Alice's squishy shoes, I can hear pitiful crying, and some laughing, a desperate kind.

"Here we are." Alice halts abruptly in front of one of the room doors. She will strip my clothes and put me into a gown that's as coarse as a sack. I remember how it was with my grandmother. Medicine dripping into her purple veins a drop at a time. Her begging us to untie her. Not looking at me, Alice says, "The nurses wanted me to tell you that we're all very sorry. We had no way—"

I think of the sheriff downstairs looking so pleased with himself. "You're just doin' what you're told. Same as everybody else." I know what my room will look like. A metal bed and table. One wooden chair. A nicked-up chest of drawers. No books. No mirror, so I can't break it and cut my wrists. No Woody to snuggle with at night, her heart beating steady between my shoulder blades.

Alice twists the knob and I wait until the door swings fully open before I look at my dismal future. The nurse has made a mistake. She's brought me to a room that's already occupied. "There's somebody in here," I tell her. In the dim light I can see the end of a bed and the shape of legs and feet beneath the sheets. I try to turn away, feeling like we've intruded upon the saddest of times, but Alice says, real emotional, "Go on in."

"I don't want to . . . ," I try saying, but I'm feeling too spiritless to put up a fight.

I peek my head around the room corner and can see the rest of the woman lying on the bed. Her honey hair is fanned out on a pillow. Her thin arms outstretched in welcome. The smell of peonies perfumes the air.

"Hello there, pea," she says softly. "I understand you've been looking for me."

Chapter Thirty-two

*M*ama?

I must have inherited Gramma Ruth Love's insanity. I am having a delusion the same way she does. The hospital doctors are going to electrocute my brain the same way they did hers. Thinking of those treatments makes me want to run and run, but Nurse Alice stops me with a small but firm hand.

I step closer.

It's not just Mama in this delusion. Sam is in it, too. My messed-up brain has him not sitting down in the jail after being arrested by the sheriff. His long legs are stretching out from the wooden chair next to the bed. His baseball cap is on his head and a leather book open in his lap. We could be at the Triple S, except it's Ivory, not Wrigley, sitting at his feet.

Woody is not at E. J.'s the way she's supposed to be

either. She is by our mother's side, smiling like she hasn't for months and months. Big and bold and joyous.

I ask my twin delusion, "I . . . is it . . . Mama?"

Woody nods.

"I . . . I . . ." I want to throw up.

Sam asks, "What are you waiting for?"

"Come here, honey," Mama says. "Don't be scared."

I don't care if she isn't real. I go to her side, take her hand in mine, kiss her arm that is jutting out of the hospital gown like an early spring branch. I bury my face in her hair. It smells like a garden, deeply earthy and luscious. She feels awfully warm for a dead person.

"I . . . you're . . . your life isn't over?" I ask, repeating what Papa told me. "You've not passed away?" I am still not sure. "Have you?" I might've died and gone to Heaven.

Mama pats the bed and I lie carefully down next to her. It is her, but not her. Not how I remember her anyway. She is as delicate looking as a piece of blown glass. She strokes my cheek, brushes her lips against my bandaged arm, and says, "You have been so brave. So independent."

The nurse who is still standing at the door, says, "Do you need any help getting ready, Laurie . . . I mean, Mrs. Carmody?" but then she throws her hand to her mouth and runs off. I can hear her shoes for a long time.

Sam stands and says to all of us, "I'm going downstairs to tie up a few loose ends. Take it easy on her, Shen."

"But . . . ," I say, still unsure, shaky and like I'm seeing all this through a kaleidoscope.

"I'll answer your questions soon enough. Help your mother get her things together, please. I brought some clothes." Sam points behind the door where they're hanging. It's a pale yellow blouse and pleated tan slacks, exactly the kind that Mama would like. Simple and to the point—not frilly. "I'll meet you downstairs."

A million questions are rolling around in my brain, too many to settle on just one. At the same time, I don't really care how Mama has miraculously come back to us, risen from the dead like Lazarus. I'm stroking her forehead, rubbing her velvety earlobes between my fingers, running my finger down her satiny cheek, making sure she's not an optical illusion. I even pinch myself. Satisfied, I look over Mama's shoulder and say to my sister, "This has got to be the best *boomba* of all times, right?" and then, I don't know why, I start bawling like a baby.

After time spent cuddling and using up a whole box of tissues to dry my eyes, which is exactly what my twin must've done before I got here, Woody and I help Mama out of the bed and get her dressed the way Sam told us to. She is as wiry as a coat hanger. Her new clothes just drape off her. We take turns brushing her hair, which has split ends and is not as shiny as it used to be. I butterfly kiss the nape of her neck and then Woody does, too. We spruce her up the best we can and then I say, "I have so much to tell you . . . I'm sure you've figured it out already, but the reason Woody is not tellin' you how beautiful you look like she usually would is because she can't talk anymore. She stopped after you . . . and she does some real peculiar things now, but don't worry. It's still Woody. I did my best to take care of her while you were gone, but sometimes I didn't do such a good job and I'm sorry."

Mama hugs me and so does Woody and that's all it takes. I feel like a lily blooming in our field after a long winter.

As we're leaving the room, Alice returns red-eyed and pulls me aside. She tells me, "Your mother is going to need some time. We gave her some powerful medications. We . . . we didn't know. When Doctor Keller admitted her, he told the staff that her name was Laurie Smith and that she was suffering from schizophrenia. She told us over and over again who she was, but . . . a lot of the patients in here . . . there's a woman who thinks she's Marie Antoinette."

I'm not sure that I have ever witnessed a living Act of Contrition, but that's exactly what Alice looks like when she goes to my mother's side and says, "I don't know what else to say, but I'm so very sorry, we all are. Goodbye and God bless."

Mama, being so forgiving like she is, takes Alice's hand in hers and says, "You were always sweet to me. Take care of yourself."

And then I tell the bony nurse, " 'To err is human.' " It's all I can think of to say that would make my mother feel proud of me, but my heart? It feels like a cannonball dropping to the bottom of the ocean. It has sunk in. All this time spent searching for Mama, thinking she'd been nabbed or had amnesia or ran off with the carnival, but then coming to grips with her death. I don't feel so forgiving. I don't care how repentant she looks. I want to throw Alice out of the window.

My sister and I are taking turns pushing Mama's wheelchair down the sidewalk in front of the hospital. Sam thought it might be a good idea to have her stay one more night and leave bright and early the next morning, but Mama told him, "No," and like he always has, he respected her wishes.

At the curb, the sheriff is leaning on the fender of his car. Doc Keller is in the backseat now. He's handcuffed. I am practically knocked to my knees when it comes to me that Sheriff Andy Nash is not at all what I thought he was. He has not been bought and sold by the Carmody men. I don't understand his part in all this yet, but if he was on my father's payroll, I'm pretty sure I wouldn't be pushing Mama towards the car. I'd be up in that hospital room taking my medicine.

Sheriff Nash takes off his police cap and says to Mama, "How do, ma'am."

She tilts her chin up at him. "Thanks to you, Andy, I'm doing a lot better than I have in quite some time. Without your help, your integrity . . ."

The sheriff says bashfully, "Good to have you back, Evelyn." And then, like it's all in a day's work, he sets his hat back atop his head and gets in his car.

I lean into his window and whisper to him, so my

mother can't hear me, "Ya might wanna go to Lilyfield and pick up Gramma Ruth Love. She confessed to me that she murdered Clive Minnow with one of her pies. And you already know she tried to do away with Mama, right?"

The sheriff doesn't seem real surprised when he says, "Sounds like you got out of there in the nick of time, Shenny," and then drives off. Like the Lone Ranger, I think. Only Doc Keller isn't his faithful companion, Tonto. He's a bad man who I'm certain will get exactly what he has coming to him, if Andy Nash has any say in the matter.

Sam picks Mama up in his arms and carries her to Beezy's beat-up brown Pontiac that's parked nearby. He says, "Evie, this is the man I've been telling you about."

Curry, who I have completely forgotten about, scrambles out to open the back door. My mother says, "I . . . thank you."

I don't know what part he played in Mama's rescue either, but he must've been heaven-sent because Sam is looking at Curry like he's an angel. I glance back up at the redbrick hospital one more time. Thinking what could've been, I throw my arms around Curry's Italian waist and say *grazie* over and over again until he pulls me off him. "You're welcome, Shenny," he says. "What say we blow this pop stand?"

I stare into his mysterious eyes. "Ya know, I have absolutely no idea what that means, but if it's something like let's hightail it out of here . . . I got your backside."

Chapter Thirty-three

We're on our way home the same way we came.

Through our beautiful Blue Ridge Mountains. Well, not exactly the same way. Sam is sitting beside Curry in the front seat, Ivory between them. Mama is wedged between Woody and me in the back. We each have one of her hands and I think that I will never let go of her again. I understand now how Papa couldn't bear letting her out of his sight.

The mood in the car is being set by the sultry night and the song that Sam found on the radio. It's not a show tune. It's something sad, but sweet. Hoagy Carmichael? Yes, it's "Stardust." That makes me think of my father again.

I have no idea how long Mama's been up at the Colony and why she never wrote or called to say, "Come get me," and how . . . well, just everything. I big-wink at my sister. "You ready to explain now, *Uncle* Sam?"

Woody's laugh reminds me of our barn door during a storm. It really does sound rusty.

Sam turns and grins at the Carmody girls with those beautiful headstone teeth that he inherited from my grandfather. He must be almost as happy as me and Woody to get Mama back. "If that's all right with your mother."

"Mama?" I ask. I am still having a very hard time believing she is here by my side and not in the ground buried six feet deep.

"Maybe just a few questions. It's so late." She puts an arm around each of her girls. "It's past your bedtime."

I never thought I would welcome those words. She'll probably make us take a bath when we get home, too. And say our prayers and brush our teeth and gargle.

I ask, "Who . . . what . . . ?" Starting down this road . . . it's like picking the right trail home when you're in unfamiliar territory. I'm completely lost.

Lieutenant Sardino shows me the way. He asked us to call him Tony, but I just can't. He'll always be Curry Weaver to me. "I guess the best place to start the story is when Sam called me a year ago and told me about your mother's disappearance."

"Tony and I go way back. He's the best investigator I know," Sam says. "He introduced me to Johnny." As always, his Adam's apple goes wobbly at the mention of his dead partner's name.

I ask Curry, real put out, "Why didn't you just tell me that Mama was alive at Miss Artesia's shop tonight? Why'd you lead me on like that? And you, Sam . . . you could've said something when E. J. and I saw you in the back of the sheriff's car in front of Slidell's. Told us you weren't really arrested."

"I'm sorry," Curry says, and really sounds so. "We wanted to tell you sooner, but Sam, the sheriff, and I decided that we had to let this all play out."

Sam pipes in with, "We couldn't take the chance that you might let something slip to your father, grandfather, or uncle. If they found out before we had the chance to . . . we couldn't risk something happening to your mother before we were able to free her."

"Besides," Curry says, looking at me in the rearview mirror, "if I had told you in the secondhand shop that your mother was alive and up at the Colony, would you have believed me?"

I don't admit it, but he and I both know that I wouldn't have. I barely believed that he was an undercover cop and not a hobo. That's also probably why the sheriff didn't tell me on the ride to the hospital that he wasn't taking me to be committed, but to see Mama. I wouldn't have bought that neither.

Somewhat mollified, I say to him, "Let's start over, all right? When Sam first called and told you that Mama had vanished, did you think she'd been kidnapped or fell down and hit her head or . . . ?" I don't say, "Or ran off to join the carnival," because that seems really imbecilic now.

"When Sam filled me in about your mother's plan to leave your father and hide nearby until he could bring you girls to her, I didn't take much of what he said seri-

ously," Curry says. "I thought your mother had not followed through because . . . well, people change their
minds. Especially scared ones. Not knowing her, I
thought that once she was safe from your father, Evie
had just kept running."

He really *doesn't* know her.

"What changed your mind?" I ask Curry, thinking
how hard I tried and how bad I failed at finding her. It
must've been triple difficult for this stranger to piece
together her vanishment. Like one of those cruel one-
color jigsaw puzzles they sell down at the drugstore.

"Many phone calls later, the more Sam talked about
her, the more your mother didn't seem like the type of
woman who would escape a bad situation with the intent
of reuniting with her children and not stick to the plan.
Her body never turned up either. That left me with a
couple of other options, none that I could act on long
distance. So I decided to take advantage of the two
weeks' vacation I had coming."

I say to Sam, "You acted like you hadn't done one
thing to find Mama, you faker." All those visits to the
Triple S asking for his help and him deflecting me. My
nose is pushed out of joint.

"I did what I could," Sam says. "I checked in at local
hospitals where I knew folks and spent time driving the
backroads. I also spent quite a bit of time trying to sort
things out with Sheriff Nash. If you take some time to
think about it, Shen . . . I couldn't tell you what I was up
to. I didn't want to let you and Woody down if the news
wasn't good. The sheriff agreed with me."

Like I normally do upon hearing Andy Nash's name, I say, irritable, "That man can't add one plus one and come up with . . ." But then I remember how he helped save Mama. And me. It's going to take some time to start thinking of the sheriff not as a dunce, but more like Albert Einstein. I've been so overwhelmed with finding Mama alive, I forgot all about what I leaned in the window and told the sheriff before we left the hospital. I don't know if the timing is right, but I can't keep it inside me anymore and Mama deserves to know and not have it sprung on her by somebody else who does not love her. "Gramma killed Clive Minnow!"

My mother gasps and says, "No."

"Yes, she did, Mama. She got me up in our bedroom and she had one of her fits and told me she did in Clive with one of her pies."

Curry says, real coplike, "The sheriff knew Clive had been murdered, but not by who. The medical examiner found—"

"Rat poison," I say. Remembering how proud she was when she told me she kneaded it to the crust on the advice of the Lord makes me shiver.

"That's right," Curry says.

Sam asks, "Did your grandmother tell you why she murdered Clive?"

"He was blackmailing Grampa for a lot of money. Clive must've been looking for UFOs the night of the carnival but heard Mama and Gramma arguing out in the clearing and he took pictures of them."

Mama stifles a cry when she wraps her arms around

me and gives me the most breathtaking hug. She knows the same way I do what it feels like to be at the mercy of my grandmother. Once she relaxes her grip, I say, "Something's been botherin' me."

"What's that?" Sam asks.

"How did the sheriff know to come lookin' for me under my bedroom window after I got away from Gramma?"

My sister tries to speak. It comes out as gobbledygook, so Sam says, "I think Woody's trying to tell you that Louise Jackson told the sheriff and me that you were in trouble."

"Lou?" I ask my twin.

She nods.

"Really?" I think of the last time I saw our housekeeper. In the kitchen. Drunk Grampa and Uncle Blackie salivating over her.

Sam says, "Lou came running to the sheriff's office crying about how your father, grandfather, and uncle were being, and I quote, 'Wicked. Something real dangerous is happenin' up at that house. I throwed the bones. Sprinkled red pepper powder. Now y'all better go get that girl outta there or I'll find me a gun and do it myself. Woody's over at the Tittle place, you get her, too. Those pups need to be in the same pod.'"

So Lou did get the hoodoo mind message I was sending her! Once again, I am astounded by how much smarter some folks are than they appear.

"Obviously, rescuing your mother in the middle of the night was not part of our plan," Curry says, "We'd intended to take you and Woody up to the hospital to reunite with her a few hours from now, but after Lou showed up frightened for your safety, we had no other choice but to act. So Sam and I left to get Woody from the Tittle place and the sheriff hurried over to Lilyfield. Lou Jackson told us that you were in the kitchen with your father and grandfather, so Andy went around to the back of the house. He found you lying unconscious."

"Why'd he have Doc Keller with him?" I ask.

"We needed Keller to check Evie out of the hospital," Curry says. "I have no jurisdiction there and the sheriff doesn't either."

Mama is biting her fingernails. "I think that's enough questions for tonight."

I want to ask how she got from the clearing after Gramma tried to murder her all the way up to the Colony. "But what about . . ."

"Shenny, hush." She nods towards Woody. My twin is doing her SOS eye blinking and twitching like crazy. Finding our lost-then-dead-and-then-found mother . . . almost losing me . . . my grandmother murdering Clive Minnow . . . it's all too much for her. I reach across Mama's lap and take Woody's other hand into mine and shut my mouth.

We listen to the hum of the car engine and the tires gripping the road. The radio has changed to something that sounds like a love song. My mother is staring straight ahead. Every once in a while, a car comes from the other direction and lights up her face in its headlights. Her cheekbones look like diving boards jutting over two empty pools. They must not have given her much to drink up in the hospital. I didn't notice earlier how her once-lush lips are chapped and split.

We have come to the crest of the mountain where we can see down into The Big Valley.

"I haven't been off the hospital grounds in such a long time," Mama says. "Everything seems bigger and smells so much better than I remember." She breathes in the fresh pine air, lets out a sigh. "I missed Christmas with you."

Thinking back on how Woody and I trimmed the tree and I sang, "Oh, Come All Ye Faithful," makes my temper flair and I cannot hold back from saying, "I wish Gramma was as dead as she tried to make you. That's the birthday wish I'm making this year." I will never tell my mother that I almost made that come true. She wouldn't like that. She is the biggest turn-your-cheek-the-other-way person I have ever met.

Mama looks down at now sleeping Woody and whispers, "Your grandmother doesn't understand the wrongness of what she did. In her mind, she was doing what was right. Defending her way of life . . . her family. She's sick. Your heart has to go out to her, Shen."

No, it does not. My heart is not going anywhere near her. Ever. I will never forgive that old woman.

When we come to the part in the road where I can see Lexington spread out beneath us, I think of Papa and Grampa and Uncle Blackie at the house. I worriedly ask, "Are we going back to Lilyfield?"

Mama says, "No, baby. Sam has made other arrangements for us. We'll be staying with Beezy for . . . I'm not sure how long."

That would probably be for the best. For a little while anyway. But in the long run, Lilyfield is our home. It's all we got. I don't tell her that. Mama looks completely drained and I'm feeling the same way, so just like my twin, I lay my head on her shoulder. She kisses me on the forehead and whispers, "Tomorrow is a river," like I knew she would. I honestly cannot imagine how all my dreams can come true, but just for the littlest bit of time, I so desperately need to.

Chapter Thirty-four

The sound of sirens blaring through my dreams wakes me. And the smell of smoke.

A fire is raging, flames licking out of the roof and windows of the second most magnificent house in all of Rockbridge County.

Lilyfield is burning.

"Papa," I scream out the car window. The heat from the blaze is toasting my cheeks when Curry pulls to a stop alongside Lee Road. He must've seen the billowing clouds of smoke from the foothills and headed right over here.

Mama yells, "Shenny, wait!" but I jump out of the car. Shout into the stunned crowd that's standing helplessly by, some in their pajamas, "Did . . . did His Honor get out all right?"

"Yeah. I saw him talking to the sheriff," someone in the crowd calls back.

Once I know that Papa is alive and well, I turn back to watch the worst blaze I have ever seen. I love Lilyfield, so I'm surprised to feel only a little distraught seeing it go up, the same way you would watching somebody else's home. I know a lot of good things happened in this house, but I can't hardly remember back that far.

When Woody, Mama, Sam, and Curry come to my side, we try to find a place amongst the other folks who've arrived to watch the firemen fighting the conflagration. The trees in the front woods have already burned so there is a clear view of the house. A couple of people say when they spot her, "Is that Evelyn Carmody?" and there is also worried speculation. "How could such an awful fire get started?" Someone else in the back of the throng—Mr. Slidell from the drugstore, I recognize his high-pitched voice—says, "Has anybody seen the twins?"

I call back to him, "We're fine, Mr. Slidell," because even though he's such a crabby man, I am touched by his concern.

When E. J. hears my voice, like a homing pigeon, he flies to our sides. Following close behind him are Louise, Beezy, and a sooty-looking Mr. Cole Jackson. All three of them just about collapse when they see Woody and me and Mama. I think Mr. Cole might be in shock, the way he is shaking. "Evelyn . . . I prayed every single night for your return."

Mama says, "Oh, Cole. It's so good to see you," and gives him a hug.

"How do, ma'am." Lou steps up and introduces herself. "I heard a lot about ya. It's Friday the thirteenth. Be careful."

Lou has no way of knowing that it's the luckiest day of my mother's life.

Blind Beezy, who's standing beside Mr. Cole, is wailing and waving her arms in the air. "Evie? Evie?"

Mama reaches for her, brings Beezy's hands to her face so she can feel that it really is her. "It's . . . so good to see you," they say to each other.

Then Beezy must've heard Sam talking to one of the firemen who has just come away from the flames to get a cool drink, because she shouts out, "Sam? Sammy, is that you?"

Her boy comes over fast to pat her little back.

Beezy blubbers, "Curry came by the house to tell me what ya were tryin' to do . . . but—"

Sam says, "It's done now, Mama."

As we are standing together listening to the *snap* and *crackle* as the fire destroys our home, E. J. belts his arm around my sister's waist and pulls her close. He says to me, "I smelled the smoke and Papa told me to run over to the Calhouns' and tell them to call the fire department. I knew you wasn't up there 'cause Curry and Sam told me where ya was when they came and got Woody. I ran over the steppin' stones fast as I could, told Lou, Beezy, and Mr. Cole 'bout your trip to the hospital, then I rushed to the tree with a bucket of water, but . . . it went up so fast. I'm sorry . . . the fort is gone."

An ambulance comes careening down our driveway and behind it, two county cars. My uncle Blackie and grampa Gus are in the first car, my father in the follow-ing one. That must mean that Gramma Ruth Love got hurt in the fire and is being taken to the hospital.

When they drive past the crowd, Papa doesn't notice his wife and girls staring along with the rest of the town. His eyes are closed. As I look at his handsome profile passing me by, still, no matter what he has done to me and Woody or even Mama, no matter how much he has hurt us, I have to grip on to Woody's hand to keep my-self from chasing the car down the road, stop myself from shouting out, "I still love you, Papa. I'm sorry your house is burning down."

Chapter Thirty-five

It's Independence Day.

There was a parade and potato-sack games and some fiddle music this morning. Mama packed a picnic of pimento cheese sandwiches and yellow Jell-O, so now we're spread out with everyone else from town. By the creek, where it winds through Buffalo Park. It's so good to eat our mother's crummy cooking again, but our blanket's up against the Tittles' blanket and I confess to stealing a drumstick out of their basket. Dorry Tittle really knows how to fry. E. J. and Woody are over at the swings acting all lovesick and moony. My mama picks Baby Fay up off the blanket and cradles her in her arms. I am pretending to nap so I can listen in on her and Mrs. Tittle's hushed women voices. Mama has resisted answering my questions. She doesn't want Woody and me to be upset. Eavesdropping runs in my blood.

"I heard some of what happened from the gals at church," Mrs. Tittle says to her. "Our plan didn't go quite like we hoped, did it."

Mama stops cooing at the baby and says back, "No, it didn't."

I remember how I found her in front of the Oddities tent that night. She was getting ready to run away, that's why she looked so sad.

"I shoulda come lookin' over to your place when ya didn't show up that night," Mrs. Tittle says with a lot of regret.

I don't know what Miss Dorry means until I remember how Vera told us that night in the drugstore, "Your mama, E. J., she was gonna borrow the Calhouns' car and give Evie a ride to the bus station."

Mama says, "I'm grateful that you didn't. In the state she was in, I believe . . . I believe Ruth Love was capable of anything."

Mrs. Tittle takes that in and says, "After she pushed you down and tried to . . . choke you . . . how did you get up to the Colony?"

The baby is fussing a little so Mama brings her up to her shoulder and bounces her. "I'm not exactly sure how I got into the boat, but that's where I woke up. Blackie was rowing."

That's where the rowboat must've been all this time. Hidden real good at my uncle's place. That's why the sheriff never found it. Despite everything, I think—my father still loves Mama. He could've drowned her that night. Thrown her over the side on the way down the creek. Knowing my grandfather, I bet that's what he urged him to do. I feel proud of Papa for standing up to him.

"I was fading in and out," Mama continues, "but I remember that Walter was in the boat. Gus, too. Once we got to Blackie's place, one of them called Doc Keller. He gave me an injection and stitched the cut on the back of my head. Early the next morning, he drove me to the hospital. I vaguely remember Doc telling the admitting staff that I was a patient of his. He left orders for strong, calming medications. Barbiturates and others. They kept me in a fog."

Miss Dorry calls out to E. J.'s little sisters, "Stay outta that creek in your best clothes." They must've done what she said because she then says to Mama, "I never did care much for Chester Keller. He's got eyes like a black racer." They're quiet for a few minutes and then Mrs. Tittle asks, "And Walter agreed with all this?" With the undying love that E. J.'s mama feels towards her coughing husband, it must be so hard for her to imagine. "To keep ya locked up in the Colony like that?"

Mama says so sadly, "I want to believe Walt tried to persuade Gus to do otherwise . . . but . . ."

She knows just like I do that Papa couldn't help himself, but it must be 'til-death-do-us-part heartbreaking for my mother to admit that her husband, the man of her dreams, the father of her children, would do something so cruel. I sneak a peek over at her. Her face is crumbling. And Bootie Young is standing right at the edge of the blanket in his best overalls.

"Miz Carmody. Miz Tittle. Shen."

I sit up and smooth down my hair. "Hey, Bootie."

"Wanna get a drink?" He points over to the metal buckets filled with ice and soda pop.

I look at Mama for permission and she nods.

That handsome boy and I stay close together for the rest of the afternoon and take in the fireworks that get set off when the sun goes down. But even though it's a dream come true to hold Bootie's big, calloused hand in mine, I cannot stop thinking about my papa's soft, small one. He is out on bail, same as my uncle and grandfather. His Honor is probably watching the show from the high hill at Heritage Farm, the way we always did when we were still a family. If he is, he's smiling extra hard at the orange and green skyrockets. Those are his favorites. I will see him in court on Monday.

Chapter Thirty-six

"Excuse us. Pardon. Thank you," Sam says as he gently guides Mama, Woody, and me through the group of well-wishers that are milling outside the courthouse.

There's not going to be a trial right away, just a hearing to decide the fate of the rest of our family. Except for Gramma. She was badly burned the night of "The Lilyfield Blaze," as the Lexington *News-Gazette* dubbed it. Mama didn't want me to read the articles, but I had to. I will never be kept in the dark again about anything. The reporters wrote in great detail about how Charlie LeClair, one of the firemen at the scene, said, "I found Mrs. Ruth Love Carmody upstairs in one of the bedrooms. When I tried to remove her, she ran down the front stairs and I lost her in the smoke. I'm sure she wouldn't have survived if Mr. Gus hadn't chased after her and pulled her to safety."

And *I'm* sure the reporter got that part about Gram saving her wrong.

The newspaper also quoted Fire Chief Al Cobb: "We know the blaze started on the second floor of the house, but the source is still not clear. Our investigation will continue."

What I think happened is that Gramma was playing with her dolls, performing her Saint Joan of Arc reenactment, and the fire got away from her.

Or maybe not.

I guess what exactly occurred that night will remain a mystery until my grandmother can recover enough to tell us what happened, which more than likely will never come to pass. She has been charged with murder and attempted murder, but is not here today because she was found non compos mentis—not of sound mind and not fit for trial. She's been taken to a special hospital in Richmond for people with criminal mental disorders. I don't believe she'll be returning to normal no matter how many electrical treatments they give her this time.

When we went to visit our bandaged Gramma last week, I whispered to Woody in the hospital room, "She looks like Gram *Mummy*," because I am still furious with her. Mama didn't think that joke was so funny. She brought a small bouquet that she picked out of her new garden to the woman who tried to murder her. When I asked her why she would do such a nice thing, as I find it truly incomprehensible, Mama told me, "Mr. Mark Twain said, 'Forgiveness is the fragrance the violet sheds on the heel that has crushed it.'"

Well, I love that sentiment, I really do, but that's all it is to me. I may have inherited my mother's hair color and her green eyes, her love of words and poetry, but clearly, the ability to forgive went right over my head.

Except when it comes to my papa.

The three tall windows on each opposing wall of the courtroom are open as wide as they will go. Outside, the full-leafed trees are still. The ceiling fans are whirring like crazy, trying to pull away the heat that has got to be dripping down everybody's neck the same way it is mine.

"They're calling your name, honey," Mama says. She and Woody and I are sitting in the second row in the courtroom. My mother is not taking up much space because she is still very thin, despite Beezy making her eat chicken potpie prison-style three times a week.

On my way up to the stand, I have to pass by the table where the Carmody men are grouped with their lawyer— Bobby Rudd. My family's attorney has the most winning record in the Commonwealth. He is Grampa's age and has gotten Uncle Blackie out of scrapes lots of times. I can tell by the way that Mr. Rudd is preening in his nice suit and lavender shirt and striped tie that he is confident he's not going to have to go to trial this time neither.

My father does not look powerful like he used to when he was the one up on the bench like Judge Elmer Whitmore is today. Papa catches my eye. I recognize that repentant look. It's the same one he'd give Woody and me when he took us out of the root cellar some mornings.

Once I take my place in the witness box, Mr. Lloyd Riverton holds out the Bible and tells me, "You know how it's done, Miss Shenny." Mr. Lloyd was the bailiff in Papa's courtroom, too, so he and I are on friendly terms. "Do you swear to tell the truth, the whole truth and nothing but the truth, so help you God?"

I hope I mean it when I say, "I do." I am afraid that I might give in to my love for Papa. Run down from the witness box, climb into his lap, and set my head on his shoulder.

Mr. Will Stockton, who is the prosecuting attorney, explains, "I'm going to ask you some questions now, Shenny. I'll be as brief as I can. Can you answer truthfully?"

I know that's what I have to do. For Mama. "I can."

He asks, "After your mother's disappearance last year, did you attempt to find her?"

"Not right away."

"Why is that?" the attorney asks.

"Well . . ." I look over at my mother. "At first, I thought she'd come back and then . . . well. There's lots of reasons I didn't set off to hunt her down, but mostly, I just didn't know how to go about finding her. I'm just a kid."

The folks in the gallery laugh a little.

The attorney waits until they settle to ask, "But recently you started a search. Why was that?"

I say, trying not to look at my father, "Papa was threatening to send Woody away, so more than ever I needed to find Mama."

Mr. Stockton asks, "So you set out to find your mother and then what happened?"

"I gave up almost immediately."

"Why?"

I don't know if I can go through with this. Papa is looking at me with woeful puppy eyes.

"Shenny?" the attorney asks. "Why did you stop searching for your mother?"

I draw in a breath, fix my eyes on my mama and sister, and say, "Because my papa told me that she was dead."

Mr. Bobby Rudd shouts, "Objection!" over the mumbling and grumbling the courtroom observers are making.

Judge Whitmore says, "Overruled. You may proceed."

Mr. Stockton nods and says, "Well, we know now that your father told a lie, don't we, Shenny? We can see that your mother is alive."

All heads swivel her way. Mama doesn't acknowledge them. She's only got eyes for me.

"Did anyone else tell you that your mother was dead?" the attorney asks.

"Yes, sir. My grandmother." This is the easy part. I don't feel bad at all telling him and everybody else, "Gramma told me she killed my mother."

There is no reaction in the courtroom. This is old news.

"And did you believe your grandmother when she told you that?"

"No, sir. I thought her nerves were breaking down again. But then she showed me a picture of her standing over Mama in the clearing near our woods and my mother looked dead."

Mama isn't smiling anymore. She's holding a hankie up to her eyes.

Mr. Stockton asks, "Do you have anything else to add?"

"No, sir."

"Then you may step down."

When I go back to my seat, past their table, Papa is not scowling nor is that vein bulging in his temple the way it would be if he was mad. He gives me his I'm-sorry smile again and that is the hardest part of all. My head knows that it's wrong to forgive him, but my heart knows no such thing.

Woody gets sworn in next and when Mr. Lloyd Riverton asks her, "So help you God?" she nods.

Judge Whitmore, who is as lean as beef jerky and has the reputation of being just as tough, says to the court reporter, Maddie Gimbel, "Let the record reflect that the witness has nodded her head yes and that all further nods or shakes of the head are to be so noted." Then to Woody he says, "Please be seated." The judge knows that my sister still doesn't speak so good. Everybody does. He has thoughtfully provided Woody with a pencil and a piece of paper to write her answers if she needs to because she is an extenuating circumstance. Mama and I told Mr. Stockton that Woody's hearing is real sensitive and not to raise his voice to her under any circumstances. And to keep his questions to a bare minimum on doctor's orders.

Mr. Stockton approaches the witness box. "Did you see somebody hurt your mama the night of June the eighth, 1968, Jane Woodrow?" he asks nice and quietly. "And if so, who was it? Take your time."

My twin looks at me and then at Mama. She doesn't reach for her pencil and pad of paper. She shocks us by saying her very first regular word in over a year. "Gramma."

It is chilling.

The attorney asks, "Do you mean Mrs. Ruth Love Carmody?"

Woody nods.

"Did you see anyone else back there that same night?"

Woody lifts her finger and points first at my father, who has hunched in his chair. Then she fingers my grandfather and, finally, Uncle Blackie, who are sitting ramrod straight, unbent by what they have done.

Judge Whitmore says, "Let the record reflect that the witness has pointed to each one of the defendants."

"That's all, Jane Woodrow. Thank you. You may step down now." Mr. Stockton helps her out of the witness box.

My sister and I are allowed to stay and hear Curry Weaver, aka Lieutenant Anthony Sardino from the Decatur, Illinois, Police Department, answer the questions that I already know the answers to. I want to hear what he has to say in case I missed something.

After Curry lifts his hand off the Bible and gives all his credentials, Mr. Stockton asks him, "How is it, Detective Sardino, that you came to our fine city to investigate the disappearance of Mrs. Evelyn Carmody?"

Curry, who looks extremely intelligent in a tan suit and shirt, answers, "The disappearance of Mrs. Carmody was first brought to my attention by Mr. Sam Moody. He asked for my assistance."

"Why did Mr. Moody feel that was necessary?" the lawyer asks. "Did he have misgivings about Sheriff Andy Nash's abilities to thoroughly investigate the disappearance of Mrs. Evelyn Carmody?"

"I wouldn't say that." Curry takes a sip of water that has been provided. "Mr. Moody understood the power the Carmody family wields over the town. He felt that the sheriff was being stonewalled by them."

Bobby Rudd calls out, "Objection, Your Honor. Prejudicial."

Judge Whitmore says, "I'll allow it."

"After you arrived in town, did you establish a relationship with Sheriff Nash?" the state's attorney asks.

"Yes," Curry answers. "As a professional courtesy, I identified myself to the sheriff and we agreed to try our best to get to the bottom of things together with the help of Mr. Moody."

"Miz Carmody was gone for almost a year. What led you and the sheriff to believe that she was still alive?"

"It wasn't so much that we believed that she could be alive, but for the sake of her children . . . well, we hoped she was alive," Curry says. "Her body hadn't been found, and in these types of cases, it usually is."

"Please tell the court how you proceeded in your search for Miz Carmody."

"The sheriff and Mr. Moody suggested that I work undercover. They were concerned that my asking questions about Mrs. Carmody's disappearance . . . well, I was a stranger in town. They were afraid that might make people reticent to speak to me. And that my nosing around might get back to the Carmody family. Sam Moody suggested that I stay up at the hobo camp."

"And were you able to use this subterfuge to your advantage?" Mr. Stockton asks.

Curry smiles at Woody and me. "Yes, the camp is where I had the opportunity to meet the Carmody children. And Miss Dagmar Epps."

Over at the defendants' table, a hurried conversation is going on. Mr. Bobby Rudd is whispering something into Uncle Blackie's ear.

That doesn't stop Mr. Stockton from asking Curry, "And how did the Carmody children and Miss Epps figure in your investigation?"

"After becoming friendly with the children, I learned more about the relationship between their parents." He's talking about our trestle-sitting conversations. "Miss Shenandoah Carmody was also kind enough to answer my questions about a few other people who I suspected might have something to do with Mrs. Carmody's disappearance."

"You also mentioned meeting Miss Dagmar Epps up at the camp." The lawyer comes in closer. "What does she have to do with Miz Carmody's disappearance?"

Curry looks to the back of the room and says, "Some thing Miss Epps told me led me to believe that there was a chance Mrs. Carmody was still alive."

I crane my neck back and see E. J. standing next to Dagmar near the courtroom doors. He is holding her hand. Curry asked our mountain man to accompany her this morning.

"And what did Miss Epps tell you that led you to believe Mrs. Carmody might still be alive?" Mr. Stockton asks, not able to hide his excitement.

"Objection, Your Honor. Hearsay," Attorney Rudd calls out.

Judge Whitmore says, "This is a hearing, Bobby. I'll allow it. Go on, Detective Sardino."

"Miss Epps made me aware of the fact that Judge Carmody had the propensity to commit what she described as 'problem people' to the hospital," Curry says. "When I asked her what she meant, she told me that ten years ago she had conceived a child with Blackie Carmody and that he'd had his brother, Walter T. Carmody, arrange for her to be sent to The Virginia State Colony for Epileptics and Feebleminded. The child was aborted and a court-ordered hysterectomy was performed on Miss Epps."

The whole gallery breaks into outraged whispers and Bobby Rudd is up out of his chair so fast he knocks it over. "Objection, Your Honor! Objection!"

Judge Whitmore says, "Sit down, Bobby. You've seen the hospital records. You're makin' an ass out of yourself."

The prosecuting attorney tries to squeeze back a smile and is not successful when he asks Curry, "After hearing Miss Epps's story, is that when you realized that the Colony might be a perfect place for the Carmody family to hide Mrs. Evelyn Carmody, so she'd be unable to testify against Mrs. Ruth Love Carmody for attempted murder?"

"Yes," Curry simply says.

"It's my understanding, Detective Sardino," Judge Whitmore says, interrupting the questioning, "that you had the sheriff suggest to me that you might benefit from spending time at the hospital." By the scarlet color the judge is turning, and the pointed way he's looking at Andy Nash, it seems like the sheriff didn't exactly tell him that Curry was really an undercover cop who was looking for my mother. "I believe I signed the papers that sent you there for observation."

Curry says, somewhat contritely, "That's right, Your Honor. I apologize to the court. It was the only way we could think of to place someone there in order to investigate our suspicions."

Judge Whitmore is still looking at the sheriff, who is nervously mopping his brow with his kerchief. "Proceed," His Honor finally says in a way that makes me think there will be quite the kick up between him and the sheriff in his chambers later on.

"Once you were admitted to the hospital, how did you go about attempting to prove your theory that Mrs. Carmody might have been committed?" Mr. Stockton asks.

"Mr. Moody had given me a picture of Mrs. Car-

mody. I showed that around, but none of the patient.
seemed to recognize her."

Mama squeezes my hand very tightly at that point. I
heard her tell Mrs. Tittle at the picnic when I was eavesdropping that she was rarely allowed out of her room.

"I also asked if they'd ever come across a patient who
might be claiming that she was somebody other than
who the hospital said she was," Curry says. "Except for
mentioning a woman who was known as Marie Antoinette, no one volunteered any information. I had no luck
until late on the second day when I overheard the nurses
talking about a woman named Laurie who insisted that
her real name was Evelyn. They were discussing which
of them should call Doctor Keller to up her medication.
I was pretty sure then that I'd found Mrs. Carmody."

I look back at E. J. and Dagmar again and think of
the poor souls up at the Colony. I wonder how many of
the patients there are truly bad off in the brain and how
many are there for reasons that have nothing to do with
them getting some help.

Mr. Stockton asks, "Once you were sure it was Mrs.
Carmody, what did you do next, Detective?"

"I waited until the nurses went about their duties and
used their phone to call Sheriff Nash and apprised him
of the situation. Since the hospital is out of his jurisdiction, he had no power to have Mrs. Carmody released.
We decided the quickest way to get Mrs. Carmody out
of there would be to come back with Doctor Chester
Keller, who was responsible for committing her in the
first place."

Judge Whitmore pounds his gavel and says, "Order." Just about everybody in the room is saying something. Doc Keller has treated them and their children for many years. It's hard for them to believe he'd do anything so hypocritical.

The lawyer asks a few more technical questions and then tells Curry to step down. He tips his hat as he walks past Woody, Mama, and me and right out the courtroom door. He's leaving to go back up north to his Indian wife and his papooses, who I am sure have been missing him so badly. I told him last night after supper *grazie* again. Woody gave him a drawing she had done of him playing his harmonica over at the hobo camp. And when E. J. coughed up one of his arrowheads as a going-away present, Curry got as emotional as one of Mama's Italian opera albums.

When Sheriff Andy Nash gets up to the stand, his testimony is to the point. Even though he is sweating so bad that his uniform shirt has turned from brown to black, he is coolly concise when he relates his part in rescuing Mama. The folks in the gallery let out a cheer for our hometown hero when he steps down from the box.

And, of course, my uncle Sam. He gets up and corroborates what Curry had to say, only in his much slower way. There's a cheer for him, too. But mostly from the colored people.

Others are waiting to tell their side of the story as well.

I'm sure Dagmar Epps will be asked by the prosecution to testify to what she told Curry up in the hobo camp about being taken away to the Colony to have that operation by order of Papa, who would only do something that awful because Grampa made him.

Doc Keller, who committed Mama to the hospital even though there wasn't a thing wrong with her except a desire to be her own untrampled person, also has a lot to answer for.

And Remmy Hawkins. He told the sheriff he found Mama's bloody blouse over at the Triple S under a rock, which was a big fat pimply lie told to incriminate Sam—I hope he gets sent to Sing Sing, but he'll probably only have to report to the detention center over in Bedford County.

My mother still has to say what happened to her, too. But she met with the judge earlier today and asked that Woody and me be disallowed from hearing any testimony that might "scar my children more than they've already been scarred."

So at high noon Judge Whitmore pounds his gavel and says, "We will break for lunch and resume in one hour without the children present."

On our way out of the courtroom, I look over at Papa, Grampa, and Uncle Blackie. They barely made it out of the burning house alive and I bet some days they wished they hadn't. I've spent enough time in my father's courtroom to know that the three of them will be bound over for trial. They will be found guilty and sent away for a very long time for what they've done. If I never see Grampa or Blackie again, it won't be too soon, but to Papa I stop and say, "I'll write to you," and then I run out of that courtroom before he can say, "Don't bother. I don't ever want to hear from you again, you little traitor."

We stop for an ice cream on the ride over to Granny Beezy's. (She has given Woody and me permission to call her that, which we took to right off.) Mama wants Woody and me to stay at her house on Monroe Street for the rest of the afternoon until she is finished up in the courtroom.

Mama and my twin and I are sitting on the banks of the Maury River, cooling our heels, eating our cones, and watching the water float by. I am certain that Mama is about to say something about tomorrow being a river ready to carry us to our fondest dreams because it seems like something she would say at a time like this, but after being still for the longest while, she tells us in a voice that sounds like it's about to break into many pieces, "Emily Dickinson wrote, 'The past is not a package one can lay away,' but . . . we're going to do our best to do just that, aren't we, peas?"

Woody nods in agreement, but I don't. I think to myself—that Emily Dickinson. She is always right on the money.

Chapter Thirty-seven

We've been settled in our new house for almost three weeks.

The gray Victorian is sort of run-down and does not show a lot of promise of picking itself up. It reminds me a lot of something you'd find over at What Goes Around Comes Around. There are no glorious woods of birch and ash and no creek with stepping stones. No wide veranda with a welcoming porch swing that invites you to while away an afternoon. No barn. In the backyard, there's a dilapidated doghouse. Ivory uses it to store his bones, but is happier snoring on the other side of Woody at bedtime.

It didn't take us anytime at all to get set up. We had nothing to unpack. Everything we owned was destroyed in the fire. Even my binoculars. We have done some shopping. Mama bought us books and clothes and a new hi-fi. She really missed her show tunes in the hospital, but she no longer sings along. She told Woody and me, "As soon as I rebuild my strength, we'll fix up the house. And I'm going to get that job at the library that I was thinking about getting before . . ."

She trails off like that a lot. I can hear her muffled crying through the thin walls some nights, but when I crawl in bed with her, she pretends to be asleep. So I just hold her hand and tell her, "*Hushacat.*" Sometimes I see Mama floating about in the garden from our bedroom window or perched stiffly on the new reading bench, staring off into the distance to the twin peaks of House Mountain. I'm thinking that once she gets her library job she'll perk up some. We don't need the money she'll make because she has her inheritance, but she tells me she *wants* to work, which is proof that she's not bouncing back as fast as I hoped she would.

Woody, Granny Beezy, and I went over to Slidell's this afternoon to pick up a few odds and ends for the get-together we're having tonight. That was kind of sad because farewells always are. Vera Ledbetter and her parrot, Sunny Boy, are preparing to fly the coop. Vera wants to go back to her old job entertaining the sailors in Norfolk. She told Woody and me over a couple of brown cows, "Thank you for wantin' me to stay and be part of your lives, but ya know, I got my own people that I've been missin'. Me and Sunny'll come back for visits. You girls take care good care of your mama, ya hear?" And then she gave us a french fry–smelling hug and some free licorice. As Woody and I were walking out the drugstore door, I heard her tell Beezy, "I tried to walk the straight and narrow, but there's a lot less nastiness in my previous line of work. More customer appreciation and less wear on my feet, too."

Since their cottage also burned down in "The Lily-field Blaze," Mr. Cole and Louise are staying with Vera until she leaves, and then they'll take over the lease on the house. They are still our help even if they don't live with us anymore. As a way of thanking Lou for taking such good care of her girls while she was gone, Mama told me last week when she was braiding my hair, "I'm going to help Louise start up her own business. The women in Mudtown don't have a beauty salon of their own. I think it's about time they do."

I am for that whole hog because Lou really does do good braids and, of course, I will never forget how she saved us by running to the sheriff that night and telling him to go rescue me and Woody. She was mighty brave to risk that. Sometimes just one courageous act is enough for you to change your opinion about somebody, don't you think? Out of the goodness of my heart, I did not tell Mama how Lou was carrying on with Blackie in the meadow after midnight or how hellaciously mean she was to Woody and me once she'd taken up with him. You know why? Because now I got something to hold over her if she gets it into her mind to quit acting like her former Louisiana self and reverts back to her unre-lenting personality self. (Like I mentioned earlier, it is always nice to have an ace up your sleeve.)

Mr. Cole offered to build Woody and me a new fort

in the backyard of the new house. I thought about that long and hard, and so did Woody. We ended up telling him, "No, thank you, but we reserve the right to change our mind." The fort came to mean so many things to us and I think we need time to sort out the good from the bad and see which one wins.

I went up to Lilyfield and the fort tree a few days ago all by myself and kicked around the rubble to see if there was anything left I could save. I found a piece of the family picnic picture that had been taken in more care-free days in the field of lilies. All that love. Gone. And just for a second, looking down at the bit of photo, I hated Papa for making that the truth. I also found the rusty coffee can altar and Saint Jude, too. I'm going to clean that statue off and give him to Woody on our birthday next month, which is very unselfish of me because she will get so above herself on that lost-causes topic.

"Evenin', Shen. Woody," Sam says, coming through the garden gate. My sister is sitting on the nearby glider, working on a drawing, Ivory's snout in her lap. I have seen Mama and Sam holding hands, stealing glances at each other when they don't think anybody's watching, but I'm still not sure if that's in a friendly family way or not. I do know that she never takes off the *Speranza* watch he gave her. We still go to the library every Tuesday afternoon, and they still talk about Shakespeare, but I think they're working their way alphabetical through the stacks because now they love to discuss Mark Twain a little bit more.

Woody smiles and nods at him. I look up and say, "Hey." He looks fancier than usual and is not smelling like gas.

Sam sits down next to me and asks, "What are you writing?"

"Just putting the finishin' touches on my diary."

Mama takes Woody and me to Charlottesville every week to a special kind of doctor who does not stick you with needles or take your temperature. He's got a comfortable office with beanbag chairs and he helps you talk about what's ailing you. Not your body, but your heart and head. Dr. Ellis Wilson, Ph.D., was the one who suggested I start writing about my feelings and just about whatever else comes up in my life. I thought that was a good idea. I mean, if Woody and me are going to move to New York City someday so she can be the next Toulouse-Lautrec and I can be the next Harper Lee, I better start practicing.

I ask Sam, "You wanna hear some of what I wrote?"

"Can't imagine anything I'd enjoy more," he says, because that's the kind of encouraging man he is.

I read, " 'Dear Diary, Big day today for so many different reasons. Remmy Hawkins got put in the detention center just like I thought he would. And his grandfather, Mayor Jeb Hawkins, got kicked out of office. I don't know why, but I'll ask Granny Beezy tomorrow, she will have heard the gossip by then. She told me this morning when Woody and I were over at her house watching E. J. mow the lawn, that she heard Muffy Mitchell tell June Harding that Miss Abigail Hawkins is dating a man who sells saddles and bridles in Farm-ville.'"

Sam chuckles at that, and so does Woody, the same way I did when I heard that news about horsey Miss Abigail.

"'And . . . ,'" I continue after I turn the page, "'Papa, Grampa, and Uncle Blackie all left for Red Onion State Prison today.'" There never was a trial. Bobby Rudd advised them to make a deal for a lesser sentence. "'A picture in the newspaper showed the three of them get-ting on the bus. His Honor looked handsome.'"

Songs of evening blackbirds and a couple of ambi-tious crickets, a dog barking the next street over, are the only sounds hanging in the air until Sam says thought-fully, "This is hard on you, isn't it, Shenny."

I look into his familiar eyes. "Only when it comes to Papa," I say, hoping that doesn't hurt his feelings. Be-cause after all, when you look at how everything un-folded, I might've got the ball rolling when it came to finding Mama, but Sam was the one who rescued her. With able assistance from Curry Weaver and Sheriff Nash.

Sam asks, "How about you, Woody?"

My sister has started talking more, thanks to some help from another doctor who is a friend of Dr. Wilson's who is particularly good with willful children. His name is Dr. Ben Abernathy. He told Mama and me that Woody quit speaking in the first place because of the horrible thing she saw—someone she loved, her own grand-mother, trying to murder someone else she loved, her mother. Not because, like I thought, she was grieving Mama's disappearance. The doctor told me that was a part of it, too, though. My sister's delicate artistic brain was not able to make sense of all the despicable goings-on, so to protect her, it made her stop talking. (That sounds weak to me, but this man has a lot of diplomas on his wall.)

Woody lifts her head up from her drawing. "What?"

Sam asks, "Do you miss your father?"

She looks down at her scarred, root-cellar knees and doesn't miss a beat. "No."

And it's not only her. Nobody seems to miss His Honor as much as I do and that can make me feel like the odd man out. After Woody falls asleep some nights, Mama and I have a cup of tea out on the back porch steps. I identify the constellations for her and we talk about him. On one of those evenings, she cried into her hands and couldn't stop for the longest time after she told me, "Yes, honey. It would be all right if you went to Slidell's and bought a bottle of English Leather to remember him by." I keep it under our mattress because the smell of it makes my sister sick to her stomach.

The back door opens and Mama, who is wearing the prettiest red polka-dot dress, calls, "Sam? Could you get the serving plate off the top shelf, please?" Then to us she says, "The rest of the guests are arriving. Please finish up what you're doing and come wash up," and goes back in.

Sam stands, brushes his hands down his pants, and says, "It's fine for each of you to feel the way you do.

The heart does not answer to the brain. If there's one thing I've learned in life it's that feelings are complicated."

When Sam heads towards the house, I go sit next to Woody and Ivory on the glider. She is drawing a picture of E. J. A hundred tiny hearts are buzzing around his face like flies attracted to a plate of leftovers. He was by her side 'til just a little while ago. He probably went into the kitchen to get closer to the food.

"So you still love him, huh," I say, impressed as all get out that she has not taken the liberty that every artist can to make their subject look better than they really do. "When you were . . . I mean . . ." We don't talk much about when she didn't talk. "Did you miss those berry lips of Ed James, yum-yum?"

Woody says, "Shut up, Shenbone," just the way she would've once upon a time, but it's not as funny anymore. I can't barely admit it to myself, but I have been told by Dr. Wilson that no matter how tragic it is, facing the truth is better than pretending even though it sure doesn't feel like it. "You can't mend a wound if you won't admit that you've got one" is what the doctor told me the last time I saw him. So the fact . . . the truth is . . . Woody and I are not the same as we were. We aren't as connected. I miss that feeling of oneness with her more than anything and can only pray our apartness is temporary. "Don't you dare tease me about E. J." Her voice is sort of slow and wobbly like your leg is when you get a cast off it. "I saw you lockin' lips at the cemetery yesterday, don't think I didn't."

Ivory and I went over there to say a final farewell to Clive Minnow. I pushed that Confederate button that I took from What Goes Around Comes Around deep into the soil of his grave. I was going to apologize on behalf of my grandmother for poisoning him, but I got distracted by bare-chested Bootie Young, who let me stick my finger in his cleft chin. All the way to the knuckle.

"C'mon," I tell Woody. "The skeeters are comin' out."

Wedding veil clouds are drifting past the moon. It's supposed to storm tonight, but not until late. When I was young, I used to think that the stars disappeared when there were showers. Like the rain extinguished them. When I told Papa that, he smiled and said, "They're always there twinkling, honey. You just can't see them for the clouds."

I think of him often during the day when I try to write him a letter that never seems to go any further than *Dear Papa . . . I miss you.* But he is most on my mind when the constellations pop up early and are kissing close. Like tonight. I know it's not a popular way to feel around here because of all the bad things that he's done, but between you and me, this half of his little Gemini wishes with my whole heart and soul that my father was by my side on this historical evening the way we planned.

It's July 20, 1969. The astronauts made it to the moon.

They fared much, much better than I thought they would.

Now all they got to do is get back home.

Tomorrow River

Lesley Kagen

A CONVERSATION
WITH LESLEY KAGEN

Q. *You became a first-time novelist at the age of fifty-seven. Have you always wanted to write or is it something that came out of the blue?*

A. I believe I'm wired to write, the same way artists and singers are born with certain abilities. Same goes for athletes. Chefs. Gardeners. Mathematicians. All of us are given something special—the trick is to find out what that is, what makes us feel most real and connected. I was drawn to words. As a kid, I'd haul my red wagon over to the Finney Library, load up, and run home to cozy up under my covers to read and write. It paid off. I won a silver dollar in fourth grade for a poem I'd written. That was a lot of dough in '59. Dreaming of retirement by age ten, I decided to expand my audience and came up with what I thought at the time was a great story for my favorite TV show, *77 Sunset Strip*. My mother, bless her heart, sent the scribbled pages off to Hollywood for me. Can you imagine what she might've been thinking every Friday night when I'd plop down in front of the television set, ready to watch my tale about the thieves who used a dog collar to smuggle stolen goods? (She would never admit it, but I think Mom was the one who sent me the eight-by-ten glossy of Ed "Kookie" Burns.)

After college, I went into radio and then ran off to L.A., where I did commercial writing and acting. Then it was the restaurant life. Motherhood. It wasn't until my daughter went away to college and all my teenage son required of me was a pepperoni pizza that I found the time to give writing a novel a shot. *Whistling in the Dark* was what I came up with a year and a half later.

Q. Whistling in the Dark *became a* New York Times *extended list bestseller. It's set in Milwaukee, where you grew up. Your second novel, the national bestselling* Land of a Hundred Wonders, *is set in Kentucky. Were you concerned about portraying a small Southern town and its characters accurately, considering your background as a city girl?*

A. Some writers can set their work in a place without having to experience it, but it's very important to me to feel grounded in a story. To taste the food, to become part of the culture, and to know the language of a certain place are essential if I'm going to make the story feel authentic. I rode horses competitively when I was a kid. Grew up in a barn listening to trainers and grooms and judges who hailed from Kentucky and other points south, so the way they spoke, the stories they told, they're part of my life, part of who I am.

Likewise for my new book, *Tomorrow River*. My daughter went to Sweet Briar College just outside of Lynchburg, and graduated from Washington and Lee law school in Lexington. I spent a lot of time in Virginia over the years, lucky me. The Shenandoah Valley is one of the most beautiful spots on earth.

Q. The settings may change but your stories are told from the viewpoint of children or, in the case of Land of a Hundred Wonders, *from the eyes of a childlike young woman. Why do you choose children as narrators? Is it difficult to write in their voices?*

A. It feels natural for me to write in a kid's voice. Maybe it's because I'm getting older and coming full circle, I don't know. Childhood seems close to me now. Kids' honesty, their unique way of viewing the world, their direct way of talking, their enthusiasm, I yearn for it. I set my books in the fifties and sixties for the same reason. It's when I grew up. I know that period. I feel it. I can still smell it.

Q. You mentioned that it's important for you to have experienced a setting before writing it. Does the same hold true for your characters? If so, what was your inspiration for Tomorrow River?

A. After I'd lived in L.A. for a lot of years, the earthquakes and mudslides, the gangs, they all began to feel scary and overwhelming. So my husband and I came back to Milwaukee and bought a house in a nice, safe suburb. We wanted our kids to have the same Midwest upbringing we'd had. Having experienced quite a bit of trauma growing up, I made it my mission in life to keep my kids safe. How we fool ourselves. I knew better. As a parent you might be able to protect your children from outside forces, at least for a while, but the real danger lies within.

Within a few months of moving into the subdivision, my son brought home a friend. I knew something devastating had happened to the boy. When you experience great loss, I believe you can sense in others that profound sadness. I asked around to see if I could find out more about him. I learned from a neighbor that a few months before we moved in, the father of my son's friend had killed his wife in their home, where the boy and his brother now lived with his grandparents.

And a couple of years ago, a business acquaintance of my husband's—a man we both knew fairly well and would never have suspected for a minute was violent—strangled his wife and dragged her onto the family room couch. The next morning, when their two young daughters tried to wake Mommy, the husband told them that she was still sleeping and not to bother her. He made them breakfast and drove them to school. Had lunch with a friend. Later that afternoon, he called 911 to report that his wife had been murdered. Of course, the police saw through his story immediately.

I could not get these kids' heartbreaking stories out of my mind. What damage is caused to children's psyches when one of the two most powerful people in their lives takes away the other? Can they forgive, or is that pain just too great to overcome?

In *Tomorrow River* I attempted to explore those feelings. I wanted to understand and, hopefully, in some small way, remind others that kids are so vulnerable. We must stand guard.

Q. You explore different aspects of racism in each of your novels, perhaps most significantly in Tomorrow River. *What makes that issue of particular interest to you?*

A. Growing up, I lived in one of the most segregated cities in the United States. The only time I saw blacks was when we drove through The Core on our way to the beach. I could see out the car window that their houses, their businesses . . . they weren't living the same way other families I knew were. It bothered me. Yeah, yeah, life isn't fair, but as a kid, I thought it should be and I still do.

Q. All three of your books deal with significant losses, yet you manage to weave both humor and hope into the stories. Why?

A. All of us deal with loss in one way or another in our lives. We lose our loved ones, our jobs, our health. Humor and hope for a better day are the only things I know of that transcend that kind of pain.

Q. You've spoken to a lot of book clubs. Are you in a book club?

A. I like to think of myself as an honorary member of each club I've spoken with over the years, and there have been hundreds. On a slightly smaller scale, my husband and I read together. We often don't agree on stories, and it makes for some great arguments—I mean, lively intellectual discussions.

Q. What's next?

A. I'm currently working on a sequel to *Whistling in the Dark* and couldn't be having a better time. It's wonderful to be back with the old gang again. I missed them.

QUESTIONS
FOR DISCUSSION

1. The story is told through eleven-year-old Shenny's eyes. What are the limitations of an unreliable narrator's point of view? What are the advantages? Are there things that Shenny overlooks or perhaps observes that an adult narrator wouldn't?

2. *Tomorrow River* is set in a smallish Southern town in 1969. Is this a story that could take place anywhere? Why do you think the author chose this setting?

3. The late sixties was a time of transition racially and socially in the South. How do the characters react to these changes?

4. Does Evelyn's Northern heritage divide the community? Does she influence any of the characters in a positive way?

5. Shenny and Woody, although identical twins, are very different. Why do you think that is?

6. Shenny has hope in the face of hopelessness. Have you ever encountered a situation in which you've had to be courageous against all odds?

7. E. J. and Shenny have a complicated relationship. How would you describe it?

8. How do you think what the twins go through will affect them later in life?

9. How did you feel about the girls' grandmother? Their grandfather? Are they victims in their own ways?

10. Of all the characters, Judge Carmody is perhaps the most conflicted. How would you describe what he's going through?

11. In life, the strong often dominate the weak. Would you say that's true in this story or is it more complicated than that?

12. What part does Beezy play in the story?

13. What aspects of Shenny's personality do you admire the most? How about Woody's?

14. Has the respect we had in the sixties for people of wealth and power diminished in any way?

15. Who is your favorite character? Your least favorite? Why?

From national bestselling author
LESLEY KAGEN
comes the funny, heartbreaking sequel to
Whistling in the Dark,
GOOD GRACES,
available in hardcover in September 2011 from Dutton.
Join Sally O'Malley and her sister, Troo,
as they experience the summer of 1960.
An excerpt follows. . . .

$\mathcal{P}$rologue

That summer earned itself a place in the record books that's never been beat. The hardware store sold out of fans by mid-June and the Montgomery twins fainted at the Fourth of July parade. By the time August showed up, we couldn't wait to send it packing.

To this day, my sister insists it was nothing more than the unrelenting heat that drove us to do what we did that summer, but that's just Troo yanking my chain the way she always has. Deep down, she knows as well as I do that it wasn't anything as mundane as the weather. It was the hand of the Almighty that shoved us off the straight-and-narrow path.

Whenever the old neighborhood pals get together, if it's a particularly sticky evening, the way they all were back then, memories get tickled up. Sitting out on one of our back porches in the dwindling light, somebody will inevitably bring up the mysterious disappearance of one of our own that long ago summer. *Do you think he was murdered? What about kidnapping? He could have just taken off.* Tying to figure out what happened to him has become as much fun for our friends as remembering our games of red light green light and penny candy from the Five and Dime. But for the O'Malley sisters, the fate of that certain someone is no more mysterious than the way he broke my front tooth that sultry August night. The two of us know exactly where that devil in the details has been for the past fifty years. He's where we buried him the sweltering summer Troo was ten and I was eleven.

The summer of '60.

Chapter One

Somebody at his funeral called Donny O'Malley *lush*. I couldn't agree more. Daddy was just-picked corn on the cob and a game-saving double play all rolled into one, that's how lush he was.

Someone else at the cemetery said that time heals all wounds. I don't know about that.

Daddy crashed on his way home from a baseball game at Milwaukee County Stadium three years ago. The steering wheel went into his chest. I wasn't in the car that afternoon. I hadn't weeded my garden so he told me I had to stay back on the farm and I told him I hated him and wished for a different daddy. I didn't mean it. I'd just been so looking forward to singing The Land of the Free and the Home of the *Braves*. Eating salty peanuts and the seventh-inning stretch.

When he was in the hospital, Daddy shooed everyone else out of the room and had me lie down with him. "No matter what, you must take care of Troo," he told me. "Keep her safe. You need to promise me that." He had tubes coming out of him and there was a *ping ping*ing noise that reminded me of the *20,000 Leagues Under the Sea* movie. "Tell your sister the crash wasn't her fault.

And . . . tell your mother that I forgive her. I'll be watching, Sally. Remember . . . things can happen when you least expect them . . . you . . . you always gotta be prepared. Pay attention to the details. The devil is in the details."

I never forgot what he told me or what I promised him, but Daddy is especially on my mind this morning. When it's baseball season, I always remember him better. The other reason I'm thinking about him is because Troo and me just got home from getting our brand-new start-of-the-summer sneakers at Shuster's Shoes on North Avenue. That's the store where Hall Gustafson used to work. He's the man Mother got married to real quick after Daddy died. My sister thinks she accepted his proposal because Hall had a tattoo on his arm that said MOTHER, but I think she did it because Daddy forgot to leave us a nest egg. I watched Mother collapse in our corn field and beat the dirt with her fists, shouting, "Donny! How could you?" but I forgave him right off. When you're a farmer, it's hard to put something away for a rainy day.

The whole time we were trying on Keds this morning, I kept imagining that slobbering Swede stumbling out from behind the curtain where the shoes are hidden, but that was dumb. Our stepfather doesn't have a job at Shuster's or anyplace else anymore because he got into a fight at Jerbak's Beer 'n Bowl with the owner, who was famous around here for bowling a 300 game but also for being quick with his fists. Hall's in the Big House now. For murdering Mr. Jerbak with a bottle of Old Milwaukee.

Sometimes in bed at night when I can't sleep, which is mostly all the time, I think about how good that all worked out and just for a little while it makes me feel like God might know what He's doing. At least part of the time. He did a bad job letting Daddy die, but I admire how the Almighty got rid of Mr. Jerbak and Hall in one fell swoop. That really was killing two dirty birds with one stone.

Troo wasn't thinking about Hall when we were up at the store. Not how he dragged her out of bed and knocked her head against the wall or any of the other rotten stuff he did like sneaking behind Mother's back with a floozy. My sister was having the best time this morning. She's nuts about Shuster's because it's so modern. They've got a Foot-O-Scope machine that's like an X-ray. Troo adores pressing her eyes to the black viewer to see inside her feet, but when I look down at my bones, they remind me of Daddy lying beneath the cemetery dirt.

"Ya know what I been thinkin', Sal?" my sister asks.

We're sitting on the back steps of the house. I'm raring to go, but she's working hard to loop her new shoelaces into bunny ears. Troo was in the crash with Daddy. She played peek-a-boo with him on the way home from the baseball game. Holding her hands over his eyes for longer than she shoulda is what caused the car to go skidding out of control and smash into the old oak tree on Holly Road. She got her arm fractured. It aches before it's going to rain and also made her not very good at tying.

"What?" I ask her.

"It would be a fantastic idea for us to get away from

the neighborhood for a while. We should go away to camp this summer," she says, batting her morning sky blue eyes at me.

My eyes are green and I don't have hair the color of maple leaves in the fall. I have thick blond hair that my mother brushes too hard and puts into a fat braid that goes down my back and deep dimples that I've been told more than a few times are very darling. I've always had long legs, but this past year they grew three and a half inches. My sister thinks I look like a yellow flamingo.

"We need to expand our horizons," Troo says.

Even though we don't look very much alike, we are what people call Irish twins. Troo will turn eleven two months before I turn twelve. I always know what she is *really* thinking and feeling. We have mental telepathy. So that's how come I know my sister isn't telling me the truth about why she wants to go to camp. It's not the neighborhood she wants to get away from. She likes living in the brick house with the fat-leafed ivy growing up the sides and bright red geraniums in the window boxes and lilacs falling over the picket fence like a purple waterfall. It's the *owner* of the house Troo's got problems with. She wants to get away from Dave Rasmussen, who we moved in with at the end of last summer. He is my real father because when Daddy was in the war, Mother accidentally had some of the sex with Dave.

For the longest time, I didn't know that Dave was my flesh and blood. When I found out, I didn't think I would get over it, but I mostly have, in my mind anyway. In my heart, Daddy is still my daddy, and Dave is Dave. Maybe someday that will change for me, but it *never* will for my sister. Daddy will always be her one and only. He looked at her like she was a slice of banana cream pie. I was his second favorite, plain old dependable cherry, and that was fine with me. When you got a sister like Troo, you gotta expect these things.

"I don't want to expand anywhere," I tell her. "My horizons are fine."

"Yeah, that's what you think, but Mrs. Kambowski told me that a person should get out and see the world whenever they can," Troo tells me in her know-it-all voice, which is not my favorite. "She said that travel is *très chic*."

"She's wrong." Mrs. Kambowski is the boss of the Finney Library who won't stop teaching my sister these French words no matter how many times I politely ask her to stop. "Ya know as good as me that goin' some place you've never been before can turn out really bad," I remind Troo. "Remember what happened to Julie Adams in the *Creature from the Black Lagoon* when she went to the Amazon? And what about Sky King? He always gets into trouble when he goes flyin' off into the horizon." Daddy and I never missed that show because he was a pilot, too. "And . . . and what about all the bad stuff that happened to us when we moved from the country to the city?"

"I knew you'd say that," she says with a smile that can bring the dead back to life. She inherited it from Daddy. He gave her her nickname, too. After she got a rusty nail pulled out of her heel and didn't even flinch, he started calling her "a real trooper," and then because that took too long to say we began to call her Trooper and then shortened it even more. Her real name is Margaret. I also call her my Troo genius because she is really smart. She can come up with plans like nobody's business. Like this camp one she's trying to sell to me harder than the Fuller Brush man tries to talk Mother into a new broom even though the old one's still got plenty of bristles. "That's why I was thinkin' we wouldn't go someplace brand-new. We could go to the same camp Mary Lane went to last year. That one up in Rhinelander. She bragged about it so much . . . it's like we've already been there, right?"

"Wrong." Down the block, Bobby Darin is singing on the radio, "Won't you come home, Bill Bailey," and that has to be a sign from God to stay put right where I am. I might not have a lot of belief in Him anymore, but I got enough to pay attention to the details.

Still struggling with the laces, Troo says, "I'm . . . I'm not thinkin' about me."

Yes, she is.

"I looked up what's wrong with you in Mother's medical book. An ocean voyage or a change of scenery is the best cure for people who have lunatic imaginations," she says in her dolly voice, which is so hard not to give in to. Even if you know she's just putting it on to get what she wants, it's adorable. "Since ya don't like being near water so much anymore, I figure a boat trip is out." When I don't agree, she doesn't give up. She never does. "I bet you'd sleep a lot better breathin' in all that country air."

I doubt it.

Troo hits the hay every night like a bale falling outta of our old barn loft. Wrapped in Daddy's sky blue work shirt that still has the smell of his Aqua Velva hidden under the collar, she holds her baby doll, Annie, up to her cheek and I feel her sweaty leg pressed up to mine and sometimes I count the freckles on her nose to see if she sprouted any new ones or walk my bare feet against the bedroom wall because it's always cooler on that wall and my thoughts go round and round and I flip over on my tummy and stare at the picture of Daddy that hangs over our bed. He's in a boat holding up a fish. His hair is blown into two horns. Troo says that he looks devil-may-care in that picture and maybe he does, but he probably isn't anymore. I didn't do that good a job last summer keeping my sister safe the way he asked me to. It seems like no matter how hard I try to be prepared, I'm not ready for the bad when it shows up. Take Bobby Brophy. He was the playground counselor who almost murdered and molested me last summer and I didn't suspect a thing. He hurt my sister, too. Knocked her out cold.

"Hey!" Troo nudges me. "I just remembered. The camp's in a pine forest. That means it'd smell like Christmas every morning and that's your favorite holiday." She brings one sneaker and then the other into my lap and says, "Tie me up."

Oh, how I wish I could. With a strong rope. I would anchor her to me.

"And ya know what the best part of us goin' to camp would be, the real *pièce de résistance*?" she says. "You won't have to visit Doc Keller while we're gone!"

Mother makes me go up to his office on North Avenue once a week so he can give me a dose of cod liver oil and a stern lecture with his breath that smells like old vase water. He warns me each and every time that I better get my imagination under control or else. "An idle mind is the devil's workshop," he says, but Doc couldn't be more wrong. My mind is never idle. Never ever. And it's getting worse. I think all that cod liver oil might be greasing my wheels.

"Whatta ya say, Sal, my gal?" My sister picks up my hand and twines her fingers through mine. She knows I'm a sucker for that. "Ya in?"

"But what about Mother?" I ask. Through the screen door, I can hear the sound of her picking up the house. She's still kinda wobbly. If somebody you know gets sick with a gall bladder that turns into liver problems and then a staph infection like what happened to her last summer, you'd better start saying your prayers. Doc Keller told all of us that he'd never heard of a person getting over something that fatal. "Who's gonna get her nummy, and what if she needs something like—"

Troo hawks and throws a loogie, which is something she has started doing lately when she wants to make a point. "What's his name can take care of her."

She means Dave, who bends over backwards for Troo, same as me, so against my better judgment, which I don't hardly have much left of anymore, I end up telling him that night out on the backyard bench that both of us want to go to Camp Towering Pines in the worst possible way. I didn't want to, but I *had* to lie to him. I know my sister. She'd figure out some way to go to that camp without me. There's no telling what kind of trouble she could get into if I wasn't there to stop her. And I made that promise to Daddy that I'll never break. Even if my life depends on it.